Celia's LEGACY

Gift of
Whispering Pines

Book SEVEN

KIMBERLY DIEDE

Gift of Whispering Pines Book Seven

Celia's Legacy

Cover by Carpe Librum Book Design – www.carpelibrumbookdesign.com.

ISBN: 978-1-961305-20-5

ISBN: 978-1-7351343-4-5 (pbk)

ISBN: 978-1-961305-13-7 (lg print pbk)

ISBN: 978-1-7351343-3-8 (ebook)

Introduction to Whispering Pines

Welcome to Whispering Pines—a quaint resort deep in the heart of Minnesota's lake country—where an unforgettable family will come together to learn how to heal and thrive, despite the inevitable wounds that life delivers. Join siblings Renee, Jess, Ethan, and Val as they struggle to make the most of the legacy entrusted to them by their dear Aunt Celia. If you enjoy a family saga filled with unanticipated twists, second chances, and the many gifts life offers, you'll love your visit to Whispering Pines!

Whispering Pines (Book 1)
Tangled Beginnings (Book 2)
Rebuilding Home (Book 3)
Capturing Wishes (Book 4)
Choosing Again (Book 5)
Celia's Gifts (Book 6)
Celia's Legacy (Book 7)

For release dates, news, and more, sign up to receive Kimberly Diede's newsletter on her website at www.kimberlydiedeauthor.com and follow her on Facebook and BookBub.

To Aunt Mary,

*Your legacy
is my inspiration*

Her legacy will live on
in the gifts
she leaves behind.

Chapter One
GIFT OF PAYING IT FORWARD

November 1973

CELIA HAD NEVER ATTENDED a funeral with so few mourners. The wind had a bite and erratic snowflakes stung her face as she approached the small group as quietly as possible. Thick, ominous clouds with rounded bellies glowered from above, threatening heavier snowfall. She watched as the young widow stood alone near the open grave. A simple pine box hovered above a hole in the earth, held there by a contraption made of pipes and pulleys.

Death is such an odd business, Celia thought as she stood awkwardly by, feeling like an outsider. She'd never met Bryce Haman, the deceased, but her heart broke over the sad tale of a young life lost and two others altered forever.

A blast of wind buffeted the knot of people and the widow next to the grave turned slightly, struggling to hold her hair away from a tear-stained face. Despite the distance between them, Celia could see that young Virginia's face had matured in the fifteen months since visiting Whispering Pines. If only Warren and Helen Arbuckle, Celia's old friends and Virginia's parents, could have reached some kind of compromise with their daughter. But they'd held firm, leading to the young woman's rebellion, and now they found themselves in a wintery cemetery on a blustery November day.

Celia knew, of course, that Warren and Helen loved all four of their daughters, though Warren tolerated their quests for independence with considerably more patience than his wife. Celia had been friends with Helen her whole life, but she secretly considered Warren the better parent. Helen fought to hold tight to a specific vision she'd created for each of her daughters—ironically just as her mother had done with her—but the girls had plans of their own. Virginia loved art, dance, and poetry. Helen insisted those were pleasant enough as hobbies but that Virginia couldn't build her life around them. Celia suspected Helen saw a piece of her own shriveled dreams in her daughter's aspirations and that it was like a painful sliver just under her skin. Helen had never fought for her own girlish dream to become a fashion designer. Did she subconsciously hold this disappointment against her youngest child?

A sudden movement, off to Celia's left, caught her eye. Relief flooded through her when she spotted Warren and Helen in the back, clothed in somber attire. When her eyes met Warren's, he offered her a brief nod of greeting, but Helen's eyes never left her grieving daughter. Even from a distance, Celia could see her back was ramrod straight.

She hoped Helen wasn't there to heap more despair on Virginia's thin shoulders.

As the minister offered a final blessing, he made a hasty retreat, probably off on more pressing business. The handful of other attendees at the service were young and unkempt, eyes hidden behind dark sunglasses despite the gloom. No one looked old enough to be Bryce's parents. The sparse crowd split up, small enough that the young people all fit in two vehicles: a rusted-out panel van and some kind of muscle car. Celia cringed when hard rock blared out of the car for a second before someone had the good sense to snap off the music. Quiet descended again as the vehicles rolled away. Only Virginia, her parents, and Celia were left beside the fresh grave.

She waited, unsure what to do. Virginia looked devastated; silent tears coursed down her cheeks. Celia wondered who they'd found to watch Virginia's child. It wouldn't have been appropriate to have such a young baby out in these elements.

Should she offer Virginia her condolences and make a quick retreat? Why had none of the younger people stayed with her?

Celia's heart broke for the young woman. She remembered Virginia's smile as she'd told her how she dreamed of traveling Europe, how she wanted to see all the beautiful paintings the world had to offer. Celia saw Virginia's musings for what they likely were: impractical dreams of a young girl, unlikely to play out, but a source of happiness regardless as Virginia planned her life. What would that life look like now? Virginia wasn't even twenty, and already widowed with a young child.

She was lucky to have parents with financial stability.

But before Celia could step forward to talk with Virginia, Helen rushed up, her face contorted with anger. Celia took one step in their direction, in case she could serve as a mediator, but Warren waved her back.

"Not now," he warned, his voice just loud enough for Celia to hear.

Clearly her friends needed time alone with their daughter. Celia turned and walked back to her Cadillac. She'd sit inside with the heater blasting to warm up and wait to see if she might get a chance to speak to Virginia.

Celia tried to give the three some privacy, and between the engine and blasting heater and the low moan of the wind against her closed car door she couldn't hear the words they exchanged, but she watched them. Warren said little, and Virginia's back was to Celia, but Helen seemed to do all the talking. There were no outward signs of compassion; no hugs or touches of any kind.

How could Helen be so harsh? Couldn't she see how much her daughter needed her now?

Celia thought back to when the Arbuckles visited Whispering Pines. Two months before their arrival, Virginia had graduated from high school, hoping to take a year to do some international travel before starting college. Her parents had other ideas. Celia found herself caught in the middle of a tug-of-war between mother and daughter. Helen refused to even consider any adjustments to their plans for her youngest daughter. Virginia felt stifled, her dreams at risk of permanent extinguishment. She was sure that if she went off to college she'd be sucked into the humdrum life her parents imagined for her. No amount of reasoning brought compromise from either side.

Helen initially thought she'd won the battle, but when the time came to move the girl into her college dormitory, Virginia slipped away in the night. She took up with an unruly crowd and refused to come home or attend class. Her parents were devastated. With Virginia's hopes to travel abroad dashed, she'd found a poor substitute for the romance and cultural variety she sought within her new group of friends. She fell into a relationship with an older boy named Bryce Haman. According to Helen, the kid wore his hair and beard long and straggly, and she could practically smell the pot rolling off him the one time she'd met her daughter's love interest.

Virginia's misguided choices continued, and it wasn't long before she'd tied herself to the melancholy young artist with a civil service at the court house. Personally, Celia was surprised someone like Bryce had agreed to marriage in the first place. But, with a baby on the way, Virginia had somehow convinced him.

Eventually she left Bryce—with a newborn baby in tow—and took refuge with Shirley, her sister. His drug use and communal lifestyle finally scared her away, and it seemed now that she'd left just in time. He was only twenty-five when he died. Celia wondered if the drugs killed him.

What will Virginia do now?

Her conversation with her parents didn't last long. Celia watched through her frosty car window as Helen brushed past her daughter and marched toward their black sedan. The uneven ground, coated with layers of snow and ice, didn't slow her down. Warren took his daughter's arm, turned her away from the casket, and walked her to her car. It was an older Buick that Celia had ridden in years earlier with Helen. The couple must have passed it down to Virginia or one of her sisters.

Warren opened the driver's door and motioned for his daughter to climb behind the wheel, then slammed the door. He didn't spare a glance in Celia's direction. She couldn't imagine how conflicted he must feel, torn between wife and daughter, both of whom Celia knew he loved very much.

With Virginia safe in her car, Warren hurried forward to where his wife waited, shoulders hunched against the increasing wind. They climbed into their vehicle, doors slamming. She felt a wave of anger and disgust wash through her as she watched Warren pull away. How could they leave their daughter alone like this? If this was tough love, Celia worried they had taken it too far.

No exhaust billowed from the tailpipe of Virginia's car. Celia left her own vehicle running and stepped back out into the bitter elements. She hurried toward the younger woman and rapped her knuckles softly on the side window. Virginia jumped in alarm. Yanking the passenger-side door open, Celia slid inside and shut the door. An uneasy tension surrounded them as the bitter wind buffeted the car.

Virginia stole a worried glance at Celia. "Do you want to yell at me, too?"

Celia extended one hand, encased in supple black leather, and Virginia took it. Tears no longer meandered down the younger woman's cheeks, but Celia could feel the angst coursing through her by how hard she squeezed Celia's fingers.

"I'm so sorry, Virginia," Celia offered, unsure what to say. "Will you be all right?"

Virginia released Celia's hand and gripped the steering wheel, squeezing hard enough that her bare fingers turned snow white.

Why doesn't the poor thing have gloves? Celia wondered, but then realized what a ludicrous thought it was. Virginia had much bigger problems than icy fingers.

"I'm sure your mother will come around. She's upset. She just needs a little time."

"Time isn't a luxury I have right now," Virginia muttered.

Celia shifted in her seat, and the stiff vinyl crackled under her in the cold. "Virginia, turn your car on before we freeze to death. We need some heat in here."

Still muttering, the girl did as she was told. Her hand shook as violently as the branches of the old elm that draped over the Buick. She seemed to be hanging on by a thread.

"Will you stay with one of your sisters?" Celia asked. "You and the baby?"

"For now. But Shirley can't afford for us to live there much longer, eating her food. She was barely getting by before I showed up on her doorstep, and I've already been there a month."

"Won't your parents let you and the baby move home?"

Virginia's shoulders shook and tears streamed down her ashen cheeks again. "No way. Mother is livid with me. And Dad always does what she says."

Celia knew that wasn't true. Warren didn't bow to everything Helen wanted. It was why they made such a good pair. But, admittedly, she wasn't so sure in this case. She'd never seen Helen so mad.

An image of her old mentor, Preston Whitby, flashed into Celia's mind. She'd turned to him years earlier when she found herself pregnant and alone. Unlike Virginia, Celia had made the choice to give her baby up for adoption. Preston had stepped in and taken care of things for Celia. She would be eternally grateful to him for all he'd done.

Virginia needed someone like Preston. Maybe it was time for Celia to step up and do the same. Her own dreams hadn't been that different, back when she was Virginia's age. She, too, had dreamed of traveling the world with a young man who caught her fancy. But her stepfather's death had forced Celia to let her Danny go and build a different kind of life to help support her own family. Preston had been part of Celia's solution. Now she'd try to be part of the solution for Helen's daughter.

"Virginia, I want you to come live with me. With me and my mother. We have plenty of room. I'll just need a few days to convert some space for you, and then I want you to bring your baby daughter and move in."

The younger woman turned to face Celia, shocked. The window behind her was white with frost, making the interior of the car feel like a cocoon against the heartbreak that lay beyond the glass. "But why would you do that for me? I'm nothing but an unthankful flake. At least that's what my mother says. I've thrown my life away. I might as well be dead, too."

Frustration, tinged with dread, filled Celia. "Don't say that, Virginia. You are a bright young woman with your whole life ahead of you. We all need help sometimes. Let me give you that now. Just until you can get back on your feet."

"But why? Why would you help me? You barely know me."

Celia took a deep breath. "That's not true. I've known you your whole life. We just never had a chance to be close. Your mother has been my friend since we were little girls. Truth be told, I don't approve of how she is handling this with you now. But she'll come around. Your father is my boss, but more than that, he's my friend, too. I found myself in a dark place once, and someone unexpected stepped up and helped me. Now I want to do the same for you. Will you let me?"

Virginia considered Celia's offer, her eyes still skeptical. Eventually, she shrugged. "What choice do I have? Thank you, Celia. This means a lot."

Celia gathered the broken-hearted girl in her arms, their hug made awkward by the confines of the front seat of the old car. Which prompted the thought: What would it be like to have an infant in the house?

"How old is your baby now?" she asked.

"She's almost two months old," Virginia replied, a small smile stealing over her expression.

"And have you gotten her baptized yet?"

Chapter Two
Gift of a Playful Kick

Early Spring 1974

"Danny would be proud of me," Celia proclaimed aloud as she stood in front of the bookshelves in her home office on a drizzly spring morning.

She thought back to the commitment she'd made to her friend to document her life in photographs. She'd made that promise after he'd given her his precious camera. It was the summer before he left home to fight a bloody war in far-off lands. In fact, she'd been Virginia's age when she made that promise.

These albums were the evidence that she'd held up her end of the bargain. She ran her fingers over the navy spines of a dozen thick photo albums, tracing the gold-embossed trim. She frowned, pausing. There was a brown age spot on the back of her right hand.

Where the hell did that come from?

She could do without the constant reminders from her fiftyish-year-old body that she wasn't twenty anymore. Nevertheless, she refused to allow a little thing like an age spot ruin her good mood. She cracked open the window next to her desk. Fresh air flowed in. She shivered in the chill. The welcome scents of freshly brewed coffee and spring showers promised a productive morning. Winter had finally moved on, but the air still held a definite chill. She wouldn't leave the window open much longer. It was still too brisk outside to throw open all the windows in the house to chase away the staleness of winter, but she'd indulge herself in here. She could always wrap up in the ivory afghan her mother had given her for Christmas.

Her goal for the day was to organize the snapshots she'd taken over the past six months. It was tough to catch up if she let too many photos pile up. She found her stack of envelopes she'd picked up from the drugstore the previous evening and settled onto the couch. With the ten sleeves of photographs next to her, she flipped open a partially filled album. Next she tore open the first envelope, the top tab gummy with adhesive. She pulled out two dozen glossy prints. Having baby Karen in the house gave her plenty of photo opportunities.

Virginia and her baby daughter, Karen, lived in Celia's basement, but they spent just enough time upstairs that Celia had the best of two worlds: plenty of privacy, but a house that felt like it had some life in it again. Winters were quiet now that her own mother, Maggie, had started to head south with two friends each January. She'd tired of the bitter winter months in Minnesota. This was her third winter away, and she'd be home in a week.

These first photos were from little Karen's baptism. While Celia didn't attend church every Sunday (a habit she knew Maggie resented), she still felt it was important for children to be baptized. Maybe it was a carryover from the many hours she'd spent in catechism as a young schoolgirl with her friends Helen and Ruby. Either way, she was sure it was what Helen would want, despite her continued refusal to acknowledge the child. She'd recognized the skepticism on Virginia's face when she suggested Karen be baptized, but Celia could be persistent.

Shortly before Virginia and Karen moved into the basement, Celia made a trip up to her attic to check something in her blue trunk and to find the old wooden crib her parents had used. She found the baby bed in a corner, covered with a protective sheet. Its carved wooden surface would gleam again after a good polish. After Celia manhandled the heavy crib over to the top of the stairs, she'd unlocked her old blue trunk.

She'd hoped the christening gown inside would still fit Karen, even though she wasn't a newborn. Maggie said no one had worn the gown since the 1920s. Both

Celia and her sister, Beverly, had worn it, but their brothers weren't baptized until they were older. Clarence, their father, hadn't believed in organized religion, and it was only after he'd died that Maggie had George and Gerry baptized. Celia had planned to mention the gown to George when he started having children, but his wife's family had their own traditions, so she'd never shown it to them. Gerry had no children.

When Virginia heard about the dress, she'd jumped at the chance for Karen to wear it. Celia smiled as she remembered the delight on Virginia's face when she first showed her the tiny gown made of linen so soft and fine it was nearly translucent. Individual seed pearls, barely larger than a pin head, topped each tiny tuck on the bodice, and intricate handmade lace ran from collar to hem.

Celia flipped through the pictures on the crisp spring morning and smiled. Baby Karen barely fit in the dress, as it was meant for a newborn, and even then they had to leave the top buttons open behind her neck, but she looked like a tiny angel. Her miniature features scrunched up in protest as the priest drizzled holy water over her forehead. Celia was thankful the child had worn the dress. She wasn't sure anyone else in her family would ever wear it.

"Hello?" came the sound of Virginia's voice, along with the recognizable creak of the heavy wooden door at the top of the basement stairs. "Are you home, Celia?"

"Back here!" Celia replied. She continued to thumb through the photographs she'd snapped before, during, and after Karen's ceremony.

Footsteps rang out on the wooden floorboards in the hallway that led back to Celia's office, and then Virginia appeared, a bundled Karen on her hip. "Why are you back here with the window open?" She glanced between her landlord and the open window. "It's cold!"

Celia set the stack of pictures aside and smiled up at Virginia and Karen. The baby's bright eyes peered around the office. Celia was always surprised at how fast she was growing, in both size and personality.

"I wanted to get some pictures organized, and it smelled stale, so I opened a window. I didn't intend to leave it open for long. I lost track of time." She reached for the afghan that hung over the arm of the couch. With her other hand, she held the stack of pictures up for Virginia. "Here, let me take her. You should look at these."

Celia settled the baby on her lap and pulled the handcrafted blanket over her little legs. She wore white tights, and shiny black shoes on her tiny feet completed the darling outfit.

Virginia closed the window before turning her attention to the photographs. She pulled out Celia's office chair and took a seat at her desk. "Oh my gosh, these are from the baptism! I'm so glad you convinced me to do that, even though Mother and Father didn't attend."

Celia hated the disappointment that tinged Virginia's words. Her tenant may be a mother now, but she was still young, and she still wished for her parents' acceptance. Hopefully they'd come around soon. The fools had missed precious time with their granddaughter.

"You're both dressed cute this morning." She held Karen tight so the child wouldn't wiggle off her lap. "Where are you off to?"

Virginia smiled at her daughter. "We're off on a mother-daughter shopping date!"

Karen arched her back in protest to fight her confinement. Laughing, Celia picked the baby up, turned her around so they were face to face, then settled her back on her lap. Karen's little feet kicked as the two of them played peek-a-boo. Celia was trying to keep Karen entertained so Virginia could enjoy the photographs.

"Do you think she'll behave for you?" she asked, unconvinced a shopping expedition with a seven-month-old would be fun or productive. "I could watch her for you instead."

"No, but thank you. I appreciate the offer. We won't be gone long. I need to buy a new dress. I could use a new wardrobe, but honestly, one dress is all I can afford right now. I probably shouldn't even buy that, but I start work at the library on Monday, remember? I want to look nice."

Celia had forgotten. She'd been busy at work and lost track of the weeks.

Karen kicked again, and her patent leather shoe jammed Celia's left breast. Celia flinched, sucking in a sharp breath.

What the heck?

The flash of pain surprised her. Karen kicked again, and she felt the stab for a second time. She must have winced, because Virginia set the pictures aside and held her arms out.

"Here, let me take her. She's quite the handful. We just wanted to stop in and say hello before we left, and check to see if you needed me to pick anything up for you."

Celia turned the child back over to Virginia. "Thank you, dear, but no."

"Are you sure? You've been so good to us, it's the least I can do. I wouldn't even have gotten my new job at the library if not for you."

"I don't need anything. I'll spend my morning on these pictures, and then I'll meet Ruby for a late lunch. You two have fun. Don't catch a chill. Spring is in the air, but it's damp."

With a wave, Virginia propped her daughter up against her shoulder so the baby could face Celia as they exited the room. When Celia waved goodbye, she'd have sworn Karen moved her stubby little fingers in a wave, too.

She watched them go. *Offering Virginia a place to stay was the right choice, even if it was a spur-of-the-moment decision,* she thought, content as the house quieted around her again.

She settled her ivory afghan tighter over her empty lap, and her hand brushed against her breast. She prodded it a bit, curious about the unexpected pain she'd felt at the baby's kicks. After a few moments, her fingers sensed a change in texture between the side of her breast and her armpit. Whatever she felt didn't belong there. Celia's lighthearted mood evaporated, turning gloomier than the weather outside her window.

Visions of her family's recent Easter celebration sprang to mind. She'd laughed as George's three children zigzagged across the lawn in search of dyed eggs and baskets filled with candy. She remembered watching George, the way her youngest brother's eyes beamed with pride over the children's antics.

But there had been another Easter weekend, years earlier, when they'd lost their precious sister, Beverly, to heart disease. Celia remembered her unreasonable level of anger over the fact that young George and Gerry missed out on treats from the Easter bunny because of their sister's death.

Time had almost healed those wounds.

But Celia had lost too many important people to untimely deaths, and she felt the pang of her own mortality.

Chapter Three
Gift of Brotherly Concern

"Knock, knock." George rapped a knuckle against the doorjamb of Celia's hospital room. In his other hand he held a pink vase filled with daisies. "Are you up for some company?"

Celia grinned. "Only if those flowers are for me." She sat up straighter in the uncomfortable bed and had to bite her lip so she wouldn't grimace. The pain pill she'd taken earlier wasn't helping yet.

"Well, to be honest, they were meant for the patient one room over, but she looked comatose to me, so I helped myself."

Celia rolled her eyes. "You're awful. You realize that, don't you?"

George stepped closer to her bed, shrugging one shoulder. "What can I say? Seeing you in here makes me nervous. I thought maybe a joke might help."

"Did it?" she asked, skeptical.

"Not much," George admitted. He rearranged two other containers of flowers on a small stand to make room for the ones he'd brought for his big sister. "I see I'm not your only admirer."

"Hardly," she said with a wink. "A girl just has to tempt the Grim Reaper and suddenly her room fills up with fresh blooms. Florists can't lose."

He chuckled as he dropped into a nearby chair and leaned forward, elbows on his knees. "I have to admit, I wasn't sure what to expect today. But you seem to be in good spirits. Has Mom been in?"

She shifted against the pillow her mother had wedged in behind her to help her get comfortable. "God, yes. She just left. She had a volunteer shift downstairs on the children's wing."

"She must be one of their most loyal volunteers."

"I suspect she'll spend time on that floor with those kids for as long as she's physically able. It's how she copes, even after all these years."

George sat back with a sigh. "No mother should ever have to bury her child."

"Let's hope she doesn't end up burying another."

His eyes flashed at her words. "Celia, don't even joke about that."

My cancer has him shook, too. She hated to see the fear in her brother's eyes.

"It wasn't a joke. I won't lie, George. This is scary. The doctors feel like they got it all, but now I have to get used to life with only one boob."

"Must you be so blunt?" he asked, shaking his head with a grim smile. "I'm glad you haven't lost your spunk. When can we break you out of here?"

Celia checked the chalkboard on the wall that faced her bed. The day and date was listed in bright white chalk: *Thursday, July 4.* "Hopefully it won't be more than a week. I hate that I'm not at Whispering Pines for the holiday weekend. I sure hope Ruby can run things out there. The place is booked solid."

George nodded. "Ruby seems like a very capable woman. Didn't she spend time out there with you when you were young?"

"Sure, but she's never taken care of guests. She's always been one of them."

"Don't you have someone out there that works full time? That old guy. What's his name?"

"You mean Nash? Sure. He's there. And I'm lucky to have him. But he's not young anymore. In fact, he told me at the start of the season that this will be his last with me. He wants to retire. I'll need to find a replacement, which won't be easy."

The thought of finding someone else, someone as trustworthy as Nash, had her worried. If she was smart, she'd hire someone before Nash wrapped things up in October so he could show his replacement the ropes.

But she couldn't think about that right now. She needed to heal.

She suppressed a sigh. The seven, nearly eight, seasons she'd owned Whispering Pines hadn't been quite as joy-filled as she'd hoped. Running a lake resort, even one as small as the Pines, was a challenge for a single woman with a full-time job. Preston used to make it look so easy. He could afford more help, and he'd *owned* the company where Celia worked. She didn't enjoy the same level of freedom in the summer months. Tripp, Preston's son, hated for her to take time away from the office. She suspected he was still bitter about the way she'd come to own Whispering Pines.

"How are we doing in here?" a nurse asked as she strode purposefully into Celia's room on soundless shoes. "Do you need something else for the pain?"

The first pill was making her feel tired, and Celia feared anything more would knock her out. She hated it when she didn't feel in control. "No. My pain level is tolerable."

The nurse smirked. "I wish all my patients could be like you. You wouldn't believe the whining I'm subjected to day in and day out."

Celia felt sorry for the woman's patients—the nurse should have expected as much in her line of work—but she kept quiet. Once the woman had checked Celia's vitals and jotted something in the chart that hung from the end of the bed, she paused before she left the room. "Anything I can get you?"

Celia declined, adding, "I may try to nap soon."

With a nod, the nurse turned and disappeared out the door.

But her appearance seemed to have agitated George. "Celia, what's your plan once you leave here? Will you go home? I'm sure Mother could take good care of you."

Celia finally let out her sigh. "Mom spent enough of her life taking care of Beverly. Eighteen years of it, to be exact. Besides, I'm sure it won't take long for me to get back on my feet. I'm on leave for the next two months. Tripp wasn't too happy about it, which is ironic. He spent time at Whispering Pines healing from his war injuries back in the forties after he lost his left hand. At least I'll finally get to spend a decent amount of time at the resort. Funny how it took a round of cancer for me to pull that off."

"Will Ruby be there to help you, then? I don't think you should be alone, at least not at first. And I doubt 'nurse' is one of Nash's job duties."

"No, I couldn't ask Ruby to do that. She can cover for me for a while, but she won't be able to stay more than a week."

George nodded, concern still etched in his expression. His hand absentmindedly brushed the hair back off his forehead, something he'd done since he was a boy. She could always tell when she saw it that he was trying to figure out a solution to a puzzle.

Celia let her eyes stray to the single window in her hospital room. The sky outside was blue, the sun bright. She'd go straight back to Whispering Pines tomorrow—if the doctor would let her, which was doubtful. George was right: she needed to figure it out before she was discharged. She hated to have to miss the annual fourth of July fireworks show, but she trusted Nash to see that no one, and nothing, got damaged.

"I might have an idea," George said. "But I'd have to check with her first."

"Check with whom?" Celia asked. Her mind was fuzzy. Had she dozed off and missed part of their conversation?

"Lavonne."

"Lavonne?" Celia repeated. She tried to follow the conversation, but her eyelids were heavy. It hit her: the pain pill was finally kicking in. "What about her?"

"What would you say if Lavonne came to spend a few weeks with you at the resort?"

Now Celia was sure she must be asleep. George wasn't making any sense. Lavonne was busy at home with their three kids. Little Ethan was the oldest, and he wasn't quite five.

"Look, sis, I can tell you need some rest. I might have a solution for you. Let me make some calls, and I'll be back tomorrow. We can talk about it then, all right?"

Celia forced her eyes open again, sure she'd only let them shut for a second or two. But the room was in shadow and George was gone.

She'd fallen asleep.

A cheerful greeting from an orderly rang out over the sound of his meal cart. "Dinner is served!"

The nauseating scent of overcooked peas and instant mashed potatoes assaulted her nostrils. Celia wished she could pull the covers up over her head to escape the unpleasant smell. Unfortunately, she doubted she could lift her left arm high enough to accomplish such a feat. She smiled wearily back, resigned to her fate.

Chapter Four
Gift of Untapped Potential

"I still can't believe George arranged for you to babysit me," Celia said, a hint of irritation in her voice. "I'm not a child." She could feel her sister-in-law's eyes on her as she stared straight ahead through the bug-splattered windshield. Her auburn hair caught on her eyelashes as it whipped around, and her open window created a vacuum of sorts inside the Cadillac. After nearly a week in the hospital, the fresh air and warm temperatures felt too good to shut out. "Keep your eyes on the road, Lavonne."

George's wife grunted. "I'm not a child either, Celia. You don't need to tell me how to drive. Besides, I'm not here to babysit. I don't see this as three weeks of playing nursemaid to you. I think of it as a much-needed holiday from my life. We both know you won't need my constant attention. Not like everyone does at home."

The bitter tone in the younger woman's voice surprised Celia. She'd always thought Lavonne loved being a mother, although she could only imagine the effort it would take to keep a five-year-old boy and his two younger sisters properly clothed and fed, not to mention entertained and out of trouble.

Not sure how to respond, she said, "They're great kids."

Lavonne tapped the fingers of her left hand against the steering wheel, and the *tap-tap* of her wedding ring against the wood grain inlay competed with the low thrum from the radio and the rush of the wind through the open window. Celia snapped off the music, unaccustomed to the noise. Unlike Lavonne, she wasn't used to a constant assault on her eardrums.

"They are great kids," Lavonne agreed, fiddling with her necklace. "Forgive me. I'm just tired. Renee woke up in the middle of the night and complained of a bellyache. She didn't make it out of her bed in time, and I rinsed vomit out of her sheets as the sun rose this morning."

Celia couldn't help but laugh. "Maybe it won't be so bad to help me after all." She glanced at the necklace. "Are those the kids' birthstones?"

Lavonne grinned, holding the three little pendants on the end of her gold chain so Celia could see them better. "They are. George gave me this necklace for my birthday. I do think he had second thoughts about his plan this morning. Renee still looked a little peaked when she came down for breakfast, and Jess refused to eat anything. If they both have the flu he'll have a miserable day."

"He isn't at work today?" Celia asked. "I thought Letty was babysitting."

"No, George took today off. Letty will come over tomorrow morning and watch the kids while he's at work. They have the schedule all planned out."

Celia recognized the flaws in her brother's plan. "Our dear sister-in-law has never seemed comfortable around your children, has she?"

Lavonne glanced over her shoulder and used the blinker, swinging out to pass a slower semi-truck. She didn't immediately answer as she concentrated on the road. Once back in her own lane with the truck in the rearview mirror, she shrugged. "I get it. Letty and Gerry haven't been around kids much. He told me once that they'd wanted children of their own, but she had too much trouble with cysts, and had a hysterectomy about five years after they got married."

Celia remembered mention of a surgery years ago, but she'd been so busy at work back then she hadn't realized the impact it would have on her brother's life. "Oh my. I figured there must be some reason they never had children. I didn't realize . . ."

She let her voice trail off. What kind of person doesn't keep better track of her own family? She squirmed, unhappy to realize how self-absorbed she'd become.

Lavonne glanced over, noticing her discomfort. "I still think I should sleep in one of your bedrooms while I'm here. I'm supposed to keep an eye on you while you recuperate."

Celia sighed. "They removed my breast, not my brain. And my brain is used to living alone. I'll be fine. You can spend time with me during the day, and you'll only be a phone call and a quick stroll away should I need you at night."

"You don't live alone. You still live at home with Maggie."

Celia squirmed under Lavonne's reminder. She hated it when people made it sound like she still lived under her mother's roof. At fifty-one, Celia technically owned their house, and it had worked out well to share her home with Maggie.

"True," she conceded. "But we're both very independent. We come and go on our own schedules. Regardless, I'm always alone at Whispering Pines."

The moment she said the words, Celia felt a pang in her heart. So much time alone wasn't something she'd ever aspired to, but it was the result of the life she'd chosen.

"Say, I forget you also have a tenant in your basement these days," Lavonne went on, oblivious to the melancholy stealing over Celia. Given Lavonne's busy home life, she'd probably relish the idea of some alone time. "George mentioned something about it. How did that happen?"

Lavonne's question shooed away her blues, and Celia's mind flooded instead with images of little Karen. She enjoyed having a child in the house again. "It's a long story. A young mother found herself in a terrible predicament and I'm able to help her out until she can get back on her feet." Celia spotted her red-lettered sign that marked the turnoff to Whispering Pines on their right. "Slow down. There's the turn."

Lavonne slowed. "You don't expect this to be a long-term arrangement, then?"

"What?" Celia asked, distracted by the welcome flush of wellbeing she'd felt the moment her eyes picked out the sign. She couldn't focus. Maybe her hospital stay took more out of her than she'd realized.

"The woman and baby in your basement."

Celia caught the glance Lavonne gave her. "Oh. Sorry. I'm tired. A quick nap might be in order once we get settled. And to answer your question, no, living in my basement isn't the perfect solution. There's no bathroom downstairs. Thank goodness we have a full bath on the main floor. But it works for now. And the baby is fun to have around."

Lavonne maneuvered Celia's Cadillac onto the gravel road that led to the parking lot of the resort. "You'd have made a wonderful mother, Celia."

A spasm rippled across Celia's chest, and she couldn't be sure whether it was her own body's efforts to stitch itself back together or the pain Lavonne's words elicited. Both the radical surgery she'd recently endured and giving up her own baby years earlier had ripped pieces of her essence away that she could never get back.

"We'll get you settled, Celia. We're almost there. I'm afraid this long drive might have been too much for you. You look positively worn out."

Celia smiled as Lavonne slipped into mothering mode. She doubted the woman even realized it. Maybe it wouldn't be so bad to have her here, at least for a while. Maggie had offered to come out to the resort to help in her recovery, but she would have had to cancel a planned trip with friends to Niagara Falls, something Celia was loath to ask her to do. Her mother had given up enough of her life for her four children.

Besides, this would give Lavonne a bit of a break, and maybe they'd get to know each other better. Their twenty-plus year gap in ages and vastly different lifestyles meant they'd never been close. This might be their chance to change that.

Celia and Lavonne settled into a routine in their first shared week at Whispering Pines. The younger woman would slip into the duplex and prepare a healthy breakfast for Celia. Celia's incision was still painful, and it made sleep difficult. As a result, she got up later than usual.

Weather permitting, Celia spent her days outdoors. At first, she rested in a lounge chair on the patio behind the duplex. Later, she'd walk down by the water and, if none of the guests were using it, head out on the dock.

After Ruby went home, Nash was a lifesaver. He went above and beyond his normal job duties, cleaning cabins when the guests turned over. Celia felt guilty about the extra work—Nash was well past the age when he could have retired—but he insisted it wasn't a burden, and she did appreciate the help. Lavonne was a quick study with the paperwork for guests, and she only needed occasional input from Celia.

Things ran smoothly at the resort while she allowed herself time to rest and heal. Perhaps the legends about the healing properties of this land were more than just talk. Like before, when she'd returned to Whispering Pines with empty arms after the birth of her child, she could feel her strength grow a little each day. She'd never see her child again, but at least she could have reconstructive surgery, when the time was right, which might help her to feel whole again.

Celia was surprised to come down to a quiet kitchen one Saturday morning. It was nearly nine o'clock. Normally, Lavonne would have a short stack of pancakes or a kettle of scrambled eggs ready for her. Not that she minded. She'd finally gotten a decent night's sleep. She felt rested. Maybe she'd go for a short walk in the woods later. All this sitting made her feel like a caged animal.

She filled the glass carafe from the new drip coffee machine she'd treated herself to earlier that spring and poured the water into the reservoir. Opening the drawer below the machine, she rooted around for the filters. Nothing. She checked the other drawers, to no avail. Maybe Lavonne moved them to a cupboard. She checked but still couldn't find any.

They must be out. She needed her morning coffee, so she'd have to settle for the old percolator pot. Thank goodness she hadn't tossed the beast. She pulled a chair over next to the counter. There was limited cupboard space in her kitchen, so she'd put the old pot on a top shelf, out of the way. As she hoisted herself up onto the chair, a wave of dizziness hit and she paused, gripping the upper cupboard door to steady herself.

Once the sensation passed, she reached up to retrieve the carafe. But she'd forgotten her limited range of motion on that side. Pain stabbed, and she wobbled on the chair.

"Celia! You'll fall!"

Confusion swirled with the pain. *This can't be happening,* she thought. She only ever heard that voice in her dreams anymore. She must be dreaming. That was the only way to explain the deep voice in her ear, the powerful hands at her waist to steady her.

From somewhere near the front entrance came Lavonne's yell: "Celia, why in heaven's name are you up on a blasted chair?"

The hands at her waist relaxed enough for Celia to turn slightly to look behind her. Lavonne was running toward her, but why? Couldn't she see Danny had already braced her from falling?

Lavonne ran toward her, but the woman didn't get any closer.

Celia looked to Danny for assurance, and he smiled up at her in that calm, loving way she'd missed so much. She placed her palms on top of his broad shoulders, and he lifted her off the chair as if she were weightless. The pain in her arm and chest ebbed away, Lavonne forgotten. Her bare feet felt the worn, cool linoleum as she pivoted to face him. How she'd ached to see his face again. Her arms came up, still free of the pain that had threatened to send her toppling off the chair, and she reached for him. His hands released her waist and came together behind her back.

Before her body could come up flush against Danny's, rough hands shook her shoulder. The scene in front of her eyes blurred. Danny's face wavered then swirled away. Lavonne's words penetrated her muddled brain.

"Celia, can you hear me?" There was a note of concern in her voice.

A cool heaviness settled across her forehead. A trickle of moisture meandered down and pooled in her ear.

"What in the blazes . . ." she murmured, reaching up to push at the wet cloth that had slipped down over her eyes.

"Thank God." Celia could hear the relief in her sister-in-law's tone.

The fog ebbed away and she felt something soft beneath her. She couldn't feel the smooth floor under her feet, and her legs felt trapped.

It *was* a dream.

She wasn't downstairs in her kitchen. She was still in bed. Bright sunshine assaulted her eyes when she pushed the wet washcloth aside. She turned her head and tried to block the rays of light with her hand.

"Why are you in my bedroom, Lavonne? What time is it?"

Lavonne stood and stepped back. She dropped into a nearby chair, ignoring the robe Celia had tossed there the night before when she'd retired. "It's just after eight. I got here about a half hour ago and made breakfast. I hollered up the stairs for you to come down, but you didn't. I thought I better check on you, and when I was halfway up the stairs, you let out this awful shriek. I ran up and found you thrashing around on the bed. Your sheets got all tangled and you looked flushed. I felt your forehead. You're feverish. That's when I got you a washcloth. It always helps when the kids are sick."

Celia used her hands to lever up to a seated position, ignoring the sharp twinge across the front cavity of her chest. "I must have been dreaming."

"Oh, you were dreaming all right. Who's Danny?"

"Danny?" Celia asked. She felt her guard come up. She never talked about Danny with her family. Her oldest friends still brought up his name from time to time, but her family knew little of the man. She doubted her brothers would remember him, and her mother never mentioned him.

"Yes, Danny. I'm sure that was the name you shouted."

"He's no one. Just somebody I used to know," Celia mumbled, although she could see curiosity mixed with concern on Lavonne's face.

"Well, I'm worried you might have a fever. Let's have a look at those dressings. We don't want an infection in your incision."

Celia opened her mouth to argue but paused. She hated being treated like a child—she hadn't even liked it when she *was* a child—but Lavonne was there to help. Celia needed to heal as quickly as possible and get back to her life. Her cancer had provided a silver lining of sorts: two uninterrupted months at Whispering Pines. They'd already made it through the first week. She didn't want to waste any more time, worn down and sore.

Lavonne helped untangle the bedding from her legs and then stripped off the top sheet. "I'll toss these in the laundry later."

Celia nodded, swinging her legs off the side of the bed. Poised there, she unbuttoned her silk pajama top and let it pool around her waist. With matter-of-fact movements, Lavonne loosened the tape that held bandages and gauze against the incisions. Celia watched as the younger woman worked quickly and tried not to wince at the pain despite Lavonne's careful movements.

"Actually, this doesn't look bad."

"You act like you know what you're doing," Celia said, still somewhat amazed at the other woman's cool nature. If their roles were reversed, Celia doubted she'd be as confident in her ability to nurse Lavonne back to health.

Lavonne shrugged. "I used to be a candy striper at the hospital when I was a teenager. I considered some type of career in the medical field, but then I met your brother, and the babies came."

Celia grinned at the old-fashioned term, despite the wistful note in Lavonne's words. "God, I haven't heard of a candy striper in years."

Did Lavonne regret giving up on a career of her own? Celia wondered but didn't want to ask. Who was she to ask those types of questions? The image of Danny in the kitchen downstairs swam in front of her eyes again. Age had taught her everyone makes sacrifices. She used to think she was so different from other women, choosing a career over a family, but life was teaching her that she wasn't so different at all. Everyone made choices. Every choice came at a cost.

There would always be days when she'd regret giving up a life and family with Danny. Lavonne likely felt the same about her own life. Everyone made sacrifices. Especially women.

"Thank you," Celia said instead. She offered what she hoped was a sincere smile. "I appreciate your help. It means a lot to me."

Lavonne smiled back as she deftly rolled out a fresh dressing, adhering it just as the nurses had before Celia left the hospital. "Maybe it'll give us a chance to get to know each other a little better."

"I thought that, too," Celia agreed. She liked Lavonne but had never taken the time to nurture more than a superficial relationship with her.

Lavonne laid the back of her hand against Celia's forehead again to test for a fever. "You're cooler now. Maybe it was nothing. Or maybe it was your dream that had you all hot and bothered."

Celia batted Lavonne's hand away.

"Why, Celia, you're blushing. I think I'll make it my goal over the next week to figure out exactly who this Danny fellow is."

"I told you. He's no one. At least not anymore," Celia insisted, sliding her feet down to touch the floor as she uttered the lie. A fresh wave of pain hit her heart—pain that had nothing to do with her surgery.

"Hmm . . ."

It didn't sound like Lavonne believed those words any more than Celia did.

Chapter Five

Gift of Helpful Hands

Twelve days post-surgery, Celia felt more like herself. She was sleeping better, and down to just one nap in the middle of the afternoon. She was ready to get some work done, and she was excited about her early morning appointment.

As she rounded the corner of the walking path on her way to the lodge, she glanced around. The guests seemed to be enjoying the pretty morning. The resort was well manicured, the green grass freshly mowed and the beach raked. Perfect. Today it mattered more than ever that the resort look nice.

A sound caught her attention. At first, she worried it was a wounded animal. Distressed animals were often dangerous. Or was it a human? She stopped to listen, hearing it again: the sound of heartbreak. Someone was crying.

She spied Lavonne on the front steps of her cabin, wiping at her face. She hurried in her direction and ignored the hitch in her side.

"Lavonne, what's wrong? Has something happened? Are George and the kids all right?"

Before Lavonne could even answer, Celia took a deep breath. The likely culprit? The woman was lonesome for her family.

Lavonne angled her face away, but Celia persisted.

"Are you all right?" she asked, laying a hand on Lavonne's knee as she sat next to her on the steps.

Lavonne shrugged. She faced forward and stopped trying to wipe away her tears. "I'm sorry, Celia. Nothing's wrong. I'm not sure what came over me."

"Do you miss George and the kids?"

Lavonne drew a long, shuddering breath. "I suppose."

Celia noticed a closed book, some type of notebook or journal, at Lavonne's feet. She took a different tactic. "Are you writing in your journal?"

Lavonne hiccupped. "No. Why?"

Celia motioned toward the book.

"Oh. That. That's just an old sketchbook I found tucked in one of the dresser drawers in the bedroom back there." Lavonne jabbed her thumb over her shoulder.

"Really? I didn't know anything was in there. Someone must have forgotten it. May I?"

"What?" She glanced down at her feet. "Look at it? Feel free."

Celia picked up the book and flipped the cover back. A pencil drawing, bearing some vague resemblance to the beach here at Whispering Pines, filled the top page. The picture, though lacking precision and detail, had an energy to it. "Did you draw this?"

"Oh no," Lavonne said. She looked at the open book in Celia's lap. "I don't know who drew that one. Keep going. I think different people have been doodling in there."

Intrigued, Celia turned the page. The next picture was like the first, but this one included a small fishing boat out on the water. It was likely drawn by the same person. Continuing on, however, she found that different artists of vastly different skill levels had taken pencil to paper inside the book. Lavonne's find fascinated her; she was surprised she'd never stumbled upon it herself.

When she flipped another page, she gasped. Unlike the other pictures, all done in charcoal pencil, this one boasted a vivid red cardinal on the branch of a tree. The tree and leaves were in the same charcoal as all the other pictures, but the burst of color made the bird jump off the page. The details were intricate and created a lifelike visage.

"This one is really good . . ."

The twitter of birds penetrated her mind. Her eyes wandered from the page to the branches high above them, half expecting to see the red bird that might have served as the model in the picture.

The drawing left her disconcerted. She remembered the myth Danny had shared with her, all those years before, that loved ones come down from heaven as red cardinals with messages. When she was twenty-one, she'd shared this cabin with her sister. Beverly had only been eighteen that long-ago summer, a new high school graduate. Celia was fifty-one now, but dear Beverly had never celebrated her nineteenth birthday.

She reached a finger out to touch the sketched bird's red plumage.

"Don't touch it," Lavonne said, catching Celia's hand. "It'll smear. Do you really think it's good?"

Celia nodded, still discombobulated by the bright red cardinal. "I think it's great!"

A set of initials, woven into the tree's foliage in the lower right-hand corner, matched Lavonne's. The rest of the pages in the sketchbook were blank.

"Wait. Did *you* draw this one?"

"Why do you sound so surprised?"

She looked between the picture of the cardinal and Lavonne's face, the hint of a smile chasing away the shadows from the woman's eyes.

"I didn't know you were an artist," Celia admitted.

Lavonne laughed out loud. "I'm no artist, but I've always enjoyed drawing." The cheerful sound was a relief to Celia after the state she'd first discovered her sister-in-law in.

She shook her head. "No, this is good. You have a real talent."

Lavonne's expression turned whimsical. "I wish I had time to do more of it. Maybe even take a class. But I'm more likely to be the one to clean up finger-paint messes or broken crayons than the one creating with paint and charcoal."

Celia closed the sketchbook, careful with the pages. Her thoughts returned to that life lesson: everyone makes sacrifices. "I never thought about how much you've had to give up to raise your kids. George still finds time to fish and golf, doesn't he?"

"He does."

She detected a touch of resentment in Lavonne's curt response.

The slam of a car door caught her attention. She glanced at her wrist and moved her old charm bracelet out of the way so she could read the watch face. "Oh my. That must be my nine o'clock appointment."

"What?" Lavonne asked in surprise. "Appointment? Celia, you're supposed to relax and heal. You just had major surgery barely two weeks ago! You shouldn't be working yet."

"Oh, this isn't really work. It's more fun than anything. I don't even know if anything will come of it."

The other woman sighed, finally wiping away the last of her tears. "You don't really need me anymore, do you? I suppose I could call George, have him come pick me up early."

Celia put a hand out and got slowly to her feet. She was stronger, but she still had to be careful. "Nonsense. We're just getting to the fun part now. If you don't have to take care of me, you can focus on some rest and relaxation for yourself. God knows you've earned it! Say, you know what? You might enjoy this meeting I have this morning. Want to come with?"

Lavonne smiled. "Sure. Why not? I have nothing else to do, given how my patient seems to be healing up nicely. But this isn't some boring appointment with an insurance salesman or anything, right?"

"It's not," Celia confirmed, her thoughts full of cardinals and messages. "And given this surprise creative side that you've hidden from me, this might be right down your alley."

"You'll include us in your book, then?" Celia asked.

Her head reeled at the prospect of Whispering Pines being included in a travel book that featured some of the most well-known lake resorts in Minnesota. She'd nearly forgotten she'd submitted an entry form after she'd stumbled on a brief article about the project in their newspaper back home. Whispering Pines wasn't particularly well known, nor was it as large as most other resorts, but Celia knew she wasn't the only one who thought the resort was special. Inclusion in a book like that could help keep her full in the summer months. Plus, a tiny part of her would welcome the flush of pride she'd feel to see her resort featured in an actual book.

"Let's not get ahead of ourselves, Mrs. Middleton," Mr. Turner said.

Turner was a handsome man somewhere in his forties. The smile he shot her was full of charm, although she wasn't sure it reached his eyes. She still hadn't decided if she actually liked the guy or not. Not that it mattered. She worked with plenty of people she didn't like. But if there was one thing she didn't tolerate in her business, it was ambiguity. She crossed her arms over her chest, her hand brushing against the bandage beneath her blouse.

"If you don't plan to feature Whispering Pines, why are you here?"

Lavonne, who had greeted Turner when he'd introduced himself to the two women but remained in the background while he explained his concepts for the book, frowned at Celia's directness. "Excuse my sister-in-law if she's getting ahead of herself. You only just arrived. Would you like a tour of the resort, Mr. Turner? Because I think you'll absolutely fall in love with the place if you give it a chance. Especially on a beautiful day like today."

The man turned his attention to Lavonne and bestowed her with the same smile that grated on Celia's nerves. She suspected the man used it to charm more than his fair share of women. Sure, he was handsome enough, but not at all Celia's type.

She paused. What was wrong with her? This was business. Clearly once she was back home she needed to go on a few dates. She was really off her stride. Lavonne was smart to step in to smooth any feathers Celia had ruffled.

Maggie's words flitted through her brain. *You can catch more flies with honey, dear.* Her mother liked to remind her of this truism whenever she thought her daughter too aggressive.

Celia remembered the forlorn look on Lavonne's face earlier, when she'd discovered her on the cabin steps. But when she'd complimented her sister-in-law's drawing, Lavonne's sadness fell away. Now she was practically charming this man's socks off, something Celia wasn't in any mood to attempt herself. Maybe she should let Lavonne run with this. It might boost her confidence, and Celia really wanted to get Whispering Pines into that book.

"Please, call me Harrison," the man said to Lavonne. "The reason I wanted to stop out today was because there has been so much interest in this project, we actually need to go through a vetting process. So yes, a tour of your little resort here would be just perfect."

Celia bristled at the condescending tone but bit her lip.

"Whispering Pines may be small compared to other venues around the state, but it's hard to beat the history and the tranquility here," Lavonne assured the man. "Celia, would you like to join us on the tour? This *is* your resort."

Celia's instincts told her Harrison Turner liked Lavonne. What wasn't there to like? Her brother's wife was pretty, younger, and apparently more than happy to butter the man up. If she didn't know better, she might have guessed Lavonne was flirting with him.

She's good, Celia thought.

"Honestly, I'm tired this morning. Why don't I put the pot on, and when the two of you get back, we can have a cup of coffee and discuss logistics."

"Are you sure?" Lavonne asked, her confidence slipping a notch.

"I'm sure. You've had to listen to me talk about the history of this place while we relaxed around the fire with a glass of wine more than once this past week."

Harrison Turner nodded, as if he could picture the scene in his mind. He, like most people, probably found the thought of relaxing around a roaring firepit to be the epitome of a perfect summer evening.

Besides, her words were true. She had shared plenty of facts with Lavonne recently. The woman would represent the resort well.

Celia walked the two of them to the front door of the lodge then headed back to the kitchen to start a pot of coffee. Nash poked his head in and they quickly discussed the plumbing in the larger cabin along the edge of the woods. She gave him permission to head to town to purchase a new water heater for the unit. Then she went back to her office and started at the top of the pile of mail. She was amazed at how much had accumulated over the past few weeks. She sorted and paid bills, as well as placing her food and liquor orders. Although she'd moved away from providing full meals to their guests years ago, she still liked to keep necessities on hand for purchase. At one point she took a break to make her way back to the kitchen for more coffee. By the time the front door opened again and voices floated back to her, her second cup had already cooled.

"Mrs. Middleton, you have a marvelous place out here," Harrison Turner said as he entered her office again, grabbed a chair from against the wall, and set it in front of Celia. He started to sit but thought better of it, instead offering the seat to Lavonne while he retrieved a second one.

When his back was turned, Lavonne gave Celia a quick wink.

Whispering Pines will be in his book, Celia thought. She bit back a grin. Well then, she was far more willing to humor the man if it meant her resort might be featured.

"It's a little slice of paradise out here," she agreed.

Harrison Turner crossed his ankle over one knee and leaned forward, a wide smile on his face. "You should know, I've only looked at half the resorts on our list, and I know I'll have to cull at least ten of them from the final project. But Lavonne made some excellent points during her tour. This resort conjures up the old mom-and-pop-type establishments of a bygone era. I truly believe that my book will be better if Whispering Pines is a part of it."

Celia felt a flush of pride at his words. And she had Lavonne to thank for it.

"It would be an honor to be included, Mr. Turner. Sorry—Harrison. What's next, then?"

"This project really took on a life of its own. I suppose I'll need to come back later, interview you, get the photographs taken. It would be helpful if I could stay here for a night or two. I'll want light from different times of day for the pictures."

She wondered if the man was half as talented at photography as Danny.

Did Danny still take pictures?

She forced her attention back to Harrison. "Stay here? Hmm . . . we're full all the way through the end of August, so that might not work."

Lavonne shifted in her chair. "What if Mr. Turner stayed in *my* cabin?"

Celia's eyes swung to Lavonne in surprise. Harrison Turner raised his eyebrows, as if intrigued by the idea.

"I could stay in one of your spare bedrooms in the duplex, Celia," Lavonne said to clarify her proposal. "You have me in my cabin for another week and a half, right?"

Celia thrummed her fingers on her desktop. "That would work. Actually, that might be our only option. Harrison, could you arrange your schedule to fit us in relatively quickly?"

The man tilted his head back and peered at the office ceiling. He tapped his index finger against the side of his nose, as if deep in thought. "It would be tricky, but I could switch some things around, perhaps come back tomorrow."

"Tomorrow?" both Celia and Lavonne asked in unison.

"Is that too soon?" he replied, lowering his head to look at the women.

Celia checked her own calendar, open on her desktop next to the phone, but only for show. She'd make this work. She wanted to be in this book. This man, a well-known author in the travel business, had done similar books in other states. His word carried weight. Whispering Pines was currently benefitting from a fully booked summer, but one never knew what the future may hold.

"Actually, we'll make it work. What time can we expect you tomorrow?"

Tripp called Celia later that same day, upset about a large project that apparently went sideways in her absence. After a perfunctory inquiry as to her health, he immediately launched into the many issues they faced on the project.

Celia found the situation ironic. Both Preston—despite all the support he'd shown her with her career through the years—and now his son, Tripp, felt men had to be placed in charge at the office, but when it came to getting the work across the finish line the details always fell to her.

Tripp hinted that she'd had enough time off to recuperate from surgery and she should consider coming back into the office early. When she didn't take the bait, his irritation came through clearly on the line, but they compromised. He'd have a courier deliver a file to her the next day; she'd take some time to see where she could help but stay at Whispering Pines for at least two more weeks.

Celia's body hadn't healed as quickly as she'd hoped. When Lavonne reminded her things seemed on track with the timeline the doctor had said to expect, it bothered her that she couldn't exceed medical expectations through sheer force of will.

Between working on the project for Tripp and Warren and getting the rest her body required, she worried she wouldn't have enough time to work with Harrison Turner. She admitted as much to Lavonne a few hours before the man was due to return to Whispering Pines while her sister-in-law again changed her bandages and made up her bed.

"Why don't you let me work with him?" Lavonne suggested. "I thought about the project so much last night I couldn't fall asleep. I have *ideas*. It feels like my creative juices are flowing again for the first time in a long time."

"I can't ask you to do that, Lavonne. You already do so much for me."

She laughed, although the sound had a hollow echo in it. "You think this is a lot? Celia, my days consist of taking care of children, my husband, and our home, from the minute I wake up until I collapse into bed every night. This feels like a guilty pleasure."

This wasn't the first time Celia had heard Lavonne complain about her life at home. "Are things really that bad for you at home?" she asked. "Does George know how miserable you are?"

Lavonne dropped the pillow she'd plumped on Celia's bed with a sigh. Turning, she fell backward onto the mattress and dropped a wrist over her eyes. "I'm sorry. Sometimes I think all I do is complain. George has been super. It's not him. And it's not the kids. It's me."

"What do you mean?"

Lavonne took a deep breath then propped herself up on her elbows to face Celia, though she still wouldn't look directly at her. "The doctor . . . he thinks I may have a touch of postpartum depression."

"But Jess is two. She isn't a newborn anymore."

Lavonne fell flat onto her back again. "Exactly. So why do I still feel like this? My doctor wants me to see someone. You know, like a counselor."

Celia felt out of her depth. She didn't know anything about the condition so many women suffered from after giving birth. She'd had her own moments of the baby blues, but nothing that stretched on for years. "Have you taken his advice?"

"I went to one session. It felt like a complete waste of time. All she wanted to talk about was my childhood, as if there were deep, dark secrets there that might be the key to helping me now."

Celia walked over to her closet, removed a simple outfit for the day, and pulled the loose top over her head. "Is there anything I can do to help?"

Lavonne sat up. "Just staying here helps. I feel like I'm finding *me* again, you know?"

Celia didn't know, but she nodded as if she followed.

"Let me help with this book project," Lavonne continued. "I felt like I connected with that Harrison fellow yesterday. You need to rest more, and now your boss's boss needs you on that project. Don't trouble yourself with the book. Have faith in me."

Grudgingly, because it felt like too much to ask, Celia smiled. "Fine. You seem like you really want to do this, and I could use the help. If you need any help at all to answer Harrison's questions or to figure out how best to highlight the resort, you know where to find me. If you think you want to do this, run with it. I trust you."

Chapter Six

GIFT OR CURSE OF INTUITION

AT FIRST, THINGS WENT as planned. Lavonne moved her things into one of the two spare bedrooms in Celia's half of the duplex. Harrison came back as scheduled, and so did the courier with the folder of work from the office. Lavonne spent the better part of the afternoon off with Harrison and gave him a more in-depth tour.

Celia lost herself in the details of the complicated construction project. The hours raced by. How could a project get so bungled within a few short weeks? In her absence, Warren put someone less experienced in charge, and when the deal started imploding the new guy walked off the job. She usually respected Warren's decisions, but it seemed the struggles between Helen and Virginia continued to distract him.

Incompetence irked Celia. Why was it always her job to clean up the mess?

She worked well into the afternoon, and as the sun set she talked with Warren on the phone to devise the beginnings of a plan to get things back on track. She ate cold leftovers then, exhausted, fell asleep on the couch. She didn't even have the strength to catch the document she held when it slipped from her fingers and fanned out across the green shag carpet.

She woke to the *click* of the front door.

"Why are you asleep on the couch, Celia? Don't tell me you worked late," Lavonne scolded as she breezed into the room. She bent to pick up the mess of papers.

"What time is it?" Celia asked, rolling onto her right side so she could sit up. "You smell like smoke."

"It's late and you should be in bed. Now come on, I'll help you up."

Celia was too tired to care that Lavonne hadn't answered her question. She made it to bed with her sister-in-law's help, and it felt like she'd barely closed her eyes when the twitter of a bird outside her open window woke her again.

The morning sun streamed around the curtains.

She thought she remembered that Lavonne said something about an enjoyable evening around the firepit with Turner and other guests, but she'd been so tired she might have dreamed that part.

They followed their morning routine, and Lavonne disappeared to work with Harrison on the book project again. Telephone conversations and permit work consumed Celia's day. Fatigue washed over her and she turned in early, proud of herself for getting into bed rather than falling asleep on the couch again. Her doctor would have admonished her for working so hard. Luckily, Lavonne didn't seem to notice—the younger woman had shifted out of nursing mode, and seemed much more relaxed than when they'd first arrived.

When she thought back on this time, Celia suspected the third day of this routine might have been where things ultimately broke down.

Against her better judgment, she agreed to drive into the office to deal with union officials behind some of their project troubles. Warren promised they'd finish in time for her to return to Whispering Pines that evening. Nash could handle any issues with their resort guests, and Lavonne expected to finish up with Turner that evening. The author planned to leave the next day.

Discussions ran later than expected at the office, and it was midnight when Celia returned. She eased into a parking spot in the outer row as quietly as possible and was careful not to slam her door. She'd worried she'd fight to stay awake during her drive, but instead she felt energized. Her extra efforts had paid off. Warren should be able to handle anything else that came up until she returned from leave. In fact, he'd ordered her to go back to the resort and rest, and said he looked forward to her return in a few weeks.

It had rained while she was away. Puddles stood in the gravel parking lot. The air held that post-rain freshness and the sky had cleared, boasting a brilliant moon and a smatter of stars. Inhaling deeply, Celia leaned against her Cadillac. Her hood was still warm against her back from her hour-long drive. She thought back to long-ago nights at Whispering Pines with Danny. He used to give her this same energized feeling. They often sat on the end of the dock together to watch the sun rise and contemplate life. She shook her head. Time here with Danny was a lifetime ago. Time to return to the now.

Despite the late hour, she felt compelled to stroll through the resort. She'd sleep better if she made sure all was well.

The deserted beach was quiet, the only sound the soft lap of waves against the shoreline. Celia often wondered why more people didn't relish the beauty of the water under the moonlight. Mystical light shimmered across the choppy surface of the dark water. She shivered at an unexpected chill. She rubbed her arms as she walked along the path that skirted the back side of the beach. At the far edge, where the woods stood tall in the moonlight, the walkway curved back.

A low fire burned in the pit in front of the newer cabins, and a sparse gathering of adults lounged in chairs around the low flames. She wondered if she'd ever stop referring to the trio of cabins as "new." The storm that took out an older row of cabins near the water had hit long ago. Celia knew the exact number of years because the storm wreaked havoc the very day she'd returned to Whispering Pines without her baby.

That baby would be nearly twenty years old now, out in the world somewhere and already older than her sister had ever been. Celia sent up a silent prayer to the twinkling stars above and wished the best for her. Life could be a challenge. She hoped that someone, somehow, sheltered her daughter from the worst of the pain.

She squinted to try to see whether Lavonne sat amongst the guests around the fire but couldn't pick her out. Celia grinned. *I might have to sneak into my own house like a tardy teenager.* If Lavonne was in bed already, listening for her patient's return, Celia would get an earful in the morning about too much work and not enough rest.

She shivered again. Why did she feel so chilled tonight? If she caught a fever, Lavonne wouldn't be the only one mad. Hopefully it was just her body protesting the long hours of the day and not the sign of a setback.

She tossed a whispered "Goodnight!" to her guests and took the fork in the path back toward her duplex. The white orb of the moon illuminated the path and reminded her of another night, back in that long-ago time when life was full of promise and possibilities. She'd met with Danny on a night like this, and their relationship had taken a new turn.

Lost in her thoughts, she wandered toward home. Nothing was out of place. She was comfortable leaving the resort in Nash's capable hands, but she wouldn't have that luxury much longer. She needed to look for his replacement.

The screech and slap of a screen door cut through the tranquility. Celia's steps faltered. A low murmur of voices and the rumble of a man's laughter floated on the soft breeze, but she couldn't tell which cabin he might have exited. Why did her stomach twist at the happy sound of guests relaxing? Her intuition sensed something. She stayed still, hidden in the shadow of the lodge. The laughter came again, followed by a woman bidding goodnight, the words barely discernable.

Celia felt a flush of embarrassment. Why the heck was she spying on her guests? People came here for fun and relaxation. She wasn't a prude. If a couple met under the cover of darkness, who was she to judge? Weren't some of her fondest memories of when she and Danny did the same?

She hurried home, appreciative that Lavonne had left a lamp on for her in the living room. She hastened back to the kitchen to take her medication, snapped off the light, and headed up the dark stairwell. Another lamp burned in the upstairs hallway. Lavonne's door was closed. Celia turned off the second lamp and slipped into her own bedroom, quiet so she wouldn't disturb her sister-in-law. Maybe Lavonne wouldn't know how late she'd gotten in after all. A hot bath would warm her, but that would surely wake Lavonne. Instead, she peeled off her clothes, put on a warm set of pajamas, and collapsed into bed, her body spent.

But sleep wouldn't come. Despite her bone-weary exhaustion, her mind refused to shut down. Desperate for sleep, she lay there, hoping all the work she'd done in recent days wouldn't set her back.

The scrape of a key snagged her attention. She wondered where Nash had been off to at this hour. It was nice to have him right next door. His presence was soothing.

But then she heard the familiar creak of the stairs on her side of the duplex. Her body stiffened in fear. The third step always groaned in protest; she kept forgetting to ask Nash to look at it.

Had someone broken in?

But she heard a bedroom door open and close, and the pieces fell into place. Lavonne hadn't been asleep in her room after all. Celia's ear hadn't recognized the woman's quiet voice in the shadows as she laughed along with the man, bidding him goodnight, but her gut did. The woman's voice, so soft she'd barely heard it, had been Lavonne's. And now she was sneaking into the house, and her hesitant footfalls hinted at secrets.

What was going on? Her heart raced at the implications. Had she made a terrible mistake letting Lavonne spend unsupervised time with someone like Harrison Turner? What if Lavonne's frustrations over too much work and not enough appreciation at home meant she'd risk losing everything to find herself again?

Despite the many unconventional decisions Celia had made throughout the first five decades of her own life, she had few regrets. She'd built a life for herself that she enjoyed, at least most of the time, and she supposed that was more than many others could say. She'd learned a long time ago that every choice comes with tradeoffs. Years earlier she'd made the heartbreaking decision to let Danny walk away—more than once. She'd given up their child, convinced someone else could offer the baby a better life. Those choices left an imprint of sadness on her soul. There were days when she regretted them, but a different course might have had undesirable consequences, too. She'd never know for sure.

She also battled her conscience, from time to time, over the lengths she'd taken to wrestle the resort away from Tripp. But she reasoned that if she hadn't, Whispering Pines would no longer exist.

She'd learned that the smallest decisions, ones that seem inconsequential at the time, can morph into so much more. Had she set the stage for Lavonne to make choices that could blow up not only her own life, but Celia's brother's life, too?

Chapter Seven

GIFT OF GRACE

CELIA SPENT THE REST of the night convincing herself that her suspicions about Lavonne were ridiculous. Her sister-in-law would never be foolish enough to risk her family for a quick romp with anyone, let alone someone like Harrison Turner, no matter how undervalued she might feel at home. She had no proof the couple she heard laughing was Turner and Lavonne. Shame on her for even thinking it.

She woke to the chatter of a noisy squirrel, the morning gray and hushed. She eased out of bed and tiptoed to the bathroom, wanting to escape the duplex before she had to face Lavonne. A few hours in the lodge office would help get her out of her own head. Coffee, too.

The lock on the front door of the lodge gave her trouble, and she was still battling with it when she heard a car door slam. Turning, she was surprised to see Turner up and moving. It was only a few minutes past six.

"Celia, I'm glad I ran into you," the man said, hurrying in her direction. "I think I've got all I need for now, and I have an appointment at another resort at eight."

"Eight o'clock this morning?" Celia asked, surprised he'd stayed at Whispering Pines another night if he was due somewhere else so early.

He checked his wristwatch. "As long as I don't get lost, I'll only be a few minutes late."

Celia pitied the individual waiting for Turner at the next resort. Her own schedule had been thrown off enough times at work by people who were careless with their commitments to know how frustrating it could be. "I'm sure Lavonne got you everything you needed, but if there is anything else you have questions about in regards to Whispering Pines, please give me a call. I'm excited to see how you tell the world about this place. I've dedicated most of my life to keeping it running, and I know your book will help with our marketing."

She watched him closely, hoping he understood that she was taking him at his word. After all their hospitality—or, more precisely, *Lavonne's*—the coverage better be good.

"Whispering Pines is a special place, Celia, and I'll do right by you," he assured her.

If he had something to hide in regards to her sister-in-law, he gave no indication, but she thought she'd test him a little more.

"Lavonne will be sorry she didn't get a chance to tell you goodbye."

Turner shrugged. "Your sister-in-law was very helpful. Please thank her for me."

See? Celia thought. *Nothing happened.* Relieved, she assured him she'd pass on his appreciation and watched as he hurried off, scolding herself. *I shouldn't be so suspicious of people.*

At dinner, Celia suggested Lavonne move back into the little cabin she'd stayed in before Harrison Turner arrived, but her sister-in-law didn't want to go to the trouble of moving her things again.

"I know you like your space, Celia, but I'm not used to being alone. To be honest, I didn't love staying in that little cabin by myself."

"Really? I thought you'd appreciate some peace and quiet," Celia said. She set a platter of fried chicken on the table. "I'm not the cook Mother was, but I found her recipe. I know you liked her chicken."

Lavonne helped herself to a drumstick. "This looks delicious! And yes, I thought it would be nice to have time to myself—and please don't think I'm ungrateful—but there's something about that cabin."

Not again, Celia thought, getting a pitcher of ice tea out of the refrigerator and taking the chair across from Lavonne. "What's wrong with the cabin?"

Lavonne broke a piece of crispy skin off her chicken, then shrugged. "Nothing. Well, nothing I could put my finger on."

"I used to love that cabin."

She nodded. "I know you did. I'm sure you made some special memories there. I just had a terrible time sleeping. I kept thinking I was hearing a baby crying." She forced a little laugh. "I was probably dreaming."

"Probably," Celia muttered, dropping a dollop of butter onto her helping of mashed potatoes. She wouldn't tell Lavonne she'd heard that complaint before. Another guest mentioned something similar last summer. *It's that damn curse again.*

"I sleep better here," Lavonne went on. "Besides, we were going to get to know each other better during my stay. I'll probably never get the chance to be here alone like this again."

"I keep telling George to bring all of you out, but he hasn't taken me up on it yet."

She nodded. "And that's kind of you. Maybe when the kids are older. I can't imagine trying to keep an eye on them out here at this age."

She had a valid point, Celia supposed. "How's Letty getting on with Ethan, Renee, and Jess?"

Lavonne squished up her face.

"That bad?"

"Well, it hasn't been great," she admitted. "George is going to take off two more days from work. Gerry is coming out to pick me up on his next free day, actually. I think Letty has reached her wit's end."

Celia tasted the chicken. "Mmm . . . not as good as Mom's, but it'll do. Well, I'll be sure to send Letty a little something to thank her, too. You have all done so much to help me get back on my feet."

"That's what family is for, Celia."

She knew Lavonne was right, and she hated herself for suspecting the woman. They spent the remaining days of Lavonne's visit talking and relaxing, enjoying the opportunity to get to know each other better. Sure, Celia was most likely getting behind in work around the resort, but she'd catch up when she was alone again. Her body was healing as her relationship with her sister-in-law was expanding.

"Gerry's here!" Celia hollered up the stairs.

"Tell him to relax!" Lavonne yelled back, irritation in her voice. "I'll be down in a few minutes!"

"He says he can't stay!" Celia shot back, shaking her head and climbing the stairs to find out what was holding Lavonne up. "I thought you said you were packed."

She pulled up short at the doorway to Lavonne's temporary bedroom at the sound of furniture scraping across the floor. "What are you doing?"

Lavonne let go of the bed's headboard and threw her arms in the air. "I can't find my necklace!"

"Your necklace?"

Dropping to her knees, Lavonne stuck her head under the bed as far as she could. "Yes, my necklace. The one George gave me. I never take it off. But it's gone."

"Oh no. I'm sorry, Lavonne. We'll find it. When did you lose it?"

Lavonne sat back on her heels, her face flushed bright red. "If I knew that, I'd have a better chance of finding it!"

Unaccustomed to getting yelled at, Celia took a deep breath and held her tongue. She wouldn't add to the drama. Instead, she tilted a rocking chair in the corner of the room to look beneath it, in case Lavonne's jewelry had somehow fallen under it. "It can't be far."

Lavonne stood then collapsed onto the bed, her face in her hands. "I'm sorry, Celia. It just means a lot to me. I can't lose it."

Celia sat down next to her. "I'll keep looking for it. I promise. But I'm afraid Gerry has a catering job tonight, so he needs to get back to town. You need to go. Do you think you've had your necklace since you've been staying in this room?"

Lavonne looked around. "I'm almost sure of it."

"All right. I'll check everything in here carefully, and if I don't find it, I'll check around some more."

"Whispering Pines is a big place," Lavonne whispered. Her eyes were suddenly full of tears.

Celia thought she was overreacting a bit, but then her eye caught on the charm bracelet she'd worn on and off for more than twenty years. It had been a gift from Danny, and she'd be devastated if she ever lost it. "Have a little faith," she said, slinging an arm around Lavonne's shoulders. "Thank you again for taking such good care of me. I don't know how I'll ever repay you."

Lavonne dropped her head to Celia's shoulder. "You already did. You gave me space to find myself again. I feel better. I can go home and be a good mom again."

Lavonne's words ended on a watery hiccup, and Celia grinned.

"You have always been a good mom, Lavonne! Nothing will ever change that. But if you don't hurry up, Gerry isn't going to think you are a very good sister-in-law."

Lavonne straightened and slapped her knees. "Right. Everyone needs to get back to their lives. It's time to get back to the real world."

Celia grabbed one of Lavonne's two suitcases and followed her out the door, thinking the woman was the luckiest one of them all, going home to a husband and three amazing children.

~ 𝓮𝓮 ~

After Gerry and Lavonne drove away, Celia busied herself cleaning the small cabin where first Lavonne then Harrison Turner stayed. Another round of guests would arrive in two days. Nash offered to clean the cabin, but Celia wouldn't hear of it. He'd gone above and beyond during her surgery and recovery, but he was slowing down. Maintaining the resort was too much for the elderly man.

As Celia cleaned the bathroom, she thought of all the people in her life who'd stayed in this particular cabin. She'd shared it with Ruby that second summer, and the following season she'd shared it with her sister, Beverly. The cabin had also been her hideaway from the world during her unplanned pregnancy. Those were—mostly—happy times.

There was also that unfortunate episode in the cabin in her first summer as owner of Whispering Pines. She'd tried to block it from her memory, but Lavonne's comments about a crying baby had brought it all back. Ten years ago, against Nash's advice, she'd allowed Eleanor and Tripp's younger sister, Iris, to rent the cabin for two weeks. She was Preston's daughter, after all, and without Preston there would be no Whispering Pines, for Celia or for anyone.

It was the last time she'd ever ignored Nash's advice.

The truth was, there'd always been something unusual about Iris.

Thinking back, Celia remembered how Iris had refused to leave at the end of her reservation. The odd woman seldom left the cabin. Celia didn't know what to do. Eleanor had been out of the country with her husband and unable to help, and Celia refused to ask Tripp for any help related to Whispering Pines, even if it involved his sister. But she'd already turned away two couples, and she hated her inability to honor their reservations. After nearly a month, she finally had to call the sheriff to help get Iris out. The scene turned ugly, but Iris eventually agreed to leave with the sheriff.

Unfortunately, that wasn't the end of the troubles.

Celia let the toilet lid clang shut. She gathered her cleaning supplies and headed to the bedroom to strip the bed and dust. As she pulled the fitted sheet off the mattress, a tiny tangle of gold glinted up at her from the dark floorboards.

Lavonne's necklace.

Celia's heart plummeted at the sight. The necklace shouldn't be in here. Lavonne was so certain she'd still had it after moving her things into the duplex.

Damn Iris Whitby. The curse strikes again.

All those years earlier, as the sheriff escorted Iris out of the cabin, she'd hissed a warning that this tiny cabin—the very cabin Celia had loved so much as a young woman—would bring pain to many. She'd uttered the words like some kind of curse.

Celia had scoffed at the idea. She'd thought it a ridiculous notion.

But then, the following summer, a guest's young dog passed away on the cabin's steps. The cause of the untimely death remained a mystery, leaving his owner distraught.

There'd been other mishaps as well. Couples left early, their vacations cut short by worrisome quarrels. Broken pipes kept Nash busy. Some guests complained of lost sleep because of the eerie sound of an infant crying.

As Celia gazed with trepidation at the thin gold chain that represented George's family, the necklace lost inside this cabin while Harrison Turner was its only guest, she was finally convinced that Iris's curse was indeed real.

It didn't take long once Celia returned home from the resort until she was exhausted again. Longer hours than usual catching up at the office after her long absence quickly negated her two months of recuperation at Whispering Pines. Warren apologized for the extra workload. She knew he still worried about her health, but there was work to be done, and that's what she was paid to do.

Today she'd decided enough was enough. She'd left at six, refusing to stay and work in the darkened office. When she got home, a bright November moon lit her path from the garage. The house was dark with shadow. Her mother must be out for the evening. Hopefully there were leftovers in the refrigerator.

The muffled ringing of a telephone reached her ears, and she hurried forward, digging for her house keys. A light dusting of snow covered the back stairs, and she had to grab the railing to catch herself as her front foot slipped. She felt a stab across her chest and paused to catch her breath, praying she hadn't done any damage to her nearly healed scars. The pain passed quickly, and she hurried inside, snatching up the receiver before the caller hung up.

"Hello," she gasped, trying and failing to not sound winded.

"Celia, is that you? Did you run to the phone?" George joked on the other end of the line.

"Yes, as a matter of fact, I did, and I damn near broke my neck," she replied, tucking the phone between her ear and shoulder so she could pull her gloves off and shrug out of her coat. Once she had one arm free, she switched ears. "I hope you're calling with news worthy of my heroic efforts to reach the phone in time."

He gave a good-natured chuckle. "As a matter of fact, I think this might qualify. Is Mom there? If so, put her on, too."

Celia tossed her coat over the back of a kitchen chair. "Sorry, her car isn't here. It's the first Wednesday of the month. I think she has book club."

"Darn. I should probably wait, then."

"No way, little brother!" Celia glanced inside the fridge and moaned over the near-empty shelves. "I ran into the house, almost broke my neck, and now there's nothing to eat. Tell me something that will make me feel better."

She gave up on dinner for the moment and dropped into the other kitchen chair that wasn't currently acting as a coatrack.

"Promise you'll let me tell Mom, then? You'll keep this our little secret?"

Celia grinned despite the dim, lonely kitchen. George's good mood was lifting her spirits. She could hear the joy in his tone. "I promise."

Without further delay, George blurted out, "Lavonne is pregnant!"

Celia wasn't sure she'd heard her brother right. The grandfather clock in the living room rang out, marking the half hour, the sound low and ominous. She sprang out of her chair and crossed over to flip the switch on the wall, flooding the room with light.

"Did you say *pregnant?*"

"I did! Isn't that exciting? We're going to have another baby! But you can't say anything to anyone. Not until I have a chance to talk to Mom. The kids don't know yet. They can't keep a secret to save their lives."

Celia nodded. "Yes, secrets can be dangerous things."

"What?" George asked. "I didn't quite hear you."

Clasping a hand over her chest, noting how different it felt post-mastectomy, she bit her lip. "I said babies are such wonderful things!"

George laughed, but there was a hesitancy to it. "Yes . . . yes, they are. I guess this means I'll need to buy another charm for Lavonne's necklace. She was so relieved when you mailed it back to her."

"I was happy to help," she muttered, doing her best to block out the dark thoughts that she'd tried banishing for good. Lavonne was *pregnant* . . . Just a few months earlier, at Whispering Pines, she'd confided to Celia that she'd been dealing with postpartum depression and feelings of overwhelm. But Celia wasn't sure her brother knew about any of that. "I didn't know you were trying for another baby," she hedged.

"Sometimes God works in mysterious ways," George replied.

This told Celia little, and she couldn't read anything but excitement in her brother's voice. "He sure does," she muttered.

The sound of young voices, talking and laughing in the background, came over the line. "There's the kids now," George said. "I have to go. But remember—let me tell Mom."

Celia nodded absently, then said, "Don't worry, I won't say a word. And George . . . congratulations. I'm happy for you."

As was tradition, both Gerry and George brought their families to Celia's house to celebrate another Christmas. Virginia and baby Karen still lived in the basement, but they'd gone to visit her sister Shirley for the holidays. Celia and Maggie waited on their front step at the designated time to wave warm greetings as everyone arrived. Their quiet home transformed as George and Lavonne's three children infused it with their youthful enthusiasm. It never felt like Christmas until the kids arrived. Maggie spoiled them all with a traditional Christmas Eve dinner of scalloped potatoes and ham. Later they opened gifts and attended Midnight Mass.

The kids woke the household early on Christmas morning in their excitement to see what Santa brought. After a huge breakfast, they convinced their Uncle Gerry and their mother to take them sledding. Letty went to lie down, nursing a migraine brought on by the constant din of excited children. Celia doubted Letty would sign up for any more babysitting gigs. Her summer experience seemed to have left her traumatized.

Maggie worked in the kitchen to get the turkey into the oven. She'd shooed everyone out of her domain. This left Celia and George—who'd had to sit out to-day's sledding adventure—to relax in the front room. Scattered strips of wrapping paper and new toys still littered the braided rug that covered the wooden floor. Lights on the Christmas tree provided just enough heat to release the evergreen scent of the needles into the air. Celia breathed in the aromas of the holiday then took a sip of her coffee, an eye on her brother as he sat in the ancient recliner, his injured ankle elevated after a slip on the ice while skating with the kids the day before.

Lavonne's pregnancy was showing, and it bothered Celia. As George's sister, didn't she have a responsibility to tell him about what might have happened at Whispering Pines?

But what if she was wrong? What if nothing really did happen, and it was just her twisted imagination conjuring up the worst?

"Penny for your thoughts," he said as he set his cup of spiced tea aside. "Come on, Celia, it's *Christmas*! It's been six months. How are you feeling?"

Her mind blanked before realizing he was referring to her cancer diagnosis and subsequent treatment plan. They hadn't discussed it lately. "I feel like myself again. There wasn't any cancer in my lymph nodes, so the doctors didn't think radiation was necessary. Lavonne probably told you all that."

Her brother nodded.

"With any luck, that whole unfortunate situation is behind me now. They're keeping a close eye on me, of course. I go back for another follow-up in January. I'm thinking of talking to them about possible reconstructive surgery."

"That's a relief. If you're feeling good, why do you look so pensive?"

She stalled with another sip of her coffee, which was now cooled. *Maybe I should just test the waters a little,* she thought.

"Thank you again for sending Lavonne to Whispering Pines to help me out last summer. I don't know what I'd have done without her."

George sighed as he clasped his hands across his stomach. The slight paunch reminded Celia she wasn't the only one getting older. "I wondered if this would come up."

"If what would come up?" Her heartbeat ticked up in pace.

"Look, Celia, Lavonne told me she's been sick with worry about what you might think of her."

Celia hesitated, unsure how to respond. She'd stewed over whether to bring up the situation with Lavonne once she learned the woman was pregnant, and here George was, taking the reins in the discussion. "What do you mean?"

"We were so relieved when you mailed Lavonne's necklace back. She was sure it was lost forever. Thank you. I should have remembered to tell you that at Thanksgiving. I can't believe that was the only time we've seen you since August.

I'm sorry about that. I know we should do a better job of spending time with you. And with Mother."

Celia waved away his concern. They were all busy. She understood that.

"But Celia, Lavonne's worried. She swears she sees doubt in your eyes when you look at her now. Your . . . suspicion."

"My suspicion?"

George glanced over his shoulder, toward the kitchen, as if to check whether their mother was within earshot. He snapped the recliner down with his good leg and leaned toward Celia, his gaze intense. "Lavonne told me about Harrison Turner," he said. His eyes held a hint of challenge.

"She did? What did she tell you?"

He shook his head. "Enough. Not long after she returned, she admitted to making a dreadful mistake. I'd had no idea she'd been feeling so low . . . so unappreciated. I'm afraid it left her vulnerable. Do you know she was even seeing her doctor? I guess *baby blues* is a real thing. I'll admit, it shocked me, and it hurt more than you can ever imagine. I walked out that day, went for a long drive, didn't know whether I could turn around and come back home. But we have a good life together. We've built a family, and neither of us wanted to give that up. It isn't easy, but we're working hard to move past it all."

She struggled to take it all in. She could read the pain in George's eyes, but she was relieved she wouldn't have to bear the weight of her suspicions anymore. If only she didn't still feel guilty about suggesting Lavonne and Turner work together in the first place.

George sighed, as if he could read her mind. "Celia, none of this is your fault. Lavonne told me she convinced you to let her work with Turner. Whatever transpired between them is not your fault. She's a grown woman, responsible for her own choices. Her own mistakes. We all are."

Celia nodded, but she doubted the guilt would melt away that easily. There was one more pressing issue, and she had to ask.

"And the baby?"

"The baby is mine," George said, the words soft but holding an unquestionable conviction. "There will be no question of that. Ever. We will never discuss this again. Understood?"

Celia swallowed; her brother's unequivocal mandate was crystal clear. He'd decided, and it didn't matter whether it was a decision based on fact, or a belief in the sanctity of the family he shared with Lavonne.

In that moment, she loved him more than she ever had before. She thought of her own baby she'd given up so many years earlier. Other people raised her daughter, and she could only hope they felt the depth of love for her that George obviously already felt for the baby his wife was carrying. He *was* the child's father.

A crash from the kitchen ended the uncomfortable silence.

"I could use a little help in here!"

The distress in Maggie's voice had both Celia and George on their feet in an instant. Celia rushed toward the back of the house; George hobbled along behind her. Their heavy conversation was over, replaced with concern for their mother.

Chapter Eight
Gift of Overdue Conversations

"Are you sure you want to take on another rental property?" Warren asked.

Celia smiled at the skepticism in the man's eyes. While she knew Warren appreciated her head for business, he clearly still struggled with her level of independence. "I'm sure. Preston always emphasized how important it was to diversify my portfolio. In fact, he helped me get started with real estate when he left me two of his rental properties in his will. I admit it scared me to death when I first found myself in the role of landlord, but I enjoy it."

"But don't you worry that you might spread yourself too thin?"

She pushed her chair back from her desk so she could cross her legs. "Are you going to lecture me, or will you take a seat?"

Warren sighed, and her smile widened. She liked to keep people guessing. Her straightforward nature, coupled with a nonconservative approach to business deals, seemed to forever keep some people on edge. Warren, for his part, saw her smile and shot her a lopsided grin in return. He stepped inside her office, shut the door, and took a seat in one of the two chairs on the other side of her desk.

"What did you need to see me about?" she asked. Warren seemed hesitant, as if he was still holding something back.

His grin disappeared. "Honestly? Tripp hounded me again about generating more revenue out of this place, or else I need to find places to make some cuts. He thinks our overhead is too high."

"And let me guess. He suggested getting rid of me again?"

Warren shrugged. "I don't think he ever really means it."

"Oh, I think he'd love to see me go. His dislike for me goes way back. But he's not stupid. I bring in many times my salary in revenue for this company. Besides, he knows I could sit down and have a little heart-to-heart with his wife and blow his life to pieces."

He scowled. "Do you ever tire of it?"

Celia knew he was referring to the secret they both held over Tripp's head. Ten years earlier, their boss had foolishly engaged in an office dalliance with his secretary, and Celia walked in on it. The fact she'd helped put the temptation right in front of the man still tweaked her conscience, but she could rationalize her own actions. Tripp's father started this company, brought Celia in straight out of college, and made it clear he wanted her employment to continue for as long as she wanted to stay, even after he was gone. What she'd done had served to ensure Preston's wishes. Tripp, she was sure, would have preferred to not have her around as a constant reminder of the error of his ways, but he had no one but himself to blame.

"Tripp is a grown man," she replied. "We all have to live with the ramifications of our mistakes. He's no different."

"You *are* a ball-buster, aren't you?"

She laughed. "I despise that term. But coming from you, I'll take it as a compliment. Look, I'm not stupid. If Tripp's marriage ever falls apart, he might just act on his threat to get rid of me. At that point, what would he have to lose?"

"Deals," he pointed out.

"Well, sure, but I imagine he's conceited enough to think he could step in and do what I do or better anytime he chooses. All that aside, I want to build up my wealth to where, when the day comes that I want to walk away from this place, I have other sources of revenue. Which is why I'm closing on this cute little single-family home at two o'clock this afternoon. I hope to pick up a few more rentals over the next ten years to give me some cash flow once I retire from here.

Whispering Pines is expensive, and my summer revenue out there doesn't always cover things. I want to build up a financial cushion."

Warren chuckled. "I should take notes. My wife is talented at spending but has no interest in the *earning* half of the money equation. I'd sleep better at night if my income wasn't all tied to this place. Helen grew up with money, and she still spends it like the well is deep. Thank goodness her father left her a sizeable inheritance."

Celia nodded. She disapproved of the way Warren contributed to Helen's spending habits, spoiling his wife much as her father had before him, but it wasn't her place to say. "Did the Christmas ornament come yet?"

"Matter of fact, it did. Helen's birthday gift this year is a glorious nutcracker, all shiny and majestic."

Celia burst out laughing, and she wondered if he even saw the connection to his earlier comment. "You call *me* a ball-buster, but then you buy your wife a mercury glass nutcracker ornament for Christmas. Are you feeling threatened by all of the women in your life?"

Warren stood, shaking his head and putting her office chair back in place. "I don't know why I even try to have a polite conversation with you."

"Oh, come on, you know you love me."

"Like a sister. And we all know what a pain in the ass sisters can be."

Celia's smile slipped at his words. She'd lost her only sister so long ago, she seldom thought about their long-ago battles anymore. Now she ached for the closeness they'd once enjoyed—a closeness she'd tried to replicate through friendships, but it was never quite the same.

"Shit . . . Celia, I'm sorry. I shouldn't have said that."

Gathering the loan documents on her desk into a neat pile, she shook her head, slipping back behind her armor of self-sufficient business woman, complete with a confident smile. "No worries. That was all a long time ago. Now, if you'll excuse me, I have work to do. My boss can be a real hard-ass."

"I'll take my leave," said boss conceded, swinging her office door open. "Good luck at the closing today! I just want you to be careful. And I hope you find renters for your new place."

Celia already had an idea for the perfect renters, and she thought Warren would approve of her plan. Now she just had to make it happen.

"I can't let you do that. You've already done so much for us. Our apartment isn't so bad."

Virginia's response was predictable, but Celia had come prepared for this debate. "Ginny, you told me last week how you wish Karen had a backyard to play in. And it sounds like a full-blown party in the apartment below you. I passed a trio of teenagers on the stairs, and one of them was carrying a six-pack of beer. It's only three o'clock in the afternoon! Karen shouldn't have to grow up in this environment."

She watched Virginia's eyes dart around the dated kitchen. Even though Celia had dropped by unannounced, Helen's daughter insisted they sit down for pie and coffee. Karen was napping, but Celia knew the four-year-old would come barreling in as soon as she heard their voices. She could read the despair on Virginia's face when their eyes met across the miniature table.

"It's the best I can afford."

"Nonsense," Celia insisted. "If I charge you the same rent as you're paying here, I'll be able to cover my new mortgage on the place and have a little left over for myself each month. You'd be doing me a favor."

This wasn't entirely true, but she could afford to subsidize the mortgage for a while. Besides, she suspected it wouldn't be for long. Virginia was blossoming into a strong woman, her confidence rising now that she was out from under her mother's influence. She talked often of wanting to marry again, to have a husband to complete the picture in her mind of the perfect family.

"Celia . . . why do you keep helping me? When you let us live with you for free that first year after Bryce died, you literally saved our lives. And still, here you are, offering more."

Taking a bite of the lemon meringue pie, Celia felt a flush of pride. Inviting Virginia and Karen into her home had been the right thing to do. She'd made a real difference. Giving them a place to stay helped her better understand why her own mother still volunteered so often. It felt good to help others without any expectation of getting something in return.

"Because, Ginny, you are like a daughter to me. Your mother is one of my oldest friends, but I admit, I don't approve of the way she treats you. I pray that someday she'll come around, but in the meantime, I'm here for you. Besides, Karen is probably the closest I'll ever come to feeling like I have a granddaughter." She jumped when something banged heavily against the other side of the wall behind her. "And I don't want her growing up in a place like this," she added.

The noisy neighbors also woke Karen. The child hollered from her bedroom down the hall.

"Let me go get her," Celia offered, pushing away from the table. "You think about it. Wouldn't it be nice to live somewhere peaceful, with a backyard, and a garage for your car? Years ago, someone took me under his wing, and it completely changed my life. Let me help you."

Karen yelled again. "Momma! Up *now!*"

Virginia laughed. "Go. Get her. I'll think about it."

Seven o'clock the next morning, Celia unlocked the outer door to the office. The phone was ringing inside, but she'd never catch it in time. A cold October wind buffeted her back and dry leaves swirled around her ankles. Weak morning sunlight barely lightened the underbellies of the thick clouds.

"If it snows before Halloween," she muttered to herself, "I'm heading south with Mother this year."

She needed to call the foreman of their roofing crew. They were most likely booked out for months, but she needed a favor. If she didn't get someone over to her house to fix the loose shingles, neighborhood kids would start to refer to it as the haunted house where the two crazy old ladies lived. Young tricker-or-treaters would steer clear of their front walk. She grinned at the images her imagination conjured up. Her house wasn't really in that bad of shape, but upkeep on her home and her growing arsenal of rental properties seemed never-ending.

As she flipped on the lights, their hum filling the still deserted maze of desks and offices, Preston popped into her mind. She knew he'd have approved of her efforts to amass more real estate. It had been his idea in the first place. And, truth be told, her heart was happy knowing her rentals were providing quality homes to good people.

Virginia and Karen were settled in her newest rental. Warren had even helped his daughter and granddaughter move. She considered it a big step toward reconciliation, though Helen was still holding out, refusing to rebuild her relationship with their youngest daughter. Celia didn't understand how her friend could continue to hold a grudge at the expense of time with her only granddaughter. Making the situation even more bizarre, Helen doted on two older grandsons. She hoped they would resolve things with time. Helen would benefit from a relationship with her granddaughter. In the meantime, Celia offered to babysit if Virginia ever wanted to go out in the evening or work an extra shift.

She smiled as she walked to her office, thinking back to Saturday night. She'd babysat Karen for a few hours while Virginia went back to work at the library for an evening class. Virginia had tried to keep Celia's babysitting duties as simple as possible. Dinner was ready on the stove, Karen already bathed, the child's favorite books set out. All Celia had to do was feed her, read her a few stories, and put her down for bed.

It all sounded simple enough.

Dinner went off without a hitch, and it impressed her when Karen cleared the dishes herself. But when Celia suggested they head to her bedroom to read books, the negotiations began. The child insisted a tea party was in order, followed by a make-believe shopping trip. When Celia countered about how late it was getting, Karen was ready with a well-devised argument, delivered with conviction, hands on hips to emphasize her points.

Virginia was going to have her hands full. Celia saw, despite their lack of time together, snippets of Karen's grandmother coming through.

God help them all, she thought as she settled behind her desk.

But the youngster didn't stand a chance against Celia. By the time Virginia breezed through the door, Karen was sound asleep and Celia was engrossed in a book she'd found on the coffee table. Virginia had immediately burst into effusive praise for the man who had spearheaded the novel-writing course that evening. That man—Celia thought Virginia had said his name was Frank—was in for a surprise. Once Virginia set her sights on someone, they stood little chance of escaping.

The back door jangled. The office was coming to life, and Celia had a full day ahead of her, followed by dinner with a man with whom she'd been on a few dates already. She'd met him in July during his vacation at Whispering Pines. She'd initially deflected his interest, given he was at least ten years her junior, but he'd eventually worn her down. They had made plans to try out a new restaurant, and she looked forward to a nice glass of wine and stimulating conversation. Her date traveled internationally for work, and she loved hearing about his adventures.

She'd never made the time to see more of the world herself. Her passport was painfully devoid of travel stamps. As so often happened, thoughts of travel brought Danny to mind. Where was he now? Was he still shooting pictures for newspapers and magazines?

She pulled her mind back to the busy day standing between her and her dinner date and flipped through her Rolodex, searching for the phone number for the foreman. A set of unfamiliar voices floated into her office, unusual given the early hour. Customers seldom stopped in before eight.

Warren's secretary tapped on Celia's doorjamb. She still wore a trench coat and her pocketbook dangled from her arm. "Ms. Middleton? There are two police officers here to see you. They met me at the door."

Ice sluiced through Celia's veins. Police? At this hour? She shot to her feet, rounding her desk in alarm. Two men filled her doorway, their features schooled into an expression that spoke volumes. She skipped any social niceties, unable to think of any plausible reason these two men might darken her doorway that didn't spell trouble.

"I'm Celia Middleton," she stated, although they'd already been told this. "What's wrong?"

"I'm afraid we have some tough news for you, Ms. Middleton. Margaret Clements is your mother, correct?"

She could only nod, bracing herself for what she feared was coming. She felt blindly for her desk, backing up to it, seeking comfort in its solid weight.

"There's been a medical emergency at the hospital," the taller of the two men said, his eyes empathetic. "We called both the home number on file and the office here. You are listed as Mrs. Clements's emergency contact. But there was no answer."

She glanced at her watch, remembering how she'd ignored the ringing of the central line when she'd let herself in thirty minutes earlier.

I should have answered the damn phone!

"Given the early hour, we thought we might catch you in person," the shorter of the two officers explained. "I'm afraid they found your mother unresponsive in an elevator. They think she was reporting for her volunteer shift in the children's wing."

Her mind flashed back to the brief greeting she'd exchanged with her mother in the kitchen that very morning. Maggie had been excited to be helping with a special breakfast for the kids that day. A group of high school students in costumes were coming in for an early Halloween celebration. Celia wished now that she'd given her mother her full attention, but her mind had already been on her own evening plans.

"But she's going to be all right, isn't she?" she implored, though she doubted these two would make a personal visit if that were true.

The younger officer shuffled his feet, as if uncomfortable, avoiding her eyes. The taller officer gave her a brief shake of the head and added, "Hurry on over to the hospital now."

Given the short distance between her office and the only hospital in town, she thanked the officers for contacting her but declined their offer of a ride. Celia hated hospitals. As she blindly navigated the familiar roads, her mind flitted back to the turning points in her life that were often preceded by mad dashes to the hospital. Would today be added to that list? The crash, years earlier, that ultimately took her stepfather and left her mother with a permanent limp. The dash to her old mentor's bedside; the fear that she'd miss out on one last chance to speak to the man. Not to mention the years before that, all the times in the hospital with a young Beverly.

She couldn't lose her mother, too. Celia couldn't remember exactly what the officer said happened. Panic jumbled her thoughts. There was still so much she wanted to talk to her mother about. Overdue discussions she never should have put off.

She bolted out of her Cadillac, across the parking lot, and through the front door. A fellow volunteer that she recognized as a friend of her mother's pointed toward a set of stairs, not wasting a moment with small talk.

"Room 245."

Nodding her appreciation, Celia took the stairs two at a time, careful not to catch a heel on the worn steps. Out of breath and disoriented, she turned the wrong way, then backtracked when another hospital employee pointed down yet another hallway.

She finally spotted Room 245.

Not bothering to knock, she flung the door open, surprising the two occupants inside. A nurse was taping an IV tube to Maggie's inner wrist. When Maggie spied her daughter's worried face, noticed her breathless state, she shook her head. "Oh, my dear, you didn't have to come racing over here! I'm fine. Just a little spell."

Celia's eyes sought the nurse's gaze. Her concerned look spoke volumes.

"I'll send the doctor in, Maggie," the nurse said, patting her patient's hand as she quickly left the room.

"Mother, what happened? Are you all right? Two police officers showed up at work this morning, leading me to believe the worst. I can't tell you what a relief it is to see you sitting up in bed like this."

Maggie motioned to the chair next to her bed. "Sit. They shouldn't have worried you. I'm sure it's nothing."

Celia did as she was told, dropping into the hard plastic chair and pulling the clinging nylon of her blouse away from her sweaty back. "Nothing? This is at least the fourth fainting spell you've had in as many years. Ever since that Christmas a few years back when you dropped the turkey."

Maggie made a *tsk* sound as she smoothed the tan blanket over her lap. "One ruined holiday dinner and you never let me live it down."

"Has the doctor been in to see you yet?" Celia asked, disliking the gray tinge around her mother's mouth.

"Yes. He wants to do some tests. He didn't like the way my heart sounds. I'm so tired of him telling me I need to quit ignoring my dizzy spells. Truth be told, the spells aren't anything new. But they've never given me too much trouble before—other than the turkey incident, that is. I'm sure Nurse Betty is going to get him back in here so he can tattle to you. She's always sticking her nose in everyone else's business."

Despite the seriousness of the situation, Celia bit back a laugh. Maggie was forever coming home from her volunteer time at this very hospital with stories about this nurse or that doctor. According to Maggie, Nurse Betty wasn't the only nosy one.

"Listen, Celia, I don't think you'll be getting rid of me soon, but there are some things I want to discuss with you."

Celia shivered, either from the clamminess of her sweat-dampened skin or her mother's tone. Even though she'd beaten herself up during her dash to the hospital over possibly waiting too long to ask her mother about some things that had always bothered her, she still wasn't so sure she wanted to have the conversation.

Maggie wasn't leaving it up to her. "Celia, dear, I want you to know how much I appreciate all you've sacrificed for me through the years. After everything that happened with your sister, and later, when we lost Clarence, I wasn't sure I could go on. I don't know how I would have managed if you wouldn't have moved home. But, also, I'm sorry. I can see now that it wasn't fair to you. You've given up so much."

Her mother's words caught Celia off-guard. "Mother, don't be ridiculous. It wasn't a *sacrifice*. We're family. Family supports each other. I gave up nothing."

Maggie stopped smoothing the blanket and pointed her index finger directly at her daughter, a stern look on her face. The unnatural bend to her finger caused by years of sewing and advancing arthritis did nothing to minimize the message: that Celia be quiet and listen for once. "Did you really think I didn't know?"

An image of another long-ago hospital room burst out of Celia's deepest memories, superimposing itself over her aging mother's. Despite her many trips to hospitals through the years, Celia had only been the patient twice. Both times she'd left a piece of herself behind.

"I'm not sure what you mean," she hedged, in case her mother was referring to something else entirely.

"You know exactly what I mean, my dear. The child."

Celia's heart skipped a beat.

"Don't tell me you have nothing to say for yourself, Celia. You are *never* speechless."

"That was all a very long time ago," she replied. "I made a difficult decision, and I eventually found peace with it. There's no sense rehashing it all now."

Maggie waved both hands at Celia, shushing her. "Rehashing? Dear, we've never discussed it. Not once. Talking about it now isn't *rehashing* anything."

"You know what I mean. It's all in the past. But that doesn't mean it isn't still painful. I don't want to talk about it."

Her mother sighed, holding her gaze. Clearly she did not want to let the subject drop.

"I suggest we hear the doctor out, see what he has to say. Maybe they can help you get these dizzy spells under control. I don't want you going to Palm Springs again if you aren't feeling better."

Maggie gave one shake of her head. "I'll go to Palm Springs if I feel strong enough. Don't forget, I'm your mother, dear. Not the other way around. And you won't distract me that easily. I've carried this secret for too long. I deserve some answers."

Celia eased back in her chair and crossed her legs, shaking her head in exasperation. "There's almost nothing to tell."

"Dear, you were pregnant and unwed, slinking off to that resort of yours for a summer and coming home empty-handed. All this time, I couldn't help but wonder. Was the baby all right? Did you have any complications? Was the baby's father involved? It was that Danny boy, wasn't it?"

She held up her palm. "Slow down. My head is spinning."

"Fine. I'll give you a chance to explain. But you need to tell me. Please. I've wondered for too long."

Surprising herself, she opened her mouth and the words poured forth. The story she'd only shared in bits and pieces with her closest friends came out in a rush.

Maggie took it all in. "Preston was involved, then? He placed the child?"

Celia nodded. "He did. In the end, he offered to tell me more, but I declined. Tempting as it was, I worried it would be like pulling the scab off a deep wound. But he let one thing slip."

Maggie angled forward with anticipation. "Do tell."

Celia grinned. "He said 'she' when he referenced my baby. Mom, my baby was a girl. There is a twenty-two-year-old woman out there somewhere with our blood running through her veins."

Maggie clasped a hand over her chest, giving Celia a start. "Relax, dear, I'm fine. It just does my heart good to finally know. You can't imagine how hard it has been for me to keep quiet about this for so long. Or maybe you can. But I didn't want to go to my grave not knowing for sure."

Celia winced at the mention of a grave. She's already buried too many family members, beginning with her birth father, Charles. Even though she'd only been five years old when he died, it was a defining moment. She thought of Preston—another defining death in her life—and what he'd said about her father. She'd always wanted to know more about his relationship with Charles, and her mother was the only one left that could enlighten her. "Well. Now you know. I've told you my deepest, darkest secret. Now it's your turn."

A wave of surprise crossed the older woman's features. "I can assure you, dear, there are no mystery babies in my past."

"I was referring to Preston."

"Preston?" Maggie repeated, confusion radiating from her eyes.

"Mother, why didn't you ever tell me that Preston worked for my father? That he helped with Beverly's medical bills? Other than the time he visited the house to talk to me, I didn't know you even *knew* him."

It was Maggie's turn to squirm.

"Mother. Tell me. I have a right to know. Did you have an affair with him after Father died?"

Her mother burst out laughing.

"What?" she asked, not sure why the question so funny.

"No, there was no affair. You're making this out to be a bigger deal than it was. It's true that Preston worked for your father. And after Charles died, he came to see me. In hindsight, I can see I probably should have let him do more. His intentions were pure. But I was skeptical. And later, when your paths crossed and he seemed to take you under his wing, I was afraid you'd waste the opportunity he offered you if you thought he was only doing it because of a promise to your father."

"I wouldn't have done that," she insisted, though now that her mother had planted the thought in her mind, it took hold. "Do *you* think that's why he hired me?"

Maggie shook her head hard enough that a monitoring tab fell from her neck. A red button on one of the machines beside her bed blinked, but she ignored it. "Of course not. But I should have accepted Preston's help years ago. I hated that you girls had to go to bed hungry, that we had to let strangers live in our house so I wouldn't lose everything. I could have avoided all of that if I'd have accepted more help. I didn't want you to mess things up the same way I had. You and I are both plenty stubborn."

A quick tap sounded on the door and it swung open. A man strode confidently into the room wearing a lab coat as white as the thick hair on his head. "Maggie, darn it, I warned you this could happen. I wasn't pleased to hear from the doctor on call this morning."

"Hello, Doctor," Maggie replied, said stubbornness clear in the set of her shoulders as she faced the intruder.

"Ah, Celia, I'm glad you're here as well," the man said. "We have some things to discuss."

Chapter Nine
GIFT OF A STUCK WINDOW

MAGGIE'S DOCTOR INSISTED SHE cut back on her volunteer time at the hospital. The woman even took his advice, at least for a few weeks. But it wasn't long before she was back to spending every weekday morning on the children's wing. Celia tried to convince her to slow down, but there was one young girl in particular that Maggie felt compelled to help. The six-year-old's mother was raising her on her own, and the woman had to work.

Celia sighed. "Mother, I understand. I do. You hate for Katy to be alone. But there are other volunteers."

Maggie slammed the cupboard door after setting a cup she'd dried inside. She tossed the dishrag to the counter, scooped her keys out of the bowl under the telephone, and hobbled to the back door. In her haste, her keys tangled in the phone cord, pulling the receiver off the wall. It clattered to the floor, but she ignored it. She turned back to Celia, her hand on the doorknob and her eyes sparkling with unshed tears.

"She reminds me of Beverly."

Maggie spun back around and hurried down the back steps, a tight grip on the handrail.

Celia watched her mother walk away, her spine straight despite the slight stoop to her shoulders. Her limp was pronounced—a sure sign of fatigue.

The discarded phone's dial tone cut through Celia's frustration. She sighed and rose from her morning paper, spread out on the kitchen table, to retrieve the squawking handset.

That evening, Maggie would tell Celia that young Katy had slipped away during the night. Maybe it was the pain of yet another loss, or Maggie's own refusal to slow down. Regardless, it would be the last trip to a hospital Maggie would ever make. Her heart couldn't withstand another blow, and just like her young patient, Maggie wouldn't live to see another sunrise.

Celia muddled her way through the days that followed, making the arrangements, all while functioning inside a thick fog of feelings. She struggled to accept the reality of the situation.

Lavonne reached across the mahogany dining table to clasp her hand. "I'm so sorry, Celia. This is such a shock."

Celia jumped at the human contact. She'd forgotten she wasn't alone in their house.

Their house. She supposed she'd have to think about it as *her* house. Only she lived here now. She was alone. Or at least she would be after her brothers and their families went home.

She sighed heavily. "I can't believe she's never going to walk through that door again, thumbing through the mail, telling me all about the kids at the hospital, their triumphs and their struggles. I'm going to have to get a cleaning lady. Mother didn't mind housework, but I hate it. What will Selma and Beth do, now that she won't go to Palm Springs with them in January? How will they afford their condo down there?"

She knew she was rambling, but her mind struggled with the vast impact her mother's untimely death was having on her.

"Her friends will figure it out," Lavonne said. "Unfortunately, Maggie isn't the first one of their group to pass."

While true, that didn't make Celia feel any better. "Why do I feel so unmoored? I'm fifty-five years old! I knew Mother's health was declining. I just thought we'd have more time."

"I think most daughters feel like that. Like they'd do anything for a little more time with their mother, regardless of how old they are," Lavonne said, her eyes awash with sympathy. "Besides, you've lived with your mom most of your life."

Celia bristled. "I have a life of my own."

Smiling patiently with the same expression Celia had watched her sister-in-law use with her children, Lavonne shook her head. "Hear me out, Cee. Obviously, you have a life of your own. So did Maggie. But you both lived under the same roof. You two did an amazing job giving each other space to come and go."

"She drove me nuts sometimes," Celia admitted.

"Sure she did. And she struggled to keep her nose out of your business, too."

Celia helped herself to a cookie from one of many trays dropped off by well-wishers. "Did she tell you that?"

"She didn't have to. I'm a mother. Offering advice comes naturally when it comes to our kids. I don't think that ever changes, whether your daughter is five or fifty-five."

She tried to remember times when she'd felt her mother was overreaching. There weren't many. "She almost never interfered. I guess we were lucky to have the relationship we did."

"Celia, you *were* lucky. So was Maggie. You had a mother-daughter relationship, but also a strong friendship. Some women grow up with neither of those things."

She'd never tried to boil down her relationship with her mother like that. She appreciated Lavonne's insight.

"I'm so glad you're part of this family, Lavonne. You're good for George, you are a great mom, and you're wise beyond your years. Thank you. Talking about her helps."

Lavonne reached across and squeezed her hand again, then stood. "George wouldn't be the man he is today if you wouldn't have stepped up when Clarence died. You gave up everything to come back here and help raise your younger brothers. Helping you through this tough time is the least I can do."

Lavonne took both of their empty coffee cups over to the sink, leaving Celia to consider her words. She seldom thought back to those earlier years, when she'd given up Chicago to move home. When she'd given up the possibility of a life with Danny. At least it wasn't all for nothing. But now that she faced a lifetime of rattling around in this big house alone, she wondered if she'd ever get used to the quiet.

"And you were there for me, too," Lavonne was saying, her back still to Celia. "None of us would have the lives we do today if not for you. We all have to live with the choices we make, but you show us how to do so with grace."

It was as if Lavonne could read her mind. No one gets to middle age without some heartache and questions of "What if?" Thank goodness her brother was smart enough to plow through the pain.

"How are your kids doing? They've never lost a loved one, have they?"

Lavonne transferred dishes from the sink to the dishwasher. She nodded, but took her time responding. "It'll be strange, I suppose. I don't think they grasp the magnitude of it yet. Maybe if we'd let them see Maggie before they closed the casket, they'd be more upset. They haven't said much about it yet."

"I hate that they don't have a grandmother or grandfather on our side anymore."

"I hate it, too," Lavonne agreed. "And my family isn't close."

The back door flew open and slammed against the wall. The kids ran through the kitchen, nine-year-old Ethan in the lead, his sisters close behind.

"Stop!" Lavonne yelled, snagging three-year-old Val from the back of the line. She settled the child on her hip and leveled a glare at her older three. "Were you born in a barn? You know better than to come barging in here like that. Slow down and apologize to your aunt."

"*Ethan* slammed the door!" Jess said, pointing to her big brother. "He should be the one to apologize."

"We *all* need to apologize," Renee said, looking between Ethan and Jess. "And then Ethan needs to go tell Dad we found Mom. He says it's time to go."

Celia couldn't help but grin as she listened to young Renee order her siblings around. The girl was a born leader. Celia liked that.

It gave her an idea. After the kids had left, she spoke up.

"Lavonne . . . maybe, given I'm old enough to be your mother, *I* could step into the role of grandmother for these four."

Lavonne laughed at the suggestion. "Celia, you are about as *un-grandmotherly* as a woman could be."

She had a point. Most grandmothers weren't career women, landlords, resort owners, or dating forty-five-year-old men, let alone all of those things rolled into one. "I suppose you're right. But can't I at least be the cool aunt they all look up to, that they can come to for real-world advice?"

Folding a dish towel and threading it through the handle on the oven, Lavonne grinned over her shoulder at Celia. "You already *are* the 'cool aunt.' "

George and Lavonne offered to host Thanksgiving at their home. It would be a first for all of them, but with Maggie gone and Celia's lack of skills in the kitchen, it seemed like the logical choice.

It was a noisy, crowded affair, and her house felt even more empty when she returned home that Thursday evening. As she wandered the hallways, glancing into all the empty rooms, she decided.

She'd allowed George and Lavonne to handle Thanksgiving, but she wasn't giving up Christmas.

She would have to enlist help from Lavonne and Gerry in the kitchen, but hers was the only house that could comfortably house everyone along with the gifts, treats, and traditions of Christmas. Gerry and Letty wouldn't mind. Their tiny house was cozy for the two of them, but it couldn't expand to hold the entire family.

Besides, Celia's nieces and nephew loved to play in the attic of the big family home, and their presence filled the old house back up with life.

For the first time ever, Celia stood alone on her front stoop, nursing a deep ache of loneliness, as she waited for her family to arrive. It was the first Christmas since Maggie's death, and the kids would expect to see Celia there waiting. But, she reasoned, if she could get through this first Christmas without her mother's steady presence, it would get easier in the future.

Wouldn't it?

Once everyone arrived, she was swept up in the holiday excitement. Maggie's absence was almost palpable, and there were lots of forced smiles, but they were finding their way through it.

Those three days passed quickly. As she stacked fresh towels in the guest bathroom, Celia could hardly believe everyone would head home the following morning. She'd worried it would be difficult to keep the children entertained, but she'd forgotten that children entertain each other.

As she went back out to the linen closet, she heard pounding feet on the wooden stairs behind the door leading to her attic.

"Celia! Celia, where are you?!"

She grinned. Why did it feel so ridiculously good to hear someone yelling her name?

The door at the bottom of the attic stairs flung open. A breathless Ethan stood there, his face anxious.

"What's wrong, Ethan?" She was again surprised at how much the nine-year-old reminded her of Clarence, her long-dead stepfather. Ethan not only looked like she imagined Clarence would have as a boy, but he liked to tinker, too.

"I can't get the window shut upstairs."

Given it was snowing and only ten degrees outside, this wasn't welcome news. "And why, pray tell, is the window open?"

Ethan flushed with guilt. "I'm sorry. I shouldn't have opened it. But I couldn't help it."

She sighed, shutting the door to the linen closet. "Show me."

The boy nodded, following her up the stairs he'd just hurried down.

As she climbed the steep steps, she remembered the commitment she'd made to herself when she'd pulled the boxes of Christmas ornaments down the weekend after Thanksgiving. She needed to do some organizing up here. It would be her New Year's resolution.

As her head crested the top of the stairs, a chilly breeze skipped across her face. There were only two sets of windows in the attic, one facing the front of the house and the other the backyard. One of the front-facing windows was halfway open, and errant snowflakes were finding their way into the darkened interior. There were no screens up here, no barriers to keep birds or squirrels out.

She glanced down at her young nephew. "Why did you open the window in the first place?"

"Because it was rattling. I was going to fix it."

"And how were you going to do that?"

He held his hands up in a shrug of defeat as he walked alongside her to the front portion of the attic. "Hadn't thought that far ahead yet."

Yep, he *definitely* reminded her of Clarence.

Celia wrapped her fingers around the top sash of the window and pulled down. The glass lowered an inch, screeching in protest, but then stuck fast. These windows always gave her trouble the few times she'd opened them to air the attic out. She knew the trick to getting the warped wood to cooperate.

"Okay, Ethan, I need you to grab me one of those old chisels in that toolbox over there. Get me the one with the thinnest blade you can find."

"Over where?" the boy asked, spinning around to face the cluttered interior of the attic.

She glanced over her shoulder as she continued to jiggle the window. "There should be an old toolbox over there by my blue trunk. You know, the trunk you guys like to play on all the time."

Ethan nodded, picking his way through the piles and forgotten pieces of furniture. "You know, Aunt Celia, you really got a lot of crap up here."

She opened her mouth to scold him for his language, but thought better of it. If she wanted to be the cool aunt, she couldn't be the disciplinarian. She'd leave that up to his folks.

"I know. Maybe I'll clean it up come January, after the holidays."

His grunt told her he doubted she'd do anything of the sort.

He's probably right, she admitted to herself.

"Here," he said, already back with the chisel.

"That was fast," she said, taking the wooden handle from his outstretched hand. "See, I think if we just shimmy this in here, like this, we can pry it loose."

He nodded and stepped closer.

But it wasn't as easy as she'd hoped. They worked on it together for a minute or two, and finally the window gave up the fight.

She twisted the lock. "Next time, ask before you open that, all right?"

"I won't touch it again," the boy promised, although she wasn't sure she believed him. The kids always came up here when they visited, and it got hot in the summer. "That box of tools is cool," he said. "Can we look through them?"

Celia glanced at her watch. It was only ten. She wouldn't have to pull lunch together for a couple of hours.

"Sure, why not?"

She followed Ethan over to the toolbox he'd found. The boy sat on Celia's blue trunk. It gave him the perfect vantage point to dig through Clarence's metal box of old tools. He held a couple up to her, quizzing his aunt on what they were called and what they were used for.

The shadows were deep in this part of the attic. The dormers were low and piles of junk blocked light from the windows. "Just a second, let me get the light."

Once they could see what they were looking at, aunt and nephew took their time digging through the collection of vintage tools. Ethan shifted so they could lay the items out across the top of the blue trunk. Their fingers became smeared with old grease off the pieces, and somewhere along the way Ethan touched his face, leaving a smudge on his cheek.

Celia appreciated his interest in Clarence's things. "Would you like to pick out a couple of these to take home?"

He looked up at her in awe. "Really? Could I?"

She smiled. "Sure. Just don't tell your sisters. They'd want to come up here and start digging through all this old junk, too."

"These tools aren't junk," Ethan said, reverence in his voice. "I can't believe these used to belong to my grandfather. I think I might want to be a carpenter someday. That's what you said my grandpa did, right?"

She nodded. "Right. In fact, he even made this blue trunk for me, as a college graduation gift."

"No way! This is the best trunk ever! I can't believe Grandpa Clarence made it!"

Grinning, Celia ran her fingers across the scarred edges of the trunk. Scuffs marred the paint and scratches were gouged into the top. It wasn't the pristine piece Clarence had gifted to her. She should have taken better care of it.

"You know my sisters think this trunk makes the perfect table for playing restaurant on, right? They kind of drive me nuts about it."

Celia met and held his eye, this nephew of hers that she'd never spent enough time with. It was high time she changed that.

"Can I take these two?" he asked, holding up the two chisels he'd deemed most worthy. One was the long, narrow one they'd used on the window. The other was short and chunky.

She nodded. "I think those two are the perfect choices. Now, don't lose those. They're extra special. If you get lots of use out of them, maybe I can let you pick out a couple more later. But only if you prove to me you can take care of those two first."

He nodded, then carefully put the other ones back, laying them in the toolbox in a much more orderly fashion than she suspected he'd found them in. "Hey, Aunt Celia, can I ask you something?"

"Sure, anything."

He wrapped his two chisels in a piece of soft, soiled cloth from the toolbox, then motioned to the blue trunk again. "How come that's locked? What's inside?"

His question caught her by surprise. Her old trunk was a favorite plaything for the kids, but it had been years since Celia had touched the things she'd locked away inside. Things like the wedding dress she'd never gotten to wear, the christening gown no one other than Virginia's baby had worn in more than fifty years.

Would she ever be willing to share some of her secrets with others? Perhaps with the next generation?

As Ethan watched her expectantly, she again felt the raw loss of her mother. She remembered the day, so long ago, when Maggie gave her some of the items locked inside the trunk. Back then, Celia had still held on to hope, even after the death of her sister, that she was destined for a lifetime filled with amazing experiences.

Maybe someday she'd open it up for all to see, but she wasn't ready yet.

"Oh, sweet Ethan. Some things are better left locked away."

Chapter Ten
GIFT OF WHISPERING PINES

"WHAT DO YOU MEAN, you aren't coming? George, when you visited at Christmas, you promised you'd bring Lavonne and the kids out to Whispering Pines this summer!"

Celia hated the desperation in her voice. She'd done her best to push through all the painful "firsts" following their mother's death, hoping the second year would get easier. But she was lonely. She'd established a monthly dinner routine with Gerry and Letty, but George's brood was so busy, she seldom saw them outside of the holidays.

"I don't remember *promising*," he said, his tone reserved.

This caught her attention. George was usually the more upbeat one during their occasional phone calls.

"You did, little brother. I invited you to come out and stay for two weeks. You agreed it would be fun."

His sigh came through the phone. "It *would* be fun. But I'm not sure I can swing it."

" 'Swing it'? For heaven's sake, you better not be talking about money. Because I'd never allow you to pay me. We're family."

"You can't afford to do that, Celia. You've told me yourself. Full cabins all summer long and into the fall is what it takes so you can afford to make your mortgage payments and pay your other expenses out there."

That's what I get for discussing business with family.

"Why won't you let me do this for you, George? It would mean a lot to me. You've never spent much time at Whispering Pines."

"But the kids—they have sports, and I only get three weeks of vacation for the entire year."

She wasn't sure why he was backpedaling. He'd seemed sincere when he'd said this would be the summer when he'd finally bring his family out.

Maybe her brother needed to know how their mother's death was still impacting her.

"George . . . I *need* you to come spend time with me this summer. It's been a long eighteen months without Mother. I need some family time."

A shuffling noise came through the phone before his reply. "Dang it, Celia, you make it hard to say no."

"Don't, then! I have a cabin reserved for you for the last part of July. I promise, the kids will love it, and so will you. Tell me I can count on you."

A child's tinny, distant voice shouted for its dad in the background.

"I'm sorry, Celia. I've got to run."

"George, do not hang up this phone without promising I'll see you in July!"

"Fine. As long as I can get the time off, we'll come. I'll call you back on Monday to confirm everything."

Click.

Celia held the phone away from her ear, the buzz of the dial tone still coming through. The sound brought back that awful morning when her mother had left the house to go to the hospital for the last time. She quickly slammed the handset on the receiver.

"They'll come," she proclaimed out loud.

But the only reply was the echo of her own words in the empty kitchen.

"If you don't hold it tighter, Celia, these babies are going to wave like the flag on the Fourth of July."

The fine metal strands of the new screening bit into Celia's fingers. "If I pull any harder, the mesh will pop off the staples on top."

"No way," said the man next to her—Wayne, the resort's current caretaker. His words sounded strained as he put his weight behind the staple gun. The awkward angle made the task difficult, and the short ladder he stood on swayed, bumping into Celia's shoulder where she crouched below. She had to let go of the screen and grab the ladder or they'd both end up in a heap on the porch floor.

Wayne expelled a heavy sigh, his arms dropping. "This isn't working. We need a different setup."

Celia let go of the ladder and stepped back to stand in the middle of the front porch. She braced a hand against her aching lower back.

"I wish Preston would have turned this screened-in porch into a third bedroom instead of just making it bigger."

"Bigger?"

She motioned around them. "The very first summer I came out here with my friend's family, we stayed in this cabin. That was way back in 1942. I was only nineteen and still in college."

Celia let her mind drift back to that long-ago time.

"This porch was much smaller back then. Just big enough for a small table and two chairs. Somewhere along the line, Preston, the previous owner, bumped out these walls to make the porch bigger. I'm guessing he wanted guests to sit out here for meals or games. Useful, I'll admit, but I could charge more if I had a cabin with three bedrooms."

Wayne stepped off the short ladder, his booted footsteps heavy. "Wouldn't take much to pull that off. You'd have to shore up the foundation. What's under here now wouldn't cut it. Might want to get that done this fall, before winter. But for now, I need to get this screen back up or your family won't have a bug-free zone to relax in."

She couldn't have that. She'd worked hard to get the cabin into the best shape possible for George, Lavonne, and their four kids. They were due to arrive tomorrow. Celia prayed this summer would evolve into an annual visit. "Well, since we can't very well wiggle our noses and turn this into another bedroom overnight, Ethan and his sisters are going to have to share a room. It'll be close quarters. The least I can do is have this porch ready to go, too."

"Don't worry, I'll get it done, even if it takes all day. What's gotten into you, huh? You seem flustered. Nothing usually rattles you."

He was right. She'd been thrilled when George finally agreed they'd come, but now her excitement was morphing into apprehension. "I just want these next two weeks to be perfect. This is the first time I've had family here in a very long time."

Pulling a tape measure out of his jeans pocket, Wayne glanced sideways at his boss then headed back to the wall on the north side of the porch, now void of screening. "That's not true. I met your mother when she and her friends stayed in one of the cabins up front. Wasn't that the first summer I was out here?"

He was right. Maggie and her snowbird friends had rented two cabins from her, spending a week lounging in the sun and around bonfires, drinking wine, and laughing late into the night. Had that really been four summers ago already? It was the summer her mother turned seventy—the trip had been a birthday celebration of sorts.

"You're right. That was lots of fun. But I didn't feel like I had to entertain them. This is different. George has four kids. If they don't have fun—if they get bored or are uncomfortable—they might never come back."

The tape measure snapped back and Wayne stooped to dig through the toolbox in the middle of the porch floor. "Celia, kids don't need to be entertained. Especially at a beautiful place like this. It's July. The weather is perfect this time of year. Trust me. They'll find plenty to keep themselves busy."

Celia wasn't convinced, but then again, she'd never spent much time around children. The kids did have fun at her house over Christmas. She wasn't sure if

Wayne had spent time around kids either. "And what makes *you* an expert on children?" she asked, curious.

He shrugged, muttering something noncommittal. He never opened up about his life before coming to work for her at Whispering Pines. He'd been an acquaintance of her previous caretaker, Nash. When Nash was nearing the end of his last summer at the resort, finally retiring at nearly seventy years old, he'd suggested Wayne to her. Nash had earned Celia's respect. Anyone he recommended warranted a second look, and she had never regretted hiring Wayne. Except maybe when he talked too much. He had a tendency to offer plenty of unsolicited advice, something Nash never did in all the years they worked together. Where Nash was quiet and a bit of a recluse, Wayne was much more outgoing. He was younger, too. Only two years older than Celia.

"Why don't you ever give me a straight answer when I ask you personal questions?"

He smirked. "Don't worry, boss, I've got nothing to hide. Besides, you don't share much either."

She supposed that was true. She considered Wayne more than an employee, but he wasn't exactly a friend either. Not because she didn't like him, but because she knew so little about him.

"Should we try again?" she asked, motioning toward the new screen that was now flapping in the wind, only connected across the top of the floor-to-ceiling windows. As she spoke, the breeze shifted and grew stronger, bringing with it the tangy scent of fresh rain.

"That'd be great. The weather's moving in—two sets of hands are practically mandatory at this point!"

Celia scooped a spare pair of work gloves out of the toolbox and got back on her knees, below the ladder. "These should help," she said, wiggling her fingers into the protective coverings then waving up at the caretaker.

They tried again, this time with Wayne bending down and around Celia. Together, they finally stretched the new screening tight. The first icy pellet of rain smacked against the screen with Wayne's grunt as he popped in the final staple. Stepping back, he returned the staple gun to the toolbox and reached down to help Celia to her feet. She straightened with a groan, earning herself another smirk.

"What?"

"You sound like an old lady," he teased.

"Some days I *feel* like an old lady."

"Oh stop. You aren't even sixty yet. We can't call ourselves that for at least another decade."

She grinned at his playful tone. Years ago, when she'd spent a summer at Whispering Pines, hiding her unplanned pregnancy, she'd gotten to know Nash. Back then, she'd considered Nash old. As she did the math in her head, she realized Nash would have been a few years younger than she and Wayne were now. It was all about perspective. Other than the occasional aches and pains, and the body image she still struggled with following her mastectomy, she still had plans for decades of more living.

Unless two weeks with her brother's children killed her first.

Celia tightened the silk scarf under her chin to keep her wide-brimmed straw hat on top of her head. The strong breeze coming off the lake kept threatening to dislodge it, but she'd learned how quickly the July sun would leach the color from her hair. Despite the cost and hassle of ever more frequent trips to see her favorite hairdresser, she had no intention of ever letting her hair go gray.

"Jess, if you won't wear sunscreen, you need to take your books and go sit in the shade for a while," Lavonne demanded, earning a sigh from her eight-year-old daughter.

"Fine," Jess replied, scooping two paperbacks off the blue wool blanket where she'd been reading while her two sisters played along the edge of the lake. She gave the books a vigorous shake, dislodging more of the sand her little sister had carelessly kicked onto her blanket earlier. She tucked the dog-eared copies into the crook of her arm, then hooked her thumb under the elastic at the bottom of her rainbow-colored swimming suit, yanking the offending fabric down to a more comfortable position.

Celia snickered as Jess shuffled toward the grass where a woven hammock drooped between two trees.

Lavonne rolled her eyes. "Not very ladylike yet."

"I've never liked to act *ladylike* either," Celia countered.

"Says the woman sitting here, looking like something out of that *Vogue* magazine under your chair. I love that coverup, by the way. It's a brilliant color on you. And if we come back next year, I expect Renee will wear a hat just like that one. The girl idolizes you."

"Oh stop," Celia said, her heart thudding at Lavonne's use of *if*. "Renee is what . . . nine now? I'm sure she doesn't give me a second thought."

"She's ten."

Celia glanced out at Renee, helping a younger Val catch minnows with a tiny net and transfer them into a glass Mason jar. As she watched, she noticed how Renee kept glancing toward the end of the dock that jutted out into the water fifty feet from where the girls were playing. She seemed intrigued by the boy who was casting his fishing line with a deftness unusual for someone so young.

"I'm serious, Celia," Lavonne continued. "My daughter has always thought you were the best, but ever since we pulled in here yesterday, all she can talk about is how amazing she thinks it is that a woman can own a place like this, quote, 'all without a husband.' And I have to admit, I think it's pretty neat, too."

"None of you would have thought it was so glamorous if you'd have been here yesterday when I was helping my handyman replace the screens in your cabin and trap a raccoon that moved in under that smaller cabin next to yours."

She laughed. "I'm sure it isn't easy. That doesn't make it any less impressive."

Celia supposed most outside observers would think she was either amazing or crazy to try to maintain a place like this without a husband backing her up. "I suspect Renee's been out there with Val this long just so she could be closer to Brandon. She doesn't seem like a girl all that interested in catching minnows."

"Celia, she's *ten*."

"Kids can have crushes at ten. I know *I* did."

Lavonne laughed again. "I don't doubt it."

Celia shrugged. Lavonne probably thought she had a much more exciting love life than she actually did. Other than her first love, she'd never again fallen hard for anyone, and whenever she *was* interested in a man, he'd either turn out to be married or the timing was off. She would never date a married man. She'd been casually dating a man ten years her junior when her mother died, and she'd introduced him to George and Lavonne when he'd stopped at the house to offer his condolences. But while she'd enjoyed his company, the six-month affair ended when she lost her mother. Her grief didn't leave enough room in her heart for any other feelings. With the passing of time, the grief no longer consumed her. Maybe she'd entertain the idea of dating again, if the right man came along, but right now she spent all her time between Whispering Pines and her work back home.

"Can I ask you something?" Lavonne said, rolling a can of Tab between her palms as if nervous to voice her question.

"Sure."

"Why didn't you ever marry, Celia? I know you've dated through the years, but you never seemed very serious about those relationships."

The question caught Celia off guard, though she supposed it shouldn't. Others had voiced similar sentiments. A generation earlier and society would have branded her a spinster. People were slightly more open-minded now. Some even whispered that she was a lesbian, working in the construction business, too, as she did. She was aware of the rumors, but she never corrected them. They'd think what they wanted. Besides, most people didn't dare ask.

But Lavonne was family. She deserved some kind of answer, though Celia vowed years ago to keep her heartbreak about Danny mostly to herself. Even after all these years, she didn't want to bring her pain out into the open. Maybe a part of her felt like keeping it to herself helped it stay real. She couldn't risk losing her memories of it all.

Reaching down into her beach bag, she pulled a slim cigarette out of a crushed pack. She knew smoking was a nasty habit, and she only allowed herself one pack a week in the summer, but she needed something to do with her hands. Lavonne's unexpected question had her nerves jumping, which was a surprise. Her relationship with Danny was such ancient history.

Perhaps Celia's reaction was because she still thought of Whispering Pines as *their* place.

She lit the cigarette and inhaled deeply, holding the smoke deep in her lungs, feeling the burn. She caught the pinched expression on Lavonne's face. "I know," she said, exhaling. "I need to quit before these damn things kill me. I'd offer you one, but I know better."

The smoke drifted over to the girls splashing in the shallow water. Val whipped her head around, sniffing the air. Celia knew the second her niece identified the source, her small face taking on an expression that mirrored her mother's.

"Auntie Celia, don't you know smoking is *bad* for you?" Val hollered, hands on her plump hips.

Celia took one last long drag and snuffed the cigarette out in the sand at her feet. "I know, honey. I'm sorry. I put it out."

With a shake of her head, Val went back to searching for minnows. Renee caught Celia's eye with an expression that might have been a mixture of revulsion and respect. She'd have to be careful—she had plenty of bad habits she wouldn't want her young niece to emulate. Turning her attention back to Lavonne, she considered how to answer her question.

Would she have married Danny and traveled the world with him? Or were those simply naïve dreams of a young woman in love? Life had intervened, and she'd moved home instead to help her family when her stepfather died.

All these years later, did she regret her decision?

Yes. She had regrets. Her daughter, the baby she'd never held, never talked to, would be twenty-three years old now, soon to be twenty-four. She would be a young woman, probably starting out on a new career. Was she married? She could be a mother by now, making Celia a grandmother, at least in the biological sense. Her decision to give the child up at birth had severed her right to know what would become of the girl.

But what had become of Danny? Where was he now, and what did his life look like?

Sometimes she could go days without thinking of her first love or the daughter she'd given up. Other days, the loneliness, the questions of what had become of them both, weighed on her.

"I'm sorry, Celia," Lavonne said, taking Celia's continued silence the wrong way. "I shouldn't have asked you about marriage. It's really none of my business. I'm sorry if I offended you."

"Don't apologize. You didn't offend me. It's just that, sometimes, thinking about it makes me sad. There was someone once. Many years ago. But it didn't work out. No one else has ever measured up."

Lavonne sighed, tilting her head back.

Celia noticed Brandon, the young fisherman, stand and gather his things. The girls probably scared all the fish away. Renee's shoulders drooped in disappointment. Celia watched the boy cross the sand and walk toward the cabin where he was staying with his grandparents. Her eyes traveled back to the old dock, reminded of the countless people that had fished as they reflected on life, poised above the water in that very spot.

"Relationships and marriage are never easy," Lavonne said, breaking into Celia's thoughts. "Add kids into the mix, and there is never enough time for it all."

The comment reminded Celia of the way Lavonne struggled with postpartum depression. Had motherhood gotten any easier for her, now that her youngest was five?

Celia watched Val playing in the water, and remembered her suspicions years ago that perhaps George wasn't the girl's biological father, a possibility her brother had quickly squashed. Did he ever think about it?

Did it even matter?

Celia had a vested interest in believing blood wasn't the driving factor in the sacred bond between a parent and a child. She had to believe the people raising her daughter treated her like their own. It was the only way she could sleep at night.

Chapter Eleven

GIFT OF GHOST STORIES AROUND A CAMPFIRE

CELIA BIT BACK A grin when Wayne asked whether she thought their guests would enjoy a ghost story. She could always count on the man to share the story of Whispering Pines' most infamous ghosts with guests around a bonfire—especially if he had an audience of eager kids.

"Don't make it *too* scary," she warned.

As she relaxed, she searched the faces of her family around the fire. George and Ethan were recounting tales of the fish they'd caught that day, promising that future expeditions on the water would yield even more. They planned to provide enough for a fish fry before they went home.

She grinned. George should know better than to promise fishing success. Maybe they'd pull it off. Or maybe they'd learn the hard way not to make such baseless claims. But it was all in good fun.

Brandon, the boy visiting with his grandparents, watched the two as they talked fish. He'd probably enjoy going with them, though she wasn't sure he and Ethan had met yet.

It was the end of day two for her family. She hoped they were enjoying themselves. Despite her earlier worries—compounded by the rainstorm that hit when they arrived—Celia was loving having them all at her resort.

"You kids afraid of ghosts?" Wayne asked. Celia watched as he made eye contact with most of the younger people around the bonfire.

He's good.

"All right," the caretaker began. "Sit back and I'll tell you all about two famous little ghosts that have been around here for a very long time."

Val stood, the blanket she'd brought out to the fire falling to her feet. She snatched it up, peeked between Wayne and the dark woods pressing in around them, and then promptly snuggled into her mother's lap.

Celia's grin grew. *He's* very *good.* She didn't want the kids to be too scared, but she trusted Wayne not to take it too far. He'd perfected this schtick over the past couple of years.

"Rumor has it," he went on, "that a family came here to spend their summer at Whispering Pines back in the 1930s. There were fewer cabins back then, and those buildings are all gone now, replaced over the years. Anyhow, there was a father, a mother, and twin boys. The boys were young, ten. The father was a lawyer and would drive into the city to work during the week, leaving his wife and sons at the resort."

"Did you know them, Aunt Celia?" Val asked.

She must think I'm really old. Celia cringed, remembering how she'd thought the same thing of Nash. All in one's perspective. "No, sweetie. I would have been very young then, and I didn't even visit Whispering Pines for the first time until I was in college."

Val's question derailed Wayne's story temporarily, but Celia worked to steer the conversation back to him. "Hush, now, and listen to Wayne."

He winked at her, then explained how the twin brothers had a tendency to disappear for hours into the woods, despite their mother's warning to stay out of the trees. They behaved when their father was at the cabin, but when he went into the city to work during the week the mischievous boys would do it again.

"Man, we wouldn't get away with that," Ethan said.

"Glad you realize that, son," Lavonne replied with a lift of her eyebrows.

An owl hooted in the distance.

"The summer weeks rolled on and the boys kept up the pattern. Finally, one day, the mother's worst fears came true: the boys didn't come back when she rang the dinner bell."

Celia scanned the group again when Wayne paused for dramatic effect. A few of the younger ones were squirming in their chairs. Val's thumb had even found its way to her mouth, something Celia doubted the five-year-old realized.

"Remember, Wayne, not *too* much information," Celia warned. At least part of the story was true, and the notion of two young children losing their lives in a horrible accident on the property always broke her heart. The story was only fun when she didn't allow herself to think too deeply on it.

Wayne nodded. "Those two little boys never made it back home to their momma. At least . . . not alive."

"So, they never found them? Never found their bodies?" Ethan asked. His dubious expression glowed palely in the shadows of the firelight. "They just . . . disappeared?"

"That's the thing about Whispering Pines, Ethan," Wayne said. "Some spirits never seem to want to leave here."

"But you never answered Ethan's question," Jess challenged. "Did they find their bodies?"

The smile slipped from Wayne's face, as if the tragedy of it all bothered him, too, despite how much fun he had talking about ghosts that still roamed the property. "They found them, but not for some time. The mother and father never returned after that horrible summer."

Jess continued to push. "Where did they find them?"

Celia had to admire the girl's tenacity. She was after the facts, unfazed by Wayne's talk of spirits.

"It turns out Arthur and Albert, the twin brothers, had discovered a cave. That must have been where they were going every day. Searchers eventually found them there, inside the cave. They found old toys and books in there, too."

"But . . . what happened?" Jess pressed. "How'd they die?"

Wayne shrugged. "No one knows. That part of the story got lost somewhere along the way. I guess it wasn't their deaths that caused the most interest, but what happened afterward."

Celia watched for reactions around the fire. This was where Wayne would really shine with his theatrics.

George, quiet until this point, chimed in. "And what started happening, Wayne?"

"Strange things. Unexplainable things. Nothing terrible, mind you. Just annoyances people couldn't explain away."

Celia listened to Wayne go into detail about all the little things people would come to blame on the ghost boys. Things like lost toys and fishing poles that someone tampered with when no one was looking. The skeptic in Celia suspected they could attribute all of that to carelessness, and she doubted a cave actually existed, but it made for a fun story, one she first heard her friend Eleanor tell during that summer she'd first visited Whispering Pines.

Wayne warned that if you saw flashes of movement out of the corner of your eye, it was likely Arthur and Albert messing with you. Her guests looked caught up in Wayne's theatrical retelling of the local lore.

Another hoot of an owl conveyed the lateness of the hour. As if on cue, George clapped his hands and insisted his children head off to bed. Amongst groans of protest, he stood and reached down to take his youngest from his wife, maneuvering the sleepy girl onto his back for a piggyback ride to their cabin. The older three were close on his heels.

Probably more spooked by Wayne's story than they'd care to admit.

"I'll be in shortly," Lavonne tossed over her shoulder to her departing family, before bending down for her forgotten can of lukewarm beer. Her eyes went straight to Wayne across the fire. "You stay in the other half of the duplex, opposite of Celia, right?"

A wary look came into the caretaker's eyes. "Yeah . . . why?"

Lavonne raised her beer to him. "Because, if my kids keep me up all night when they're too scared to sleep, it'll be me knocking on your door, not your ghost boys playing pranks."

Her warning elicited a hearty round of laughter from the guests still relaxing around the fire, and the conversation flowed to other topics. There would be no more talk of dead children or spirits that roamed the property that night.

Eventually, Celia had to stifle a yawn. She rose to her feet, and Wayne followed suit. Placing two additional logs on the fire for those inclined to remain, they said their goodnights and headed for the duplex on the eastern edge of the resort.

"You did well tonight," Celia complimented him. "It wouldn't be a proper summer vacation without an old-fashioned ghost story told around a campfire, would it?"

"It wasn't too over the top?" Wayne sounded concerned. "It looked like your youngest niece was scared."

"Val? She'll be fine. Lavonne warned me she's always had a thing about the dark."

"I hope I didn't make it worse."

Their sure steps had brought them to the stairs of the duplex, the familiar pathway easy to traverse even in darkness. Wayne's concern for her family touched Celia. He always seemed to enjoy interacting with the guests, much more so than Nash had ever done, but this concern was new. She didn't know what to make of it.

"I've got an early morning, so goodnight," the man said.

He politely motioned for her to precede him up the steps. The exhaustion she felt over entertaining her family must have shown on her face, because Wayne never cared too much about social niceties.

After all her anticipation of her family's visit, the days with her nieces and nephew flew by. Celia would have preferred time to slow down, to enjoy their days together even more.

Afternoons on the beach under a hot summer sun morphed into evenings around the fire. A friendship blossomed between Ethan and the other boy staying at the resort, Brandon. Celia saw little of them. They kept busy fishing and whatever else eleven-year-old boys do with their time. When rain or too much sun chased the girls indoors (except for Jess, who often went inside with a book all on her own), they'd end up at Celia's duplex. Discussions ranged from their teachers and classmates to Celia's love life and everything in between. It was during those unfiltered discussions, when their mother wasn't around, that Celia felt like she was getting to know her young nieces.

One morning, with only a few days of their vacation remaining, Lavonne surprised Celia by showing up alone, empty coffee cup in hand. "I'm out of coffee, and I'm not sure I can survive my girls' constant chatter without some caffeine this morning."

As Celia held the screen door open for her, the other front door, next to her own, opened. Wayne stepped outside, pulling his door shut behind him.

"Morning, ladies." He grinned, slipping sunglasses on. "Heard there's a good chance of thunderstorms rolling through in the next couple of hours. If you need me for anything, Celia, I'll be working on that big old red maple that fell over last winter. We're running low on firewood. It should burn nicely, but needs time to dry out."

Celia hadn't noticed their firewood supply. "Good catch, Wayne, thank you. Be sure to head in if the weather turns bad. I don't want anyone out in those woods in a storm, including you!"

He slid his glasses down his nose far enough for her to see his eyes. The look he shot her spoke volumes. She wasn't to worry. He'd been taking care of himself for a good long time. He gave another quick nod in Lavonne's direction, then jogged down the front porch stairs and out of sight.

A cold gust of wind stole up the porch steps and danced around the two sisters-in-law, confirming the caretaker's weather prediction. Despite her shiver, Celia welcomed a break in the monotonous summer heat.

Lavonne followed her inside, pouring herself a cup from the full pot of coffee on the kitchen counter. She proceeded to wrap her hands around the steaming mug and inhale the fresh scent with a sigh.

"Perfect."

The coffee smelled good, and Celia filled a cup, too. "Let's sit on the back patio, enjoy a cup of this before figuring out lunch. What's the rest of the family up to?"

"George went golfing with two of your other guests he met at the firepit. Ethan is off somewhere with Brandon, probably fishing on the dock. The girls are making pet rocks on the picnic table outside our cabin. They'll be fine by themselves for a bit. I needed a break from the bickering."

"They seem to get along as well as most sisters do," she pointed out. She remembered the near constant arguing she'd done with Beverly when they were young girls. It was almost a game. They fought, but they always had each other's backs. She suspected it was the same for Renee, Jess, and Val.

Lavonne shrugged. "I suppose."

They exited through the kitchen back door, Celia bringing a glass coffee carafe along. She set it on the small table between two wooden chairs that creaked when they sat.

Lavonne wiggled in hers. "Will these hold us?"

With a grin, Celia assured her they hadn't failed her yet.

Glancing behind her, Lavonne eyed the duplex. "I've been dying to ask you about him, but didn't want to mention it when the kids were listening. Which is most of the time."

"Him? Who?"

"Why, *Wayne*, of course!" Lavonne grinned at her like a girl gossiping about boys at a slumber party.

"What about him?"

"Come on, Celia, don't play dumb with me. I've seen the way he watches you."

Celia honestly didn't know what Lavonne was talking about. *Wayne?*

"He doesn't *watch* me. He works for me. He does a great job. I worried when I had to replace the old caretaker. That man had been here since long before I bought the resort. You remember Nash?"

Lavonne nodded.

"When he retired, he suggested I talk to Wayne." Celia frowned. "I don't recall how they knew each other."

Lavonne's face fell. "You mean that's really all there is to it? He just works for you? I was looking for a juicy story this morning."

The younger woman's questions surprised Celia. Did Wayne look at her, *think* of her, as anything other than a boss that showed up occasionally, usually with a new list of ideas about what he needed to fix or update? She'd always suspected his days at Whispering Pines were more pleasant when she wasn't there to boss him around. The woman she'd hired to oversee the resort guests when she was at her office job didn't seem to interact much with Wayne.

"Mom? Auntie Celia? Where are you guys?"

Lavonne sighed. "Back here, Val! In the backyard."

Scuffling sounds got louder and louder.

"That break didn't last long," Lavonne muttered.

Val came bursting around the corner. "Mom, Jess and Renee are teasing me!"

"Val, what have I told you about tattling?"

As Lavonne slipped into mom mode, Celia only half listened, thinking still about her earlier comments about Wayne. While their relationship had evolved from a simple boss-and-employee comradery to something more akin to friendship, she'd never thought of him in the way Lavonne seemed to imply. She supposed he was handsome enough. She'd worked with so many men through the years, and she'd always made it a rule not to mix business with pleasure. While women were making inroads in the world of business, it was still easy to get sidestepped with entanglements that could mean trouble for a career. Tripp and his dalliance with a secretary were proof enough of that.

But . . . Wayne?

Damn Lavonne for planting the idea of something more in her head. Celia cherished the summer days she spent at Whispering Pines above all else, and so made sure to carve out as many as possible between time at the office. Lately, however, she was feeling more and more alone. Her mother was gone, her friends were busy with their own lives. But other than Danny, she'd never spent time with another man at Whispering Pines.

More yelling pulled her attention back to the patio. Something in the urgency of the voices, the touch of panic, sent a rush of adrenaline through her veins.

"Something's wrong." Lavonne scrambled out of the unreliable wooden patio chair, her words silencing a whiney Val.

Both Renee and Jess rushed around the corner of her duplex, panic radiating from their eyes. "Aunt Celia! Mom! Come quick. It's Ethan. Something bad happened."

Fear shot through Celia, and she sprang to action.

"Slow down, Ethan," George was saying, having dropped to one knee in front of his son.

Celia hadn't heard her brother return from his golf game, but she was relieved he was here. That relief grew at the sight of her nephew.

Ethan gulped, struggling to catch his breath as his mother, aunt, and sisters all rushed to his side. Wayne was there, too, standing slightly behind the boy, a steadying hand on his shoulder.

"Now tell me again," George insisted.

"I think we found the cave. But Brandon fell into it. He's hurt. Come on, I'll show you!"

Celia looked from her flustered nephew to Wayne. With a curt nod, he motioned for her to step to the side with him, away from Ethan and the rest of the family. Once they were a few steps away, she grabbed his arm, shifting so their backs were to everyone else.

"What happened?" she hissed. Her stomach churned with a jumble of emotions: relief to see Ethan in one piece, yes, but also a nearly overwhelming sense of responsibility and fear for the welfare of the other boy.

That damn cave. Maybe she should have believed it actually existed after all.

Sensing her angst, Wayne placed a comforting hand on her shoulder, much as he'd done for Ethan. "I'm not exactly sure. Ethan found me. He must have heard my chainsaw. Apparently the boys went into the woods to find that damn cave."

She let out a quick snort over his exact replication of her own thoughts.

"That story about the ghost boys," she said. "I'm sure plenty of people have gone looking for it in the past. But why would Ethan and Brandon go alone?"

"Celia, they're *boys*," he replied, as if that explained everything. "It's what kids do. We can worry about that later. The important thing is we need to get some help. Ethan wanted to take me to Brandon right away, but I told him we needed to come back here and get help first. If that boy fell into some kind of hole and hurt his leg, there might not be much I can do alone. Maybe if I was pushing thirty instead of sixty . . ." His voice trailed off, frustration on his face.

Celia waved the comment away. Wayne might not be a young man, but he was no slouch. She'd scolded him often enough about lifting heavy things around the resort. But then she remembered his right shoulder gave him trouble from time to time. In fact, she'd noticed him rubbing at it in recent weeks.

"You made the right call," she assured him. "So you think we need to call for help?"

"Yeah, I do. Ethan said the kid's leg looked busted. If that's the case, you're gonna need a stretcher to get him out of there."

Celia nodded, then turned back to face her brother's family. "I'm calling for help. Stay put, I'll be right back."

Celia suspected the wait for help to arrive had to be the longest fifteen minutes of Ethan's young life. Brandon's grandparents were distraught as well. The boy's grandfather wanted to join the search party but had ultimately agreed to stay, as the man's slow, uneven gait would hold them all back. They didn't need to end up carrying *two* people out of the woods.

Speaking of . . .

"Wayne," she said, "I need you to stay here and keep Brandon's grandparents calm. I'll go with Ethan, George, and the rescue team."

"Bullshit. I don't want you traipsing around in the woods out there."

"Excuse me?" She was shocked and maybe a little offended at the man's audacity to question her. "I've spent plenty of time in these woods. I know them better than anyone, and I feel responsible for the fact one of my guests is currently out there somewhere, hurt. How well do you know these woods?"

The look on his face told her that he saw her point.

"Look, we don't have time to argue about this," she continued. "I need you to stay here. Keep the grandparents calm and be here in case any of our other guests need anything."

"Fine, but I'm going to at least walk you in to where I was cutting the tree. That will get you started in the right direction. Do you know where this cave is that Ethan claims they found?"

"No, unfortunately. Hopefully he remembers the path."

Wayne ran a hand over his brow, frustrated. "I shouldn't have told that damn ghost story. This is my fault."

"That's ridiculous. You said it yourself: boys will be boys. Sure, maybe they were looking for the cave, but they probably would have headed back into those woods at some point, regardless."

The sound of the ambulance cut her assurances off. Everything was a blur of activity after that. Lavonne also stayed behind with her girls and Brandon's panicked grandparents. Wayne led everyone who'd responded to the call about an injured boy in the woods—two EMTs and an off-duty fireman—along with Ethan, Celia, and George, to where he'd been cutting wood. Celia could still sense his desire to continue on with the group, but she turned him back. She'd worry less, she'd assured him, if she knew he was keeping an eye on things at the resort.

Ethan's ability to focus, to recognize things along the path he was now traveling for the third time so he could lead the group back to his friend, impressed Celia. It wasn't until they caught sight of a red sweatshirt, tied partway up the trunk of a tree, that they could hear Brandon answering their calls.

"Great job leaving a marker like that, young man," one of the EMTs complimented Ethan. "You stand back now. Let us do our job. You did yours getting us here."

The man's reassurances caused some of the pent-up energy to seep out of Ethan. Celia could feel the boy's body relax under the comforting arm she'd wrapped around his shoulders.

"He'll be all right now," she told him.

"I hope so. He sounds pretty weak."

She squeezed her nephew's shoulder as the two of them watched George help the three rescuers. The fireman eased himself down into the hole that must have opened up in the ground under Brandon's weight.

She felt a shiver pass through Ethan's body. "They know what they're doing," she assured him.

She was right. It didn't take long before Brandon was once again traveling the path back to the resort, though this time it was flat on his back, laid out on a stretcher. Celia caught the thumbs-up he gave her nephew, along with a comment about being even.

She wasn't sure she wanted to know what that meant.

"I think the kids would have fun playing on this, don't you?" Wayne asked, appearing at the back door of the lodge with a large, bouncy black inner tube.

"Where in heaven's name did you find that?" She laughed at the man's enthusiastic expression. "It looks like *you're* the one who wants to play on it."

"I admit, I played some pretty wicked games of King of the Hill on one of these bad boys when I was younger. No idea what tractor it was for, just found a box with two of these in it over in the shed. I doubt it's ever had air in it before now." He must have rolled it over from the air compressor. Still balancing it on end, he gave it a bounce on the grass. "Should hold."

"Wayne, weren't you the one who said kids don't have to be entertained?"

He gave her a sheepish grin. "That was before I planted the idea of a cave, hidden out in the woods somewhere, into the brains of eleven-year-olds. Ethan's new friend left for home with a thick white cast on his broken leg, and now your nephew's bored. I thought I'd give them something fun to do."

She shook her head. Wayne had never shown any interest in any of their guests. "Why are you so worried about the kids having fun?"

"Guilt, I suppose," he admitted. "But mostly because they're important to you."

His response caught her off guard—much like Lavonne's earlier observations just before chaos descended with Ethan and Brandon.

Is he just trying to please his boss? It felt like more than that.

He waited and watched, as if weighing her reaction.

"I think the kids will love playing on that thing," she said. "They're already down at the water. I'm headed that way now. Come on, let's go see what they think."

He rolled the tube back a step to give Celia room to step outside. "Lead the way."

She took a deep breath, allowing the fresh, pine-scented air to chase away the slight hesitation she'd never felt in Wayne's presence before. "What a beautiful day. I'm glad the weather has been decent for the kids. Come on. They'll be excited to take that thing out."

The caretaker hoisted the large tube over his head. "They will as long as I don't pop it before I get it down to the beach. Hopefully they won't play too rough on it. I don't want anyone else to get hurt this summer on my account."

Celia remembered Wayne's prophetic words as she hurried into the lake, her feet sinking into mucky areas and getting poked by the occasional rock. The kids' screaming meant something was terribly wrong—again—but she couldn't see what was happening. The ruckus drew her into the water. She could still count all four of their heads, so at least no one had gone under on her watch. One hand shielded the glare of the sun as she tried to see what all the screaming was about. George had left her in charge while he and Lavonne went up to the cabin to get dinner on the table. Her brother would never forgive her if one of the kids drowned after he'd left them in her care.

Young Val, buoyed up by a bright orange lifejacket, reached Celia first.

"What happened?" Celia asked, grabbing hold of the shoulder straps on the vest, pulling Val up so the water was only as high as the child's waist.

"Renee's hurt! There's blood, lots of blood!" Val said in a rush, looking back over her shoulder at her siblings. They were floating closer now, Ethan pushing the slick black tube toward shore.

Celia nodded, pushing the girl toward the beach. "Get out of the water, Val. Be quiet now. Everything will be fine."

Val splashed her way onto shore, for once doing exactly what she was told. Jess and Ethan were both on the far side of the tube, their arms wrapped around its shiny surface, their feet splashing behind them. Renee sat on the tube, her back to her brother and sister. Her face was pale, but there was a red wash of blood on the child's thighs.

"Ethan, when you can touch bottom, spin the tube so Renee's closer to me. I'll take her from here. Jess, run up and get one of your parents. Tell them to bring a towel, maybe a first-aid kit." She turned and called out, "Val, go sit up on your towel."

She scooped Renee off the tube, one arm under the young girl's knees and the other around her shoulders, her wet skin making it difficult for Celia to hold her securely. Her niece felt weightless as she transported her out of the water, depositing her into a nearby lawn chair.

His children's screams must have alerted George before Jess could even reach him, because he was at Celia's side in a flash, taking over. Celia was more than happy to step back, out of the way. Once Ethan could hoist the inner tube out of the water and onto the sand, he came to stand beside his aunt. Now, out of the water, she could see that there was a gash on Renee's thigh.

"What happened?" she asked, glancing between Renee and Ethan.

"We were screwing around and she must have caught her leg on that metal thing that sticks up out of the tube in the middle," the boy said. "I think it's where the air goes in."

Damn, Celia thought. *Poor Wayne. He's going to blame himself for this, too.*

Chapter Twelve
GIFT OF SHELTER FROM THE RAIN

CELIA EYED THE BEAT-UP old tackle box sitting in the middle of her desktop. She'd neglected most of her regular duties during her family's two weeks at the resort, but she'd holed up inside her office as soon as they'd driven away, hoping to lose herself in work to squelch the loneliness threatening to swamp her. She'd just hung up with her liquor distributor when Wayne strode into her office and set the tackle box down in front of her.

"What's that?" she asked, looking between him and the box. The sight of his clean-shaven face gave her pause. She'd never seen him without a beard. His hair looked different, too. "And what's with *that*?"

His grin slipped. His hand came up to self-consciously touch his cheek. "Oh, this? It's nothing. This hot weather was making my beard itch. I thought a shave and cut might help. Want to help me hide that?"

He pointed, and her attention went back to the old box he'd set on her desk. "Hide it? I don't understand."

"It's a time capsule. Ethan and his sisters put it together. After your niece hurt her leg, they were looking for something else to do besides swimming. I caught them digging around in the garden shed for a box they could use to put together a time capsule. Figured I'd help them out, since it was my fault the poor girl needed stitches."

Celia sighed, dropping into her desk chair. "Wayne, we've been over this a hundred times. Neither Brandon's nor Renee's accident was your fault. Kids will be kids. You were just trying to help me show them a good time. If anything, it's *my* fault they got hurt."

That grin came back, and she had to admit to herself that the shave and haircut looked nice. He looked years younger.

"We are quite the pair, aren't we?" he said.

"A pair?"

"I mean . . . I think we need to both stop blaming ourselves for those kids. They had fun. Everyone's survived the summer—so far—and now they're back under the sole responsibility of their families. We can breathe a sigh of relief."

She leaned back in her chair, considering his words. The kids *had* seemed reluctant to leave. Renee even cried, and when Celia asked her why she was so upset, the girl only cried harder. She made both Celia and George promise they'd come back every summer from now on. Renee's words had warmed Celia's heart.

Wayne was right. Despite a few hiccups, the long-awaited first visit was a success.

Now she could relax. She'd have to travel back and forth for her office job throughout the rest of the summer, but the pressure of entertaining family was behind her. At least until next summer.

"Are you going to help me hide that or not?" Wayne asked again, nodding at her desktop. He was clearly excited at the prospect.

"Sure. Why not? Where were you thinking?"

"Follow me," he said, grabbing the kids' time capsule.

He held his free hand out to her. She took it without thinking, allowing him to tug her out of her chair and around the corner of her desk. He dropped her hand as she came alongside him, spun on his heel, and strode out.

She had to skip to keep up with him. "Where are we going?"

"Just follow me. I have the perfect spot in mind."

She laughed, and any vestiges of loneliness at the departure of her family ebbed away. The sun was shining, her work done, and she didn't need to leave until the next day. Wayne was enjoying this, and his attitude was infectious.

A young family passed them on the walkway, heading for the beach. The mother, having looked flustered and harassed upon their arrival three days earlier, smiled warmly at Celia and Wayne. "Beautiful day," she said, looking relaxed as she passed by. The brief encounter was a potent reminder of what she loved most about Whispering Pines.

"And that's why we work so hard," Celia murmured.

"What?" Wayne said, slowing so she didn't have to hurry to keep up with him.

"Oh, I just said 'that's why we work so hard.' That mother. She was a mess when they arrived, but she looks like she's having fun now."

He nodded. "That happens all the time. There's just something about this place."

He turned slightly, and her heart leapt. She grabbed his arm, pulling him to a stop.

"You aren't thinking you want to hide it in there, are you?"

Wayne sighed and stepped back so he was again even with her. "Cee, you need to give up this ridiculous notion that there is anything wrong with this cabin."

Crossing her arms, Celia regarded the smallest of her cabins with a mixture of trepidation and guilt. The cabin, previously her favorite, was falling into disrepair. The memory of Lavonne's gold necklace, tangled on the bedroom floor next to the bed, flashed through her mind. She couldn't shake the feeling that the cabin was cursed. She'd even played around with the idea of tearing it down and rebuilding a new, history-free structure in its place, but she couldn't afford it.

"It's the perfect hiding spot," Wayne was saying. "I had to get at a leaky pipe leading into the tub a while ago, and I haven't closed it back up yet. I think I can fit this thing"—he shook the time capsule—"between the studs, in the wall in the back of the closet."

"How in the world do you think the kids will ever be able to find it again if you put it inside a *wall*?"

He shrugged then walked toward the cabin again, glancing back at her over his shoulder. "We can't make it too easy for them. Besides, you hide time capsules away for many, many years. If the kids ever try to find it again, who knows? Maybe they'll be adults by then."

Frustrated, Celia followed him up the stairs and into the cabin. Because of the plumbing problems, she hadn't rented out this cabin since June. Maybe she wouldn't even try to rent it out again until next year.

Or maybe I never *will,* she thought, a chill sending goosebumps racing down her forearms.

Wayne, always a practical man, headed for the bedroom. He already had several tools laid out on the old dresser next to the closet. He pulled the bulb string dangling from the ceiling of the closet, and light flooded the tiny interior.

Sure enough, the back wall of the closet was open. Celia could see the pipes snaking around and disappearing into what she knew to be the cabin's bathroom on the other side of the partially disassembled wall.

"See?" He tipped the old metal box up on its side, the contents rattling. "It fits perfect, right between these studs."

She leaned against the doorjamb, arms crossed, shaking her head. "There is no way anyone will ever find this again. What did they put in it?"

Wayne set the repurposed old tackle box on the floor, brushing past her as he stepped back out of the closet into the bedroom. "No idea." He returned a second later with a small array of tools in one large hand, screws clenched between his lips, and a board in his other hand. Once his hands were free again, he spat the screws into one, and turned to face her. "Ethan made me promise to find a great hiding spot. He said he didn't want to find it when they come back next year. He wants it to be like a game. Maybe this will be too hard to find, but I'm a man of my word."

"But . . . what if no one ever finds it?"

He sighed and dropped to one knee. "Would that really be that big of a deal? I could tell the kids had fun putting this together. Maybe that's all that will ever come of it. Maybe they'll forget all about it, grow up and move away, and some plumber will find this the next time this old tub springs a leak. *Someone* will get a kick out of finding this, even if you and I are long dead by then. It may disappoint them when they open it and find a collection put together by kids and not a stash of stolen cash or something, but it'll still be a kind of adventure, don't you think?"

She laughed, despite her reservations, and watched as he wedged the box between the studs. It was a tight fit, but it *was* a fit.

He held the panel up again. "I cut this last week," he explained, then groaned. "Damn, it's about an inch too short."

Celia squatted next to him. "That isn't a big deal. Line it up on top. A gap on the bottom doesn't matter. This is just the back of a closet."

He sighed. "I hate doing anything half-assed."

"Wayne, it's a *closet*."

"Fine. Who knows, maybe the gap will serve as a kind of clue. Hold it here so I can get this straight, will you?"

Celia grinned. She appreciated that Wayne always tried to make the best of any situation. He may not like to do things half-assed, but he was still much more relaxed compared to her. Wayne compromised. He could teach her a thing or two.

The space was so small, there was no way she could hold her body away from his. She could feel the muscles in his back strain as he twisted at an odd angle to get the last screw in. The hand drill he was using must have slipped because his body jerked forward, and he cussed under his breath. She lost her balance, and they ended up in a heap at the bottom of the closet.

"I am *so* sorry," she said, trying to find a safe place for a foothold, embarrassed to be on top of the man.

He started laughing, his heavy hand falling onto her back. His humor, like his excitement over finding a hiding spot for the kids, was infectious. Celia giggled, imagining how ridiculous they must look.

She gave up the struggle and let herself relax on top of him. It felt good to laugh, *so* good. She hiccupped. Tears welled and dripped down her cheeks, falling onto Wayne. His other arm came around her, but it took her a minute to realize he wasn't laughing anymore. Their positions trapped her arms between their bodies, and she wriggled one hand free to wipe the tears from her eyes. Wayne was looking at her closely now, the hint of a smile still hovering, but there was also concern in his eyes.

"Are you all right?" he whispered.

She knew he wasn't worried that she'd hurt herself, but maybe he could sense there was something more to her wave of nearly uncontrolled laughter. She quieted, and they both stayed where they were, despite the awkward position. His hand came up to touch the back of her head, and she let her eyes drop to his lips, so close now to her own.

It was all the encouragement he needed. His hand applied a pressure so light she barely noticed it, and as she lowered her head to touch her lips to his, she felt a mixture of pleasure and dread.

Maybe Lavonne was on to something. Celia was coming to see this man in a whole new light.

But as she kissed him, her mind flashed again to the notion that nothing good ever seemed to survive the energy of this cabin.

Celia fought the overwhelming desire to let her eyelids drift shut, instead trying to stay focused on the small rectangle of rain-slicked blacktop revealed by her headlights. The rhythmic back-and-forth of the windshield wipers wasn't helping.

"Only ten more miles to the turn," she said, her voice sounding odd within the empty confines of her car. She'd given up on the radio, lightning interfering with the reception enough to cause the songs to cut in and out. The choppy music grated on her already tense nerves.

It wasn't as if this drive was any different from so many others. She often arrived for her weekends at Whispering Pines after dark, but tonight she'd gotten an even later start because of a work dinner. The weather wasn't a surprise either. They were experiencing a summer much wetter than usual.

The real difference this time was how little sleep she'd had beforehand.

In truth, she hadn't slept well all week. After foolishly kissing Wayne the previous weekend, she'd tried to act as if it hadn't happened. Even now, she felt a flush of embarrassment at her clumsy exit from the bottom of the closet.

I'm too old for this foolishness, she thought, rubbing a hand over one tired eye.

But she hadn't felt too old at the time—at least until she'd struggled to get back on her feet. Wayne had let her go without a word, as if he could sense her need to be alone, to sort through her reaction to what had just happened between them.

After she'd exited the cabin, squinting in the sunshine after the gloomy closet's interior, her feet had led her down to the beach, across the sand littered with relaxing guests, and out onto the dock, which was thankfully empty. She'd sunk down onto the end, pulled off her sandals, and plunged her feet into the cool water. It took time for the blistering sun to relax her tense muscles and the caress of the water to ground her.

She remembered the unusual sensation of feeling like she was floating high above the woman sitting on the end of the dock, looking down at her. She'd wondered how she was always the only steady presence at Whispering Pines while everyone else seemed to rotate through. She imagined seeing the ghosts of all those she'd spent time with here through the decades.

Preston was there, nodding his approval at her.

Beverly, her sister, telling her again how the summer they'd spent together at Whispering Pines had been the best three months of her brief life.

Memories of others were there with her as well as she floated above the lake and her dock. Her friends—Helen, Ruby, and Eleanor—their youthful faces like shadows behind their now aged silhouettes.

None of them came out here anymore. Celia was the only anchor.

She could imagine seeing Danny's mother, Mrs. Bell, exit the lodge far below, perhaps carrying a stack of clean linens. The kitchen would smell of her famous baked bread or chocolate cake.

And of course, the strongest memories of all included her time here with Danny. She remembered back to her first day of that second summer when Danny picked her and Ruby up at the bus depot. It would be the start of the summer that forever changed her.

How different her life might have turned out if the stacking of future events hadn't kept her home instead of building a life somewhere with Danny.

Was it the misty memories of her past that both tied her here but also left her feeling forever alone, isolated?

Something cool and slick, hidden in the shadows of the water, had brushed against her foot, slamming her abruptly back down into her own body, bringing her focus back to her confusion over the kiss. Fish flashed silver in the water below.

Behind her, the laughing voices of children and scolding parents caught her attention, and she glanced back over her shoulder at them. She hoped they were all creating their own memories of Whispering Pines as they frolicked in the soft waves.

That possibility was why she still worked so hard to keep the resort going.

She'd decided then, as a rambunctious toddler gave her a friendly wave with his sand shovel, that she needed to create more happy memories of her own at Whispering Pines. She had to quit living in the past. It was time to let go of the old memories that were preventing her from enjoying her time now.

She wouldn't let fear hold her back from new experiences, even if that included taking a chance with Wayne. If that was what he wanted, too.

She'd slid easily into that decision, sitting in the warm sunshine. But now, in the dark gloom of a stormy night, alone in her car, doubts crept back in.

Neither she nor Wayne was young anymore, both closer to sixty than fifty.

Had the kiss even meant anything to him, or had it been a chance event, one quickly forgotten?

What did she even really know about the man, other than how dependable he was around the resort, and the soft spot he seemed to have for her nephew and nieces?

As her headlights bounced off the bright red letters of the sign marking the turn to Whispering Pines, she slowed and eased the Cadillac onto the gravel road.

She thought back to the conversation she'd had with Virginia two nights prior. She'd seen little of Virginia or her daughter all summer, so when the woman asked if Celia could watch Karen for a few hours, she'd jumped at the chance. Virginia was finally dating the man she'd met two years earlier through her job at the library. Frank, a creative writing professor, seemed so different from light-hearted Virginia, but the woman was positively glowing with happiness when she'd returned home after their date with a fresh bouquet of roses in her hand.

Is that what new love looks like?

Would Celia ever feel like that again, or was she too old to expect butterflies and flowers?

The dark façade of the lodge came into view in the glow of her headlights. Several cars were there, but given the rain and the late hour, guests would likely be in bed by now.

The clock on her dash showed nearly midnight as she turned off her engine. The only light was the dim glow of a solitary streetlight at the edge of the parking lot. Celia twisted in her seat and reached behind her, fumbling for her umbrella. It wasn't there.

She gasped as a blur of movement crossed her back windshield, a shadow in the night.

Someone tapped on her window.

She spun back around. Her hand clutched at her galloping heart.

Wayne's face glowed in the weak light, his features obscured by rivulets of rain coursing down the outer glass.

She dropped her forehead to the steering wheel, laughing at her own foolishness.

The door handle rattled and she had to unlock it so Wayne could pull it open.

"Sorry, didn't mean to scare you," he said, swinging the door open. He already held an umbrella open above his head. It was the same rainbow-colored one she'd been searching for in her backseat. He grinned. "I thought you might need this. You forgot it on the porch next to your door when you left."

He held out a hand and helped her out, and when his warm, steady fingers wrapped around hers, she decided an umbrella was even more useful than flowers.

Chapter Thirteen
Gift of Diversification

Summer 1983

"Thank you for agreeing to meet us here," Virginia said, squeezing Celia's hand. The two women stood close on the sidewalk as Frank, whom Virginia had recently married, fumbled with the lock on the old storefront.

Celia patted her hand in return, then stepped closer to the plate-glass window. She cupped her hands around her eyes to block the glare of the hot sun and allow a view of the interior. "Well, I admit you have me curious."

"Don't let the inside scare you," Virginia said, joining her to look through the window while Frank continued to struggle with the lock.

Celia had heard a hint of both excitement and trepidation in the younger woman's voice when she'd called that morning to ask if she had time on her calendar for a quick meeting downtown. Intrigued, she'd gladly rearranged her schedule to free up an hour.

She stepped back from the window when the lock clicked open. "Frank, is your brother thinking of expanding his store?"

Frank held the door open for the two women, his eyes moving to the sign over the adjacent building. "No, but he mentioned this place last month at the wedding. We were talking about Virginia's big dream."

Virginia stopped in front of Frank, laying her hands on his chest as she brushed a quick kiss across his cheek. "Marrying you *was* my big dream, Frank. If none of my other dreams ever come true, I'll still die a lucky woman."

Celia grinned at the color creeping up the studious man's cheeks at his wife's display of affection. He rolled his eyes, but clearly the man was crazy about Virginia. Celia had hosted their small wedding in her backyard, and the love these two shared was impossible to ignore.

"Come on in, Celia, and I'll explain why I dragged you down here like this during what I'm sure is a busy day for you," Virginia said, entering the hushed interior, her heels clicking on dusty tile.

Celia followed, her eyes sweeping over the inside of the store, pleasantly surprised at the coolness of the air after the heat on the sidewalk. Despite the bearable temperature, there was an unpleasant mustiness to the air.

"Keep an open mind," Virginia suggested, making her way to a wooden cabinet near the center of the large room. Various shelving units stood at haphazard angles around the floor.

"Enough with the suspense," Celia said. "Why am I here? Why are *we* here?"

Frank stepped around the counter to stand beside his wife, putting an arm around her waist as they both faced her. "Celia . . . we have a business proposition for you."

A distant memory flitted to her mind, and the pieces clicked into place. Her face must have reflected her awareness as she set her purse down on the wooden surface between her and the couple. Virginia reached for her hands, and she could feel the excitement coursing through her young friend.

"Remember when you helped me land my job at the library, Celia?"

"Sure, I remember," she said, enjoying the excitement in Virginia's expression. "You thanked me profusely, then went on to explain the library wouldn't be the last step on the ladder of your career. You insisted that one day you'd own a bookstore of your own."

"That's right. I did. And you said you'd help me with a bookstore, too, if you were able. Do you know that I've been shushing little kids for ten years already?"

She laughed. "Ten years? That hardly seems possible!"

"Ten years," Virginia confirmed. "I've learned so much about books over the past decade, and obviously Frank loves books, too. I *know* it's the right time. I've been keeping an eye open for the perfect location, but nothing ever seemed quite right. But when Philip mentioned to Frank that this space was vacant, I knew the time had come."

Frank squeezed Virginia's waist, then let his hand drop. "There is another interested party meeting with the realtor this afternoon, so if we want it, we have to move quickly."

Celia took another look around the interior space, now imagining it as the bookstore Virginia always wanted. It wasn't that hard to envision. The large windows in the front allowed for a flood of natural light. Depending on how they chose to set it up, there would be plenty of room for several sections.

"There is a small apartment upstairs," Virginia was saying. "Perhaps we could rent it out for extra income, to help cover costs. There's a basement, too, but they've had some water issues down there."

That would explain the unpleasant odor. Celia had learned through her work that water issues needed to be dealt with quickly to prevent further damage. "I might suggest some resources to help with the basement problems. Would you like me to have someone check for any additional structural issues, too? Is the space for sale or lease?"

She noticed a look pass between the two. Frank gave his wife a brief nod of encouragement.

"It's for sale. We'd appreciate your help, thank you, Celia," Virginia agreed, wringing her hands. "But I actually had something more in mind."

"More?" Celia asked, unsure where the woman was heading and why she looked so much more nervous now instead of excited. "Come on, Ginny, you're killing me here."

"We want to ask you if you'd come in as a partner," Virginia said in a rush.

"Partner? You want me to be part of your business?"

She nodded and strode toward the front of the space, motioning at the massive front windows. "Can't you picture it? Tables draped with white linen, stacked with beautiful books and a display to catch the eye of shoppers outside. We'll change the display with the seasons. Bright colors and beachy covers in the summer. A beautiful Christmas display. The possibilities are endless."

The younger woman's excitement was obvious, but Celia wasn't understanding her own place in it. "But, Virginia dear, I'm still working. I don't have time to work a second job. Or a third, if you count Whispering Pines."

But Virginia waved this away. "Oh, heavens, I'm making a mess of this. I'm just so excited. Frank, please explain to Celia what we were thinking."

"Of course," he said, smiling a patient smile that reminded Celia how well he balanced Virginia's happy-go-lucky nature. "Celia, I'm going to be completely honest with you. Everything about this situation is perfect—except for the timing. This building could meet all of Ginny's needs for her store. The only problem is we can't afford it. I'd hoped to have a few more years to save up the capital we need to get started. But we don't have that luxury. When I suggested we might need to bring in a partner, the only person Virginia would even consider was you."

Celia was already appreciating the possibilities for herself, now that the initial shock was wearing off. "But why not ask your father for money to invest? Warren would certainly consider it."

As she spoke, she caught another look pass between the two, as if this was an old argument they'd rehashed many times.

Virginia shook her head. "I don't want my parents involved in my bookstore. Father would be fine on his own, but you know as well as I do that Mother would stick her nose in where it doesn't belong."

Celia laughed. "You're probably right. But didn't you say Karen was spending the day with Helen today? It seems to me that they've been spending lots of time together. Are you finally on better terms with your mother?"

Pacing now, Virginia rubbed her upper arms, the turn in the conversation seeming to make her uptight. "A little."

Frank cleared his throat. "Why don't we stick to today's business, shall we? Whether Ginny is comfortable with Karen spending time with Helen is a sore subject, best left for another day. But what do you think about our suggestion? Would you have any interest? I know your work keeps you busy, plus you have rental properties, but you have such a head for business. We'd welcome your expertise. And maybe you'd appreciate the variety. You've been at your job for a long time."

Too long, Celia agreed, but only to herself. They were correct to guess she might be ready for a new challenge. And she'd always loved to read. Maybe it was because she'd always believed that if Beverly had lived long enough, she'd have become an author.

Her head was already spinning with the possibilities.

"I admit, I'm interested. Tell me what you envision with this bookstore, Virginia."

Celia's invite was all it took to infuse the younger woman with energy again. She launched into her desire to carry a full range of books for all ages and tastes.

"But you can't be everything to everyone," Celia countered.

"Maybe not," Virginia admitted with a shrug, "but my time at the library has given me a keen sense of what people like. Many books sit on the shelves gathering dust, while others always have a long waiting list. I may be new to store ownership, but I know my way around books. The other thing I'd really like to do is feature new authors, especially those from the Midwest. I don't have as much input as I would like in the buying decisions at the library. Helping Frank with his creative writing courses has helped me see how much undiscovered talent is out there. I want to give *those* authors a way to get their work into the hands of readers, too."

Authors like Beverly, if only she'd had the time, she thought. Celia had never expected something like this to come her way, but she already knew she wanted to be involved.

"I couldn't work at the store," she cautioned. "Between my work and Whispering Pines, I barely have a spare minute, especially in the summer months."

Frank nodded. "We realize that. But would you have time, say quarterly, to help me with the financials? I can't guarantee we'll be able to get you a large return on your money in the short term, but we will share any profits with you, and do our darndest to protect your investment."

"I love what you are considering, and I think you've found a great space here," she conceded. "I tell you what, Mr. and Mrs. Fisk, I'll give my lawyer a call when I get back to the office this afternoon. I can set up a time for the three of us to meet with him. He's young and just building his clientele, so he should be able to get us in right away. But don't worry. He's smart and dependable. If you would like to have legal representation present, too, let's invite them as well."

Virginia rushed over to her, arms extended, catching her up in an unexpected hug. As the younger woman's fragrance wafted around her, Celia hugged her back. Her enthusiasm for this project was exactly what had been missing from Celia's life lately.

Celia headed back to the office. She shut her door and sank into the chair behind her desk. Her fingers itched for a cigarette, even though she'd given them up after her nieces admonished her for the nasty habit during their first visit to Whispering Pines. She'd been caught up in Virginia's excitement about the bookstore, but now she worried she might have been too rash. She didn't know the first thing about retail or selling books, and the Fisks were looking to her for help.

A brisk knock on her door interrupted her musings.

"Come in."

The door swung open. Immediately, she had to school her features to remain neutral when she spied her boss's boss, Tripp Whitby, in her doorway.

What's he doing here? He wasn't due in town until later in the week.

"Nice of you to grace us with your presence, Celia," he admonished, letting her office door bang against the wall. "Are you in the habit of extra-long lunches these days?"

She bit her lip. Tripp used to be notorious for his long lunches when he worked out of this office. "No, I had a client meeting," she said, offering nothing more. He didn't need to know her meeting was a private matter. She'd earned some latitude, given her many years of dedicated service to this company, and Tripp knew it, too. "What can I help you with?" she prodded.

"Join us in Warren's office. We need to discuss the project out on Twenty-eighth and Third."

"I'll be in shortly. I have one phone call I need to make first."

He waved a hand over his shoulder as he left. "It'll have to wait. I need you in here right now."

As his voice faded, she collapsed back in her chair in frustration. Tripp didn't often visit their office anymore, but when he did he drove her nuts.

Her eyes sought the framed picture of her brother's four children, all smiles in their swimsuits, standing on the beach at Whispering Pines. She couldn't remember if they took the shot during their second or third summer vacation out there, but the joy emanating from their faces always made her smile. George and Lavonne had given her the framed photograph for her sixtieth birthday.

She'd planned to work until sixty-five, then spend the rest of her days—or at least her summers—at her resort. But could she stand to work for Tripp for another five years?

The niggling doubts that started to plague her after her quick meeting with Virginia and Frank dissipated. She needed something other than this place to keep her mind occupied for the next five years. She'd call Jack Poole as soon as she could extricate herself from Tripp's impromptu meeting. Besides, Jack was a bright young man. She was transitioning all of her legal work to him, intent on helping her best friend's son get a strong start at his law office. Ruby had always been there for her through the years, and it was her turn to do the same.

Setting up a limited partnership like the Fisks suggested should be a relatively straightforward task, even for an inexperienced lawyer. She and Jack would have to learn together. Celia liked the idea of further diversifying her business interests. She wasn't sure she could stand Tripp for much longer.

Chapter Fourteen
Gift of Moving On

Summer 1988

"Well, this is it." Celia's words bounced around the interior of her Cadillac. In a last act of rebellion, she pulled into Tripp's prime parking spot in front of the office. He would be in attendance at her retirement party, and wouldn't like that she'd parked in his spot. He hadn't worked at this office on a regular basis in years, but Tripp's sense of entitlement never faded.

Today is my day, Tripp, like it or not.

She turned off the car but didn't get out. She rested her left arm on the sill of her open window and reached for the dash with her right hand. Without conscious thought, she pressed on the cigarette lighter.

"Old habits die hard."

What was the matter with her? She hadn't smoked in eight years. This damn party was jangling her nerves. She still battled strong cravings, especially on a day like today. Good thing the lighter wouldn't work with the car turned off. That, coupled with the fact she didn't keep an emergency pack of cigarettes in her purse anymore, kept the old habit at bay.

She pulled fresh air into her lungs, tasting the scent of rain. She'd knew the old wives' tale promised wealth to a couple if it rained on their wedding day. Did rain also signify abundance on someone's retirement day?

After today, she'd be free. Free to spend her days doing whatever she wanted. Free to spend her summers at Whispering Pines. To go watch her nieces and nephew play their sports. She had a pile of books stacked high on her nightstand, novels she'd picked up while visiting the Fisks' bookstore.

"Correction, *our* bookstore," she said. She glanced around again, but decided she better get used to talking to herself.

Maybe that was why she wasn't feeling as excited as she'd expected when she started counting down the days to retirement way back in January. Seven months of red check marks should have left her feeling better prepared.

She'd wrapped up the last items on her list the previous afternoon and handed off the remaining customer files to her replacement. A soft peach sunrise tinged the eastern skyline by the time she finally fell asleep after her last day. Her mind raced all night, replaying the wins, the challenges, and even the mundane moments of her forty-year-plus stint inside this building. The years she'd spent working for the Whitbys were mostly good. She'd accomplished things most women only dreamt of, and she'd amassed a comfortable nest egg. While there was still too much discrimination, she hoped she'd helped pave an easier path for younger women climbing the ladder behind her.

It was time for her to go. The past twelve months had been challenging after Warren retired the previous summer. New management always brings change. Celia had no desire to prove herself to anyone new at this point in her life.

She was ready for a different kind of work.

She jumped when someone banged on the roof of her car, smacking her elbow against the doorframe. Pain shot up through her arm and into her shoulder and neck.

"What are you doing sitting out here, Celia?" her old boss laughed. "Isn't the party inside?"

"Don't you know better than to sneak up on somebody like that, Warren?" she scolded, rubbing her tingling elbow. She eyed him, standing just outside her door, looking relaxed and stylish in a casual sport coat. "Retirement looks good on you. Where's Helen?"

He checked his wristwatch. "She'll be here by two. She was doing something with Karen today."

Celia gathered her purse and opened her door, but she had to turn the car on so she could roll up the window. "I can't imagine Karen wants to come to my retirement party. Not exactly something a fourteen-year-old would be interested in."

"Actually, your party was the perfect excuse for Helen to take Karen shopping for a new dress."

She got out and he pushed her door closed. He motioned for her to take the lead as they walked toward the office. Neither of them would be back here much after today. This was Warren's first time back in months.

"How was Florida?" Celia asked as he opened the door for her. "You've worked on your tan."

He smirked. "Only indirectly. I'm *working* on my golf game. Shaved five points off my handicap. Beautiful courses around the Naples area. Will you try golf?"

Hours on a golf course sounded mind-numbing to Celia, even though Warren seemed pleased to be honing his skills. "I thought golf stood for *Gentlemen Only, Ladies Forbidden*."

He snorted. "You sound like my wife. She could golf at the club if she wanted to. Plenty of other women do. Thank God for Men's Night."

She slugged him on the shoulder. He'd proven to her time and time again that he was *not* a male chauvinist, but he did like to annoy her for good fun.

The door behind them opened and closed again. A familiar voice cut into their banter. "Lucky you're the man—or woman—of the hour, Celia, parking in my spot like that."

She didn't even bother to hide the roll of her eyes at Tripp's comment. Tripp had plenty of chauvinistic tendencies.

She leaned in to Warren and lowered her voice. "Just wait," she whispered. "Next, he'll ask if I picked up the cake for the party today. He probably expects me to put the coffee on, too."

"Play nice," Warren cautioned. "You can do it one last time."

With that, her friend turned to face Tripp, hand extended.

Celia took a fortifying breath and turned as well, plastering a half-smile on her face. The party would be more pleasant if she behaved herself. But the hairs at the base of her neck bristled when she noticed Tripp's wife at his side.

What is she *doing here?* she wondered in dismay. *She can't stand me. If she had her way, Tripp would have fired me years ago.*

Warren turned slightly, catching her eye. He mouthed the word *nice* again.

Oh, she could play nice.

"What a pleasant surprise, Sophia. I didn't expect to see you today," Celia said, trying her best to infuse warmth into her words. "Thank you for coming."

"Dear Celia, I wouldn't miss it for the world," Sophia purred, extending a limp-wristed hand in her direction.

Celia was accustomed to returning firm, sometimes bruising handshakes with men. She wasn't sure what to do with Miss Hoity-Toity's limp fingers. She gave them an awkward squeeze, then stepped back for a buffer of space.

A commotion near the front of the office saved her from an extended conversation with the company's owners. The party was starting early. She recognized Renee's laughter and a warm round of hellos from George.

"If you'll excuse me, I must greet my family," Celia said. She'd thank her brother for saving her from small talk with the power-wielding woman.

She passed a pair of frazzled secretaries as they hurried to set out punch and coffee cups next to the cake. She almost apologized for inconveniencing them like this, but stopped herself. She'd earned this party. If they weren't organized enough to be ready early, that was on them. Celia's ability to anticipate things ahead of time was foundational to her success.

Renee rushed toward her with arms extended. Celia took in her niece's sharp navy dress and pumps as the girl enfolded her in a congratulatory hug. "Aunt Cee, I'm so excited for you! Gosh, aren't you excited? This means you can spend all your time at Whispering Pines now! I'm *so* jealous."

Celia hugged her back. Of her brother's four children, all teenagers now, she knew Renee loved the lake resort the most. "You are welcome anytime, dear. You know I'd love to have you out again. *All* of you. I missed you last year."

Renee stepped back but kept one hand on her forearm. "I appreciate that. Unfortunately, if I want to drive, I need gas money. They give me all the evening and weekend shifts at the restaurant since I'm the new kid."

Celia understood, but summer at Whispering Pines wouldn't be the same without her nieces and nephew. Renee gave her arm one last squeeze and then backed out of the way to allow the rest of her family to greet the guest of honor.

Sixteen-year-old Jess wore a pretty sundress. Celia almost didn't recognize her. "You got contacts!" she said, giving the girl's hand a squeeze. Jess didn't like hugs.

"I did," Jess said, the blush on her cheeks killing her attempt to appear cool and aloof in the room full of adult strangers. "Now that you're retiring, does this mean you'll spend more time at your bookstore, Aunt Celia? I bet you can get all the books you want for free."

Celia laughed. She appreciated that she and Jess shared a love of reading. "I don't know if the Fisks will want me hanging around too much, but I am hoping retirement will mean I'll have more time to read."

She accepted warm hugs from George and Lavonne, then greeted her youngest niece, Val. New to the teenage years, Val had a mouth full of metal and a body that was just starting to transition from child to woman. Her short stature was accentuated next to her big brother, and she looked ill at ease.

In contrast, Ethan was all smiles. "Thanks again for picking up the tab for everything my football scholarship didn't cover."

The young man hugged Celia. Her heart panged when she realized how much her nephew still resembled Clarence, the grandfather he'd never met. The way his longish hair fell over his forehead and the twinkle in his eye . . .

Our loved ones do indeed live on.

When Celia developed her financial goals for this next phase of her life, she'd set money aside for all four of George and Lavonne's kids to attend college.

The money would only be enough to cover attendance at a state school, but she wanted to give them a leg up, and with no children of her own to support she was thankful she could help.

"You are very welcome, Ethan. I know you'll make us all proud."

Small talk continued between Celia and her family. She'd heard from Gerry the night before. He'd called to pass on congratulations from him and Letty, but he was working and couldn't attend her party.

Tripp approached, a hand extended in greeting to George, Lavonne, and Ethan. The three girls hung back. Celia stifled a bark of laughter when she noticed Val giving the tall man in his business suit the stink eye. Renee poked Val for her lack of manners.

She's a better judge of character than I gave her credit for, Celia thought, introducing her family to the company's owner.

After Tripp exchanged social niceties with them all—pausing for a heartbeat when he caught Val's unexpected glare—he turned to Celia. "I'm sorry to interrupt, but a reporter from the paper is here."

"The newspaper?" Celia asked, shocked the press was at her party.

He nodded. "It was Sophia's idea. Remember that piece they did on you years ago? About how unusual it was for a woman to hold a role like yours in a construction company? Sophia thought it would be good press for the company to bring them back, to have them document the longevity of your career. To showcase the commitment we have to helping women and this community."

Renee and Jess looked impressed with the idea of their aunt being featured in the local newspaper. "Wow, Celia, that is so neat," Jess said, giving up her fight to remain apathetic. "I'd love to be a career woman just like you some day."

"Me, too," Renee chimed in.

"Come on, kids, let's get out of the way," Lavonne insisted, ushering her family toward the cake table.

Celia turned back to Tripp. "Sophia's idea? I didn't think she liked me much."

She held her breath, unsure how Tripp would react but unable to keep up the polite façade any longer.

"You've always been a fair judge of character," he conceded, surprising her.

"So, you admit it. She hated having me in the office."

Tripp shrugged. "*Hate* is a strong word. You have to understand, Sophia comes from old money. She has a tendency to feel a certain level of, shall we say, *distrust* when it comes to women trying to improve their stations in life. Her and some of her girlfriends get suspicious of other women that don't come from money."

Celia snorted. "Your wife needs better friends."

Before she could say anything more, a graying man carrying a notepad approached, followed by a younger man with a camera. The photographer reminded her of her old friend Danny.

Danny . . . where was he now? Their paths hadn't crossed in so long. Thinking back, she realized she'd last talked to him the weekend she turned forty. He'd surprised her with a visit, and she'd told him everything. Even about the baby they'd conceived together, and how she'd given it up for adoption without consulting him. Maybe now that she'd have more time, she could look him up. He used to drop in on her, unannounced. Could she do the same thing to him?

This young photographer, with his earnest face and clunky equipment, was all it had taken to bring back so many memories. She pulled her attention back to the bustling room and the task at hand. She'd talk to this reporter and say all the right things to promote the Whitby Company. After all, she'd been doing it for decades, and she owed a lot to Preston's old company.

The well wishes continued. Customers she'd worked with through the years showed up to thank her for her partnership. Tears threatened when representatives of a local affordable housing group presented her with a bouquet of flowers and a card. The retirement card was full of notes of gratitude from families now living in their own homes thanks to her perseverance. Frank and Virginia stopped by, having closed the bookstore for an hour to attend.

"I'm not sure I would have *closed* it," Celia said, laughing. "Aren't I supposed to help you make smart business decisions? Not encouraging you to close up shop in the middle of the day!"

Virginia dismissed her concern. "This is a special occasion, Celia. We wouldn't miss it for the world."

"Will I get to see Karen today?" Celia asked, looking around them. "Warren mentioned Helen would bring her by. It's been so long since I've visited with her."

She caught the hesitant look that passed between Virginia and her husband.

"What?" she pressed. "Is Karen all right? I know the teenage years can be especially tough for girls."

Frank gave a quick shake of his head. "Karen is fine. Virginia just worries that her daughter is an awful lot like her mother, especially now that they spend so much time together."

Celia had known Helen, Virginia's mother and Karen's grandmother, for her whole life. While she'd always consider Helen one of her dearest friends, the woman could certainly try one's patience. "Helen has many wonderful qualities. Karen could do worse in companions than her grandmother."

"Speak of the devil," Frank interjected with a nod toward the front door. "Here they come now."

Warren must have spied his wife and granddaughter, too. He joined them as they made their way toward Celia, Frank, and Virginia.

Helen caught Celia up in an uncharacteristic hug. Surprised, Celia pulled back, but Helen held tight. "I see Sophia is here to celebrate. She's finally getting rid of you!" Helen whispered in her ear before taking a step back and giving Virginia and Frank a quick greeting.

"Hello, Mother," Virginia said, her face expressionless—something Celia rarely saw on the younger woman. The tension between mother and daughter was palpable.

"Why don't we see about getting a piece of that cake, Virginia? Let Celia visit with her other guests. It's nice to see you, Helen. Warren," Frank offered. He actually smiled at his in-laws, unlike his wife. "Karen, come with us."

"But, Dad . . ." Karen whined. The look Frank gave her cut the girl off before she could make a scene.

Celia was glad to hear Karen call Frank "Dad," and to see the teenager listen to him. Virginia was already halfway to the refreshment table. She wished Helen would make more of an effort with her daughter, but at least she was building a relationship with Karen. Maybe that was the best any of them could hope for. But there would be a more appropriate time for her to broach the subject with Helen. Again.

"My heavens, Helen, you're even more bronzed than your husband. Don't tell me you spent time on the course in Florida, too?"

Helen held up one arm, as if to inspect the color of her own skin. "Certainly not. But the pool was delightful. Saltwater instead of chlorine. I wish we could switch our pool to saltwater here."

Warren crossed his arms over his chest. "If I do anything with the pool at our house, it'll be to fill it in with cement. I pay too much in maintenance for that beast every summer and no one uses it outside of our Fourth of July picnic."

"That's not true. Karen has been over to swim almost every day since we got back from California," Helen corrected him.

Ever since Warren retired, he and his wife had traveled somewhere special at least every other month. Celia hoped she'd find time to travel now, too.

A pair of arms wrapped around Celia's waist. She'd recognize Ruby's freckled arms anywhere. She spun around and gave her best friend a proper hug.

"Look at this turnout, Celia! I'm impressed. And look who I found in the parking lot," Ruby said, turning slightly so Celia could see a more subdued Eleanor standing behind her.

"Oh, my—*Eleanor*! I wasn't expecting to see you today. Thank you so much for coming! Your brother and sister-in-law are here, too," Celia shared, glancing around but not finding Tripp and Sophia in the crowd.

"I'm not here to see *them*, Celia. I'm here to celebrate *you*! Father would be so proud of you today."

Celia studied her for a moment. The woman had lost her husband four years earlier and she hadn't seen Eleanor since the funeral. While both Helen and Ruby—and, hopefully, herself—still exuded a youthful energy despite hitting the halfway mark of their sixth decade, Eleanor's face looked colorless. The frown lines between her eyes were deep. Celia couldn't help but wonder where the young girl she'd met during her college years had gone. The memory of a young Eleanor floated to her mind, laughing and joking as she met them outside the lodge at Whispering Pines for the first time. The Eleanor in front of her bore little resemblance to that girl. Had the loss of her spouse caused this radical decline in her old friend, or was she simply tired from her drive from Chicago?

"If you ladies will excuse me, I see some old customers I'd like to say hello to," Warren said, leaving the four women to catch up.

Celia turned her attention back to the party at hand. She felt honored they'd all made the time to join her on her special day. "I can't believe you're all here! I've missed you so. I see Ruby often, but with all of your recent travels, Helen, and with you still in Chicago, Eleanor, it's been too long since we've had time together."

The three women nodded, and Celia thought Eleanor's expression softened. Inspiration struck.

"I have an idea!"

All three watched her expectantly.

"Why don't you come spend a couple weeks with me out at Whispering Pines in August? It'll be just like it was when we were girls!"

"Can we skinny-dip again?" Helen asked, her expression so sincere Celia worried for a moment that she was serious.

"Um, well . . ." she stammered.

Helen cracked up. "I'm kidding! Motherhood and age stole my perky breasts! My days of skinny-dipping are over."

"Helen, keep your voice down," Eleanor scolded their friend.

Celia cringed when she noticed a few heads turn in their direction. Her friends had called her a prude all those years ago when she hated shedding her clothes to swim naked in a pond in the forest. Looking back, she realized they were right. And maybe she was *still* a little prudish. Eleanor, on the other hand, had quickly joined in back then. Celia doubted this matronly version of her old friend would be as fast to shed her clothing.

Eleanor sighed. "While that sounds like a fabulous idea, Celia—well, other than the skinny-dipping part—I'm afraid I'm all booked for this summer. I'm heading to England next week for a month with my daughters and grandchildren."

If Celia were the one heading off on a European vacation, her excitement levels would be off the charts. By comparison, Eleanor looked resigned to the idea.

"I'm sorry, Celia," Ruby chimed in. "We have a family reunion on Edwin's side in Wyoming in two weeks. Then I'm babysitting my grandson, Seth, until I head back to school in the fall."

Helen shook her head. "When are you going to retire, Ruby? Aren't you tired of teaching by now?"

Ruby shrugged. "This will be my last year. And would you believe, I finally get to help chaperone a group of students heading to Venice next spring! It's something I've always wanted to do, but the foreign language teachers usually get to do it. This year, the French teacher will have an infant at home, so they asked me to go. I can hardly wait!"

Helen nodded and turned back to Celia. "Sorry, dear. We're busy, too. I simply can't squeeze one more week into our full summer schedules at this point."

Celia felt some of her enthusiasm seep away. For the first time in her adult life, she'd have plenty of time to entertain at Whispering Pines this summer—but it seemed everyone else was busy as usual.

"Why don't we plan for a week or two next summer?" Eleanor suggested. "If we get it on our calendars now, there won't be any excuse for us to miss it. I, for one, could benefit from time at the old resort. How I've missed Whispering Pines through the years. Is it still as special as it used to be?"

Celia smiled, heart swelling at her appreciation for Eleanor. "I like to think it is. Yes. Let's plan on that, then. No excuses for next summer! The four of us will make Whispering Pines our own again, just like we did back in 1942!"

Chapter Fifteen
GIFT OF A NEW CHAPTER

CELIA SNAPPED OFF THE television, cutting off the rambunctious greetings of bar patrons on *Cheers*. Quiet settled around her as she took a seat on the couch under the front windows. Tomorrow she'd leave for Whispering Pines to celebrate her freedom and enjoy a whole month of sunshine. Maybe she'd stay for *two*.

It felt strange to have an open schedule. It was the last Thursday of July. Many in the business community would gather for drinks and socializing at one of the local restaurants in town. The Chamber hosted the event. Celia seldom missed it.

She'd miss it tonight. That meet-and-greet was part of her old life.

Instead, she'd relax at home. She picked a dessert plate up off the coffee table, her generous slice of three-day-old cake hanging over the edges. They'd pressed what was left of the sheet cake into her hands at the conclusion of her retirement party. Chocolate crumbs fell onto the cover of the novel Virginia had pushed into her hands the last time she'd stopped in the bookstore. "You'll finally have time to read, Celia," the woman had reminded her after insisting she'd love *Vows*, LaVyrle Spencer's latest romance.

Celia supposed she'd get used to retirement eventually, but it felt strange to not be going out. The white frosting cracked under her fork as she cut through the upper crust to the still-moist cake beneath. She hadn't wanted to buy groceries, since she was leaving so soon, so the left-over cake from her party would be her dinner. There was something liberating about eating dessert for a meal.

"You are turning into quite the wild child," she said to herself.

Her only answer was the creak of a board somewhere within the walls of her old, empty house.

When nothing but crumbs remained, she set the plate aside and picked up the book. She was pulled into the story, reading until the setting of the sun made it too hard to see. The telephone rang. A glance at her wristwatch revealed it was after nine.

"I really need to install a phone in here," she sighed, pushing off the couch and heading to the kitchen, the insistent clang of the phone like the irritating buzz of a mosquito.

Snatching the receiver from the wall, she took an extra second before answering to stretch the tangled cord. "Hello?"

"Celia, what did you say to my wife?"

Her left hand quit trying to untangle the phone cord. "Tripp?"

He was the last person she'd expected to call her at home, now that she was officially retired.

"I mean it. What did you tell Sophia?"

Celia held the receiver away from her ear to stare at it in confusion. She considered the tempting idea of hanging up, of leaving the man to his own drama, but curiosity was replacing her irritation. The growl in Tripp's voice might have cowed someone who didn't know him as well as she did.

"Did that wife of yours finally wise up and leave you?" she asked, shocking herself at her own audacity. But once the words were out of her mouth, she couldn't take them back.

"You think you've won, don't you?" the man hissed into the phone. "You think I can't touch you now. But you're wrong."

A shiver ran down her spine at his menacing tone.

"Look, I don't know what you're talking about. You either need to start making sense, or I'm hanging up."

She thought she heard the *psssch* sound of a can being opened. She could picture him tucking the beer between his stump and body to easily pop the tab. Years of practice meant his missing left hand seldom slowed him down.

"Tripp, are you still there?"

She heard him swallow, and could imagine him swigging a can of beer on the other end of the phone.

"I mean it, Tripp. I have better things to do than listen to your heavy breathing."

She moved to hang up the receiver but heard him shout her name. Against her better judgment, she again put the phone against her ear, curiosity winning out.

"I know you said something to Sophia at that damn party of yours. She barely said two words to me during our drive back to Chicago." He paused. "That was actually nice, come to think of it."

Now Celia was sure the man was drinking. Even Tripp wasn't usually so belligerent or easily distracted.

"I'm glad you had a peaceful drive home. Now, if you'll excuse me—"

"It had to be you. Who else would tell my wife about that damn secretary? I thought we put that problem behind us more than twenty years ago. In fact, you promised you took care of it. In exchange, I practically *gave* you Whispering Pines."

A headache blossomed behind her eyes. She untangled her hand from the phone cord and rubbed her forehead. A tiny part of her had always worried this day would come. She wasn't proud of the way she'd wrestled Whispering Pines away from Tripp, but it was the only way she could think of to protect the property. Preston, his father, had entrusted it to her, and she'd done what she'd done in remembrance of him.

Could Tripp take Whispering Pines away from me after all these years?

If he made a play for it, it would be out of spite. Tripp never liked her. He never cared about Whispering Pines. But maybe, just maybe, she could convince him to leave it alone.

"Tripp, I promise. I said nothing to your wife. You were standing right there during the only conversation I had with her at the party. Maybe someone else said something?"

A growl echoed in her ear. "No one else *knows*."

That wasn't true. Warren and Helen knew. But she wasn't about to bring their names into the conversation. She didn't think Tripp ever suspected their involvement in the plot to save Whispering Pines and to secure their positions in the company. Besides, why would they have said something without telling her?

"Annemarie might have said something to someone in the office. It wasn't like she was exactly trustworthy. She was shocked and mad when you terminated her after what happened."

"I still think it was you," he spat. "I'm calling my lawyer. You shouldn't have played me like this, Celia. The minute you finished at the company, you thought you could bring me down. Destroy my marriage. But you won't get away with it!"

Click.

"Bastard!" She clenched her teeth as she put the receiver back on the phone base. She should have hung up on him the moment she heard his smarmy voice.

She'd thought—*hoped*—all of this was behind her. Tripp's marriage to his socialite wife had been precarious for years. While it was true Celia had taken advantage of that once, she'd played no part in any last nudge that was now apparently sending it to its ultimate demise.

Maybe no one had said anything specific. Tripp's womanizing, gambling, and drinking weren't exactly a secret. Sophia wasn't dumb.

But that didn't matter. His narcissism would demand someone else be to blame.

Celia dug out a fork and popped the plastic lid off the remaining quarter of her sheet cake. Not bothering with a plate this time, she dug in, her mind elsewhere.

Why did Tripp have to keep casting doubt on her ability to protect Whispering Pines? She'd battled him over that special property for much of her adult life.

Suddenly disgusted at mindlessly eating countless calories, she threw her fork in the sink and tossed the last of her cake in the garbage. She took a swig straight from the milk carton—something she'd swatted her younger brothers over the head for countless times. It didn't matter. Tomorrow she was leaving for her extended celebratory trip, and she'd toss everything in the garbage before she left.

But thanks to Tripp's call, she had one more stop to make in the morning before she could leave town.

"You can wipe that grin off your face right this minute, Jack," Celia said, frowning at her young lawyer. "It's not professional."

Ruby's son struggled to school his face into a neutral expression. He failed.

"I apologize, Celia. I had no idea of the lengths you went to when you purchased Whispering Pines."

Celia squirmed. She'd known Jack all his life; cheered him on from the sidelines as he struggled to put himself through law school. His parents were teachers, and they'd helped with his undergraduate degree, but he'd been on his own when he pursued a career in law. Ruby had burst with pride over her son's accomplishments, and Celia felt compelled to give him all her legal business once he passed the bar. He worked for a well-respected local firm; the partners would help him develop into a properly trained lawyer.

But now that she was retired, she would need more legal support than ever. She didn't plan to sit home and eat bonbons. Cake on the couch was an anomaly. Without the demands of her office job, she intended to keep busy with other endeavors. She'd need an excellent lawyer and felt confident that Jack would grow into the role. But right now, his grin reminded him of the kid he used to be, and it annoyed her.

Or maybe she was embarrassed to share with him how low she'd stooped to wrestle Whispering Pines away from Tripp. But she'd promised Preston that she'd protect the resort no matter what.

Hopefully, it wouldn't all come back to haunt her now.

"The fact remains, I purchased Whispering Pines from Mr. Whitby," she reminded Jack, intent on keeping their discussion on a professional level. "And it's your job to make sure that purchase stands any additional scrutiny Tripp may demand his lawyers give it."

Jack had the good sense to sit up straighter and shift into a no-nonsense frame of mind. "I understand. I'll look through everything. And, with your permission, I'll sit down with Mr. Lemon and walk through the transaction with him as well."

"I'd appreciate that."

For the first time since Tripp's unpleasant phone call the evening before, she felt her shoulders relax. She'd been right to come here, to have a fresh set of eyes review everything surrounding her purchase of Whispering Pines. After all she'd been through, and how long she'd waited to have time to enjoy the resort, nothing could disrupt her plans now.

She stood, prompting the younger man to rise and walk her to the door of his tiny office. He shook her hand before opening the door.

"Celia, I wanted to thank you again for bringing me your business. I know the only reason you're placing so much faith in me is because you've been friends with my mother for forever."

She opened her mouth to dispute his statement, but he raised a hand to quiet her.

"I'll do my very best to earn your trust. Go enjoy your time at the lake, and we'll make sure everything is taken care of here," he assured her.

The ring of confidence in his tone was a welcome surprise.

She held his gaze. "I look forward to a long, mutually beneficial partnership with you, Jack. Now, if you'll excuse me, I think it's about time I get on out to Whispering Pines. I have a retirement to celebrate."

Chapter Sixteen

GIFT OF THE UNEXPECTED

CELIA SCREECHED IN PAIN. Her hammer clanked to the floor.

"Everything all right up there?" a voice cried from the depths of the lodge.

"I'm fine, Mary!" she hollered back, shaking her wounded thumb. It didn't take away the sting. She shoved it in her mouth and stepped back to survey her work.

The perfectionist in her railed against the mismatched frames, but the display was impressive. She'd wanted to update and add to the framed photographs on the wall inside the front door of the lodge for years. She finally made the time to do it, buying out all the frames in the sizes she needed that the nearest store had for sale. Some were wooden, others metal, in a wide range of colors.

"These pictures were taken over many decades. Since it's an eclectic assortment of frames, we can pretend these went up over the years, too."

"You know what they say about women who talk to themselves, don't you?"

Celia spun around at the voice behind her. Her foot caught the dropped hammer, sending it skidding across the floor until Mary's big toe stopped it.

"Ouch!" Mary grabbed her injured foot, her sandal no match for the kicked hammer.

"Sorry," Celia apologized, grinning at the pair of them and their injured digits.

The front door opened, allowing light to flood the persistently shadowed alcove. Celia glanced back and threw an arm over her eyes at the bright intrusion.

"What the hell are you two doing in here?" the man in the doorway boomed. What Ed lacked in height was balanced out by girth. His wide shoulders stretched from one side of the doorjamb to the other. "I can hear you clear outside."

His bark didn't faze Celia. Her years in the construction industry had numbed her to colorful bursts of swearing. "Your wife snuck up on me. Practically gave me a heart attack!"

Mary dropped her injured foot. "So you threw the hammer at me?!"

Her words shocked Celia into silence. But only for a moment. Then she burst out laughing at the absurdity of it all. "I didn't *throw* the hammer at you, Mary! I wouldn't do that. I dropped it a minute ago. And when you scared me, I accidentally kicked it."

Ed shook his head. "If you two are done messing around in here, I wanted to let you know you have a visitor, Celia."

Mary grunted at her husband. "Messing around? I'll have you know I've—"

Celia laid a hand on the other woman's arm. "We both know how hard you work around here, Mary. I'm sure he didn't mean to imply otherwise. Besides, we can't have guests hearing the three of us bicker."

Mary harrumphed and rolled her eyes, but said nothing more.

"Is it the Smiths?" Celia asked. "They're early."

Ed shook his head. "No, it's some old guy. Says he's a friend of yours. Didn't give me his name."

"Why didn't you get his name?" Mary chided. "You're not much of a welcoming committee."

Celia picked up the troublesome hammer, smoothed her hair, and resisted the urge to scold Mary for more bickering. This was the couple's third summer under Celia's employ, and they did a great job running things at Whispering Pines. Working so closely with a spouse was bound to create tension.

He shrugged. "I was filling the low spots in the parking lot when he pulled in." He turned his attention back to Celia. "The guy didn't see me at first. Just got out of his car and stood there, staring at the lodge and then out at the water. Real intense, like. Something tells me he's been here before, but I don't recognize him."

A shiver of apprehension raced down Celia's spine. "Was he missing his left hand?"

Ed narrowed his eyes at her, confused by the unusual question. "Not that I noticed."

A car door slammed and Celia looked beyond Ed's silhouette in the open doorway, squinting at the bright sunlight. Gravel crunched as someone approached the lodge.

If it wasn't Tripp, who could it be? Had Wayne come back after all this time? Ed was only forty-five, and he might consider anyone closer in age to Celia's sixty-five to be "old."

A man stepped into view, thick white hair falling across his forehead. The bright sunlight behind him threw his features into shadow.

Ed turned back to the man. "Found her," he told the visitor, as if Celia had been lost. "If you'll excuse me, I'll get back to it out here."

Ed brushed past the man. If he was a guest to be checked in, Ed left that business to Mary. Even with Celia back at Whispering Pines for an extended period, Mary insisted on keeping up her duties. Celia was spending the rest of her summer at Whispering Pines relaxing and learning to enjoy retirement.

"Hello, Celia. You look well."

Celia gasped. She knew that voice. It wasn't Tripp, come to harass her. Nor was it Wayne, back from wherever he'd disappeared to.

"Danny?"

The man stepped inside. He reached both hands out to her, but paused when he noticed the hammer in her hands.

Stunned by the man's sudden appearance, she couldn't move.

When she said nothing and made no moves toward him, he dropped his hands. "I should have called before dropping in on you like this."

Mary cleared her throat. "If you'll excuse me, I'll get back to the laundry."

Nodding absently to Mary, Celia kept her eyes on Danny. "What are you doing here?"

"I heard from Eleanor. She told me you retired and that you were spending the rest of your summer out here."

Inclining her head, she waited for him to say more. Her head spun. His sudden appearance didn't make sense.

He laughed, but he sounded nervous. "I've done it again, haven't I? Popped in on you from out of the blue."

Celia wagged the hammer at him. "Danny, the last time we spoke was the weekend of my fortieth birthday. In case you lost count, that was twenty-five years ago."

His eyes searched her face. "The years have been good to you."

She snorted. She might not look bad for her age, but she certainly didn't look forty. Unless he was blind, he could see that. The years had left a mark on his face, too.

"Could you please put that hammer down? You're making me nervous, waving it at me like that. I promise, I come in peace."

She glanced at the hammer, having forgotten she still held it. "Where are my manners? Why don't you come in to the office," she instructed, turning away without making sure he followed her. He'd come here unannounced to see her. He'd follow.

Her office, once holding only functional furniture for running a resort business, had morphed through the years. The original desk was still in the middle of the room, facing the door, just as Preston Whitby had set it up in the early 1940s. But Celia had made the office her own through the years. The walls were a sunny shade of yellow, an oval rag rug warmed the floor, and a green couch now filled the wall facing the windows. Pretty prints hung on the walls, and a lime-green electric typewriter stood on the small stand next to her desk, replacing Preston's manual one, the hunk of black iron no longer practical. She'd scored a deal on the green couches from a wholesaler that did business with her old company. There were matching couches in every cabin. The final touch: plants graced most surfaces, softening the atmosphere.

Danny whistled as he crossed the threshold. "Sure looks different in here!"

Celia thought back to that long-ago summer when she and Danny had sat at this very desk with Preston Whitby, discussing the business of running Whispering Pines and the impact of the war on all of them. As a college girl, she had been struggling with what she'd do when she graduated. Unbeknownst to her, Danny was considering enlisting in the war efforts. It would be the only magical summer they'd ever share.

She could remember the date on Preston's desk blotter: *July 28, 1943*.

Why would she remember something so inconsequential?

Her current planner was open on her desk and bold gold lettering listed today's date: *August 28, 1988*.

Everything had changed over those forty-five years. Those two young people, sitting across from Preston on that long-ago July day, could never have guessed the different paths their lives would follow.

Celia settled into her ancient office chair. It groaned under her weight, the same way it had when Preston used to sit in it. "Why were you in touch with Eleanor?" Her mind was careening from question to question, but this seemed the logical place to start. "I didn't know the two of you kept in touch."

Danny pulled one of the two chairs that faced Celia back from the desk and he settled his tall frame into it. He crossed an ankle over a knee and relaxed, his hands draped over his legs. "Our correspondence through the years has been sparse, but Preston planned for my mother in his will. If she ever needed to go into a nursing home, or needed money for medical care, Preston made me promise to reach out to his estate lawyer."

"How is your mother?" Celia asked, concerned. The woman, if she was still living, would be nearly ninety.

"She has dementia. That's why I talked with Eleanor. Well, initially I contacted the law office, but they told her I'd been in touch. It's so sad. Mom did so well through the years. She married again, traveled all around the states in an RV."

Celia's mind snagged on his comment about Mrs. Bell marrying again. "Wait—married? Seriously?"

He shrugged. "Sure. Mom was still young when my dad died that winter, back in '43. Do you remember when she ran into that delivery man when we were back here for Eleanor's wedding? Would have been . . . '51."

"No!" Celia whispered. They'd gotten a kick out of watching Danny's mother flirt with the man that used to deliver produce to Whispering Pines, back when she'd worked here as a cook. "They got married?"

"They did. Eventually. I could hardly believe it myself. It bugged me a little, to be honest, but I knew Mom was lonely. My job took me all over the world and I hated that she was alone so much of the time."

Celia understood. Her own mother blossomed during her second marriage, too. "I can see your mother remarried, living out of a camper. I bet she'd host potlucks for the whole campground."

Laughing, Danny agreed. "No one could lay out a spread like Mom . . ." He sobered as he continued his story. "But her husband died a couple of years ago. Mom took it hard, and I started to notice things when I'd visit. Small things at first. But three months ago, the police called. She'd stopped at a rest stop in central Nebraska, fell asleep in her car, and by morning the battery was dead. When a Good Samaritan tried to help, she got belligerent. I'm sure she was scared. They called the cops. Thankfully, my name was on the car's registration, so they reached me right away."

Danny's sad tale hurt Celia's heart. She hadn't thought about her old friend's mother in a long time. "Did you have to put her in a home, then?"

"Sadly, yes. She needs to be in a facility equipped to deal with dementia. Do you have any idea how expensive a place like that is?" He reached up absently and flipped his mop of white hair out of his eyes, the still-familiar gesture twisting Celia's gut.

"Thank goodness Preston set something aside for her," she said, hating the idea of sweet Mrs. Bell, waking up in a roadside rest stop, alone and confused. She sighed when she realized she couldn't even remember Danny's mother's first name, nor did she know her new last name since she'd remarried. The woman would always be "Mrs. Bell" to her.

Danny stood and ambled over to the window that faced the beach, hands in his back pockets. "His generosity was a shock. Still is. I think he was feeling his own mortality by then. He got emotional, talking about how important my parents were in those first years after he'd bought the resort."

"When did you last see Preston? After Eleanor's wedding? He was healthy as a horse back then."

"I don't remember the exact year. He wasn't happy about his restricted diet his doctor had him on. He'd had a heart attack. I could tell he didn't have the same stamina as the man I remembered."

Celia was better with dates. Preston had his first heart attack in 1965, a few days before Thanksgiving. "Did he reach out to you?"

Danny was slow to respond. Celia thought he might not have heard her. But then he shook his head and turned to face her. "No, I went to see him."

His body didn't block her view of the beach, and her eyes caught on the dock. The dock where they'd spent so many late nights, talking and dreaming about life as only twenty-year-old kids can do, before the weight of life's trials provides a cold dose of reality. It was hard to reconcile that summer, so long ago yet still vivid in her memory, with the white-haired man standing in front of her now. Ed had called him old, and she'd certainly noticed the years, but now, when she took more time to study him, she thought he looked much as he did so many decades earlier—if you ignored the white hair, missing finger-tip, and scars mixed in with a few wrinkles on his face.

Celia suddenly knew why Danny would have wanted to see Preston back then, but she hated to think about what else they discussed beyond future support for his mother. "Why?"

Danny searched her face, his mouth firm. Then, like the fast flick of a butterfly's wings, his serious expression fell away. "It doesn't matter. What matters is how generous the man was, and how thankful I am that my mother is at a place that's providing her with the care she deserves."

Celia knew Danny wasn't being totally honest with her. His smile didn't quite meet his eyes. She would have pushed, but the truth was she didn't really want to know if they'd discussed more that day. She went along with his change of topic with something approaching relief.

"I'm glad you could get your mother placed. How did you think Eleanor seemed when you spoke with her?"

"What do you mean?" he asked.

"She came to my retirement party. It was wonderful to see her. I just thought she seemed awfully reserved. Nothing like the fun-loving girl we used to have such a good time with when we were younger."

"Seemed fine to me, I suppose." He scratched his jaw. "Now that you mention it, she didn't tell me much about what she's been up to. After we caught up on the situation with Mom, she switched the topic to you."

"To me? Why would she do that?"

Instead of answering her directly, he turned back to look out the window again. "Remember all the dreams we talked about, sitting on the end of that dock? Is it actually the same dock? I don't see how it could be."

She pushed out of her creaky chair and moved over to stand beside him. "Parts of it, at least. We've had to replace the wooden boards on it a few times, and it's probably about time to pull the whole thing out and start over. But I haven't been able to bring myself to do it."

He stood there, nodding slowly, lost in his thoughts.

"Have things changed much out here since 1951?"

She unlocked the window and worked to shimmy it open. The old sash stuck, but brute force worked. The window screeched in protest. "The resort is like a time capsule. In fact, remember my youngest brother, George?"

"Sure," he said, glancing down at her.

"The first year he brought his brood of four kids out here, they got bored near the end of their trip and put a time capsule together. Remember that tiny cabin, the one I was staying in with Beverly, the one summer you worked here? My caretaker helped me hide the kids' capsule in the wall. I doubt they'll ever find it, if they even remember to look for it down the road."

"The guy out there working on your parking lot?"

"Oh, no, that's Ed. Back then it was Wayne. Ed and his wife, Mary, have been here three years now helping me out. With luck they'll stick around for a long time."

"The Wayne guy didn't stick?"

"No."

Celia didn't want to discuss Wayne with Danny. She still felt bad about how things had ended with him. Come to think of it, her relationship with Wayne shifted when they were hiding the time capsule. She shouldn't have let their friendship morph into something more. Wayne was a great guy, but he'd eventually wanted a commitment out of her. But she'd worried that she would only come to think of Wayne as a stand-in for someone from her past.

That someone was now standing right next to her.

Why was Danny back?

What was she supposed to do with him now that he was here?

She watched as the last family on the beach packed up their belongings and headed for their cabin. The light was fading. It was getting to be dinnertime.

"I'm not sure what came over me," Danny finally said, bringing them both back to the present. They were two old friends who'd once meant the world to each other but who'd drifted apart, destined for different paths. "I should have called instead of dropping in on you like this. But I wanted to see you. I wasn't sure what you'd say over the phone, so I came in person instead."

"Danny . . . we missed our chance."

He gave no sign he'd heard her. "Eleanor mentioned your retirement party. I took that opening to ask all the questions I'd been wondering about for years. I think she finally tired of me peppering her, because she suggested that if I was so curious I should just come out here to talk to you myself."

"She did not!" Celia said, feeling a twinge of betrayal. Was her old friend trying to set her up with her old flame? She should have at least warned her. Celia would have to give Eleanor a piece of her mind the next time she saw the woman.

Danny chuckled. "I don't think she thought I'd actually come here," he said, crossing back over to sit down again. "Have a seat, if you don't mind. My leg gives me some trouble these days."

Her stomach rumbled. She pressed a hand to her noisy midsection.

Danny glanced at his watch. "I didn't realize how late it's gotten to be. Please do me the pleasure of allowing me to take you somewhere for dinner. You're hungry, and if I don't eat something soon, these butterflies are going to gnaw a hole in the lining of my stomach."

That admission did more to strip away Celia's defenses than anything else he could have said. Did she dare? Danny was the only one that had ever touched her heart in a way that always seemed to leave her shattered when he walked away. And he always walked.

But part of her was curious. What had he been doing with his life in the years since she'd last talked to him? The age span from forty to sixty-five was filled with a lot of living.

"I'll agree to dinner, Danny, because despite all our time apart, I still consider you a dear friend." She hoped he caught the emphasis she'd intentionally put on the last word.

"Grab your purse. I have the perfect spot in mind."

Chapter Seventeen
GIFT OF "REMEMBER WHEN"

CELIA TOOK A DEEP breath as she waited for Danny on the beach at Grand View Lodge. She soaked in the glorious riot of colors that stretched across the horizon, casting the water an indigo so deep it was almost black, an overlay of gold shimmer across the top. He'd run inside to check on a table. She adjusted her light wrap, pulling it tighter across her shoulders.

She'd dressed quickly for dinner, doing what she could with her hair and slicking a warm coral shade across her lips, as Danny waited downstairs in the duplex. She had wondered what he'd been thinking, standing there in the entryway of a building he'd helped build with his own hands when he'd been a young man of barely twenty. He'd been back here one other time, for Eleanor's wedding, but it all seemed so long ago. Did the memories haunt him, as they did her?

She wasn't surprised when he'd turned left at the end of the lane leading away from Whispering Pines. They'd first met at the larger Grand View Lodge. It seemed fitting to return there for dinner, for a chance to reconnect after so long.

Celia used her time alone on the beach to collect her thoughts. Three hours ago, she'd been hanging pictures in the lodge at Whispering Pines. It was ironic that Danny had snapped several of the photographs she'd finally dug out of her old blue trunk in the attic at home before this latest trip to the resort. Enough time had passed that she was able to pull the pictures out of storage without her heart fracturing again. To touch the smiling faces of her and her girlfriends, when they'd sparkled with youth, warmed her heart. She'd even started making plans for their promised visit next summer. She'd already decided they'd make this same drive next summer, down the road from Whispering Pines to Grand View Lodge, the place where they'd danced away their summer nights so long ago. They used to dance with handsome young men and dream about their futures. Helen and Warren had connected here, marrying a few years later.

Celia first met Danny here, too, the summer before he came to work at Whispering Pines.

Some of their dreams were born here. Danny's came to fruition: to become a famous photographer, traveling the world. There were costs involved with pursuing that dream that he couldn't have guessed, but he'd found his success nonetheless.

Had Celia achieved the things she'd dreamed of, back when she was fresh-faced and unjaded?

"Our table is ready, Celia," Danny said, appearing at her side.

When she turned to him, the setting sun caught in his hair, turning it to a golden shade similar to the color it had been when she'd first met him.

Maybe time wasn't so linear after all.

"I can't believe you got a table on such short notice," she said, looking away from his earnest eyes, from the hair she used to love to run her fingers through.

He held out his arm and she slipped her hand through it, fingers resting on the sleeve of his dinner jacket. She'd opted for shimmery silver flats, so it was easy to keep up with Danny's long stride. He didn't lead her inside as she'd expected, but angled her toward an open table on a patio, positioned perfectly to witness the sun's final dip below the horizon.

"I didn't even know this patio was tucked back here," she said, allowing herself to relax into the moment.

Once they'd ordered and wine sparkled in their glasses, Celia raised her glass. "To catching up with old friends."

"To catching up," Danny echoed, tapping her glass with his.

The ring of vibrating crystal danced across the air.

"What a magical evening," she whispered, tipping her wine goblet toward the sinking sun.

The discordant sounds of someone tuning instruments caught their attention.

Danny's smile widened. "Did you ever learn to enjoy dancing?"

She flexed her toes, more satisfied than ever with her decision to don comfortable shoes. "Why won't you believe me when I tell you my feet were sore from my blasted heels when you caught me wandering the hallways that night?"

"I'll be forever thankful for those shoes. If not for your sore toes, we might not have struck up a conversation that night."

She laughed, and it sounded foreign, even to her own ears.

There's a distinct quality to a woman's laugh when she's sitting across from an interesting man, especially when that man is someone special. Someone she's loved, she thought. *Past tense,* she reminded herself, watching Danny say something to a passing waiter.

The last time she'd shared a meal with this man—if you could count a cup of coffee and a doughnut as a meal—he was uneasy, blaming his lack of proper table manners on years in the field; they'd rushed from story to story, grabbing food on the go. The man sitting at her table now, with the last sliver of a golden sun setting behind his shoulder, was more polished. Easing her glass out of the way, Celia clasped her hands on the tabletop and gave Danny her full attention. She hoped to get some of his story out of him before their meal arrived.

"Tell me, Danny, where have you been hiding for the last twenty-five years?"

"I'd hoped to find out what *you've* been up to. I don't want to talk about me."

She wagged a finger at him. "No, you don't. You show up, unannounced—as usual, by the way—and insist I accompany you on an unplanned dinner date. You owe me. Spill."

"You're just as bossy as ever, I see," he said with a wink.

"Wasn't my assertiveness the thing you loved about me?" she shot back.

He paused, as if considering several comebacks to her teasing.

She was flirting with him. And damn if it didn't feel good.

Careful, a little angel on her shoulder whispered.

Lighten up, the devil on her other shoulder teased.

Danny slid his glass out of the way, mirroring Celia's movement, but then reached across the table, inviting her to put her hands in his. Instead, she fiddled with her napkin until he pulled his hands back. For all she knew, his mother wasn't the only one to marry. A lot could have happened in twenty-five years.

If her rejection stung, he hid it well. "All right. But let me know when you're getting bored. My life up until I saw you the last time around our fortieth birthdays was much more exhilarating than more recent years."

"I'll be the judge of that."

She buttered a fragrant slice of warm bread from the basket at her elbow and offered it to him, making herself another. He took a bite and chewed it slowly. Celia wasn't sure if he was savoring the bread or stalling.

"If you don't start talking, I'll still be waiting when our dessert arrives."

He grinned and set his half-eaten slice down. "Fine. Let's see. I suppose most of what came next, after the last time you and I talked, was your doing."

"My doing?" she asked. Her stomach clenched at the notion that maybe he'd built a family with someone else, after he'd shared how part of him wanted a child and she admitted to giving theirs away.

"Well, not immediately. For the next couple of years, I buried myself in my work. I missed Roberts. Remember my buddy that got killed when we were covering the war in 'Nam?"

She nodded. She'd never forget that horrific story he'd shared with her.

"I took one week a year to spend with Mom. And I tried to drop in to see Roberts's kid once in a while, but then his wife got remarried, so that got awkward."

A waiter arrived with their food, artfully slipping plates in front of each of them so unobtrusively that Celia barely noticed.

"What part of that was *my* doing? My workaholic tendencies?"

He laughed as he picked up a knife and fork, cutting into his juicy steak. "No, I think both of us suffered enough from that. Isn't it part of what kept us apart for all these years?"

"Touché."

He seemed to appreciate her acceptance of the fact they'd each built their lives around work, perhaps to the detriment of other parts of their lives. "Actually, what I mean is that last conversation we had weighed on me."

"About the baby?" she asked, her voice soft with dread.

He nodded. For the first time since they'd sat down, he seemed reluctant to meet her gaze. "Celia, Preston was willing to tell me anything I wanted to know. Did you ever talk to him about what happened? What he'd done with our child?"

She could tell he was choosing his words carefully, weighing how much to say. She shook her head, her pulse pounding in her temples. "I rushed to his side, at . . . the very end . . . and he offered to tell me. He knew he was dying. But I had never expected to speak to him about it again, and his offer was so unexpected. It terrified me. I said I didn't want to know, and he seemed to accept that. But I admit, he let it slip that our baby was a girl. That's all I know."

"Do you want to know more?"

It was her turn to avoid his gaze, although she did nothing more than slice up her walleye into bite-size pieces and stir it into her rice medley. Her appetite had deserted her.

"What did you learn?" she hedged, unsure.

"I know her name. I know where she lives."

"Where she lives *now*?" Celia asked, shocked. She looked up. "Have you *met* her, then?"

He shook his head, chewing a piece of steak.

How can the man eat at a time like this?

He must have read something in her expression. "What? I eat when I'm nervous."

There was something so honest about his response, Celia felt a sliver of tension ebb away.

"I haven't met her," he said. "Believe me, I considered reaching out to her, but in the end I didn't want to disrupt her life. Preston said the adoptive parents didn't intend to tell the girl the truth. Or at least not initially. I didn't feel it was my place to blow up her world."

Celia forced herself to take a bite of food. She was relieved, but she still had so many questions.

Did she really want the answers?

"I respect that," she said eventually. "You would have made a great dad, and I'm sorry you never really got the chance. Have you at least seen her, maybe from afar? You're a photo journalist, for heaven's sake."

"*Was* a photo journalist, you mean. I hung up my camera years ago."

This breadcrumb about his life caused her breath to hitch. Danny's camera was like a third arm for the man. They'd talk about that later, but she wanted to stay on topic about their daughter. The one she'd never met but never forgotten.

"Have you ever gotten close enough to see her? To see what she looks like? *Who* she looks like?" These were some of the questions that kept her up at night.

He set his fork on the edge of his plate. This time, when he reached one hand out to her from across the table, she took it. His thumb caressed the back of her hand. His eyes focused on something behind her. Finally, he spoke.

"I couldn't resist. I found out where she works. It's a public place, so I went there. Talked to her briefly, even. Of course, she had no idea who I really was, but she was delightful. You know how sometimes you can feel someone's energy?"

Celia did know. Sometimes you can recognize in an instant when someone is good, is kind. Or the opposite can hold true: some people put off a negative energy that immediately sets you on edge. She'd run across plenty of both during her working years. She nodded, searching Danny's eyes, even though he still stared off into the distance.

How much more did she want to know?

"She mentioned a daughter. A husband. She's happy. Content. I could tell."

Celia squeezed Danny's fingers, realizing what this meant. "We're grandparents?"

He laughed, squeezing her back. "I suppose, in a biological sense."

A large group of diners at the table next to them stood to make their way to the door. One man gave another a light shove, scolding him in a teasing tone for picking up the tab for everyone. That tab might have included an impressive quantity of alcohol, because the shoved man stumbled, bumping into their table. Celia's wine sloshed, spilling onto her plate.

"I'm so sorry," the man said, his demeanor switching from jovial to contrite in a flash. "Please, order a new meal if you'd like. I insist on paying for you both. I didn't mean to ruin your dinner."

Celia insisted it wasn't necessary. She wasn't even hungry anymore. But he persisted.

Danny intervened. "That would be kind of you. Thank you."

"I'll talk to the maître d'. Please, be sure to order dessert, too." The man sauntered away, flagging down a member of the staff.

"Why did you let him do that?" Celia asked.

Danny reached over and picked up her plate, her walleye now a pinkish hue in a pool of red wine. He switched their plates out. "You, my dear, have to learn to accept someone's attempt to atone for their sins. People feel better if they can help. Accept it, then give them a simple thank-you. Here. Try some of my steak. It's delicious."

"What makes you think I'm not good at accepting help?" she asked, sensing hidden innuendo in his words.

"See, you're trying to figure out whether I just insulted you, when I really just want to help."

The steak in front of her held more appeal than the fish, even before the wine bath, so she cut off a corner and tasted it. "This is good."

He nodded, watching her eat. "Celia, I know I've dumped some heavy information on you tonight. I apologize if it's upsetting you."

She stabbed another tidbit of meat with her fork, waving it in his direction. "I think I need time to process it all. Other than seeking out our long-lost daughter, what else have you been up to since I saw you on my birthday?"

"Twenty-five years is a long time," he said. "In fact, our daughter isn't my only child anymore."

Celia's stomach did one slow roll, and any hint of appetite she'd garnered evaporated at his words. "You have other children? Are you married?"

"I have one other child. A son. But no, I'm not married—at least not anymore. I was for a short time. My ex-wife is ten years younger than I am. The marriage was a mistake. My son was not."

When the waiter stopped at their table again, Celia asked him to take their plates and declined dessert. After their table was cleared, the two old friends sat quietly, studying each other over a flickering candle.

"Are you disappointed in me?" Danny asked.

"Disappointed? Why ever would you ask that?"

Instead of answering, he brushed at the white linen tablecloth, splattered now with red wine and breadcrumbs. "Why don't we go for a walk on the beach. Maybe we can find a dock to sit on, like we used to?"

She nodded, and they made their way to the entrance, making sure the clumsy passerby had indeed paid for their meal.

Danny turned toward the water, but Celia tugged on his arm. As he gazed down at her, she saw his disappointment.

"I'm sorry," he said. "Would you prefer I take you home instead?"

She dropped his arm. "Let's go back to Whispering Pines. It's a beautiful night, and I'd rather sit on our . . . I mean, *my* dock. It'll be quieter there."

"Whatever you'd like, Celia."

Grand View Lodge may be known for its magnificent sunsets, but the moon hanging over the lake at Whispering Pines glowed bright and full, majestic. To Celia, it felt like home.

"Do you sit out here as often as you used to?" Danny asked, rolling his pant legs as high as possible. He dropped his shoes and socks onto the worn boards behind them. "Aww," he groaned, his feet dipping into the cool, dark water below.

Celia removed her shoes, pulled her skirt up so it wouldn't accidentally dip into the water, and lowered her own bare feet beside his. "Every chance I get. I've never understood why so few guests try it."

The events of the day felt surreal to Celia. One minute she was hanging up old photographs in the lodge, smashing her thumb with a hammer, and the next she was sitting next to Danny on their dock.

"Tell me about your son," she invited.

During the drive back to Whispering Pines, she'd processed the news that her Danny had married and divorced. That news didn't upset her. A child was more troubling. She was happy for him, even if it left her with a sense of melancholy.

"He's a great kid. We named him Finnegan, but he goes by Finn," Danny said, leaning back on his hands to stare at the moon. "He played basketball in high school. He even earned a scholarship to play ball at a private college. I traveled too much for work when he was growing up, so my ex practically raised him. I wish it would have been different."

"His name sounds Irish. Is it a family name?"

"It was my father's name."

"I don't think you ever told me his first name before," she said, suddenly sad that they'd never shared much about their parents. "You said you aren't working anymore. When did you quit?"

He took in a slow breath. "Five years ago. Finn was getting into trouble, and it was too much for his mother. I think he acted out because he was mad at me. I missed important events. Other times, I'd show up unannounced. It created too much instability."

She considered pointing out that he'd made a habit of showing up unannounced with her, too, but she didn't want to interrupt.

Danny leaned in to drape his left arm over Celia's shoulders, pulling her against his side. Her arm wrapped around his back without hesitation.

"It was tough. My family suffered because of my job. You knew that would be the case. Traveling the world isn't conducive to raising kids. But we made the best of it, he and I, and things got easier when I was around more often. I didn't quit work altogether, but cut back over time."

She gave him a comforting squeeze. "Does he look like you or have any of your mannerisms?"

Danny squeezed her shoulder, then lowered his arm to take his wallet out of his back pocket. He pulled a picture out.

She held it at various angles to see it in the moonlight. "He has your mouth," she concluded, disappointed there was little other resemblance that she could see.

Laughing, he took the picture back. "I know. He doesn't look like me. But sometimes, when he opens his mouth, I hear myself talk."

She smiled, but his comment made her wonder again whether their daughter displayed any similarities to either of them. Had nature been strong enough, regardless of who had raised her?

"Enough about me," Danny said, stowing his wallet and glancing her way. "What have you been doing since I saw you last? Come on, dish."

"I'm not sure there's much to tell," she said, her eyes scanning the rippling water in front of them. "I never married. Never had more children." *Couldn't have more kids* would have been the full truth, but she didn't want to make Danny feel any worse about their unplanned pregnancy so many years ago. "I worked. Lived with Mother until she died at seventy-four. I'm still in the same house. I suppose my biggest news is my retirement. But you already knew about that."

Danny squeezed her hand, then swatted a mosquito off his cheek. "I'm sorry you lost your mother. She wasn't very old."

"Thank you. It was tough."

There was a splash in the water as a fish jumped nearby.

"But, Celia, aren't you forgetting something? Aren't you now the proud owner of this place? That is an amazing feat, my friend! How did you manage it? Preston informed me he was passing the resort on to Tripp, even though he had serious reservations about his son's willingness to keep the resort going."

Something buzzed close to her ear. "You wouldn't believe me if I told you," she said, waving away the annoying insect.

"Try me."

"You'll think less of me."

He nodded. "I'm duly warned. Now, come on. You have me really curious now."

She told him, leaving nothing out. He didn't interrupt as she explained how she set a trap for Tripp, using the man's own vices to ensnare him in a sticky web of mistakes she then used to basically force him to sell her Whispering Pines at a price she could afford.

"I promised Preston I'd protect this place, no matter what. And that's exactly what I'm trying to do," she concluded.

He remained quiet for a beat, as if letting it all sink in. "I'll be damned. You bested Tripp Whitby. Few can claim that."

She squirmed. She wasn't proud of the drastic measures she'd taken to purchase Whispering Pines. She admitted as much to Danny.

He shook his head. "Celia, you need to let that go. Do you think Tripp would have acted any different if the roles were reversed? When that man wants something bad enough, he doesn't let his conscience stop him."

She thought back to her phone conversation with Tripp a few days after her retirement party. She'd said nothing to his wife, but Tripp had her worried. She was glad she had Jack digging into the legal aspects of the sale, making sure everything would stand up in court.

"I hadn't thought of it like that," she conceded. "Maybe it's about time I forgive myself for stooping so low."

"I'd advise it."

The two old friends let a comfortable silence settle between them.

Celia shivered in the cooling night air. "I'm glad you came to see me."

"It's been a real treat," he agreed. "But I've kept you out too late, and now you're cold."

He popped to his feet like a man half his age, extending a hand to help her up. His leg couldn't be bothering him *that* much. They stood face to face in the moonlight, neither one sure what should come next.

"I'll walk you back to the duplex, then head over to my hotel. I'm going home tomorrow for Finn's birthday party. Celia, I've loved catching up. We shouldn't wait another twenty-five years to do it again."

She looked at the moon, so high in the sky. She hated the idea of him driving so late at night. Mary and Ed hit a deer driving back late from their daughter's home. It was still in the shop for costly repairs.

"Why don't you stay here? There are lots of deer this year. We had a mild winter, so their numbers are way up."

He shook his head. "I can't let you put me up. It would be too much of an imposition."

She wasn't dissuaded. The easiest solution was for him to stay in one of her spare bedrooms in her duplex, but she wasn't comfortable with that idea. "I'll tell you what. I have one open cabin tonight. It's the small one. I've got renters coming tomorrow, but you could stay there tonight."

She could see he was tempted, and she was suddenly glad she hadn't closed up the tiny cabin for good, though she'd seriously considered it.

"I don't know . . . That means someone will have to clean it again in the morning. It seems like extra work."

She waved away his concern and started up the dock toward shore. "What's a little work amongst friends? Come on. Let's get you settled. I watched plenty of sunrises out here with you when we were younger, but the only sunrises I see nowadays are the ones I get up early enough to watch."

Danny fell into step next to her. "Sunrises are beautiful either way."

Chuckling, the two old friends headed for the resort's smallest cabin. Danny remembered the way.

Chapter Eighteen
Gift of Purpose-Driven Work

Late Winter 1989

"I swear, you're busier now than before you retired," Ruby complained, dropping onto the passenger seat in Celia's Cadillac and pulling off her wool-lined leather gloves. "I hardly see you anymore. I'm sure glad we have these monthly historical society meetings. At least I know I'll see you once a month, unless you are at Whispering Pines. Thanks for the ride, by the way."

"We still see plenty of each other, Ruby. Besides, what would you rather I do? Sit home all day learning needlepoint?"

Ruby grinned. "I'd like to see that. By the way, why didn't you make me retire last spring? These kids are killing me."

"Don't be so dramatic," Celia countered, earning a grunt in return. "And don't forget the real reason you stayed. Venice. In the spring. I bet you have a calendar hanging on your fridge right now, filled with red X's for every day you survive in that classroom leading up to your trip."

"You know me well. But Edwin is afraid he won't be able to get time off to come with me."

Celia pulled away from the curb, watching Ruby instead of the road. Tires screeched and a horn blared. She slammed the brakes to avoid a collision.

"Didn't you just get this out of the shop after another of your fender benders? I'm not sure it's safe to ride with you," Ruby teased.

"Don't exaggerate. That dent was the first one in quite some time, and it wasn't my fault. My neighbor backed into me from across the street. I wasn't even in the car!"

"But you also slipped through that stop sign last winter," Ruby reminded her. "I was with you."

"It was *icy*. But enough about my driving. What were you saying about Italy and your hubby?"

Ruby pouted. "He claims he might not get time off from work, but I think he's afraid to fly over the ocean."

Celia laughed. "Boat or plane are the only way to get to Italy, and I doubt he can get the time off it would take to go by ship. He's crazy if he doesn't want to go. I'd give anything to go to Venice. Even if it meant following a bunch of promiscuous teenagers through the canals, trying to get them home in one piece."

"Tell you what—if Edwin doesn't come with, you can be my plus-one." Ruby pulled her seatbelt on as Celia sped through a yellow light. "Unless you kill us on the way to this meeting tonight. Then neither of us will get to go and I'll spend eternity wishing I retired *last* year!"

Celia grinned, loving the possibility of seeing some of the world with Ruby once her oldest friend retired from teaching. She still had a desire to travel, and maybe if Edwin turned out to be a terrible travel companion for Ruby, Celia would have herself a sightseeing partner.

The next morning, Celia was still thinking about the property they'd discussed at the previous evening's meeting. She knew Ruby enjoyed the heated discussions at the monthly meetings. Her friend would love to save every decrepit building in town. But after working in a business that focused on progress, she didn't feel the same. She'd never tell Ruby how many projects she'd been part of that included tearing out the old to make room for the new. She liked to think she brought a needed balance to the group of old cronies.

Not everything should—or could—be saved.

The dilemma kept replaying in Celia's mind as she sat with her morning newspaper. They'd discussed one of the oldest buildings in town that was slated for demolition to make way for a new apartment complex. The building had significant water damage. The problem had never been adequately addressed, and now mold was everywhere. In Celia's experience, it would be too expensive to mediate.

A local savings and loan association used to rent the lower half of the building. They shirked their maintenance responsibilities, and then the financial institution was forced to close its doors a year ago when it didn't survive the burgeoning S&L crisis. The landlord had nowhere to turn to recoup the damages.

Celia wasn't concerned for the shuttered S&L or the landlord. She worried about the dozen elderly tenants living in the seedy apartment units on the second floor of the doomed building. Lack of affordable housing was still a significant problem in town. She'd battled the issue for years, trying to direct some of her company's resources toward the development of properties that served the most vulnerable populations. Her stance was never popular, particularly with Tripp. He valued profit over humanitarian efforts. But the flowers and cards she received at her retirement party from those she'd helped reminded Celia her efforts made a difference.

If the landlord sold to developers, there would be a net increase in rental units, but the rent would skyrocket. Where would the current elderly tenants go?

She flipped through the newspaper, but nothing held her interest. Out of habit, she scanned the back section. Employment postings, invitations to bid, and various for-sale advertisements could sometimes be a better gauge of what was actually happening in town. She was glad to see a job posting for Homes Sparkle.

The woman Celia initially hired to clean her house after Maggie died experienced health struggles of her own, so Celia had to find someone else to come in. She'd hired a cleaning service owned by an old friend. Joyce and John Robins owned Homes Sparkle. Joyce worked at the Whitby Company with Celia before having kids. Celia had worried the small company was growing too fast. The cleaning crews they'd send to her house were often short-staffed and rushed. Since she knew Joyce personally, Celia had reached out to offer her assistance. The last thing she wanted to spend her time on was cleaning her house. She'd rather help Joyce and John's cleaning company stay afloat. They welcomed her assistance, but only if she agreed to accept a small ownership percentage.

And just like that, Celia had suddenly found herself a partial owner in not one but two local businesses. She was glad to see Joyce was trying to bring on more employees.

She ignored the invitations for bids—something she'd watched closely while still working. She didn't have to worry about that anymore. But she always monitored the real estate ads. She had Preston to thank (or to blame, depending on how she looked at it) for spurring her interest in investment properties. She'd amassed a small portfolio of little rentals. Headaches were an inevitable part of the process, but she enjoyed the challenge of making sure each property cash flowed.

A new advertisement caught her eye. The listing mentioned a fourplex.

"Forty-second and Eighth," she read aloud.

She was familiar with the area. Residential, and within walking distance of a grocery store. The price looked reasonable. She didn't own any properties larger than a duplex. Could she keep up with a building with four units?

Her interest piqued, she refilled her coffee and wandered to the back window overlooking her snow-covered garden. A fourplex wouldn't house everyone in danger of displacement if the building they'd discussed was demolished, but it could help.

Did she dare take on another property?

She bought the property. Jack helped with the legal aspects of the purchase. Her lending officer at the bank was comfortable with her growing expertise in managing a portfolio of rentals.

When the historical society failed to save the downtown building, Celia was prepared to offer a partial solution for the displaced renters. She had more applicants than units available. It was a good problem to have, because her margins were too skinny to allow for any vacancies.

Ruby was right. Her days were even busier now that she wasn't "working." But for the first time in her life, she was busy doing things on her terms, and she hoped she was making a difference.

Celia flipped the page on her desk calendar, outlining the 1989 in the upper right-hand corner of the new sheet.

"How is it March eighth already?" she muttered.

The weather outside her office window was typical for early spring in Minnesota. Piles of dirty snow remained, but the sun had melted enough of it to reveal swatches of green grass. A late-season snowstorm was forecasted for later in the week. If they were lucky, the mild temperatures of the past few days would keep the accumulation light.

Celia was ready for spring. She planned to spend her entire summer at Whispering Pines—something she'd been unable to do since her college years.

"Except for the summer you spent hiding there, when you were pregnant with Danny's baby," she reminded herself.

She'd looked forward to unrestricted summers at the resort ever since she'd started dreaming of retirement. Now that the time was finally here, why wasn't she more excited? Her eyes strayed to the framed world map hanging on the wall opposite her small desk. A retirement gift. Her co-workers hadn't missed her occasional mention of her dreams of traveling the world.

Celia planned to keep Mary and Ed Dixon on at Whispering Pines. She'd paid extra money down on the resort's mortgage in recent years, had even refinanced to lower her monthly payment so she could afford to pay the couple out of the summer's income. She'd worked too hard for too long at the Whitby Company to fall into another full-time job running Whispering Pines. She wanted to enjoy the resort, not spend her days working from May through September.

There was one glitch. Mary had asked for the month of June off. Their only daughter, Isabelle, was due with their first grandchild. Ed would only be gone for a few days, but Celia would need to handle all of Mary's duties for the month. She started making a list of the things she'd need to accomplish before she headed to the resort for five months.

The doorbell interrupted her thoughts. That would be Joyce at the door.

She may be planning to spend June changing beds and cleaning floors, but she didn't have to clean her own house today. Grabbing the envelope containing a check that should help Joyce and John meet Homes Sparkle payroll obligations for the next few months, she headed for her front door.

She tapped the envelope against her leg. Her real estate holdings were growing, and she was again part of the local business community. If she wasn't careful, she'd prove Ruby right. But, worse yet . . .

Too many irons in the fire might mean she'd never see the world.

She opened the door.

Joyce set her bucket of cleaning supplies down on the floor inside the front door and gladly accepted the check. "You don't know how much this means to us, Celia. If you hadn't called, we might have had to close up shop. I don't know how we'll ever repay you."

Celia grinned, optimistic that her new investment would stabilize the ground underneath the company's feet. "Actually, now that you mention it . . ."

Joyce returned her smile. "I know that look. You always find a way for everyone to benefit from a business relationship. What's it going to be?"

"I could use some help cleaning up a property I just purchased. The previous owners left a mess behind, and I have four new renters moving in at the beginning of next month. Any chance I can hire you to do a special deep clean?"

"You can throw any new business our way that you like. And now you'll get a small percentage of what you pay in business dividends," Joyce laughed, waving the envelope Celia had handed her high in the air.

Chapter Nineteen
GIFT OF OLD FRIENDS

CELIA OPENED THE DOOR to her half of the duplex, her other hand braced against her aching lower back. She grinned at the sound of the vacuum cleaner next door. Mary was due back tomorrow, and Ed was probably cleaning for the first time since she'd left Whispering Pines a month ago.

She couldn't wait for Mary's return. Stripping beds was tougher on her sixty-six-year-old back than she'd expected. The past month reinforced Celia's desire to find any way she could to keep the Dixons on; Mary took care of things inside, along with the basic record keeping, while Ed maintained the grounds and buildings.

She wondered again whether she was crazy to hold on to a place like this. It wasn't a lucrative financial investment.

"It was never about the money," she reminded herself out loud as she dug through the fridge for a cold drink.

She found a can of Miller Lite in the back. She wasn't much of a beer drinker, but a group of fishermen left a few stragglers behind earlier in the month. Not finding any better options, she popped the top.

The window over the sink looked out to plush grass surrounded by tall-reaching pines. Celia gazed outside, enjoying the muted sunshine of the late June day. Danny used to call it the golden hour: the perfect time to take pictures outdoors. She let her mind wander back in time to that summer when she'd stood inside the yet unfinished shell of this duplex. Danny had been helping Preston build it.

"I promised you I'd take care of this place, Preston, no matter what," she muttered. "And I will."

A flash of red at the birdfeeder caught her eye, reminding her of a conversation with her niece, Jess, a few summers ago. They'd spied a similar bird, its bright plumage out of place in a sea of green during a walk in the woods that surrounded the resort. Jess wanted a head start on the science project both Ethan and Renee had to do at the beginning of their freshman year in high school. Celia had welcomed the one-on-one time with the girl. Jess spied the red cardinal when she'd reached for the perfect leaf on a low limb of an oak tree.

"Did you know some people think red cardinals are visitors from heaven, coming back with a message?" Celia had asked her niece.

"Visitors from heaven?" Jess replied, and Celia could still hear the skepticism in the teenager's voice. "You mean like angels? You don't really believe that, do you, Aunt Celia? There's no proof any of it exists."

Celia remembered a split-second of dismay over Jess's cynicism. Personally, Celia needed to believe in something beyond the here and now, beyond the things we can see with our eyes. Later that evening, she'd overheard Val ask her father if red birds were angels. George had assured Val it was indeed possible. Jess had to have told Val about the cardinals. Maybe her dismissive attitude was all show.

The red cardinal outside her kitchen window flew away, gone in a flash, the swaying feeder the only evidence of its visit. Maybe it was Preston, paying her a quick visit from heaven to assure her how much he appreciated her efforts.

Would George and Lavonne ever bring their kids back to the resort? Despite her brother's assurances during her retirement party that they'd try to make it this summer, he'd called later to say they couldn't make it work. She knew Ethan's summer was consumed with football practice and his summer job—she helped pay for his tuition, but he had a football scholarship he needed to work hard to keep—but she had hoped her nieces would be back. Especially Renee, since she loved Whispering Pines almost as much as Celia did.

Her family wasn't coming, but Helen, Ruby, and Eleanor were coming in three weeks. She was excited for their visit, and would enjoy some peace and quiet before their arrival.

After years of waiting, she could finally relax like a guest.

It would turn out to be the longest three weeks of her life. She didn't know how to relax. Hopefully, with time, she would learn how to do nothing without suffering a bout of crippling anxiety.

"What time is our dinner reservation?" Ruby asked, checking the slim silver watch on her left wrist.

"Eight," Celia replied, glancing first at her old friend and then at the plethora of summer blooms gracing the familiar old bench behind her. She'd smelled the yellow roses even before she'd spied them. There they were, climbing up and over the trellis that outlined white-trimmed windows. When she'd come back to Grand View lodge with Danny the previous summer, they had parked on the other end of the lodge, missing the roses altogether. Tonight, the familiar sights and smells sent Celia back in her mind to the dances she and her girlfriends attended at this very resort, forty-seven years earlier. They'd been so young that summer between their freshman and sophomore years at college.

Helen stepped up onto the sidewalk, her arm looped through Eleanor's. "I can practically hear the band playing," she said, the dreamy look on her face telling Celia they were both traveling back to similar times in their memories.

"I wonder if they still hold dances here like they used to," Eleanor said, her gaze skimming the impressive façade of the majestic old lodge.

Celia nodded. "They hold the occasional dance, but they rarely have live bands anymore."

Ruby lifted her right foot and rolled her ankle from side to side, grasping Celia's forearm to steady herself. "Promise me you aren't going to make me go dancing tonight," she said. "My bunion is killing me in these shoes."

Helen laughed. "I told you not to wear those if they hurt your feet."

"And I should have listened," Ruby acknowledged. "All those years standing in front of a classroom raised hell on my feet."

"Remember how we used to dance for hours back then? Blisters and sore feet never bothered us," Eleanor said. "Those were the days."

Celia took a deep breath, enjoying the heady scent of the roses along with the underlying notes of fresh-turned earth and rain. "Come on. Let's go out back and watch the sunset like we used to. Ruby, if your feet hurt, take your shoes off. I wonder what changes they've made around here. We aren't so old that we can't explore a little until our table is ready."

"I was thinking a nice glass of wine before dinner would be the perfect start to the evening," Ruby countered, adjusting the strap on her handbag. "But the shoes stay on. I don't want to snag my pantyhose."

Celia sighed. "It's nearly ninety degrees. I can't believe you wore nylons."

Ruby shrugged. "What can I say? Two pregnancies ruined my legs. Varicose veins banished my bare legs for good."

"Fine. We'll compromise. How about a bottle of red on the patio while we wait for them to call our table?"

"Perfect," she agreed, motioning ahead of her. "Lead the way."

"Eleanor? Helen? Does that work for you?" Celia asked. She'd slipped into hostess mode when her oldest friends arrived at Whispering Pines earlier that morning. She hoped inviting them back would help her remember why she'd always loved her time at Whispering Pines. Keeping up the resort, with Nash's help, wasn't stimulating enough after her high-pressure career. It was turning out to be too quiet, too lonely.

"Absolutely," Eleanor agreed, pulling her arm out of Helen's. "We're too early to watch the sun go down yet. Remember how late we used to get here for the dances? Back then, we'd watch the sunset *first*, and then we'd dance the rest of the night away. We weren't even old enough to drink yet!"

Helen smirked. "Not that it stopped us from enjoying the spiked punch."

The foursome made their way through the familiar entry and hallway to the resort's premier restaurant, letting the hostess know they were there and would wait out on the patio for their table. It was like stepping back in time. Little had changed.

Once settled with two bottles of wine on a low table between them, a sense of peace settled over Celia. This time together was exactly what she'd been missing. She raised her glass of rich, burgundy-colored wine in a toast. Molten sunlight glinted off the crystal and the ever familiar call of a loon complemented her words. "To old friends."

"To old friends," the others echoed.

"I'm so glad you suggested we all get together this week, Celia," Ruby said, settling back into her seat and enjoying a sip of her wine. "I still can't believe I don't have to start school in a few weeks."

"To Ruby and her retirement," Helen said, holding her wine glass up again in another toast.

"Welcome to the world of leisure-filled days," Eleanor added, clinking her glass against Helen's.

Ruby joined the toast. "I hope you're right. I don't want to work as hard in retirement as Celia still does!"

Celia laughed. "You can work as much, or as little, as you want to. Tell us all about your trip to Venice. I left for Whispering Pines before you got back, so I've been dying to hear all about it. By the way, I'm so sorry I missed your retirement party."

Ruby waved away her concern. "Don't be. It was a bunch of teachers and administrators crammed into the home economics room for thirty minutes after the last bell of the school year. Four of us retired, and the celebration consisted of one crummy little cake and a room full of people eager to start their summers. It wasn't a party for family and friends."

Helen frowned. "That's unacceptable. We'll celebrate you this whole week, Ruby. Anyone who dedicates their life to teaching the youth of this great country deserves more than a quarter of a cake."

With another round of toasts to Ruby's transition into her retirement years, the women drained their first bottle of wine.

Ruby sniffed. "I don't know what I ever did to deserve the three of you."

Celia caught the telltale shimmer in Ruby's eyes. Mixing tears and wine never boded well with her old friend, so she took the conversation back to Ruby's trip to Italy. "Our table won't be ready for a while. Let's hear the good, the bad, and the ugly about your last trip as a high school teacher."

"Oh, sweetie, it'll take way more time than that to cover everything, but I'll start with the horrendous flight over. The next time I tell you I'm going overseas with my husband, you have to talk me out of it! Which breaks my heart, because that trip made me realize how much more travel I want to do in retirement."

The conversation flowed, along with the wine. There were plenty of belly laughs over Ruby's recap of her much-anticipated chaperoning trip. Her husband, Edwin, would be mortified if he knew how much his wife shared, but the chance to get things off your chest was the point of time with your besties.

Their table was ready, but the move into the dining room didn't stifle their conversation. Ruby finished her story with a vivid description of Edwin dropping to his knees in their driveway to kiss the ground when they finally arrived back home.

Talk moved on to children and grandchildren. Eleanor spent time each week with her granddaughters in Chicago. They helped keep her busy after the death of her husband. Ruby pulled out a picture of her only grandson, Seth, and handed it to Celia.

"I haven't seen Seth since he was a gap-toothed toddler. What grade is this? Front teeth and glasses make him look so old," Celia pointed out.

"He's got some growing to do before the rest of him catches up with those teeth," Ruby admitted. "And the poor dear inherited his grandfather's eyesight. That's from a year ago. He'll start fourth grade this fall. He's a good boy."

It was hard for Celia to believe Ruby already had a grandson more than halfway through grade school. She passed the photo on to Eleanor.

"Helen, are you still spending lots of time with Karen?" Ruby asked.

Helen set her menu aside. "Every chance I get. She's fifteen, and interested in boys, but she still makes time to hang out with her old grandma."

Eleanor wagged a finger at Helen. "Watch who you're calling old, Helen. I have to admit, I had a tough couple of years after Harry died, but the past few days at Whispering Pines, and sitting here reminiscing with the three of you, feels good. We're *hardly* old. Sixty-six used to sound ancient, but now I won't consider myself old until I'm at least eighty. Isn't it funny how our interpretation of *old* shifts?"

Helen shrugged. "Maybe what they say about Whispering Pines is true after all. That walk we took early this morning left me invigorated. My knees have been bothering me, but they feel great today. Getting out of bed tomorrow morning might be a different story."

A waiter arrived to take their order, and Celia used the quick break in conversation to study each of her friends' faces. What Helen said was true. Whether it was the wine, the conversation, or their short time back at Whispering Pines, each looked more relaxed—softer, even—than when they'd first arrived. But Celia hadn't found the peace she'd expected, having spent the past three weeks trying to relax at Whispering Pines for the first time in a very long time. Instead of enjoying herself, she'd felt bored. Unhinged.

When the waiter left with their orders, Celia cleared her throat. "I'm glad the three of you are enjoying your time at Whispering Pines."

A pause followed her words.

"But . . . ?" Ruby prompted, eyeing Celia. She found herself at a loss for words, so Ruby kept digging. "Celia, aren't you enjoying your summer at the resort? You've looked forward to this for so long."

She fingered the burgundy napkin, neatly folded next to her now empty wine glass. "I know. That's why I hate to mention it. But you're right, Ruby. I did look forward to this, but I'm having a hard time relaxing. My caretakers don't need me to keep things running."

Eleanor squeezed her hand. "Competent staff is exactly what you want, Celia. Don't be so hard on yourself. You don't know how to slow down yet, to stop pushing so hard. You spent your career trying to prove yourself in an industry dominated by men. And working for my big brother couldn't have been easy."

You don't know the half of it, Celia thought, her mind going back to the previous summer when Tripp had lashed out at her over his failing marriage. She still had no idea who'd told Sophia about Tripp's infidelity. The lawyers hadn't found any weaknesses when they'd reviewed Celia's two-decade-old purchase of Whispering Pines. They didn't think Tripp had any recourse, but the man's blatant animosity disturbed her more than she'd admit.

"I can't believe you two were raised by the same parents," she pointed out to Eleanor. Despite their friendship—or maybe because of it—she'd never been completely honest with her about how deep Tripp's hatred of Celia ran.

Eleanor sighed. "That awful business with Mother was ugly, and his experiences in the war scarred him, too. I'm sorry if he made your life difficult through the years. I know Father tried to protect you."

They let the conversation die off, each in her own thoughts.

Just as the quiet started making Celia uncomfortable, Ruby laid her forearms on the table and leaned in. "Tripp's animosity toward Celia started way back when he had a thing for her little sister. I vote we leave Tripp alone with his demons and get back to *you*, Celia. Do you think time has chipped away at your love of Whispering Pines?"

The question was like a stab to Celia's heart. She didn't want to entertain such a thought.

"Celia, dear, this might be hard for you to consider," Eleanor said, "but we've all been through so much. The trials we survive change us. It's okay if you want something different now than when you were younger."

"But I'd never walk away from Whispering Pines," Celia insisted, trying to ignore the glimmer of hope that was rising inside her at Eleanor's words. "I promised your father I'd protect it."

Eleanor reached for her hand again, this time holding on to it for a beat longer. "And you've done that. Celia, you bought Whispering Pines from Tripp twenty years ago. Which, by the way, I've never understood how you managed to pull off."

Celia's eyes flew to Helen. She and Warren knew the depths to which Celia had dipped in her desperation to fulfill her old mentor's dying wish. Should she finally share the whole sordid tale with Eleanor and Ruby?

Ruby jumped into the conversation before Celia could decide. "Eleanor is right. Let's take a little walk down memory lane, shall we?"

The arrival of their dinners interrupted the conversation, but as soon as they were alone again, Ruby continued.

"You helped your mother with Beverly from the day she was born. You collected rent from the tenants living in your home to help keep food on the table and the lights on. You weren't even as old as my Seth here." Ruby waved the picture of her grandson in Celia's direction, then stuffed it back in her pocketbook. "You never wanted to stay home as a wife and mother. I think it was because you never wanted to depend on anyone."

"And I never did," Celia said.

"Right. No need to get defensive," Ruby retorted, as only a woman secure in a long-lived friendship could say without fear of offending. "There was a time when you might have let someone in. I know how hard it was to let Danny walk away when you had to help your mother with your little brothers after your stepfather died. And don't even get me started on how hard it was on you when Beverly died. Celia, you've weathered more than your share of tragedies."

Celia drained the last inch of liquid in her wine glass with one big gulp. She narrowed her eyes at Ruby. "You make me sound pathetic. I've had a good life. I accomplished everything I set out to do."

Eleanor squeezed her fingers again and released her hand to sit back. Celia hadn't even realized her other friend was still holding her hand. The knowing grin from Eleanor as she leaned back in her chair did nothing to calm Celia's ruffled nerves.

"I feel like something's happening here, ladies," Celia said, setting her knife and fork down across the meal she'd barely touched. "Are you ganging up on me?"

Ruby folded her hands across her heart. "I promise we aren't ganging up on you. But you could call this an intervention of sorts."

"An intervention? What, exactly, do you think I need to be saved from?"

"Why, from yourself, of course," Helen tossed in, finally joining back into the conversation. "Don't you think it's about time to throw all the 'shoulds' out the damn window and start living for yourself?"

"But I thought that's exactly what I was doing by moving out here for the summer. I've wanted this for so long."

Helen nodded, then scooped another bite of her salmon cake. "And are you happy now that you're here?"

It was a simple question. *Was* she happy? She'd certainly expected to be.

"Celia, you've always dreamed of traveling the world. But you retired from a forty-year career and jumped right into more work. How many rental properties do you own now?"

She swung her gaze to Ruby. Apparently, the woman was still set on picking on her. "That isn't any of your business."

Ruby rolled her eyes. "You can be so prickly, Celia. All we're trying to say is that you need to live a little. You have Whispering Pines running on autopilot now."

"Have the three of you discussed this behind my back?"

Eleanor sighed. "Don't be difficult, Celia. Yes, in fact, we *have* discussed this. You're more reserved than we expected you to be. When were you going to tell us Danny came out here to visit you last year?"

Celia groaned. "Did Mary say something? Ed?" She'd have a talk with the Dixons about their big mouths when they got back to Whispering Pines. They had no business telling her friends about that surprise visit. "What makes you think I was ever going to tell you?"

Ruby shook her head. "It was a rhetorical question, Celia. It's obvious to us you had no intention of telling us. And why is that? Why all the secrecy where Danny is concerned?"

She couldn't believe Ruby would even have to ask. As far as Celia knew, there were only three people remaining in this world who knew she'd born Danny's child, and two of them sat at this table. The wounds from that time still ran deep; this conversation felt like a scab being ripped off.

"I don't want to discuss it."

But her hissed retort fell on deaf ears.

"Is he married?"

She blew out a breath in frustration. "Not anymore, if you must know. He's single, with a son in college."

"How did it feel to see him again? Mary said he showed up out of the blue one day. Said it took you completely by surprise."

Ruby wasn't going to drop it. Celia looked to Helen and Eleanor for help, but they both looked as interested in her response as Ruby.

She paused, considering the question. How *had* she felt? "Honestly, I'm not sure. It was strange to see him again, after so many years. A shock. But . . . a nice shock."

Eleanor nodded, chewing the last bite of her meal and pushing her plate out of the way. "I apologize if I played a part in that. I may have mentioned you were back out at Whispering Pines."

Celia picked at her food. "I'm aware."

"Don't hold a grudge. When he mentioned he was divorced, I got a tad bit excited over the possibility of playing matchmaker. Didn't the two of you have a thing, way back when?"

Dropping her napkin onto her plate, she collapsed back against her chair. "We had more than a 'thing.' You could even say there's some unfinished business between us. And his showing up like that stirred up things I thought I wanted to forget. Now I'm not so sure."

"*That* sounds interesting," Helen said. "Is the spark still there? Will the fires flame again?" She rubbed her hands together excitedly.

Helen's comment brought back the conflicted feelings she'd experienced during Danny's brief visit the previous summer. She couldn't deny a spark remained, but the bigger issue was his offer to reveal more to her about their daughter. She'd put him off. They'd talked on the phone twice during the winter months, and he'd written her a handful of letters. He filled them with platonic reports of happenings in his life, but she knew Danny well enough to understand he'd be interested in more—if she was.

"Perhaps," she hedged. And then she let the secret she'd intended to take to her grave slip out. "I got pregnant with his child when I was in my early thirties. I gave her up."

That shut everybody up.

"He didn't know, but he found out later. He knows where she is now, and he'll tell me everything if I want him to."

No one said a word. Shock registered on everyone's faces.

Nothing like revealing one's deepest, darkest secrets to squelch conversation around the dinner table.

Helen gripped the edge of the table. "Celia . . . what are you talking about?"

In that moment, Celia would have given anything to stuff the words she'd spilled back into her mouth. But it was out now. She couldn't take back the words, so she might as well admit the rest. She started over.

"I had a baby. Thirty-three years ago. Danny was the father. I never told him. I didn't want to tell anyone, but Preston knew."

"Father knew?" Eleanor whispered.

"He did. He was a smart man. He realized it before *I* did. I was outside, vomiting in the bushes, during the company Christmas party. It could have been the end of my career. But Preston agreed to help me. I knew my only option was to give up the baby. I was never cut out to be a mother."

Ruby gave a vicious shake of her head. "You would have made a *fabulous* mother."

Celia paused. "Do you really think so?" she asked, taken aback.

Ruby's expression reflected the sincerity of her words. "I know so."

"Wait. You gave up a child *thirty-three years* ago?" Helen asked, color draining from her face. "How did I not know this?" She spun on the others. "Did you two know?"

Eleanor whispered a negative reply. Ruby's shrug spoke volumes.

Celia stood. "I need some air."

Everyone stumbled to their feet. Eleanor pulled a stack of large bills from her wallet, shoving them under her plate. She reached for Celia's arm, leading her out of the restaurant with Helen and Ruby close behind. She sent the host a nod of acknowledgment on their way out. Celia allowed Eleanor to guide her toward the main entrance of the resort.

How had the evening ended up like this? Whatever had come over her?

As they stepped outside, the heady scent of roses assaulted her senses once more, and she collapsed in tears on the old wooden bench.

Chapter Twenty
Gift of an Epiphany

A LIGHT MIST DANCED along the water's surface, golden tendrils shimmering as the sun began its inevitable climb. Celia worried her revelations the night before might have shone a much harsher light into corners of her life she'd wanted to keep in the shadows. What had possessed her to reveal so much to her friends after all this time? What would Helen and Eleanor think of her now? What would they think of Ruby, for keeping her secret from them, too?

They'll think less of me.

Each had raised daughters of their own; Helen raised four and Eleanor two. They'd never understand how she could have walked away. Celia never walked away from *any* responsibility. But that was what hurt the most. She'd walked away from the most important thing in her life.

Footsteps on the wooden treads meant her peaceful moment on the dock was over.

"Unless you brought me a cup of coffee, I don't want to see you this morning," she said without turning toward the sound.

"That's a relief. We'd hate for you to send us packing."

The welcoming aroma of fresh-brewed coffee floated ahead of the footsteps. Celia glanced over her shoulder and saw Ruby wasn't alone. She'd brought the whole gang.

"I've never known you to be up at this hour, Helen," Celia teased. Maybe if she pretended nothing unusual had happened over dinner, she could stuff it all back into the shadows.

"It's true. I haven't witnessed a six o'clock sunrise since my girls were babies. But sleep was elusive last night."

Celia accepted the second mug Ruby carried. Her three friends took seats around the edge of the dock. Ruby sat next to her, while Eleanor and Helen took the corners, facing out in opposite directions. Turning her eyes back to the rising sun, Celia took a quiet comfort in her friends' proximity. She sipped her hot coffee and allowed herself the space to breathe. A loon called from nearby. Ripples pulsed out from her left where Eleanor's bare feet swirled in the water. Celia's dangling feet did little to hamper the outward rush of concentric circles. As predictable as the sunrise, displaced water would travel far, eventually lapping against the shore on the other side of the lake.

Had her revelations the previous evening started a similar chain of events?

"Celia, what are your plans for the rest of summer?"

Ruby's question came as a surprise. "You know I'm planning to stay until after Labor Day. You're taking care of my house plants, remember?"

Ruby set her mug to the side and turned to face Celia's profile. "You've already been here for three months. Why don't you come home with us on Monday? It's not too late to plan a late summer trip. Remember how you used to want to see the world?"

Celia suppressed a sigh, reminding herself that they were just worried about her. "You three discussed this behind my back this morning, didn't you?" She kept her gaze forward, imagining Eleanor's ripples tickling the shore at the faraway water's edge. Clearly her uncharacteristic mini breakdown the night before had them questioning her ability to function out here on her own.

Helen snorted. "This morning? Honey, I just rolled out of bed into this sundress and accepted the cup of coffee Ruby handed me as Eleanor rushed me out the door. No, once we got you settled in your bed, the three of us were wide awake. Your other renters had turned in, but a low fire still burned outside our cabin, so we stayed up and talked."

"About me."

"You gave us plenty to discuss, didn't you?"

"I suppose I did, but I'd give anything to take it all back this morning." Celia refused to look at any of them. "Can we just forget everything I said? It must have been the wine."

"I'll admit, I felt fuzzy this morning from the wine, too," Eleanor said. "In fact, we should have brought the coffeepot down with us. Celia, we want to respect your privacy. What you shared last night about the baby is something we don't need to discuss after today. But let me say, I, for one, respect the decision you made so long ago. And knowing Father, he would have made sure she went to a wonderful home. I'm sure she's grown into a lovely woman. You can't spend the rest of your life second-guessing yourself."

Celia only heard sincerity in her friend's words. "You don't think I'm a monster, then?"

Eleanor leaned over with a laugh, wrapping an arm around her shoulders and squeezing her. "You did what was best for everyone involved. Honestly, I don't think you'd be second-guessing yourself now if Danny hadn't come back into your life with news about her. Your integrity is unquestionable. Don't beat yourself up over it." She gave her one last squeeze and stood. "I'll be right back. More coffee."

The three remaining women let quiet descend once more as her footsteps faded. Celia focused on Eleanor's words. She had a point. It was only over the past year that her guilt came bubbling back up to where it was always right there, just below the surface. After Danny left, she'd pushed herself to stay busy: more meetings, additional rentals, even another business interest.

She felt a wave of relief that her big revelation hadn't scared Eleanor off. But what about Helen? She'd said nothing specifically related to Celia's secret. With the benefit of hindsight, she could now see how much Helen had given up to raise her children—even Virginia. Helen's dreams of traveling to Paris to design clothing never got off the ground. Raising four headstrong girls had pushed her to her limits, and the struggles with Virginia had nearly broken her. What must she think of Celia for choosing a different path?

"I'm sorry I never told you, Helen." She braced for one of Helen's notorious retorts. Helen never liked to be kept in the dark about anything.

Instead, her friend merely sighed and whispered, "I wish you would have."

The hurt in Helen's voice was undeniable. Which left Celia feeling more ashamed than ever. She'd have preferred an angry outburst.

"Celia! Helen and Ruby! Come up. Mary made us a scrumptious breakfast!" Eleanor stood near the lodge, yelling and waving a red napkin.

Celia jumped to her feet and hurried toward the noisy woman, motioning for her to be quiet. *It's not even seven yet. Other guests are still sleeping,* she thought, cringing.

But as her bare feet sunk into the cool sand at the end of the dock, it reminded Celia of a much younger Eleanor, running toward them to first welcome them to Whispering Pines on that summer nearly fifty years before. Her jet-black curls still bounced in the sunshine, and it didn't matter if Eleanor's biweekly trip to the salon kept her gray hair at bay.

Celia had the oddest sensation that she'd come full circle with these women at this place. Was she holding on too tight?

Was there still time to do more than this?

Eleanor must have realized she was being too noisy. She slapped both hands over her mouth, turned, and disappeared into the lodge. Celia slowed, giving Ruby and Helen a chance to catch up. She scanned the grounds as she walked, taking in the neatly trimmed grass and fresh paint around the windows. The gravel parking lot was smooth.

It was like waking from a dream. The Dixons had things under control out here. They didn't need her physical presence. There was a big, beautiful world out there to see.

Maybe she would head home with her girlfriends when they left.

She wasn't getting any younger. She hadn't worked her whole life to stay within the narrow swatch she'd unconsciously created for herself through the years. And since Ruby's husband was turning out to be a terrible travel companion, her old friend might jump at the chance to explore the world with her.

Or she could always call Danny.

Whispering Pines would still be here, waiting for her, when she was ready to come home.

Chapter Twenty-One
Gifts from Grandma Maggie

Late Winter 1995

CELIA PEEKED INTO HER noisy kitchen, drawn by the racket that comes with party preparations. Gerry was pulling a tray of deviled eggs from the refrigerator while Lavonne stirred something on the stove.

"How are things going in here?" she asked, wandering over to see what was in her sister-in-law's pot. "Did the cake arrive yet?"

"Not yet," Val reported, peering out the frost-rimmed window in the back door. "I hope they hurry. We can't have a baby shower without a cake."

"Two cakes, remember," Lavonne said, flicking off the burner. "A blue one for my sweet grandson Nathan and a yellow one for Ethan's little bundle."

"I'm sure Virginia's friend will get the cakes here in time. She's running a new bakery downtown, close to the bookstore. Cake deliveries will be an important part of her business. Could be she's learning how to get the timing right," Celia said. "I see you dressed up for the party, Val."

The twenty-year-old glanced down at her maroon-colored collegiate sweatshirt and dark jeans. "I didn't think you'd mind. I'm working the concession stand at the hockey game tonight and this is what we're supposed to wear."

"Concession stand?"

She nodded. "It's a work-study thing. Besides, I wore a dress to Jess's first baby shower her girlfriends held for baby Nathan before he was even born. I figured I didn't have to be fancy for this family shower."

"And you were right," Celia confirmed. "But I wouldn't mind a new sweatshirt from your school for myself. Do you think you could arrange that? But I don't want a hood on it. Those snarl my hair."

Val laughed. "I'm sure I could find you the perfect one. It's the least I can do, since you just paid my spring tuition bill. I hope you know how much I appreciate that. I'm not sure what I would do without your help."

"Just keep those grades up, missy. One more year and you'll all be through college. I can hardly believe it!"

Lavonne set her kettle of melted white chocolate on the small kitchen table, then retrieved a bowl of strawberries from the fridge. "We should have dipped these *hours* ago so they'd set up," she grumbled. "Val, get away from that door and come help me. *You* can hardly believe it, Celia? I can't believe I'm a grandma! I'm not even fifty!"

Gerry sprinkled paprika over his tray of chilled eggs, his years of working in the food industry evident in his practiced movement. "What did you decide to study, Val?"

"Hospitality."

Lavonne snorted.

Val spun around. "What? Not this again, Mom."

Lavonne held up a bright-red strawberry in her youngest's direction before plunging three-quarters of it into the white chocolate. "I'm sorry, sweetie. I just worry. I don't know what you're going to do for work in that industry. I wish you would have stuck with computer science. There are guaranteed jobs in that field. You wouldn't believe how everything is moving to computers at the hospital these days."

Val rolled her eyes. "I *hated* coding. It bored me to tears. You know that, Mom. Besides, I could barely understand a word some of those teacher's assistants said. Their accents are so strong."

"If you're going to do anything in the travel field, you have to get used to accents," Celia warned. "Trust me."

A car door slammed out back, pulling Celia's attention from the bickering. "The cakes must be here. Val, be a dear and run back there and help Mable."

Val shot her a grin, happy to be saved from yet another round of arguments with her mother. Cold air rushed in when the girl failed to push the back door closed as she hurried to escape. Gerry pulled it shut.

Lavonne rolled her eyes, unconsciously mirroring her daughter. "That girl will be the death of me. She can't make a decision to save her life. I sometimes wonder if you'll get your money's worth out of that one. The other three picked something early in their college careers and stuck with it. They all landed jobs after graduation, and now they're getting married and having babies. Val, though . . . she's not focused."

Celia supposed Lavonne felt it was her job to worry, but she personally liked Val's gumption. Since finally making travel a part of her life a year into her retirement, she thought Val had vast career opportunities ahead of her. Maybe after today's joint baby shower wrapped up, she'd try to have a talk with Val. Encourage her. Celia could see her potential.

Oh, to be twenty again, with my whole life still ahead of me, she thought.

When Gerry turned his back, she snuck an egg off his artfully arranged tray and popped it into her mouth.

It felt good to have her whole family back, gathered in her home. She'd missed too much of George's kids' younger years, spending too much time at the office. The five or six summer vacations they'd spent with her at Whispering Pines were her favorite memories as the resort owner. But life had eventually become too busy for them. They stopped coming out, then even Celia cut back on her time out there. Once she'd committed to seeing the world with Ruby—not to mention her trip to Ireland with Danny—she hadn't been back to the resort.

Today was a poignant reminder of how fast time passes. Jess and her future-doctor husband, Will, welcomed their first child shortly after Christmas. She could hear the baby's hungry cries even now through the closed kitchen door. She smiled at Ethan's very pregnant young wife, Stacey—the other beneficiary of today's baby shower—as she waddled through the door, a hand on her extended belly.

"Jess asked me to grab Nathan's bottle," Stacey said. "With any luck, he'll nap once the party starts."

Lavonne pulled out a kitchen chair and guided Stacey into it. "Here, sit for a minute. I'll get his bottle ready. Has the swelling in your ankles gotten any better?"

Celia slid the bowl of strawberries closer and picked up where Lavonne left off. She exchanged grins with Gerry. It was fun to watch their younger brother and his wife navigate the different stages of parenting life: from being young parents to the challenging years of raising teenagers, to now, finding themselves as both in-laws and grandparents within a few short years. Both Ethan and Jess were married and becoming parents of their own. Even Renee was planning a wedding. Only Val was still enjoying the total freedom of single young adulthood. Celia could only hope the kids weren't rushing into things.

But who was she to judge?

The back door opened and another rush of cold air burst in.

Pregnant Stacey held her long, dark hair up to bare the nape of her neck. "That feels heavenly. Can't we just leave all the doors open?"

Lavonne handed her daughter-in-law a warmed bottle, a content smile on her face. Celia loved the way Lavonne welcomed spouses and grandbabies into their family unit with a glad heart. Years earlier, when the woman visited Whispering Pines to help Celia recuperate after her terrifying bout with breast cancer, Celia had her doubts about the future of George's family, so new back then. But George and Lavonne had bravely weathered those storms, and their willingness to work through their challenges together had brought them to today, to the house where George was raised, near bursting with his own kids and their budding families.

Celia had missed out on too much while the kids were growing up, but she vowed to change that going forward. This was her family, too, and these young people could benefit from her guidance.

Besides, similar to the magic of Whispering Pines, they might just keep her young.

"I don't see why we have to play these silly games," George muttered, his reading glasses perched on the tip of his nose while he worked on a word search. He swore under his breath when the pencil broke through the thin paper, poking him in the thigh.

"Careful, brother," Celia warned, nodding toward the sleeping newborn in the arms of Renee's fiancé, Jim. "You can't be swearing around your grandchildren."

George tossed his paper and pencil on the coffee table. "The boy is three weeks old, Celia. Don't be ridiculous. The only place those stubby pencils are worth a damn is on the golf course. Here, Jim, give me Nathan. It's your turn to play the next stupid game."

Renee slapped her father on the knee. "What the heck is wrong with you, Dad? You aren't usually so crabby. This is a happy day."

George removed his glasses, tucking them in the front collar of his shirt, then reached for the baby.

Renee held out a hand. "Dad, give me those. You'll poke him. I'll put your glasses on the table."

As Celia watched the exchange, she had to wonder. Renee was right. George was seldom so uptight. But as he took baby Nathan in his arms and sank back into the recliner, his face relaxed.

Jim stood, now liberated, and offered to fetch more punch for anyone.

"No, you don't," Renee laughed, pulling him back down beside her. "Good try, though. You're almost as big of a spoilsport as Dad! There's one more game, then we'll let the two mommas open their gifts. After that we'll eat."

The front door opened and Jess's husband rushed in, pulling his coat off. "I'm sorry I'm so late! Our experiment went sideways in lab and we had to do it over. What'd I miss?"

Lavonne pressed against Celia's side on the crowded couch. Celia could *feel* the woman's irritation at her son-in-law's late arrival. Lavonne leaned even closer. "Nice of him to show up."

Celia caught the look Lavonne and George exchanged. *That's probably what George was cranky about,* she thought. His son-in-law almost missed his infant's baby shower.

It wasn't the first time Will had arrived late to a family function, always blaming it on some exam or mishap in the lab. Before Jess gave birth to Nathan, she worked a second job in the evenings, doing what she could to support their family financially. Things would be tighter now. There was no way Jess could work two jobs and take care of their new son. Celia hoped Jess was happy in her marriage, but she didn't like the twist in her gut when Will offered yet another excuse.

Will leaned down and kissed the top of Jess's head, then spotted Nathan in George's lap. He stroked a hand over the baby's fist but made no move to take the child. Jess suggested Will join them for the last shower game, but unlike Jim's willingness to do as Renee asked, Will waved off Jess's suggestion and wandered back to the kitchen.

After a moment of uncomfortable silence, the noise ramped back up and the family finished the last game. Lavonne stood and started bringing over gifts. Stacey moaned from her spot on the loveseat. Ethan sat in front of her on the ottoman, taking her feet into his lap to massage them. Even from her seat across the room, Celia could see the girl's swollen ankles.

"Ethan, hon, open the gifts, please?" Stacey asked. "I'm not sure my arms are long enough to reach around my swollen belly to hold a present."

Ethan patted his wife's feet and shifted his position, accepting a wrapped package from his mother. Lavonne handed a similar-sized gift to Jess.

"Your Grandmother Maggie asked me to save these for any future great-grand-children," Lavonne said. "She gave me five gift-wrapped packages months before she died. Maybe she had a sense she wouldn't be here today. If we're blessed with more than five grandbabies in the years to come, I'll need to learn to crochet so no one's left out."

A wave of sadness and awe washed over Celia. She hadn't known her mother had taken the time to make things for future babies—babies she somehow knew she'd never meet. "What a wonderful thought," Celia muttered.

George nodded his agreement at his sister's whispered words and the baby stirred in his arms, clasping his finger. Celia's heart warmed at the sight.

Jess pulled back white tissue paper to reveal more white. A blanket unfolded as she raised it high, the softness of the threads and intricate design a true work of art. She touched the special gift to her cheek. "What a thoughtful thing for Grandma Maggie to do. This is *so* soft."

Ethan pulled a matching blanket from their box, showing it to his wife. Celia could tell from their expressions that Maggie's thoughtfulness touched them all. She'd never given much thought to the legacy one leaves behind, but her mother certainly had done more than think about it. Ethan gave the blanket an easy shake, draping it across his wife's extended belly.

"I wish I would have met your grandmother before she died," Stacey told him, her eyes misty as she ran a hand over the silky threads covering her round stomach. "It's almost like she's giving this little one a hug from heaven."

A round of oohs and aahs filled the room, and Celia had the strangest sensation. She thought again of the others that lived in this house long ago, family long dead, and it was as if not only Maggie but others were in the room with them during such a touching moment. Her sister, sweet Beverly, would have loved to get to know the people in this room now—George's ever-growing family. She liked to imagine Clarence was here in the room with them, too. He'd have loved these great-grandbabies. He'd have fashioned rocking horses and doll cradles with his own hands, much as he'd done when he'd built the old blue trunk for her.

Long before Clarence lived in this house with her mother, Celia's biological father, Charles Middleton, built the house. He'd left Maggie widowed with two young girls when he died in a work-related accident. Her father came from family money, but his death, shortly before the stock market crash of 1929, left them nearly destitute. Only five when he died, Celia's memories of the man were mere shadows. But this had been his home, and it was the one thing, other than her daughters, that Maggie had held on to. In that way, Charles had left them a legacy as well.

What kind of legacy would Celia leave behind? It was one thing to be the fun aunt to her brother's children. But now that those children were having babies of their own, and Celia was feeling the aches and pains of her own advancing age, maybe it was something she should think about.

Conversation flowed around her as she studied the faces of her family. Gerry and his wife, now in their fifties, had never had children. But George's expanding family promised to keep them all busy in the years ahead.

Celia turned to Renee. "How are the wedding plans coming?"

"I can't believe we're only a month away!" her niece replied, threading her fingers with Jim's. "Hopefully all these babies won't scare him away."

Jim brushed a quick kiss on Renee's knuckles. His cheeks bloomed with color when he caught Celia's eye. She liked the man Renee was marrying. Jim seemed solid and dependable. Celia worried Will's primary concern was his future career rather than his young wife and new baby, but she thought Jim would treat Renee like a priority, like an equal. At least she hoped he would.

"How soon do you want to have children, Jim?" Celia asked.

Lavonne gasped. "Celia, that's awfully personal."

Celia shrugged. "Lavonne, I'm Renee's seventy-two-year-old eccentric aunt who lives alone and travels the world like a drifter. I've earned the right to be nosy. Every family needs a crazy old aunt. Guess that's me."

Anyone listening to the exchange laughed. No one disagreed.

"So?" Celia persisted. "Jim?"

He shrugged, chuckling. "I love kids. Anytime Renee wants to start will be fine with me. We don't want Ethan and Jess to get all the blankets your mother crocheted!"

Another round of laughter commenced, and Celia was sure she was right about Jim. He'd make a wonderful husband for Renee.

The laughter stopped when Stacey hissed Ethan's name. Her tone had a bite to it. Celia watched, alarmed, as the mother-to-be scrunched Maggie's blanket into a heap and tossed it to Val, who was standing beside the loveseat.

"Jeez, Stacey, careful!" Val scolded, shaking out the snowy white gift to refold it.

Stacey grimaced, attempting to sit up straighter. "I think my water just broke."

Chapter Twenty-Two
Gift of Advice

"Sorry I'm short on ham this week, Ms. Celia, but I can slice up this nice beef roast if that would serve your needs."

Celia regarded her butcher with a sigh. The man seemed to apologize for one thing or another every time she stopped in. "Beef will have to do, if that's all you have on hand. I'm sure the kids won't care between beef or ham. The sandwiches are just a little something extra to feed a hungry crowd near the end of tomorrow's wedding dance."

The heavy wooden door into the shop creaked open and a bell tinkled above. "Everything all right?" Val asked. "I was getting worried. If you want to pick up those extra flower bouquets, we need to be there by five."

Celia glanced at her diamond wristwatch, angling it to make out the tiny hands. She'd had no trouble reading her watch face until recently. Her vision wasn't what it used to be. Turning back to Clyde Klaus, she checked his progress at the meat slicer. He was only halfway through the roast. "Val, be a dear and run over to get those flowers without me. They should have them ready to go. I've already paid for them, and by the time you get back, Clyde should have everything ready for me."

"But I thought you called ahead for this order, too," Val said, frowning at Mr. Klaus's back.

Celia had indeed phoned ahead. But she needed to talk with Clyde. He'd run this business alongside his only brother for forty years. That brother died six months earlier. She hated to think Clyde might not be able to keep the shop going on his own.

"Never mind that. Please, we need to get these last-minute details wrapped up for Renee and your mother. Go. I'll be ready when you get back."

Val shrugged, then jangled Celia's car keys. "You're the boss, Auntie. I'm just here to chauffeur you around today."

"I don't need a chauffeur," Celia said, but her niece was already gone through the same noisy door.

Why did everyone question her driving ability?

Ah, well. She was happy to have an extra set of hands given her long list of wedding to-dos. Jess was home with baby Nathan as he battled yet another ear infection, and Renee had her own long list of last-minute details to attend to. Lavonne was at Ethan's, helping Stacey with their one-month-old daughter.

Poor George and Lavonne, trying to juggle two new grandbabies and a wedding—all in one year, no less. When Celia offered to help with some of the logistics, their relief was obvious.

"Will it just be the roast beef then, Celia?" Clyde asked, setting her large stack of carefully wrapped meat next to the register.

She studied the old chalkboard behind his head, considering the list of daily specials. "You better give me ten pounds of sliced turkey, too. I'll take the peppered variety you have on special."

Clyde shook his head. "I forgot to change the board. That was last week's special. I'm plum out of that, too."

"Do you have anything else we can slice up to use for sandwiches? I'm afraid I need more than just that," she said, motioning to the beef.

"Let me go in back and check. I'm sorry. I'm having trouble with my supplier these days."

She frowned as he disappeared into the back room, stooping to avoid hitting his head on the top doorjamb. It reminded Celia that he used to be the town's basketball star. George and Gerry used to talk about Clyde Klaus when they were in the fourth and eighth grades. Clyde led the high school basketball team to capture the state basketball championship for the first—and, so far, only—time. They'd worshipped Clyde. Celia did the quick math. He was likely ten years younger than herself. Only sixty-two, and not likely ready to give up on this place yet.

"You're in luck," the butcher said in his booming voice, holding a wrapped parcel high in his large hand much as he would have palmed a basketball in his youth. "It's not peppered, but it's fresh."

Celia nodded her agreement as he unwrapped a smoked turkey loaf and took up his position at the slicer again. She took a deep breath, unable to mind her own business. "Have you considered getting some help in here, Clyde? Maybe a part-time student? I hate to see you trying to do it all by yourself now."

The butcher glanced her way but didn't reply. She hoped she hadn't offended him. He and his brother had been good to both her and her mother through the years. It was the reason she hadn't stopped coming here, despite the adequate selection of meats at the larger grocer across town. Neither Ruby nor Helen understood why she bothered to take the extra step to support the Corner Market.

The door creaked open again and a man Celia recognized from the Italian restaurant on Main hurried in. Clyde eyed the man warily over the stainless-steel machine as it reduced Celia's turkey to shreds. "What can I do for you, Esposito?"

"You shorted me two sirloins in this week's order, plus the one I was short last week."

Clyde switched off the machine as it reached the end of the slab, and Celia caught the sound of his heavy sigh. "I'll credit your account. It won't happen again."

"See that it doesn't," the man demanded, knocking his fist on the sales counter. "I've worked with you for years, Klaus, but if this continues, I'll have to take my business elsewhere."

Two more quick wraps with his knuckles and the man spun away, exiting as quickly as he'd appeared.

Two bright spots of color stained the butcher's cheeks. He avoided Celia's gaze, methodically wrapping the second stack of meat in white butcher paper.

"Clyde?"

He finally looked up. "I don't need a snot-nosed kid underfoot, chopping off a finger or selling bratwurst instead of liverwurst to Mrs. Potts."

Celia raised her eyebrows. "Why would anyone buy either bratwurst or liverwurst?" she asked with a shiver.

He grinned. It was the first smile she'd gotten out of him since she'd arrived. "We're famous for our liverwurst around here," he assured her.

She noticed he still said *we* instead of *I*.

"Clyde, I love your store. You offer excellent product at reasonable prices. But you've got some stiff competition across town," she reminded him.

He pulled a large bag out from under the register and set her two packages inside. "Don't I know it. But I can't afford to hire someone. I don't need another person to work at the counter. I can handle that. It's the bookkeeping end. And ordering. My brother had a system for all that. I handled everything else. He went so fast, he never had time to show me how to do it. It's not like I can hire a kid to do that for me."

Celia snapped open her wallet and paid the man. Val would be back any minute. "Maybe I could help."

He snorted. "I don't see what you could do. No offense."

Leveling a look on him that she'd used often during her days working with men who underestimated her, she looped her fingers through the handles of the bag. "I may not be an accountant, but I have plenty of contacts in town. I could spend some time helping you develop your own ordering and tracking system. And I could recommend a reputable bookkeeper. You can pay me with a good steak once in a while, and the cost of an accountant is one you can't avoid if you don't have the knowledge to do it yourself. Think of it this way. This place only needs to support one of you now, not two."

He crossed his thick forearms over his chest and eyed Celia, considering her offer.

The door opened and Val scurried back in. "You'll be glad to know the interior of your Cadillac now smells like a funeral home."

"Val! That's a terrible thing to say. The flowers are for your sister's *wedding*."

"Trust me. Those white-and-pink lilies are suffocating. I know, they're one of Renee's favorites, but man!"

Celia laughed as Val waved a hand in front of her wrinkled nose.

"Here, let me take that. It looks heavy," Val insisted, taking the handles of the bag from her aunt. She even grunted with the full weight of the wrapped meat when she pulled the sack off the counter. "Good Lord, how many people are you planning to feed?"

Grinning, Celia turned her attention back to Clyde one last time. "I'm serious. I can help. You think about it. We'll talk about it again when I come back next time."

She followed her niece out of the Corner Market, hoping the butcher would take her advice. She'd love to help Virginia's daughter land a new client. Karen had recently gone to work for an accounting firm following her college graduation.

Val kept the keys, so Celia climbed into the passenger's side of her own Cadillac. She sneezed as the strong scent of lilies assaulted her senses, and she popped open the glove compartment to rummage for a tissue. Sneezing a second and third time, she pulled a single tissue out of the crushed box she'd found and held it over her nose.

"Open the damn windows in here before we get asphyxiated!"

Val jammed the keys in the ignition, checked over her shoulder, and pulled away from the curb. Once driving, she pushed the buttons to roll down all four windows. "Told you. Funeral."

Celia gave her shoulder a playful push. "Don't joke about funerals when we're planning a wedding. It's bad luck."

"I never would have guessed you to be the superstitious type," Val said, stopping at a red light.

"Well, I don't believe the wedding couple will automatically be rich if it rains on their wedding day like some people claim, but even *I* wouldn't joke about funeral flowers."

"Fine. I won't tell Renee. *She* picked them out. But if I ever get married, remind me to stick to red roses, please."

The light turned and Val advanced through the intersection.

"Yellow roses are nice, too," Celia said. "Head to the reception hall, please. We still need to make these sandwiches and get them in the cooler for tomorrow night."

Val groaned. "I thought someone would do that tomorrow."

"Too bad, dear. *We* are that someone, and tomorrow we'll both be busy getting pretty for the big shindig. We can help ourselves to some sandwiches for our dinner, and it won't take us more than a couple of hours. Besides, I've been wanting to talk to you about something."

Val turned left, then glanced at her aunt. "That sounds ominous. Should I be worried?"

Laughing, Celia shook her head. "Not a bit. I just thought it would be fun to talk about what you're considering in hospitality. I've done lots of traveling these past five years and I might have some ideas for you. I wanted to visit with you about it at the shower last month, but then baby Elizabeth was in such a hurry to join us, I didn't have a chance."

"Really? You'd do that?"

"Why are you so surprised?"

The reception hall where Renee and Jim would celebrate with their family and friends the next day came into view. Celia knew the owner and had borrowed his keys earlier, knowing they'd likely arrive after the staff had left for the day.

Val pulled into the empty parking lot, turned off the car, and turned to face her.

Celia patted her niece's arm. "I get the sense your mother doesn't approve of your career choices. When I was your age, my aspirations differed greatly from all my friends, and Mother didn't quite know what to make of it, either. But a talented business man took me under his wing and mentored me. Maybe I can do the same for you."

Val reached over and gave her a hug. "Thank you, Auntie."

Celia squeezed her back, their embrace awkward in the tight quarters of the front seat. "Now, we have flowers and sandwich fixings to attend to. Let's get a move on."

"You are fantastic to all of us," Val said as they crawled out of the Cadillac. "I hope you know how much we appreciate you."

"That's what family does, Val. And don't you forget it," Celia ordered, removing a large box containing one of the flower arrangements.

Val grinned and took the box, heading for the hall. For a second, the setting sun emphasized her profile, shocking Celia with the resemblance between Val and Beverly. She'd never noticed it before, but now she wouldn't be able to unsee it.

Family forever.

Chapter Twenty-Three
Gift of Music and Dance

After a beautiful wedding ceremony, Jim and Renee led a boisterous parade of family and friends through the streets of downtown in their balloon-festooned, rusty gold Monte Carlo, arriving at the reception hall, ready to celebrate. A generous group of Lavonne's girlfriends served the happy couple and guests a tasty meal. The only unfortunate incident of the whole day came when the cake top wobbled, leaving the crowd gasping. Jim did his best to catch it, but gravity won out, and he ended up falling down himself, knocking down the cake top, too. Celia noticed the sheen of tears in Renee's eyes, but young Val stepped in, scooping the miraculously unbroken figurine of the bride and groom out of the splattered cake. She promised her big sister to bake the newlyweds a fresh cake, complete with the salvaged figurine, on their one-year anniversary.

Crisis averted.

As Celia watched Lavonne stoop down in her wedding finery and clean the mess up with a stack of personalized napkins, an old memory surfaced. Her mind took her back to the lodge kitchen at Whispering Pines, to Mrs. Bell on her hands and knees cleaning up a mess of dropped chocolate cake and fudge frosting. It was the same night Celia finally got up the nerve to ask the woman how her son was doing off at war. Even then, after spending just one summer with Danny, Celia already knew he'd be an important person in her life. If he survived the war. He survived, but poor Mrs. Bell didn't live much longer after Danny had to make the excruciating decision to put her in a home when her memory started failing. Celia missed the dear woman. She'd taken Celia under her wing, much as Preston had back then.

"A penny for your thoughts," Ruby said, nudging her arm. "You look a million miles away."

Celia pulled her attention back to the festivities, and to the other three women seated at her table near the cake. She'd appreciated Renee's phone call six months earlier, asking who Celia would like added to the guest list.

"You are family, too," Renee had said. "We wanted you to celebrate our wedding with your friends, too."

She didn't add, though Celia suspected she was thinking it, *Since you'll never have a child get married.*

"I wouldn't say I was a million miles away," she told Ruby. "That ruined cake reminded me of the time Mrs. Bell dropped a big chocolate cake. You weren't there that summer, but Helen, you might have been there that night. Do you remember?"

Helen paused. "I can't say that I do. But I remember what a fabulous cook Mrs. Bell was, and how kind she was to us all."

"I was so sad to hear of her passing," Eleanor added.

Celia lifted her champagne flute into the air. "To Mrs. Bell—for feeding us well, and not ratting us out to Preston when we spilled wine on our picnic blanket."

The four women tapped their glasses and sipped champagne, each lost in her own memories of their girlhood summers at Whispering Pines.

As she set her glass down, Celia studied the faces of her three friends. So much had changed for all of them in the five years since she'd retired. Before that retirement party, Eleanor had been newly widowed, and over the course of the next five years, both Helen and Ruby also suffered the deaths of their husbands. Celia had felt another tiny crack form in her heart at Warren's death. A sudden stroke. She'd worked with Warren for so many years, it felt like losing a brother. After Edwin's one disastrous trip to Italy, Ruby's husband never boarded another plane in the few remaining years he'd lived.

She wondered how each of them was feeling in this moment, surrounded by youth and laughter, celebrating the beginning of a new marriage, when each of them was now beyond the endpoint of their own unions.

Toward the end of Edwin's life, Ruby had taken a year off from her travels with Celia to nurse her ailing husband. Maybe now she'd consider another international trip. There was still more of the world Celia hoped to see, before age made travel too difficult. Besides, she thought it would be good for Ruby's healing heart.

Helen was still miserable over Warren's sudden and unexpected death just six months earlier. They'd been busy enjoying their lifestyle after he'd retired. Age had mellowed Helen's sharp tongue, but the bitterness she felt over her sudden widowhood had left her jaded. Celia had to work hard not to be affected by her friend's nasty moods.

Eleanor seemed well adjusted. She'd even admitted to seeing someone occasionally, an old business associate of her departed husband. When Ruby screeched her enthusiasm over this, Eleanor insisted they weren't *dating*. Whatever that meant.

Celia could only hope they'd all enjoy their evening celebrating with her extended family. Everyone experiences losses. That didn't mean they should stay home and wallow in their grief. Life was for living.

Family moved tables out of the way to clear the dance floor, but they'd seated Celia and her friends out of the way. All four older women smiled as they watched Renee and Jim hold each other in their first dance. The couple's feet didn't take them far, but no one noticed their lack of finesse. The two looked lost in each other's eyes, oblivious of the crowd watching them with rapt attention.

"To be young and in love like that again," Ruby sighed.

Helen let out a soft snort. "No, thank you."

Eleanor shook her head, saying nothing. The girl who'd been so full of fun and vitality during their college years had matured into a much more reserved woman. Celia wondered if old money did that to a person.

After Jim and Renee finished on the dance floor, there were other dances with the wedding party and parents. When the band announced one last family dance before they opened up the dance floor for everyone, Celia noticed George making a beeline in her direction.

"I already know what you are going to say, but I won't take no for an answer, sis," he declared, extending his hand to her.

"Show him how it's done, Celia!" Ruby clapped, encouraging her, and the others joined in. All her friends knew she'd never been much of a dancer.

Touched that George would even think to ask her to dance, Celia graciously accepted. Hopefully she could dance to one song and then settle back at the table to visit with her friends for the rest of the evening. Or until they all called it a night, before they turned into pumpkins, well before the younger generations would wrap up the celebration. She rested her cheek on his shoulder as they executed a slow waltz around the dance floor, both tired after a full day of wedding festivities.

"Thank you for your help with the wedding, Celia," George was saying.

She raised her head and smiled up at her brother. "Oh, I didn't do much."

He laughed. "Always so humble. You do more than you know. For starters, if you wouldn't have paid for Renee's schooling, she might have had to settle for a two-year community college, and never met Jim."

"Tonight is all *my* doing, then?" she teased.

"You could say that," he agreed, leading her in a graceful turn. He was paying more attention to the music and steps. She let him lead. "Seriously, though. Thank you for taking on some details for the wedding. Lavonne is so busy with the two new babies, and I've been helping Ethan out on a few of his construction jobs to earn some extra cash. All these weddings have depleted the funds."

She pulled back a smidge more in his arms. "George, if you're having money troubles, I can certainly help. You need only ask."

He chuckled. "No. That won't be necessary. But thank you for the offer. Seeing as how Val isn't dating anyone these days, I think I'll have time to restock the coffers before it's her turn. And, much as I'd like to help Jess and Ethan with the costs of their new babies, I think it's better for them to figure things out on their own."

Celia didn't disagree. All of them learned as much from their struggles as from their successes. "I think that's wise. But come to me if anyone finds themselves in too deep. Promise?"

"You could always offer to pay for Will's schooling. He'd probably take you up on that."

It took a beat for her to realize he was teasing. "I hope things work out for Will and Jess. Of the three new spouses, he's the only one that worries me a little, if you don't mind me saying."

"I don't mind," George said. The familiar song was ending and he paused, dipping Celia ever so gently as the last notes drifted away. "I admit I have similar worries. But tonight is a time for celebration, so let's have fun."

Celia stepped out of her brother's arms and executed a quick curtsy. "Yes. Let's."

Celia didn't end up limiting herself to one turn around the dance floor. The groom insisted on a dance, thanking her for her many contributions to their special day. Then Ethan appeared, insisting he owed her a dance. Even Will got her out on the dance floor once. Gerry was the only male in her family who left her alone. He disliked dancing even more than Celia.

Eleanor slipped away while Celia was on the dance floor with Ethan. "She said to be sure to tell you again how much she appreciated the invite and she'll call you tomorrow," Ruby reported.

"Did she say anything more about this mystery man?" Celia asked as she sank back into her chair, winded from dancing. Her feet were killing her.

"Not a word. That woman is like a steel trap. If you ever have any secrets, you're safe to share them with her. She'll take them to the grave."

Helen laughed. "Right. Like any of us have lived a life exciting enough to have *secrets*."

Ruby and Celia exchanged a knowing glance.

"Wait . . ." Helen's smile fell away. "I'm sorry, Celia. I guess you do have some big secrets. Does your family know about—"

"Helen," Celia interrupted, her voice loud enough to drown her friend's words out. "How is Karen liking her job these days?"

She'd noticed Lavonne approaching their table and didn't want her to overhear anything revealing Helen might spill. As Lavonne took the empty seat Eleanor had vacated, Helen mouthed *Sorry!* to Celia.

"You have to be pleased with how today turned out, Lavonne," Ruby said. "But I bet you're about ready to go home and put your feet up!"

"Believe it or not, I'm still raring to go. I love to dance, and we hardly get to anymore."

"You are so right," Helen agreed. "Growing up, we went to fancy dances most every weekend. The world is a dimmer place now that no one dances much anymore."

"It was a beautiful ceremony, and Jim is an amazing man," Celia said, watching her niece's new husband dance around the floor with a toddler in his arms. "Who is that?"

Lavonne followed her gaze. "His cousin's little girl. I think Jim will make a wonderful dad someday."

"My, this family is growing by leaps and bounds," Celia declared. "Mother and Clarence would be so proud." She reached over and squeezed Lavonne's hand, her fingers brushing the baby's-breath in the corsage at her wrist. "You did good, momma."

"*We* did good, Celia. They are all turning into perfectly respectable grown humans."

The women laughed over Lavonne's pronouncement. With any luck, these young people would float through life relatively unscathed.

If only life worked that way.

Chapter Twenty-Four
GIFT OF LEARNING TO FISH

Summer 2003

CELIA WIPED SWEAT FROM her forehead with the back of her hand before it rolled into her eyes. If the temperature stayed this high through the next day, her party would be a scorcher. The early morning rain she'd woken to contributed to the thick, humid air and a riot of color throughout her backyard. Even though the party would be outside, guests would be in and out of the house. She needed to finish weeding and dead-heading before the cleaning crew arrived. Just one more flowerbed to tend. The neighbor boy would mow the next morning. Her youngest guests would run around barefoot in the heat of the summer day, and she wanted the grass to be a soft carpet underfoot.

As she snipped away the spent heads on her yellow rose bushes, she wondered again if planning a gathering of family and friends at her own home to celebrate her eightieth birthday party had been a good idea after all. A party for upwards of thirty people was a lot of work at any age.

She was proud of her yard. The flower gardens rimming the lawn were more lush than the summer she'd hosted Virginia's wedding twenty years earlier. She'd still been working back then, tending to flowers as time permitted. But this summer was different. Now she had plenty of time to putter around back here.

Her traveling partner, Ruby, was still nursing her shattered heart after her daughter and son-in-law died on Valentine's Day in a horrific car crash. A drunk driver sideswiped the couple's car on their way home from an evening of dinner and dancing. Celia's heart ached for her dear friend. The suddenness of it all left Ruby unmoored, wallowing in her grief. Nothing Celia or Ruby's remaining son, Jack, did seemed to help her find her footing again. Only time with her grandson, Seth, seemed to give Ruby any sense of joy.

Like his grandmother, young Seth was struggling to find his way out of the haze of grief. Celia knew Ruby worried about the young man. He'd barely kept his grades high enough to graduate from college in the spring, and, according to Ruby, he'd done nothing to land his first career job. Architects sit at a desk, something the young man swore he couldn't bring himself to do yet. Maybe in a year. Ruby told Celia she had her doubts about that. Seth was drinking more than he should, and he'd even scuffled with the law.

He was lucky his uncle was a lawyer. Though Jack didn't practice criminal law, he had connections, and between Ruby and Jack, Seth had managed to stay out of jail. Celia prayed Seth would clean up his act. Ruby didn't need any more heartbreak, and her relationship with her grandson could be a lifeline or the final straw.

Ruby's struggles had brought an abrupt halt to her travels. Celia understood, and would give her all the time she needed. At least her gardens were looking spectacular for tomorrow's party. Maybe, after the festivities were over, she'd cut a bouquet from back here for her friend. Ruby loved having fresh blooms in the house.

Celia still couldn't relax in her free time, so she was discovering new hobbies. She'd consulted more with the Fisks, discussing ways to maintain sales at their bookstore. She enjoyed the mental challenge. There were also monthly meetings with the local company she'd hired to oversee her rental properties. Keeping the buildings in decent repair, even if she couldn't afford to make them top-notch, was important to Celia. Her tenants deserved to live in nice, respectable homes. Next week she planned to sit down with the Robinses to help them figure out ways their small cleaning business could support both of their daughters plus themselves. Celia had some ideas but wasn't sure if John would be receptive to them. The man didn't like change.

Slamming car doors signaled the arrival of one of John's cleaning crews. Celia braced a hand on one knee and grabbed hold of the handle on her trusty old spade, hoisting herself up. Everything creaked, but she did her best to ignore her aching joints and back.

She'd done what she could to prepare her backyard for the party. It was time to shift her focus inside.

She almost missed the clang of the doorbell over the persistent roar of a vacuum cleaner on the floor above.

"Who can that be?" she mumbled.

Lavonne was bringing groceries for the party, but not until after her volunteer shift at the hospital. Setting her ice-cold glass of lemonade on the kitchen counter, Celia made her way to the front door, trying not to let the crick in her knee slow her down.

But Wendy, the Robinses' eldest daughter and head of the day's cleaning crew, beat her to the door. "I've got it!"

Grateful for the younger woman's help, Celia slowed. She noticed a van pulled up to the curb in front of her house, its sliding side door flung wide open.

"Flowers?"

"Must be for your birthday." Wendy smiled, pulling open the heavy front door. "Hello, Pam!"

"Well, hi, Wendy," the girl on the threshold said. The two large bouquets she balanced obscured part of her face. "I have a delivery for Celia Middleton?"

"Those look heavy. Here, let me help," Wendy insisted, dropping her dust rag and taking a white vase brimming with at least two dozen yellow roses.

"Danny," Celia whispered. Only her old friend would send such a large arrangement of her favorite flowers. They'd practically met over yellow roses, sixty years earlier, back when he was a gardener at Grand View Lodge.

"Follow me," Wendy instructed, leading the delivery woman back to the dining room. "Let's put them on the table in here, and I can help Celia get them placed wherever she'd like. How is the new job going, Pam? I'm so glad Jill hired you. Has she let you design any arrangements yet?"

It was nearly as hot inside the house as outside, and the new flowers perfumed the air. Celia watched the two women, who obviously knew each other, bring in the flowers. She didn't have to see the card to know the roses were from Danny, but she was curious who'd sent the second bouquet.

The two women visited for another minute before Pam said her goodbyes. "I still have a big delivery for the hospital. I helped design a few of those arrangements. I need to stay in Jill's good graces, so she'll let me continue to do more than just deliver. Thanks again, Wendy, for helping me get this job."

After a quick hug, Wendy saw the girl to the door. Once the door was closed, she caught her long hair up with a rubber band and scooped her dust rag off the floor. "Celia, why don't you turn on that air-conditioning unit? It is blazing hot in here!"

Nodding, Celia gimped her way to the window unit on the north side of the living room. "I've never liked air-conditioning, but you're right. I need to cool things off. My guests will need somewhere to escape the heat. Say, that reminds me. Could you send one of your girls down to the basement? I'd appreciate it if they could do a quick dust and set up the ping-pong table. It'll give the kids something to do if it's too hot outside."

"Sure, I'll send them down when they finish upstairs. Hey, why are you limping?"

She waved away the question. "I'm fine."

Wendy shook her head. "You never complain, do you?"

"Complaining solves nothing. My left knee gives me some trouble, but I see the doctor next week. Say, I was treating myself to a cold glass of lemonade. Why don't you join me for a few minutes? Cool off."

She checked her wristwatch. "I think I can manage that. We're ahead of schedule."

Celia added fresh ice to her glass and poured one for Wendy. The two settled at the dining table, Celia doing her best to stifle a groan of relief when she took weight off her bum knee.

"These flowers are gorgeous. Would you like to read the cards?" Wendy asked, pulling the miniature white envelopes out of each bouquet and handing them to Celia.

She didn't recognize the handwriting on the front of either envelope. Opening the one from the mixed arrangement, she smiled when she realized the Dixons had thought to send birthday greetings.

"Not to be nosy," Wendy prodded, "but I'm dying to hear who sent these."

"The carnations are from Ed and Mary Dixon. Dear friends of mine. They've worked for me for going on twenty years."

"Twenty years? Do they help you with your rentals?"

"No. I actually own a small lake resort in central Minnesota. They maintain it for me."

"A lake resort? Are you *kidding* me? I didn't know that!"

Celia sighed. "It's true. I spent lots of fun summers there, back when I was about your age. How old are you?"

"I'm twenty-three. Do you still go there in the summer?"

"Sadly, no. I hoped to spend lots of time out there after I retired, but it wasn't the same. My friends and family were too busy with their own lives to visit often, and I was lonesome. I guess sometimes memories can be too powerful."

Wendy sipped her lemonade, rubbing at the ring of condensation it left on the tabletop. "But you've held on to it?"

It wasn't exactly a question, but Celia felt the need to explain herself. "I started going there with friends during college. Eventually, I did some work for the man who owned it. His name was Preston Whitby. Unlike all my friends, I was more interested in building a career than landing a husband. Preston helped."

Wendy grinned but didn't interrupt.

"When I graduated from college, Preston hired me in a role usually filled by men. He was wealthy, and Whispering Pines—that's the name of the resort—provided an escape for him. I worked for him at both his principal business and out at the resort for many years."

Her voice trailed off as she fell into the rabbit hole of memory.

"Interesting! Preston passed the resort on to you, then? When he died?"

Celia's shoulders tighten in irritation at the younger woman's assumption. "I should say not. I think he would have liked to have done that, but he felt compelled to leave it to his son. Even though Tripp didn't care about the place."

Wendy shifted uncomfortably in her chair. "I'm sorry, Celia. I didn't mean to offend you."

Realizing her reaction wasn't fair to Wendy, Celia toyed with the edges of the envelope containing the Dixons' birthday greetings. "I'm the one who should apologize. It's just that even the thought of Tripp and the difficult relationship I shared with him through the years still sticks in my craw. I don't know why I can't let it go. The man has been dead for five years now."

It was true. Even Tripp's death hadn't tempered the conflicted feelings she still felt toward him. If not for the bond he'd shared with Celia's long-dead younger sister, she knew she'd have hated the man. But that surprising relationship, so terribly long ago now, had been one of the reasons Celia tolerated him through the years. The other main reason, of course, was the respect Celia had for Tripp's father, Preston.

She realized Wendy was waiting for the rest of the story.

"Truth be told, I might have been a bit underhanded when I bought the resort from Tripp back in the sixties. But I'd promised his father that I would protect Whispering Pines, no matter what, and I'm not one to break promises."

"You are such a badass, Celia," the girl said, grinning as she sipped her lemonade. "Are you going to sell it? Since you don't go out there anymore?"

Celia smiled. She liked to think she was still a bit of a badass, too, even at eighty. "That would be the logical thing to do. But, since I seldom do what people expect of me, no. Even though it's been years since I've spent any length of time at Whispering Pines, I know it's safe in my hands. I just need to figure out how to protect it after I'm gone."

Wendy's expression reminded her she should probably figure that out sooner versus later. No one lives forever. She'd lost enough people through the years to be painfully aware of that truth. But Wendy was too polite to point out that someone turning eighty should probably already have her affairs in order.

"Enough about me," Celia insisted. "How are things going for you, young lady?"

Wendy shook her head, pointing to the other envelope Celia hadn't opened yet. "I'm fine. I'm more interested in hearing about who sent you those gorgeous yellow roses. I've always loved the yellow rose bushes in your yard." A sly smile crept on the girl's face. "Something tells me there's a story behind this arrangement."

Celia laughed. "Oh, my dear, you'll be late for your next appointment if I tell you that entire story."

Not that I'd share it, even if we had all the time in the world, she thought. Her story with Danny was complicated, but also it was special. One she only ever allowed herself to examine when she was alone, lost in her thoughts.

"Let me guess," Wendy said, still smiling. "They're from a man. A man who was dumb enough to let you get away a long time ago, and he still regrets the fact he let you slip through his fingers."

Celia laughed at her saucy tone. The guess wasn't wrong, but it wasn't exactly accurate either. Celia held many regrets. She suspected Danny did, too. But life has a funny way of moving on, and while the deep love and respect they felt for each other remained, they'd both come to accept they were never meant to live life together.

"You might say that, but I'm sorry I didn't hold on to him, too," she conceded. She knew she couldn't make Wendy understand. She'd never understood it herself. "Sometimes our lives intersect with people, but we can't walk the same path as them. Does that make any sense at all?"

Footsteps thumped down the wooden staircase, along with chatter. Wendy stood. "Actually, it does. I'm only twenty-three, but I dated someone special a few years ago. It didn't last, but I know I'll never forget him. He left to join the Marines. Maybe our ill-fated love affair will turn out like yours did with . . . I'm sorry, what did you say his name was?"

She hadn't said it. But his name always brought a smile to her lips. "Danny. His name is Danny. I'll read the card later. I know he wasn't able to come because his son is getting married this weekend."

"You haven't even *opened* the card," Wendy pointed out. "How can you be sure they're from him?"

Celia smiled knowingly. "I'm sure. Now, if you don't mind, could I get you to give me a hand with the decorations for tomorrow's party? It'll take your girls some time downstairs, I'm sure. There's a box on my desk back in the office. Be a dear and bring them out here, would you? I'll get help with the balloons and streamers outside tomorrow morning, but I'd like to make the table look nice in here, too."

Wendy nodded as she gathered their lemonade glasses. "I'll go grab that for you."

Celia toyed with the unopened envelope as Wendy put their glasses in the kitchen and headed down the hallway. Once she was out of sight, Celia slid a finger under the envelope's seal and pulled out the card.

My dearest Celia,

Wishing I could be with you as you celebrate your 80th. But I've learned age is irrelevant. No matter our age, you'll always be that beautiful, timeless woman I fell in love with at the end of our dock at Whispering Pines. Thank you for warming my heart for as long as I can remember.

Yours,
Danny

As she brushed away a tear, she appreciated the truth behind his words.

"Are you all right, Celia?" Wendy asked from the doorway. The words were low and soft, meant to comfort and not startle. In her hands she clutched the box Celia had asked for.

Celia tucked Danny's note back in its envelope and set the missive aside. "I'm perfect. Now, bring that here. Let's see what all I've been squirreling away for today. I forget."

Wendy set the heavy box down in front of her. "I'm not sure what you want to do with all this stuff."

"I suppose we could toss most of it," Celia admitted, standing up to reach inside. She pulled out an old, dusty wine bottle, the label partially gone, its print faded. "But I have a hard time letting some things go."

Wendy chuckled. "You don't seem the sentimental type."

"I have my moments. Maybe after my party, I'll go through some of this old junk and get rid of things. God knows I have time now. Do you know I've lived in this house almost my entire life?"

Helping her remove items from the box, Wendy shook her head. "I didn't know that. And what do you mean you have time *now*? You always seem so busy! In fact, I've been wanting to ask you for a favor, but I haven't gotten up the nerve. I wasn't sure you'd have time for it, what with all your traveling and such."

Celia picked up the dust rag Wendy had dropped on the table earlier and tried to polish the pitted glass of the old wine bottle. This was one item she'd never toss. It dated back to her very first picnic at Whispering Pines with Helen, Ruby, and Eleanor. Finding it in the tall grass years later, when she'd been back at the resort to help rebuild after a nasty late-summer storm, had felt miraculous.

"Would you like me to take that into the kitchen and run it under the water?" Wendy offered, motioning to the bottle Celia couldn't get clean.

"Heavens no, child. The corrosion is part of its charm. Besides, water would be the end of what little label remains. What was it you wanted to ask me about?"

The door to the basement opened and Wendy's two cleaners came back into the dining room. "Anything else, Wendy?"

She looked to Celia. "Did we miss anything?"

Celia did a quick mental check of the list of things she still hoped to accomplish before Lavonne arrived with the food. "The only thing I'd appreciate some extra help with—and I realize this goes above and beyond cleaning my house—is if you could bring out a stack of tables and folding chairs from the garage." When Wendy nodded, Celia turned to the two cleaners. "If you two wouldn't mind setting them up in the backyard and hosing them off, I'd be forever grateful. I'm not sure my back could take that today."

"It's no problem," Wendy said, smiling. "Ladies, just head out through the door in the kitchen to the garage. Any place in particular you want them set up, Celia?"

"No. I'd appreciate it if you rinsed them off. We'll get everything to the proper spot tomorrow morning."

The two women offered Celia birthday wishes, then hurried out back.

"They certainly seem like good workers," she said once they'd left.

Wendy agreed as she removed the last of the items from Celia's box. "In fact, what I wanted to visit with you about is somewhat related to those two."

Celia, seeing the box's contents scattered on her tabletop, sat back down. Between the heat and the morning's gardening session, she'd need a nap. "I'm intrigued."

Wendy set the empty box on the floor and sat across from her again. "I think Mom or Dad probably mentioned to you that I've had luck hiring cleaners from a local women's shelter. I was having trouble finding dependable help, but, except for one case, all the women from the shelter have done a great job for us."

Celia did recall John mentioning Wendy's success in finally finding a source of workers. "I love that you're helping those women out. When I was young, after my father died, we nearly ended up in a shelter ourselves. He left us this place, but it was around the time of the first big stock market crash, and Mother nearly lost everything. I was only five, but I learned a lot."

"Wow, you really have been in this house a long time," Wendy said, looking around. "Sorry. I'm getting off topic. The women are great workers, but they can only stay at the shelter for a short time. Most of them don't save any of the money we pay them, so when it comes time for them to leave the shelter, often with their children, they have to move to another shelter—or, worse yet, go home to an abusive situation they tried to escape in the first place. All because they can't afford a place of their own."

An image of a much younger Virginia popped into Celia's mind: the two of them standing in an icy cemetery. If Celia hadn't taken in Virginia and her baby those many years ago, there's no telling what would have become of them. "That's awful. I'm sorry to say that I've never considered donating to the local shelters. Is that what you were curious about? Are you on a fundraising committee?"

Wendy laughed. "We always appreciate money, and yes, I am on the fundraising committee, but that isn't why I brought it up today."

"Well, if it isn't my money you're after, how can I help? I know this is a big house, but I'm not sure I'm up to opening up my home to strangers at my age. Mother did it, but I'm beyond that."

Pipes rattled. The women had found the hose in the backyard.

"No. I'd never dream of asking you to do that. I'm just wondering if you'd ever come in and visit with some of the women." Wendy leaned toward her. "Celia, I know you had a very successful career and now you own properties all over town. I didn't know you owned a resort, too, on top of it all. You know how to handle your money. Most of the women in the shelter don't have a clue about finances. Could you help them?"

"Help them? How?"

She shrugged. "Come talk with small groups, maybe? Give them pointers? As a board member, I have a new appreciation of how important it is to teach these women to fish, instead of giving them a handout. If you catch my metaphor. Would you at least give it some thought?"

Celia chuckled as she reached for an old photograph Wendy had taken out of her box of memorabilia. It was a picture of her standing next to Helen's brother, Leo, back in the early 1940s. Both of them held a fishing pole. Leo had *literally* taught Celia how to fish.

"I'm honored that you think I have anything worth sharing," she said, her eyes skipping between the framed photo and Wendy's hopeful expression.

Could she do it? Could she help those women who'd already suffered so much?

In a flash of insight, she realized she probably could. She'd learned to fish years ago—literally and metaphorically—when a few kind people took the time to show her how.

Maybe it was time to pass that lesson along.

Chapter Twenty-Five
Gift of Family

"What's a woman to wear to her eightieth birthday party, Bev?" Celia asked, looking to the ceiling of her dead sister's bedroom. "Can you believe I'm turning eighty? Some days I feel so damn old. Everything hurts. Other days, I feel like I'm thirty again. Or maybe forty. But eighty? God, time's gone so quickly."

The sound of party preparations floated from below as she dug in the closet. She probably shouldn't be talking to herself like this when other people were in her house. It's no big deal to talk to yourself when you're young, but if someone overhears you doing it at eighty, it could be a quick ticket to the nursing home.

Not that Celia would ever allow that. But no sense tempting fate.

She liked to think Beverly was somehow near, especially on special days like today, even though she'd never lived to see twenty. If her spirit was close, she'd have no tolerance for Celia's pity party. She'd remind her how blessed she was to live for so long.

Shaking off the funk that had threatened to envelop her since her eyes popped open that morning, she pulled the new dress she'd purchased for today's party off the hanger and dropped it on the spare bed. She'd loved the bright colors and the way the loose shift skimmed over her expanding midriff. As she unbuttoned her housecoat, she realized her half-slip was in the dresser in her new bedroom. Scooping her dress off the bed, she crossed the room and swung open the door, laughing at the notion that the room she'd moved into after her mother's death twenty-five years ago was *new*.

"Whoa, slow down, Celia," Ethan warned, catching her by her upper arms to avoid a collision in the hallway. "You mustn't have heard me call your name, then?"

She'd been so caught up in thoughts of Beverly and dressing for her party, she'd failed to hear her nephew outside the bedroom door. She took a step back. "Lord, I *didn't* hear you! You startled me. You shouldn't do that to an old lady, it could kill me!"

Ethan shook his head. "It would take more than a good scare to do *you* in, Cee. Hey, why aren't you dressed yet? Should I send Mom up to help you? The family is pretty much all here."

Tossing the dress still clutched in her hand over her shoulder, she fixed him with a stare. "I may be old, dear, but I can still dress myself."

Holding his hands out in front of him defensively, Ethan assured her he didn't doubt that. "I'm just up here to look at that broken window in the attic like you asked. I thought I'd get that taken care of now, so I don't forget."

Footsteps on the wooden stairs interrupted him. He waved over Celia's shoulder.

"There you are, Ethan," Stacey said. "I thought you were going to grab the diaper bag from the car. Drew needs to be changed."

A pungent scent reached Celia before Stacey did. She turned to face her nephew's wife, smiling at the dimpled two-year-old in her arms. "You certainly do need a diaper, little man."

Drew grabbed for Celia's finger, pulling with his chubby fingers. Laughing, she pulled her finger back and shook her head. "Sorry, little guy, I need to finish getting cleaned up for my birthday party."

Weaving around his aunt, Ethan took the smelly little boy from his wife and settled him on his hip. "What the hell, Stacey? Why didn't you send Lizzy out to the car for it? I need to help Celia with something."

Stacey shrugged, resting her now empty hands on her hips. "Lizzy is only eight. She's too young to go out to your truck. It's parked on the street. Besides, you have the keys."

He started to reply, but Celia cut him off with a hand on his forearm. "Don't worry about the window, Ethan. I had a sheet of plywood in the garage, and I braced it against the broken pane to keep anything from crawling in. If you can't get to it yet today, you can come back in a day or two."

"Where's the broken window?" Stacey asked, peeking into the bedroom behind Celia.

"Upstairs. In the attic."

She grinned. "The attic? I've been dying to see your attic. Come on, Ethan. Let's run up there quick so I can see it."

He bounced little Drew on his hip. "This kid needs to be cleaned up."

"I know," she said, a hint of impatience in her tone. "Let's run upstairs real quick. I love this house. Then I'll take your keys and go change him."

Celia fought the urge to wave a hand in front of her nose. *The poor kid shouldn't have to wait to be changed,* she thought, even though the boy was all grins, grabbing for the rim of his dad's baseball cap.

With a sigh, Ethan turned on his heel. "Fine. Come on, then. Celia, we'll leave you to get dressed for your party. I'll see what it'll take to get your window fixed and either do it later today or stop back tomorrow."

"That's fine, dear. Show Stacey the attic. Although I should warn you, Stacey, it's nothing special. Just a big old room at the top of the stairs, filled with lifetimes of junk."

Stacey stopped and gave her a quick hug before following behind Ethan and her youngest. "I think everything about this house is special, Celia. And just yell up at me if you need any help getting dressed."

Celia watched as the attic door swung shut behind the three, cutting off Stacey's offer for help. The sharp odor lingered behind.

"Why does everyone think I suddenly need help *dressing*?" she muttered, slipping through the door into her own bedroom, careful not to leave it open any longer than necessary. She didn't need to show up at her own birthday party smelling like dirty diapers.

～ eℓℓ ～

Celia came down the stairs, her summery party dress flowing around her, to a chorus of shouts.

"*There's* the birthday girl!"

"The woman of the hour!"

"Love the dress!"

She kept her right hand on the stair railing, but she clapped the other over her mouth in delight. Her family had transformed the dining and living rooms.

"What do you think?" Renee asked, motioning around. "Too much?"

Laughing, Celia shook her head. "Never. It's not every day a girl gets to celebrate turning eighty. The balloons and streamers—I thought those were going outside? I *love* them!"

Jess straightened from arranging a massive tray of frosted cupcakes. Sandwiched between the cupcakes and dishes was an impressive display of finger foods and more desserts. "Don't worry, the birthday fairies worked equally hard outside! All of this is just the extras. We got our wires crossed. I ordered three dozen helium balloons—aaand so did Renee. Mom accidentally told us both to see to the balloons."

Lavonne finished arranging the family china and silver on the opposite end of the table and hurried toward the stairs. She caught Celia up in a hug at the bottom of the stairs.

"Happy Birthday, Celia. This is shaping up to be a heck of a party!"

Celia checked her watch. "Are people arriving already?"

"No, it's still early," Val piped in from behind her mom. "Just family so far. And we don't count!"

"You *all* count," Celia countered. "Is it terribly hot outside?"

The front door opened and Renee's husband entered holding a toddler wearing nothing but a diaper. Jim's shirt looked damp with sweat, giving Celia her answer.

"Where's his cute outfit?" Renee cried, crossing the living room to take little Robbie from Jim.

"Let me guess—*he* soiled himself, too," Celia said, drawing a round of laughter. "I'm telling you, Ethan's little guy stank up the hallway upstairs. I should have set up a changing station in the downstairs bath!"

Jim pulled at his damp shirt and shook his head. "No, his diaper's clean. He's just hot. I figured it was safe to take his romper off for a while before the party gets hopping. We probably shouldn't have put it on him before we made the drive over."

Jim excused himself to run downstairs and check on the other kids. Celia watched him go, delighted they'd made the trip over from Minneapolis for her party.

She clapped her hands together. "What can I do?"

"I think everything is about done," Lavonne said. "George and the rest of the men should have the tables and chairs set up outside by now. Why don't we grab some punch and go out there? We want to give you your birthday gift before everyone else arrives."

Celia scooped nuts out of a bowl on the table and dumped them into her hand, adding mints to the mixture, too. "I do like gifts, but I distinctly remember putting *no presents* on the invitation."

"Oh, Celia. We wouldn't come to your party without a gift! And we probably won't be the only ones to ignore your instructions, either. I had George set up a gift table outside, just in case," Lavonne teased as she poured two cups of pink punch. She nodded toward the kitchen. "Come on. I've got your punch."

Ethan clomped down the stairs, quickly followed by Stacey, who held young Drew. "Celia, I'm afraid your windowsill is rotted through, but I took the measurements and then nailed your plywood in place. I'll get a new window ordered and fix it up next week for you."

Celia thanked him, then, wrinkling her nose, suggested they change the boy quickly and join them out back. "Apparently your mother has a *gift* for me."

"Ah, yes—you'll want that before the party officially starts," Ethan agreed, turning back to Stacey. "Here. Give him to me. Grab me a beer out of the fridge and Drew's bottle. I'll go out to the truck and change him, then meet you in the back."

"Fine by me," Stacey agreed, waving the air away from her nose—much as Celia had wanted to do—once her hands were empty. "It's nice to see you haven't forgotten how to change a diaper."

"Now, now, no fighting, kids," Celia teased, making her way to her back door, hurrying as much to escape the smell as to keep things moving.

Stacey followed close behind. "That's not us fighting. That's just me reminding Ethan he could stand to step it up a little in the father department."

Celia caught the look of frustration on Lavonne's face as she held the screen door open with her foot, a punch cup in each hand. "Stacey doesn't know how lucky she has it," she whispered as Celia passed.

Celia agreed. Both Ethan and Jim seemed like involved fathers to her. She tried to give the spouses of her nephew and nieces the benefit of the doubt, but today wasn't the first time she'd heard Stacey complain. And would Will even show up today?

Deciding to let it go, Celia took in the party preparations in the backyard. She giggled at the pretty sight in front of her. There was indeed an abundance of balloons and streamers out back, too, just as Jess had promised. White linen tablecloths covered the assortment of card tables, positioned to take advantage of as much shade as possible. Someone had brought out both of the flower arrangements delivered the day before her party, placing them on the two largest tables.

"What a perfect day," she proclaimed, a rush of appreciation swelling within her. "You all take such good care of me. I wish there was a way I could do something nice for all of you."

George stuffed the handkerchief he'd wiped his sweaty face with into the back pocket of his slacks and approached his sister, taking her arm. "Come—sit over here, in the shade. It's not too bad if you stay out of the direct sun."

Patting his hand, she allowed her youngest brother to lead her. "This is so nice. You have a beautiful family, George. And everyone is so helpful."

"It's the least we can do. We wanted to help you celebrate. You've always taken such good care of all of us, we thought it was our turn to return the favor."

Celia hugged him then sat on the folding chair, careful not to tip over on the grass. Accepting the ice-cold punch from Lavonne, she waited while her extended family gathered around her. Renee sat next to her, bouncing a near-naked Robbie on her knee. Jim came out the back door, followed by four more children.

"I can't believe you're up to *six* grandchildren!" Celia said, smiling over at Lavonne and George while the youngest generation plopped down on the grass at her feet.

"Yep, there's six of us now!" a gap-toothed Lizzy proclaimed from her grassy spot closest to her great-aunt. "And can you believe I beat Nathan at ping-pong already?"

"That's because I let you!" the tallest of the children shot back. "We'll have a rematch in a few minutes."

"Maybe I'll play you left-handed, give you a chance," Lizzy countered.

"All right, that's enough, you two," George said, the soft-spoken reprimand immediately silencing his grandchildren. "Now. Who has Celia's present?"

"We have them, Grandpa!"

Two small girls in pastel party dresses, matching pink ribbons dangling from their blond and dark-brown pigtails, stepped out from behind Jim. One was slightly taller than the other, and they wore the cutest matching yellow sandals. Each held a beautifully wrapped gift in her hands.

"Don't you two look beautiful," Celia exclaimed, waving them over to her. "Come here and let me look at you."

The girls scampered over to her, but the younger girl tripped over Nathan's outstretched foot and fell to her knees, dropping the pretty gift she'd held up so proudly a second earlier. The gift rolled once, ending upside down, the bow squished into the grass.

"You did that on purpose!" the child screamed, scrambling to her feet and taking a swing at Nathan, all in one fluid motion.

"Hey, now—you two know better than to act like that," a deep voice declared, and Will rushed forward to scoop the little girl up into his arms. "Girls don't hit."

So he did *show up after all,* Celia thought.

"And gentlemen don't trip their little sisters," she added, catching the telltale glint in Nathan's eye. The eight-year-old had the good sense to look embarrassed.

Jess looked horrified at her children's antics. "Mother, tell me you gave Lauren the present that wasn't breakable."

Lavonne stood and took the girl, now weeping, out of her father's arms. "Here, I'll take her. Thank you, Will."

As she sat back down, Lavonne wiped the tears from her granddaughter's face and tightened her drooping hair bow. "Don't worry, Jess, I'm not brand new at this grandma gig. The present will be fine. Julie, give your Aunt Celia the gift you have first. Nathan, pick up the other present and hold on to it for a minute."

Jess let out a sigh of relief and Celia downed the last of her punch, handing Julie her empty cup in exchange for the present. Julie accepted the plastic cup and stood next to Renee and her little brother.

"Should I open it now?" Celia asked, to which she received the expected round of agreement from the kids. "Should I . . . *shake* it?"

This question earned a sharp "No!" from the adults in the surrounding circle.

"Just kidding," she said, grinning.

"You are as bad as the kids," George said, watching from behind Lavonne, a comforting hand on little Lauren's shoulder. Aside from an occasional hiccup, the girl's tears had stopped. "Open it already!"

Enjoying the camaraderie of her family, Celia did as she was told. She really had no idea what the package contained. But it didn't matter. Their presence was the real gift.

As the paper fell away, the cardboard box offered little clue. Pulling the flaps apart, Celia was shocked to find another box inside, this one boasting a full-color picture.

"A new camera?!" She looked to George for an explanation.

"Ruby told me your old one was on its last leg. We thought it was about time you tried a digital camera. No more film!"

Taking the inner box out, Celia turned it around in her hands, studying the package. "This looks pretty fancy. I'm not sure I'll know how to use it."

"The salesman assured me the basics of it are easy. But we also signed you up for a six-session photography course so you can master some of its other features, too."

Celia was touched by the thoughtfulness of their gift. "I've always wanted to learn more about photography." Suddenly her voice could only come out as a whisper.

"Ruby mentioned that, too," George confirmed.

"Aunt Cee, open mine, too," Lauren insisted from the safety of her grandmother's lap. "Nathan. Give it to her."

Lavonne gave the feisty little girl's pigtail a playful tug. "Hey there, missy, don't be sassy."

Lauren snuggled into her grandmother, putting on a bit of a show after her stumble made her the center of attention.

Nathan handed Celia the second package. She fluffed up the bow, pulled it off the wrapping paper, and stuck it to her dress, near her heart, earning laughter from the kids. Inside, she found a carrying case for the camera.

"You all know what this means, don't you?" She looked from face to face, feeling her heart swell with love for all of them.

"No, what?" Lizzy asked.

"It means that if I can figure out how to work this thing, I'll be snapping pictures of all of you, all afternoon long!"

This brought another round of groans from the children and laughter from the adults.

George walked over to take the gifts from her. "The woman at the store gave me an abbreviated lesson. I'll take it inside and get it set up, then show you the basics. Why don't you kids run and play now?"

"Can we have cupcakes yet?" Nathan asked as he stood and brushed off the seat of his pants.

"No, you cannot," Jess said. "Don't touch the food on the table if you're going back in the house to play ping-pong. After everyone else gets here, we'll eat."

The eight-year-old boy shook his head, whining about starving to death as he held out a hand to his cousin. When Lizzy took it, he yanked her to her feet. But she looked unfazed by his roughness and ran ahead of him toward the house. Not wanting to miss out on the fun, Julie and Lauren followed close behind, holding their dresses up in an unladylike fashion. Renee opened her mouth to scold them, but Celia shushed her.

"Let them be. They're having fun. If they get bored, someone can walk with them down to the park."

Robbie squirmed in Renee's arms. "I wish he would have napped earlier," she said, trying to soothe the fussy child.

Jim stepped forward to help. He picked up the diapered boy and settled him on his shoulders, keeping a tight grip on the toddler's upper thighs.

"Be careful, Jim," his wife warned, watching with apprehension.

Jim nodded, smiling. "The Twins are playing. Celia, would you mind if we took the boys inside where it's cooler? I thought maybe we could get them to nap before the rest of your guests arrive."

"I think that sounds like a smart idea," Celia agreed.

She watched, smiling, as Jim, Ethan, and Will all went inside with the kids, leaving the women alone in the backyard.

"I hope you like your gift, Aunt Celia," Val said. She sat in the grass to Celia's left, leaning against the trunk of the closest tree. "The man giving the photography class is a friend of mine."

"I'm *thrilled*. That was very thoughtful of all of you. Thank you again."

Jess reached over and picked a yellow rose petal off the white linen on the table next to her chair. "These roses are beautiful, Celia. Who sent them?"

Celia's eyes twinkled. "Just an old friend that couldn't make it today. His son is getting married."

Nodding, Jess held the petal up to her nose as if to smell it. "Anyone we know?"

Celia shook her head. "No. He's not from here. Someone from way back. We were friends when we were kids. In fact, he's the one who first got me interested in photography."

"That's cool!" Jess dropped the petal to the grass. She looked as if she had more questions for Celia, but Lavonne, who hadn't been paying attention to their exchange, asked Renee how long she'd be gone.

Eager to steer the conversation away from any more questions about Danny, Celia picked up on their thread. "Where are you going, Renee?"

Renee sighed. "Just to St. Louis. It's work. But I have to be gone all week. I leave early on Monday. I hate all this traveling they're making me do."

Jess snorted. "I'd kill for a work trip. Four nights alone, in a fancy hotel room, all by myself? I don't know what you have to complain about, Renee."

"It's just so hard with the kids. Jim has a tough time juggling it all when I'm gone."

A welcome breeze flipped the corner of the tablecloth up. Lavonne stood to smooth it down. "Honey, be sure to tell him to call us if he needs any help."

Renee nodded, but she didn't look any happier about the situation.

"If you're that miserable, why don't you just quit?" Jess said, a note of impatience in her voice.

"It's not that simple, Jess. I have to work. So does Jim."

"Yeah, but you could find a different job," Val suggested. "I've had *lots* of jobs. It's no big deal."

Celia glanced down at Val. Secretly, she wished George's youngest would take her own career more seriously. She'd held such high hopes for the girl back when Val studied hospitality. But in the years following her college graduation, she'd flitted from job to job, none of which Celia would have considered professional. She simply didn't understand the girl, was maybe even a little disappointed in her, but she'd never admit as much out loud. As the baby of the family, maybe she would just be slower to mature.

"Are you telling me you always look forward to working on Mondays?" Renee was asking Jess.

Celia tuned back into the conversation, letting go of her worry over Val, if only for the day. George and Lavonne didn't seem to be worried about their youngest. Why should she?

"Usually," Jess said, earning an eye roll out of Renee. "What? It's true! I like my work. I'm sorry you don't."

Celia was sorry, too. She'd never forgotten how much Renee loved her time at Whispering Pines when she was younger. She'd been a smiley, agreeable girl. In fact, now that she thought about it, she realized Renee didn't laugh nearly as often as she used to. She seemed happy with Jim and was good with Julie and Robbie, but anytime she talked about work, she lost some of her sparkle.

Not a good sign.

A shout came from the side of the house.

"Hey, is this where the party is?!"

And just like that, Celia's eightieth birthday party was in full swing.

Chapter Twenty-Six

Gift of Forever Friends

"Smile!" Celia said, aiming her new birthday gift at Ruby and Eleanor. "Lean closer to each other."

Eleanor grinned and scooted her chair closer to Ruby's. "You remind me of Danny Bell when you boss us around with a camera in your hand."

Celia smiled. "He sent those roses." Danny's yellow roses graced the center of their table.

Eleanor breathed them in and sighed. "Oh, Celia. I'm afraid you let a good one get away."

"She didn't let him get *too* far away," Ruby said. They were the first words she'd uttered since taking her seat in the shade, and the challenge in her tone was unmistakable.

Celia rested her free hand on her hip. "Do you have something on your mind, Ruby?"

Her best friend shrugged. "Not really. It's just that we all know you've kind of been stringing him along for all these years. I'm not surprised he didn't come today."

The animosity in Ruby's words shocked Celia. "I have not! I'll admit that our relationship—or whatever you want to call it—is anything but traditional, but we've always been friends foremost. He'd have come if he could, but his son is getting married this weekend."

This seemed to take some of the bite out of Ruby. She slumped in her chair, blinking her eyes as if fighting tears. "For Pete's sake. Ignore me, Celia. I don't know what's the matter with me. I'm so ornery, I can hardly stand myself. I'm terrible company. I should have stayed home!"

Celia skirted the table and wrapped a comforting arm around her shoulders. "I don't take any of that personally. You've been through too much lately. I can handle ornery. What I couldn't handle would be for you to stay away. Friends should feel comfortable venting to each other."

Squeezing Ruby's shoulder one last time, she straightened and waved to the new guests arriving. Val happened by with punch and cake. "Val, honey, will you be a dear and fetch some refreshments for Ruby and Eleanor? I don't want them to give up their seats in the shade. And ladies, I apologize, but I need to go greet my guests. Will you be all right?"

Eleanor shooed Celia away. "We aren't going anywhere. We'll catch up later, once Helen is here. We'll stick around after everyone else goes home so we can make this a party for the ages."

Celia grinned. There was a time when she'd have believed she and her friends could outlast the rest of the partygoers, but unless this shindig wrapped up by seven, tonight wouldn't be one of those nights. She set her camera down and left the women in Val's capable hands.

John Robins and his wife, Joyce, were handing a smartly wrapped gift to Renee to take to the gift table.

"You two know we said *no presents*," Celia scolded as she reached her hands out in greeting.

Joyce wore a sheepish expression. "Don't think of it as a gift. It's a pretty picture frame, and it's simply a replacement for the one our cleaning team broke yesterday."

Laughing, Celia thanked Renee and turned her attention to the Robinses. "I told Wendy not to worry about that old thing. Come, sit. I'm so glad you came today. I've been meaning to stop by the office to catch up. How is business?"

John held out a chair for Celia at the table she'd indicated. "Only *you* would want to talk business at your own birthday party. I hope that by the time I'm eighty, running a business will be far back in my memory."

Celia picked up a paper napkin, stamped with a silver happy birthday, and used it as a fan. "Business never feels like work to me. I enjoy it."

"Your place looks so festive," Joyce broke in, scanning the backyard. "I can't seem to get my rose bushes to produce. How do you manage?"

"A friend taught me a very long time ago not to overwater them. I'm careful not to fuss too much. Telling you to leave them be probably doesn't sound like the best gardening advice, but it works for me."

The three continued with small talk as other guests mingled. Eventually, their conversation did loop back to their cleaning business, Homes Sparkle.

John cleared his throat. "We've made a decision."

The comment caught Celia's attention. "Don't tell me you've decided to sell? Or close up shop? Because that would be a shame. I was just visiting with Wendy yesterday about the luck she's having in giving work to women from the local shelter."

"Oh, no, we aren't there yet. But we've both worked so hard in the business for so long, we want to let Joyce step back from all the bookkeeping. You wouldn't have any suggestions for a local accountant we could hire, do you? And don't say you'll take it on yourself. I simply won't allow you to work that hard anymore."

Another fresh set of guests arrived, distracting her for a moment. She spotted Helen.

"I do have someone I could suggest, actually, and there she is now."

Joyce and John turned toward the noise of the greetings in progress near the back corner of the house. Celia waved to Helen. Her granddaughter, Karen, and the younger woman's husband must have given Helen a ride.

"You must mean the young woman," John said, nodding in the trio's direction. "Because Lark owns the bank downtown."

"That's right, you do your Homes Sparkle banking at Stuart Lark's bank. Karen is his wife. She's a talented accountant. I've referred several business associates and friends her way. We could talk to her and see if she has time to take you on as well."

Joyce poked her husband. "See, John, I told you Celia would know what to do."

When Celia braced herself on the table to stand and greet her old friend and the Larks as they wandered over, Helen raised a hand. "Stay seated, my dear. No need to get up. It sure turned out to be a hot one, but it looks like you've got a good turnout. I bet there's a cold drink inside. I'm going to grab something and go say hello to Ruby and Eleanor. How is Ruby doing? The poor dear."

Celia felt a stab of irritation over Helen's comments. Unlike Ruby, Helen had finally bounced back from the death of her husband. She'd developed the new habit of acting like she was the only young one in their friend group, despite their all being the same age, give or take a few months. But Celia tapped down her annoyance. The time may come when she'd need to knock Helen down a step or two, but today wasn't it.

"Ruby is struggling today," she said. "Maybe you can cheer her up." That much was true, Celia thought as she watched Helen walk away, still *tsk-tsk*ing about their friend's mindset.

Once Helen moved on, Celia introduced Karen and Stuart to the Robinses. She provided the bridge to a potential future business arrangement and then artfully steered the conversation to lighter topics. While Karen seemed pleased with the referral, Celia thought she looked ill and insisted she sit down in one of the vacant chairs at the table. Maybe she wasn't feeling well, and the heat certainly wouldn't help.

"Do you know if your parents will have time to stop by today, Karen?"

Karen nodded as she eased into the metal folding chair. "The bookstore's normally open until four on Saturdays, but I know they wanted to stop by before it got too late. I think they're closing at three."

The Robinses excused themselves to find refreshments.

With John and Joyce gone, Celia allowed her concern to show. "Karen, are you feeling all right? I know it's hot out. Head on inside to cool off and grab something to eat. I have the air on inside, though I doubt it can keep up with all the coming and going."

Karen shook her head, insisting she was fine, but Stuart stood and put a hand under her elbow, nudging her to stand.

"I think it would be wise for all *three* of us to get out of this direct sunlight," he said. "Karen, go grab a few of those chairs over at that table in the shade near your grandmother. I'm sure that man and little girl won't mind."

The heat wasn't giving Celia too much trouble. "That's Will, my niece's husband, and his daughter, Lauren. Go, join them! And why don't you go inside, Stuart, and get the two of you some punch? I'd like to take a few more pictures. My family gave me a brand-new camera for my birthday. I'm even going to be taking some lessons with it, so I need to practice."

Karen laughed, some of the weariness in her features melting away. She did as she was told, and Celia watched as she shook hands with Will. Celia smiled. She liked Karen. She was all grown up from the baby living downstairs, and had developed a head for business. She reminded Celia a bit of herself when she was younger.

She retrieved her camera from Eleanor and Ruby's table, where they were catching up with Helen. More petals were falling from the roses, the heat zapping the life out of the flowers, too. She brushed one off her new camera. It was as if a part of Danny was there with her, celebrating.

A bossy little voice caught her attention, and she spied little Julie leading Jim across the grass toward the sprinkler in the far back corner of the grass. "Come on, Daddy! Mommy said I could run through the sprinkler to cool off."

"But what about your dress?" Jim asked his daughter as she pulled him along by the hand.

Celia quickly held the camera up to her eye, focused, and pressed the shutter, praying she'd captured the cute shot. *Time goes by so fast. Next thing you know, Jim will be walking Julie down the aisle at her wedding,* she thought. He'd appreciate a picture with his young daughter.

"Is that new?" Helen asked.

"*Brand* new. George and his family gave it to me, along with photography lessons so I can learn to use it properly."

"Very nice," her old friend said, and Celia nodded her agreement before going in search of more shots of her guests.

Stuart had returned with punch and was sitting with Karen, Will, and young Lauren. Another perfect picture opportunity. Will often missed family events like this, blaming his busy doctor schedule. Lauren was enjoying her father's company.

"Say cheese!" Celia ordered, snapping off another shot. Lauren was grinning up at her daddy in the first one, so she took a second when the girl faced her. "Perfect. Thank you!"

"You're welcome, Aunt Cee-Cee!" Lauren giggled, snuggling into her dad.

The dear girl had called her "Cee-Cee" since she first learned to talk. Celia was so happy the kids came to her party. George's grandchildren were precious, even more so with the knowledge that she could send them all home with their exhausted parents when the party was over.

"There's Mom and Dad now," Karen said, pointing over Celia's shoulder.

Celia made her way over to Frank and Virginia, delighted to see them again. She thanked them for going to the trouble of closing early to stop by. They chatted for a few more minutes before a new round of guests arrived.

Lavonne appeared just as Celia was greeting Clyde Klaus, her old butcher, and pressed a dripping glass of ice water into her hand. "It's hotter than blazes, Celia, and I'm worried you're going to suffer heat stroke out here. At least have the good sense to get in the shade. And hello, Clyde! It's been a long time. I've been meaning to stop over and pick up some of those New York strips from you. I told George that you just can't beat the steaks from the Corner Market."

"You stop by anytime, missy," the old butcher replied, and Celia would have sworn he blushed at Lavonne's compliment. He'd likely give her a deal, too—something Celia cautioned him against doing too often. Clyde was another friend she'd referred to Karen, and while Karen handled most of his accounting tasks, Celia helped with ordering and placing advertisements once in a while, too. Like she'd told John Robins, business was like play to her.

"Karen's here, too, if you want to say hello to her," she said, encouraging Clyde to follow her to two empty chairs set in the shade cast by the garage.

"Oh, I'll leave her be. No one wants to think about work at a birthday party."

"I *always* think about work," she said. Even to her own ears it sounded odd, but she didn't much care.

He nodded. "That's where you and I are alike, Celia. Not much for me to do outside of work. Ever since my brother died, I got no one to fish with anymore."

She sighed and took a drink of her water. The ice cubes had already melted.

Clyde's situation was like her own. He hadn't made the effort to find a new fishing buddy. She had the time to spend at Whispering Pines now, but it no longer held as much appeal. Too many ghosts.

"Do you ever think about retiring, Clyde? Aren't you almost seventy?"

"Yep, turned seventy back in April. But what would I retire *to*?"

Jess appeared, carrying a silver tray of clear plastic glasses full of punch. Celia waved her over and insisted Clyde take one. She didn't have a good answer to his question. The two old friends sat quietly, watching the other guests mill about, the sound of shrieking kids floating over to them from the sprinklers.

"All right. Tell me your best fish story, then."

Clyde downed the last dregs of his punch and dropped the plastic glass out of the way on the grass. He crossed his arms over his barrel chest and stretched his legs out in front of him. He allowed himself a beat to collect his thoughts, and then launched into a tall tale about a dark and stormy night when he and his brother fought to land a monster sturgeon while fishing up at Leech Lake near Walker back in the sixties. Celia let him talk, encouraging him to describe the memories she suspected had grown to soaring heights over the years. As he spoke of his brother, dead for nearly ten years now, he looked happy.

"You miss it, don't you?" she said, finally interrupting.

"Fishing?"

She nodded. "And your brother."

Clyde pulled his feet in and leaned forward in his chair. "I haven't thought about that night and that damn fish for years. Maybe I should call Stick. See if I can't get the old trawler running again."

"Stick? Is that a person?"

He glanced over at her and snorted. "He was a friend of my brother's. Mine, too, I suppose. He stops in for ground chuck once a week. Keeps hinting about fishing reports he's hearing. But ever since Buck passed, we've never taken the boat out again. Maybe it's about time."

Celia sipped her punch. "If you won't retire, maybe you could close the store one day a week. Maybe it's rich coming from me, but life's too short to work all the time. Go fishing on Wednesdays, and see if you can't hunt down another trophy sturgeon. And then come tell me the story."

Clyde grimaced. "I can't close the store on a Wednesday."

"Why not? People can adjust their schedules. Your customers know you work too hard keeping that place going by yourself."

He chewed his lip, considering.

Celia checked around the backyard to make sure everyone appeared to be enjoying themselves. Stuart must have gone back inside. Lauren had scampered off somewhere and Karen and Will were visiting. Frank and Virginia hadn't stayed long—and now that she thought about it, she hadn't noticed any exchanges between Virginia and Helen. Their stubbornness frustrated her to no end. No mother and daughter should have such a cold relationship, but neither seemed to try. At least Helen had developed a bond with Karen.

Clyde slapped his knees, huffing as he bent over to pick up his empty punch glass. "I best be on my way. Think I might go home and tinker on the boat."

Celia stood as well, worried she may have neglected her other guests too long. Clapping Clyde on the shoulder, she made him promise to save some walleye for her if he decided to go out fishing again. They also planned for Celia to stop in the butcher shop later the following week so they could come up with a promotion for the upcoming Labor Day weekend.

Her stomach gurgled, and she had to grab the back of her folding chair when a soft wave of dizziness stole over her. She should get a plate of food, perhaps cool off inside for a few minutes. Swooning out in this heat would ruin her party. Plus, she'd never hear the end of it from her family.

As Clyde took his leave, she headed inside with her water glass, waving to Jess and Renee. They were in a heated discussion about something while Jim looked on. Celia wondered if Jess was giving her big sister more career advice. It was such a shame Renee didn't enjoy her work.

The handle on the back screen door stuck. She wiggled it, but the lock must have caught. She'd had trouble with it before, and with so many people passing in and out, the faulty mechanism must have finally broke. Just as she was about to turn and yell to Jim for some help, the inner door opened. Jiggling the handle, she shrugged to the man standing inside.

Nodding his understanding, Jack Poole fiddled with it on the inside, then held the screen door open a few inches after it released, careful not to knock Celia back.

"Once again, saved by my lawyer!" she laughed, opening the screen farther and stepping inside. "I'm so glad you made it, Jack. And on a perfect Saturday afternoon for a golf game!"

"What is it with people? Why does everyone think all lawyers do is golf?"

She laughed, setting her empty glass on the counter, and caught Ruby's son in a quick hug. "Seriously, thank you for stopping by. I know you work every bit as hard as you golf. And your mother mentioned you are knee-deep in a complicated tax case. I appreciate you taking the time for me."

Jack rolled his eyes. "Mother needs to learn not to talk about the cases I mention to her."

Grinning, Celia picked her glass back up and filled it from the faucet. Though not as cold as when Lavonne had included ice, the cool water was easier to drink, and Celia felt rejuvenated. "It's a scorcher today."

"Speaking of Mother, where is she?" Jack asked. "I let myself in the front. There are quite a few people milling around, but I didn't see her."

"She's out back, talking with Eleanor and Helen."

"How is she?"

Celia understood the look of concern in his eyes. She was worried about Ruby's peace of mind, too. "It helps when she keeps busy."

Jack relaxed against the closed back door with a sigh. "It was hard on her, losing Dad. But since losing Sharon and Ron, too, I worry that it's all too much. At least the other driver will do some hard time. No one with that many convictions for impaired driving should ever see the light of day again. Throw away the key, I say."

Setting her empty glass in the sink, Celia considered Jack's words. Maybe it was time she did something more impactful to try to pull Ruby out of her funk. "Do you think I could get her to agree to travel somewhere? You know, a short trip? She's always wanted to go to Nashville. Maybe getting her out of the house would help?"

He shrugged. "I doubt she'd agree to it, but you could ask her. Truth be told, I worry she won't be able to move beyond this."

"I should ask how *you* are doing, too, Jack. Yes, your mother has lost a lot. But so have you. Sharon was your only sister."

Jack nodded, rolling his shoulders, and his eyes settled on something high in the kitchen's corner. "I'll be fine. It's an awful tragedy. I'm trying to spend more time with my nephew, but the kid's only twenty-three. He's lost both his parents. Seth's not interested in a round of golf or dinner at the club with his old bachelor uncle."

The door behind Jack bumped open, and he stepped out of the way. It was Jess, leading a muddy Lauren inside by the hand.

"I doubt that mud will come out of her pretty party dress," Celia said in dismay.

"It's okay, Aunt Cee-Cee. It was pretty while it lasted," Lauren declared as her mother pulled her past them, presumably on the way to the bathroom to get cleaned up.

Jack and Celia watched the mother and child cross the kitchen and disappear out of view.

"Try not to worry about Seth too much," Celia counseled. "Kids are resilient. He'll find his way through his grief. In his own time."

"That sounds like a voice of experience," Jack said, shutting the door again to keep the heat out. "Say, Celia, you still haven't stopped by to update your estate planning. I thought you were going to do that a few months ago."

She leveled a stare at him. "Jack Poole, why are you here right now? Why are all these people running in and out of my house?"

Her question seemed to confuse him. "Hmm. Because it's your birthday?"

"Right. It's my birthday, and turning eighty is enough of a hit for one day. I don't need my lawyer reminding me I'm going to kick the bucket soon. Can't we talk about that whole nasty business another day?"

He had the grace to laugh. "I'm sorry. Bringing it up today was in poor taste."

"That it was," she agreed. "Now, I came in here to fetch one of those delightful cupcakes and try a few other treats. Would you like to join me, or do you want to go out and check on your mother?"

Jack recognized the dismissal, promising he'd get something to eat after he stopped outside to greet his mom. As he was leaving out the back, Val popped into the kitchen, her purse over her shoulder. "Oh good, there you are, Auntie! I wanted to say goodbye. I'm headed out."

Celia glanced at the ticking clock above the kitchen sink. It was nearly five. She supposed others would leave soon as well. "Thank you for all your help with the party, Val. Where are you off to now?"

Val grinned. "I have a date."

"And who's the lucky boy today?" Celia teased. Val seemed to go through men even faster than she changed jobs.

"His name is Luke. I'll bring him by sometime to meet you. He's nice."

To meet her? *That* was new. Maybe this boy was different. "That sounds lovely. Go have fun, honey."

Celia finally made it to the dining table and filled her plate from the delicious selection. A few guests sat in the living room, watching the end of the Twins game. Celia sank into the empty recliner with her plate, groaning with relief as her bottom came into contact with the cool, soft leather.

"Having fun?" George asked from his corner of the sofa. An empty plate rested on the coffee table in front of him and young Drew—who smelled much better now—slept alongside him, curled in a ball with his thumb in his mouth. Ethan was snoring softly from the other corner of the couch.

"I am," she assured her brother. "I appear to have more stamina than my nephew there. Ironic, don't you think?"

George chuckled. "Celia, you've always had twice the stamina as the rest of us. Has everyone gone home that was outside?"

She pulled the wrapper off the yellow cupcake she'd selected, hoping it was lemon-flavored. "No. So I need to eat quick and get back out there."

George twitched as the crack of a bat emanated from the television. "Damn. That's the third out. Not sure the Twins are going to pull this one off."

The two turned their attention to the last inning of the close game, giving Celia time to enjoy her birthday treats and cool down. When a Twins player smacked a home run out of the park, George's silent cheering was comical to watch. He wouldn't risk waking a sleeping baby, even for a victory by his beloved team.

Once the excitement of the win had passed he asked, "Are you getting some pictures with your camera?"

"I think so. Thanks again for the quick lesson. As long as I have the settings right, I think I'll have some fun ones to put in an album."

He laughed. "Have you ever counted the albums you have back in your office?"

"Not recently. Developing my film and getting the pictures into albums or frames quickly is a habit I picked up years ago. They'll give you something to remember me by when I'm gone."

He eased carefully away from Drew, doing his best not to disturb the two-year-old. Celia nodded her appreciation when he picked up the empty plates littering the coffee table, including her own.

"He won't sleep tonight if he takes too long of a nap," she pointed out.

George whipped his head comically between the toddler and Ethan, both on the couch. "Who? Drew? Or his father?" he teased. "That, dear sister, is not my problem. It's one of the many perks of being a grandfather. I get to have fun, play with them, and then send them home for their parents to deal with."

"I suppose that's true," she agreed. She'd given up on the opportunity to ever be a grandmother many years earlier, but she tried to think of George's brood as her own. She pushed out of her comfortable chair with a sigh. "I better see to my guests before they all think I deserted them. But I'll use the powder room first. Thank you for cleaning up, George."

"My pleasure, sis."

She stayed out of his way as he headed for the kitchen with a precarious pile of her good dishes. If he tripped and dropped them, she'd kill him.

As she made her way toward the back of her house; the cool air and quiet was a welcome respite, if only for a moment. She was lucky to find the bathroom empty. After using it, she paused at the door to her office before heading back outside. The large wall map drew her in. She'd amassed a decent assortment of pins in the many locations she'd visited since her decision to travel instead of spending her retirement working at Whispering Pines. While she missed her resort, she never regretted seeing the world—even if she'd had to wait until her seventies instead of doing it in her twenties and thirties with Danny.

A light rapping sound caught her attention. Initially she thought it was someone wanting to use the bathroom down the hall, but when she turned to look, she was surprised to see Will standing in the doorway to her office.

"Hi, Will. If you're looking for Jess and Lauren, I think they might have gone downstairs to check out the ping-pong contest the kids have going down there. Your daughter was a muddy mess," she said, smiling at the memory of the smudge of brown mud on Lauren's forehead.

"Actually, I was hoping to catch you for a minute."

Something about that simple statement raised a tiny warning bell in Celia's gut. Was this why he'd stuck around at a family event longer than he usually did?

"All right, then. What is it you wanted to talk to me about?"

Jess's husband meandered into her office, snapping his fingers while tapping his fist with an open palm. He seemed nervous, an emotion she'd seldom, if ever, seen him display.

That's when she knew. He wanted something.

Before he said another word, disappointment welled up inside of her. She'd become accustomed to people in the community approaching her to ask for funding or her time, as she'd made it a point to be generous with her hard-earned resources. But neither of her brothers or their families had ever come to her to ask for money. Granted, she'd done things without being asked, like footing the bill for George's kids' college education and some wedding costs, but she'd never done it because someone asked her to.

Was Will about to spoil that now?

He finally spoke, stilling his hands. "Did Jess mention the new house she loves, by the new school?"

Celia walked over to stand beside her desk. She felt like she needed something solid between her and Will. Her instincts had served her well through the years, and she wasn't going to ignore them now. "No, she hasn't mentioned anything."

Dropping his hands to his side, almost as if attempting to relax, he gave her his most charming smile. "Really? That surprises me. We stumbled across the For Sale sign by accident while taking the kids out for a Sunday drive. Jess wants to get the kids into the new school district."

She wasn't buying into the notion of Will taking a "Sunday drive" with his family. The whole *Leave it to Beaver* vibe he was going for didn't fit him at all. And she suspected she knew exactly where he was going with this.

"And?"

He had the grace to look away for a split second, as if what he was about to ask made him uncomfortable. Though, again, she wasn't buying the act.

"*And* . . . Jess really wants that house. I'd love to give it to her, but the down payment would be a stretch. I've crunched the numbers, and I'm having a little trouble getting comfortable with it. Then I had an idea. I know how much you like helping your family. I thought you might get a kick out of helping us out."

His faux-earnest expression and high-wattage smile were meant to entice. She supposed he expected her to smile back, to jump at the chance to spend her hard-earned money to help his family move out of a perfectly suitable house into a showier neighborhood. She didn't smile.

"No."

His face fell. "No?"

Celia shook her head. "No. You see, Will, I have a simple philosophy with money. Those of us that can, should work hard to earn it so we can take care of ourselves and those we are responsible for. If we're lucky to have some left over after that, we give it to those unfortunate souls who can't take care of themselves. You are a well-paid doctor, a young surgeon. You are more than equipped to provide for your family."

His crestfallen expression at her flat-out refusal to entertain the idea had quickly morphed into something else entirely. Color dotted his cheeks. "But I don't understand. You're a wealthy woman. We've never asked you for a dime. I thought you'd be happy to help."

"Does Jess know you are discussing this with me?"

He clasped his previously relaxed hands in tight fists. "Of course not. I wanted to surprise her."

Lavonne's voice floated down the hallway. "Celia?! Celia, are you back here?"

"Will, the most important thing I can give you right now isn't money. It's a piece of advice. Never live beyond your means. I promise you that if you take that to heart, you'll never have to grovel to anyone again, ever. Now if you'll excuse me, I have guests to see to."

"I wasn't *groveling*," he muttered as she brushed past him.

She maintained a steady pace as she exited her office, her back to Will. She hoped she appeared calm—collected, even. But inside, her emotions were roiling. Had she been too blunt with the young man? Had Jess's family outgrown their current home? She knew her niece worked hard as a wife, mother, and employee. Should she have considered Will's request instead of cutting him off so abruptly?

Torn though she was, she fixed a smile on her face and sought out Lavonne where she waited for her next to the dining table.

She would put the whole nasty business out of her mind. No one had given Celia any handouts. If Jess's husband wanted a new house, he'd have to figure out how to make it work on his own. *That* was the best lesson she could teach him.

Chapter Twenty-Seven

Gift of Answers

"I'd say your party was a huge success," Lavonne said, smiling as she picked up a silver tray. It held the remnants of a lavish meat and cheese tray Clyde Klaus had thoughtfully contributed to the eightieth birthday celebration. As she straightened, she narrowed her eyes at Celia. "Are you all right? You look a little green. I wish you would have listened to me earlier when I asked you to come inside and cool off."

Celia shook her head. "I'll be fine. The heat doesn't bother me. You know how I hate air-conditioning. Actually, Will cornered me in my office."

Lavonne set the tray back down and settled her fists on her hips. "What do you mean, he 'cornered' you?"

Most of the dining chairs stood against a far wall to allow easy access to the table and party fare, but one remained. Celia pulled it out to take a seat. She hoped Will wouldn't saunter back into the dining area and catch her in conversation with Lavonne. He'd suspect she was tattling. At least she *felt* like she was tattling. But she hadn't liked the way her stomach tumbled when she'd witnessed his frustration—his *fury*—over her denial of his request. After making sure no one else was within earshot, she gave Lavonne an abbreviated version of Will's request and her own response.

"I don't blame you one bit." Lavonne's smile was gone, her mouth now pinched. "How dare he come to you for money! Is this the first time he's done that? Jess would kill him if she knew. Wait—*does* Jess know?"

"Not according to Will. This was the first time he's ever come straight out and asked for money. But he's hinted in the past that a little help with his medical school bills would be more than welcome."

Lavonne shook her head in disgust. "Do you want me to talk to George about it?"

Celia shrugged. "I don't know what good that would do. I don't think Will is his favorite son-in-law. I wouldn't want to feed those flames."

The door from the basement burst open and a gaggle of kids flooded around the table.

"Grandma, we're hungry! Is all the food gone?"

"Julie, how can you be hungry? Every time I've seen you the last two hours, you've had food in your hand!"

Julie gave an impish smile. "I'm probably growing again."

Lavonne laughed. "Do you see anything here on the table that looks good? Everything is getting pretty picked over."

The front door opened and Jim entered with little Robbie on his hip. "Julie—*there* you are. I've been looking for you. Your brother needs to get home for his bath."

She skipped to her father. "I'm hungry! Grandma was just going to get us some food."

Jim dropped a firm hand on her shoulder. Celia couldn't tell if it was a gesture of affection or a way to settle the child down. Her fast chatter and the bounce in her step meant she'd had plenty of sugar. "All I see on that table are cupcakes and cookies, and I'd say you've had plenty of sweets already."

"There might be one last platter of those little sandwiches in the fridge, Jim," Lavonne said. "Should I run and check?"

Julie nodded emphatically, but Jim shifted his hand until it cupped her scalp. "Settle down, please."

The child ceased her incessant bouncing, but her foot started tapping instead. It was as if she had more energy than she knew what to do with.

Turning his attention back to his mother-in-law, he shook his head. "Renee needs to get home and start on laundry. She leaves on that work trip of hers early Monday morning. We should get going."

Julie wriggled out from under his palm. "But *Daddy*, I have to go to the bathroom!"

"Too me!" a previously quiet Robbie chimed in. The toddler fought Jim's hold.

"Has he started potty training already?" Celia asked, surprised. Robbie was barely two. She might not know much about raising kids, but she'd thought boys were usually slower to get potty trained.

"Hey, what about us? We're hungry, too," Nathan chimed in, and the smattering of cousins around him voiced their agreement.

George popped his head out of the kitchen doorway. "Are you guys bothering your grandmother and great-aunt? And did I hear some of you are hungry? Get in here, and I'll see what we can do about that."

George's announcement was met with hollers of approval, and the children moved almost as one unit in his direction. Julie tried to follow them, but Lavonne caught her by the arm.

"Not so fast, little missy. Grab your brother, and I'll take you both back to the bathroom. Then you'll listen to your father and find your manners. You'll thank Aunt Celia for the nice party and act like a gracious guest."

Julie, clearly disappointed over the way her ploy to stay longer had backfired, returned to her dad's side and stuck her little arms out for her brother. With a half grin, Jim handed the boy over, and his daughter struggled to hoist Robbie onto her hip. Biting her lip, Julie followed her grandmother down the hall to the bathroom, sparing an envious glance at the remaining cupcakes on the table.

Once they were alone, Jim thanked Celia for the fun afternoon.

"I should thank all of you," she replied. "You've all worked hard and taken care of all my other guests this afternoon. Are people leaving?"

The young man grabbed a spare chair and took a seat beside her. "Most have left. Your lady friends are still out at the table, in the shade. I'm not sure what they're discussing, but it looked rather animated. One couple left, saying they had another party they needed to attend but that they'd be back to pick Helen up in an hour."

Celia crossed her legs and settled more comfortably in her chair. She welcomed a few minutes to visit with Jim. "That would have been Karen and her husband, then. She is Helen's granddaughter, and they are unusually close." Jim nodded, distracted, and Celia added, "You know, Renee didn't sound excited about her work travels earlier."

He ran a hand through his short black hair. "She's not. I wish she enjoyed her job more. It's hard to be away, you know—especially now with the two kids."

"I wish she liked her job, too. When I was her age, I loved what I did. And when I wasn't working, I'd escape out to Whispering Pines to recharge."

Jim rested his elbows on his knees, hands clasped between them. "Whispering Pines," he repeated. "Why does that sound familiar?"

"I'm sure Renee mentioned it a time or two. She used to love going there as a young girl. Believe it or not, she used to tell me the resort was her favorite place in the, and I quote, 'whole wide world.' "

He chuckled. "Man, I'd love for her to have time to get away somewhere. To relax. But it seems like she ends up using all her vacation time with the kids. Robbie has chronic earaches, and when he spikes a fever, the babysitter gets nervous. It's harder for me to get away, so Renee usually handles it."

Celia gave her mind the freedom to travel back to the weeks when Renee and the rest of her family would come out to Whispering Pines in the summer. She used to cry every time they had to head home. Renee might have loved the resort as much as Celia did if she'd had the chance to go there as an adult.

"Whatever happened to the resort?"

Jim's question pulled her back. "To Whispering Pines?"

He nodded, curiosity etched on his face.

"Believe it or not, I still own it. Though I haven't been out there for quite a few years now."

"You're kidding! How did I not know this?"

She laughed. "I don't know. It's not like it's a secret or anything. George and Lavonne used to bring the kids out, but then they got busy, as teenagers do, and their visits eventually stopped altogether. I'd intended to spend time out there once I retired, but I'd always had a dream to travel, so I ended up leaving the upkeep of the resort in the capable hands of a couple I hired as caretakers years ago. They sent that pretty flower bouquet for my birthday."

"The yellow roses?"

Celia could feel a blush of heat rise to her cheeks. "No, not that one. The other one."

Jim gave her a strange look, clearly curious at her reaction. She steered the conversation back to his wife. "Do you think Renee has any desire to change careers? She's much too young to be unhappy at work."

Footsteps approached.

Jim rose to his feet. "To be honest, Celia, I'm not sure what would make her happy. I think she feels stuck right now."

"Daddy! Robbie went pee on the bathroom floor!"

Lavonne hurried behind her granddaughter. "Julie, where are your manners? You don't talk about things like that at a birthday party! Celia doesn't want to hear about that."

Julie's bottom lip quivered.

Celia took pity on the young girl and pulled her in for a quick hug. The child smelled like a combination of sweat and lavender. "Did you help yourself to a little spritz of my perfume when you were in my bathroom?" she asked when Julie pulled back. She was careful to smile into the little girl's eyes so she knew she wasn't mad.

"Maybe . . ." Julie whispered, obviously not wanting Lavonne or her father to know she'd used her great-aunt's perfume without permission.

"That's all right," Celia whispered back. "You smell pretty."

The quiver disappeared, and Celia would have sworn Julie stood up straighter. She turned to her father as he took Robbie from Lavonne. "Come on, Daddy. Mommy has work to do. We should go home so she can give us our baths and read us our bedtime stories." She turned to Celia and said, "She likes to do that whenever she has to go on trips without us."

Celia smiled at that. She braced herself with one hand on the table and stood, the long day catching up with her. "I should probably get this cleaned up."

But Lavonne wouldn't hear of it. "You'll do no such thing. Go say goodbye to your guests, and if Helen, Eleanor, and Ruby aren't ready to leave yet, go join them in the shade and catch up with your friends. I'll see to the rest of this and shoo everyone else out. You've entertained all of us long enough."

Celia didn't have to be told twice. Thankful for the reprieve, she gave Lavonne a quick hug then headed back to her friends in her backyard with a plastic pitcher of ice water and a stack of Styrofoam cups.

As she made her way toward their table, the spark of an idea hit.

What to do with Whispering Pines was like a burr in her side, causing her to delay making any formal arrangements. But maybe she'd finally stumbled on the solution. She'd make that appointment with Jack to update her affairs.

After all, she wasn't getting any younger.

As Jim had warned, her three friends were locked in an animated discussion. Celia hated to intrude, so she quietly poured them each a cup of water and sat down. They barely glanced her way.

"I'm just not sure how I feel about the whole topic," Ruby was saying. "It feels a bit like playing God."

"I disagree," Helen shot back.

Eleanor picked up her fresh cup of water, nodded her appreciation to Celia, and faced Ruby. "Did you ever have trouble conceiving? Or carrying your children to term?"

Ruby crossed her arms over her chest. "My two were five years apart."

"Did you lose any babies in between Jack and Sharon?"

Looking uncomfortable, she downed her water in a few large gulps. "No."

Eleanor lowered her voice. "Well, I suffered through three miscarriages after I had our two daughters. I told none of you that. It was too painful to talk about. We wanted more children, but it wasn't meant to be. We had our two princesses, and we had our family. But I shudder to think of how I would have felt if we'd had no children. Back then, couples didn't have the options they do now."

Finally, unable to resist any longer, Celia cleared her throat. "I'm sorry to interrupt, but I'm not following."

Helen pulled a tissue out of her purse. She blotted at her face and eyes. Celia couldn't be sure if she was sweating or crying. Her eyes looked glassy. "One of them mentioned that Karen looked wiped-out today, and when I mentioned that's because of the fertility treatments she's going through, it sent us into this *lively* debate about the *ethics* behind it all."

There was an edge to Helen's voice that told Celia the "debate" was more likely an argument. She glanced between her three friends, regretting her intrusion. She was not at all sure she wanted to be part of a conversation around such a charged topic. "I didn't realize Karen and her husband were having troubles conceiving. I'm sorry."

Helen tucked the tissue back into her purse. "They are, and it's been extremely difficult. I wish people would have more empathy for situations like theirs."

Ruby returned Helen's pointed stare without cowering. "It's not like *you're* known for your empathy, Helen. You shouldn't sit in judgment of my opinion. Besides, you can't really relate either. You have more children than any of us. Four beautiful daughters. And you expect us to believe you can relate to Karen's situation?"

A car door slammed out front.

"That would be my ride," Helen declared, still visibly upset about the conversation Celia only caught the tail end of. "You should never assume you know the trials other people have been through. I'll have you know my second pregnancy was especially difficult, and I had problems after that. Warren and I found our own way to pull together the family we wanted, and I'd hope if you all knew the details of that you wouldn't sit in judgment the way Ruby is of Karen right now."

Ruby's shoulders sagged. She stood and rushed around the table to Helen's side. "Please accept my apologies," she said, reaching for her friend's hand. "Sometimes I'm a silly old woman who doesn't know when to keep her trap shut."

Celia held her breath. Ruby's apology sounded sincere, but Helen could be incredibly stubborn. After a beat, Helen took Ruby's hand and gave her a small smile. It wasn't much, but it was better than a complete snub.

She dropped Ruby's hand and faced Celia. "This was a lovely party. Thank you. You clearly put lots of work into it and had a nice turnout. I'm sorry it had to end on a sour note like this. I'd planned to suggest we make a regular habit of getting together more often, now that we all find ourselves single and living within twenty miles of each other for the first time since college."

Celia loved the idea. "We *should* do that! Why don't we start next week? Thursday night, perhaps?"

Karen rounded the corner of the house. "Grandmother, are you ready to go?"

"Yes, yes, I'm coming!" Helen hollered back as she hurried in her granddaughter's direction. "You don't need to come all the way back here and walk me out to the car like I'm an invalid."

The three remaining friends watched Helen leave.

"Oh, dear," Ruby said, breaking the silence. She slid into Helen's empty chair. "I really set her off this time, didn't I? I wonder if I'll ever find my way out of this funk . . . I think I'll take myself home now, too. Helen was right, Celia. This was a wonderful party. You always make these milestone birthdays feel like a true celebration."

Celia had never thought about the parties she threw in that light. But Ruby was right. Every birthday, not only the big ones, was a blessing. "I figure that as long as we're still kicking, we should celebrate."

"Isn't that the truth," Eleanor agreed. "No one else in my immediate family has lived to see eighty yet. How did we get so lucky? Thank you, Celia, for reminding us we aren't done living yet. I do like Helen's idea of a weekly dinner. Harry liked to go out to eat often, but I've gotten out of the habit."

Ruby stood. "Celia, would you mind picking us up? I always feel fancy when I ride in your car."

Laughing, Celia agreed. "You realize my Cadillac is over ten years old, don't you? I'm not sure I'd consider that anything special."

"Let me keep my little fantasies, would you?" Ruby dropped a kiss on first Celia's cheek and then Eleanor's. "I can help you finish cleaning up, if you like."

"That isn't necessary. Lavonne sent me out here with the promise that they'd clean up inside and then head home. George and Jim were kind enough to put away all the tables and chairs out here except these. I don't believe there is anything left to do. Thank you for coming, Ruby."

Ruby folded her chair and tucked it under her arm. "I'll set this in the garage on my way out. I parked in the alley."

Eleanor and Celia followed her lead with the chairs. Eleanor offered to take her flower arrangements in the house while Celia stowed the last table away, adding, "Be careful with your back. I'll meet you inside."

Celia didn't need the reminder. Her aging body had taught her to be careful a decade earlier. During a flight to Florida with Danny, she'd hoisted her own suitcase into the overhead bin. He'd offered his help, and she'd said no, and then spent weeks heading to the chiropractor for relief. It was the last time she'd ignored such an offer.

By the time she returned to the kitchen, Eleanor had two cups of iced tea set out on the kitchen table. Celia groaned as she sank into a chair. It creaked under her weight. The old set had graced the corner of this kitchen for as long as she could remember. It might be time for an upgrade. She accepted the drink and sighed.

"That looks delicious. What a day."

"Such a delightful party," Eleanor agreed, but Celia could see her friend's mind was elsewhere.

"I'm glad you didn't rush off right away. It's been too long since the two of us caught up. How are your daughters and their families? Do you have any trips planned with them this fall?"

The question brought Eleanor more fully back to their conversation. She shared that she did indeed have a trip to New York City planned with her grandchildren. Her excitement over the upcoming travels made Celia envious.

"I need to convince Ruby it would be good for her to take another trip. I think it would help her mood. God knows it would help mine. I'm feeling restless these days."

Eleanor nodded, understanding Celia's need to keep busy. The thread of conversation trailed off after that, and the two sat in silence for a moment. The quiet felt deeper after the house full of party guests.

Finally, Eleanor said, "Celia, something has been weighing on my mind for the last couple of weeks, and I wanted to visit with you about it in private."

Celia smiled. "So that's why you stayed."

Eleanor nodded but didn't immediately respond. Instead, she stood and paced to the back door, peering out the small square window as if gathering her thoughts. When she did speak, her words sent a jolt through Celia's system.

"I sold the Whitby Company."

"Really?" She chose her words carefully. "I suppose that makes sense." But the implications had her head spinning. Would the sale of her old company impact her retirement income? Was that what Eleanor wanted to talk to her about?

As if her friend could read her mind, she turned back to Celia and strode as quickly across the kitchen as her orthopedic shoes would allow. She patted Celia's shoulder before sitting down again. "Don't worry, dear. We kept everyone's pensions funded."

Celia stammered, saying, "I wasn't really worried."

"Of course you were worried. You've never been one to take your financial situation for granted."

She conceded Eleanor's point with a shrug. "True. With that piece of the business out of the way, why don't you tell me about the new buyer. Will they keep the name? Will they keep the local office in town here open?"

Eleanor nodded. "There won't be any drastic changes, at least initially. But the real reason I bring it up is because the company we hired to get everything in order brought a few old boxes over to my house last week. With Tripp gone, his wife remarried, and Iris in a nursing home, they didn't know what else to do with them. The records were more family-related than business, so they were hesitant to toss them. I'm glad they didn't. One box contained some of Father's old papers."

"Preston's? Oh, my. How I miss that man." Celia smiled at the thought of her old mentor and dear friend. Her life would have looked completely different if not for him.

"I do, too. I'm not sure how life would have looked for me if not for Father," Eleanor agreed, practically echoing Celia's own thoughts. "Going through the boxes was like an unexpected, much-welcome surprise visit from him. There was even a notebook containing his early plans for Whispering Pines, back in the late thirties when he first purchased the property."

Celia gasped at the notion. "I'd love to see that someday."

Nodding, Eleanor promised she'd give it to her to read. "I knew you'd get a kick out of seeing that. He pulled off most of the things he'd dreamed of, too. At least related to the resort. The only one that never came to be was bringing Mother back there."

Celia nodded. She knew it couldn't have been easy for her friend. She'd never be able to fully appreciate how Eleanor had felt when her own mother abandoned her as a teenage girl. Eleanor's mother had never returned to the states after she'd run off to England with her youngest daughter. She'd died over there. It was her anticipated death when she fell ill that had prompted Preston to put Celia in charge of Whispering Pines all those years ago.

"I'm sorry, Eleanor."

Her friend waved a hand, as if to say all of that was pain that subsided long ago. "Even *that* isn't what I need to talk to you about. I've been debating telling you. Honestly, I wasn't even sure when I came here today whether I'd mention it if the chance arose."

"Heavens, Eleanor, spit it out! The suspense is killing me."

"I'm sorry. I'm not trying to be dramatic. There was an old manilla folder in the mix. It had your name on it. Curious, I read it." Eleanor avoided her eyes, as if guilty for invading Celia's privacy. "Part of me wishes I would have left it well enough alone."

A wave of unease passed through Celia at the ominous words. But now that Eleanor had cracked open that particular door, she had to know what was on the other side. "What was in the folder, Eleanor?"

Taking a deep, fortifying breath, Eleanor met and held her wary gaze. "It was a single legal document. It was quite lengthy, and I admittedly skimmed parts of it, but it was clearly to support the adoption of a baby girl. Dated September 1956."

Panic sluiced through Celia's veins. Surely the document would have named the baby's adoptive parents.

Eleanor took in her alarmed expression. "I feel like I've opened Pandora's Box."

Celia took a beat to consider the ramifications of knowing who Preston gave her baby daughter to so long ago. Maybe it was time to learn the truth. First Danny and now Eleanor had come to her with important information about her child. She needed to open herself to the truth. "Out with it. Please. At this stage, I want to know what was in the document. I won't do anything with the information, though. Danny located our daughter years ago, but I chose not to reach out to her."

Eleanor's eyes skirted away from Celia's, and she played with the impressive diamond she still wore on her ring finger despite her widowhood. "This piece of the puzzle might make that approach impossible."

"Whatever does that mean?"

Eleanor chewed on her lower lip. "It listed the adoptive parents."

Celia closed her eyes, nodding impatiently. "I figured that. You might as well tell me. I can't imagine it makes any difference one way or the other at this stage."

"Actually, it might make a difference. A big one."

Those words settled around them. Celia held her breath. If Eleanor didn't tell her what she'd discovered soon, she might pass out.

"The names on the document," Eleanor said, "were Warren and Helen Arbuckle."

Celia blinked. She couldn't have heard that right. Eleanor continued to twirl her wedding ring. The sound of water plopping in the kitchen sink echoed around the silent room. The floor above them, as floors do from time to time in an old house, gave an errant creak. The sound pulled Celia's eyes upward.

Finally, she whispered, "How is that even possible?"

Eleanor shrugged.

"Helen . . . adopted . . . *my* baby? But she had four girls of her own."

Her friend gave her space to absorb the news.

Celia felt as if she were in quicksand. None of this made any sense.

Then things clicked.

Virginia . . .

When, as a young woman, Virginia found herself widowed and the mother to a newborn, Celia jumped at the chance to offer her a home. She had often wondered if the fact that Helen's youngest daughter was similar in age to the daughter Celia herself had given up was one reason she'd felt compelled to help Virginia.

"But Virginia's birthday is in November," Celia uttered.

From the look on Eleanor's face, she'd already reached the same conclusion Celia was now coming to. "They could have changed it," she pointed out. "If they knew who they were adopting from, then sharing the same birthday as your baby would have been a sure giveaway."

A tear plopped onto Celia's hand. She hadn't even realized she was crying.

"I couldn't believe it either," Eleanor went on. "If it were true, how could Helen keep a secret like that for so long?" Before Celia could answer, Eleanor provided her own counterpoint. "But she did get upset today when Ruby questioned whether Karen's infertility treatments were a good idea."

If Virginia is my daughter, Celia thought, *that means Karen is actually my biological granddaughter.*

The edges of her vision were turning gray. She needed to get ahold of her emotions or her heart would give out on her. Like Maggie's had. And Beverly's. As it was, Celia's heart was breaking. Or maybe it was actually coming back together. That fifty-year-old crack, finally repairing itself.

"It's possible that Helen doesn't even know," Eleanor offered. But from the sound of her voice, even she wasn't convinced.

Celia shook her head. "Don't be ridiculous. Helen would know perfectly well whether she gave birth to Virginia."

A tiny smile played at the corner of Eleanor's mouth over her friend's outrage. "Of course she'd know if Virginia was adopted. But *she* didn't sign the document. She was listed, but only Warren's signature was on there. Well, and Preston's. You must have signed something giving Preston the authority to handle the adoption."

Celia nodded. The details from that time were so murky. Clouded by the pain she'd experienced over having to give up her baby all on her own, without input or comfort from Danny. She looked at Eleanor. "Do you think it's possible Helen doesn't know Virginia is the baby I gave up so long ago?"

It was Eleanor's turn to nod. "I think it's entirely feasible. Think about all the trouble she had with Virginia when the girl was a teenager. She struggled so with the girl. If she'd have known you were her birth mother, she might have dropped her on your doorstep and washed her hands of her."

What had actually happened bore an uncanny resemblance to what Eleanor suggested. When Celia pointed that out, Eleanor shook her head.

"But none of that was at Helen's suggestion, was it? It's true that Helen finally took a stance with Virginia—one I never really agreed with, by the way. When she cut her off, you stepped in and helped the girl, but Helen never instigated it. Am I right?"

Celia thought back to that wintry day in the cemetery when Virginia buried her estranged husband. Eleanor was right. "But surely *Warren* knew," Celia said. "He was my friend. If this is all true, how could he never tell me?"

Eleanor crossed her arms on the tabletop. "I don't know. Maybe raising your daughter for you, and sparing you the pain of knowing, was the most selfless thing he could have done for a friend. Or maybe he did it as a favor to my father. I remember Helen saying they always wanted a big family. That stuck with me, because it wasn't something I'd have expected her to say. Remember how self-centered she always was? But she softened with Warren. They seemed happy."

This was all too much to take in at once. Celia needed time to think. Time to herself.

Eleanor, once again, must have reached the same conclusion. She stood and took Celia's half-empty glass of tea, the ice cubes long melted, over to the sink. "I should be going. It's been an endless day for you, and I know this bombshell has to be incredibly unnerving. Even *I* needed time to digest it, and I'm not directly involved. Or I can stay, if you'd prefer someone be here with you. I can give you all the space you need, but maybe you shouldn't be alone right now."

Celia considered this. But she was used to her solitude. She'd never been afraid to be alone.

"No. You go. I'll call you tomorrow. I need some time. And don't worry, I'll be fine."

She could feel Eleanor's eyes on her, trying to ascertain her state of mind. But she didn't want to meet that gaze at the moment. She felt too fragile, as if everything might shatter at any moment.

"Do you plan to confront Helen about this?"

Celia could only shrug. She didn't know what she'd do with the information Eleanor had stumbled upon by chance. If Helen truly didn't know who Virginia's biological mother was, the news might destroy her. Despite the tenuous bond between Helen and Virginia, her old friend's relationship with Karen, Virginia's daughter, was a whole different story.

Celia got to her feet, smoothed the colorful sheath she'd donned for her party over her churning middle, and finally met Eleanor's eye again. "I'm not sure. I need time."

Eleanor hugged her and then let herself out the front door.

When quiet again descended, and Celia found herself completely alone for the first time all day, the full implication of what Eleanor had shared hit her again. As if in a trance, she trudged to her recliner near the front window. Her friend had set Danny's bouquet of yellow roses on the side table next to her chair. She plucked a velvet petal from one of the sunny blossoms and rubbed it against her cheek as she sank into the recliner. Instead of putting up the footrest, she rocked softly, as one would rock a baby.

Unbidden, her sister's face swam before her eyes.

"Were you listening to all that, Beverly? All this time, I wondered what became of my daughter. Who would have guessed she was right here, within my bubble, all this time?"

She waited for a creaking reply from the old house, a sign she often attributed to the spirit of her long-gone sister. But this time there were no sounds other than the whispers of a lifetime of memories. Exhausted, Celia allowed her eyes to drift shut to dreams tinged with an extra glow.

Chapter Twenty-Eight
GIFT OF A BIRD'S NEST

Winter 2005

"WHAT A DELIGHTFUL CHANGE of pace," Eleanor said, unwrapping an elegant cashmere scarf from her neck and handing it to the young man behind the desk at the country club. The years had leached most of her color away, but her cheeks held a hint of pink and her eyes sparkled in a shade that matched her emerald wrap. "I enjoy our weekly dinners, but it'll be too cold to venture out tonight. Besides, it's easy right now to get a reservation during the middle of the day. Everyone is either still home recovering from the holidays, or back at work kicking off the new year."

Celia dropped her car keys in her purse and shrugged out of her own jacket, also handing it to the coat check. "A benefit of being a retiree."

Eleanor laughed. "Or the widow of a wealthy businessman. I can't claim to be a retiree."

"You worked hard, too, back in the day," Celia reminded her.

A woman walked by, capturing Eleanor's attention. Celia didn't recognize her, and so she stepped away to allow the two some privacy while she waited for Ruby and Helen to return from the ladies' room.

Thursday evening dinners had become a regular occurrence ever since Helen suggested it two years earlier at Celia's eightieth birthday party. Celia appreciated the weekly contact with her girlfriends. She spent plenty of time with Ruby, between their Monday afternoon bridge club and local historical society meetings, but she might have lost touch with Helen and Eleanor if not for their dinners.

Following that fated conversation after the party, Eleanor had passed the adoption papers on to Celia, but she'd never broached the subject again. Celia appreciated the discretion. She'd decided to keep this particular revelation a secret. Revealing it would hurt too many people, including dear Virginia. Virginia struggled in her relationship with Helen, but she'd been close to her father. Celia couldn't steal that pearl from her. No one else needed to ever know the whole story. And since Warren was gone now, as was Preston, it was likely to remain that way. If Danny knew the names of their daughter's adoptive parents, she had to trust he'd keep the knowledge to himself as he'd always done. There was nothing to be gained from sharing the news.

Unfortunately, despite ongoing treatments, Karen still hadn't gotten pregnant. Helen mentioned that she'd suggested adoption to Karen and her husband, but apparently she'd refused to consider it. Perhaps she would at some point, if the pain of infertility continued.

Life was funny sometimes. Helen's granddaughter, also secretly Celia's, struggled to start a family, while Ruby's grandson, Seth, found himself in the unenviable position of expecting a child with a woman he'd barely even dated.

It surprised and delighted Celia that Ruby was being so supportive of him. Celia had also gotten to know Seth better over the past six months, as he'd started offering Ruby and her rides to historical society meetings. At first he'd just dropped them off, but eventually he'd joined them in the meetings, too. He seemed to have inherited his grandmother's love of protecting old buildings.

Ruby and Helen returned from the bathroom.

"Thank you for dropping us at the door," Ruby said. "You know how my arthritis acts up when it gets this cold."

Celia waved this away. "It was no problem. The ice in the lot was treacherous, too."

Once the foursome settled at their table and placed their orders, Eleanor held up one hand, something important she wanted to share. The red polish on her fingernails accentuated her skin, still porcelain-white but now lined with blue veins and liver spots.

Between her friend's elegant ivory pantsuit and the winter-white landscape beyond the large windows lining the dining room, Celia felt garish and out of place. She'd never enjoyed eating at the country club. Feeling unusually self-conscious, she fluffed the back of her auburn hair, matted from the high collar of her winter jacket. Perhaps she should tone down the bright rinse she still used on her hair. But resistance welled up inside of her at the idea of going gray. She was eighty-two years old. She could wear her hair any damn way she pleased.

"I don't know about the three of you," Eleanor said, pulling Celia back to her surroundings, "but I've decided I've had enough of these brutal Minnesota winters."

"Winter can certainly be long," Celia agreed.

Ruby leaned forward. "And don't forget, Celia, we have that trip to Florida next month. We may want to extend it a few weeks if this extreme cold sticks around."

Celia smiled at this idea. "You know, I have to get someone over to the house with a tractor. I'm running out of room for the snow piles along the alley."

"I don't mind the cold," Helen said. "And I have a service that takes care of my snow."

Eleanor gave a slight shake of her head. "I don't understand why you two still want to keep those large homes of yours."

"I agree," Ruby said. "I'm so thankful Edward insisted we downsize a few years back. With him gone now, I'd never have been able to keep our old place."

"But what did you mean when you said you've had enough, Eleanor?" Celia asked.

Eleanor placed both her hands, palms down, on the white linen tablecloth and met the eyes of each of her lunch companions in turn. "I've decided. When I visited my eldest daughter and her family in South Carolina over Christmas, I fell in love with the area. She's been pestering me for a while to move closer. I resisted the idea, as I didn't want to become too reliant on her. But her girls are both out of the house now, and they have a large empty wing in back. It really would be perfect. So . . . I'm *moving*."

Their salad delivery coincided with Eleanor's announcement. Celia was happy for Eleanor, but she would dearly miss her friend. She admitted as much when their waiter moved on to another table.

"I'll certainly miss you, too. *All* of you. Which is why I have an idea. There is a quaint cottage in her backyard. They use it for guests, and I've already asked if it's free next winter. It is! You must come for a visit. Stay for a month—more, even, if you like."

Helen snorted. "Eleanor, who's to say any of us will still be able to travel by then? That's a year away."

Celia hated it when Helen cast her negative cloud over a discussion. "Speak for yourself, Helen. As long as I'm still breathing, I plan to travel. In fact, we booked a cruise for next September."

"And I admire you for it," Eleanor chimed in. "But I have to admit, I'm not as keen to travel without Harry. Do you do any traveling with Danny Bell these days, Celia?"

Celia sighed. "It's been years. He traveled so often with his work that now he'd rather stay home. He has a grandson, and he doesn't like to miss any of the boy's sports. Truth be told, we seldom talk anymore."

The *real* heart of it was that, ever since she'd learned the truth about their daughter, she was reluctant to see Danny again. She knew if they spent any amount of time together, she'd feel the need to discuss the situation with him.

Helen, unaware of the thoughts racing through Celia's head, spoke. "I don't understand why you and Ruby love to travel so much, Celia. What if something happens when you're away from home?"

Ruby shrugged. "Would that be so terrible? Both Celia and I waited our whole lives to do this. Besides, what are you so afraid of, Helen? You're so ornery, you'll probably outlive all of us." She kept her tone light, but there was a noticeable tension between the two friends.

"Would your daughter mind having guests?" Celia asked, bringing the discussion back on point.

"Not at all," Eleanor assured them. "The cottage has a kitchen and its own carport. Not that you'd want to drive. The traffic is terrible."

Ruby pulled a pocket-size calendar out of her purse and flipped toward the back. "When were you thinking? Remember, I'm going to be a great-grandmother soon, and I won't want to miss Christmas with Seth's new baby."

Eleanor grinned. "You'll love spoiling that child. I was thinking perhaps the month of November, or even part of December. We could have Thanksgiving together on the coast."

Helen shook her head. "Ladies, I'm afraid I'm going to have to decline. It all sounds like far too much of a commitment for me. But you three go ahead and make your plans."

Celia experienced a flush of guilt over the relief she felt at Helen's announcement. Helen wasn't exactly an ideal travel companion.

Ruby finally found a pen in her purse. "I'm ready to pencil it in to my calendar if you are, Celia. I think a month out East would be fun."

Celia always spent Thanksgiving with her brothers and family. But George's grandkids were growing, and the house was getting crowded. Surely they wouldn't miss her for one holiday. "Let's do it."

Eleanor clapped her hands, reminding Celia of a long-ago memory when they'd all been young women, arriving at Whispering Pines for their first summer visit. That had been Eleanor's place, too. It was like they were bookending their adult lives with their travels to stay with Eleanor.

The scream of a siren racing by on the road below echoed through the frozen air beyond the club's windows, red and blue lights glancing off the snow-covered grounds.

"Oh dear, I hate seeing that," Ruby said, a haunted look coming into her eyes. "It always means someone is suffering."

Celia shivered, despite the stuffy air in the dining room. Ruby was right. This acted as a reminder that they needed to keep on living life as long as possible—even if they had to move at a slower pace these days.

Using the key Clyde had given her years earlier, when she first started helping him in his store, Celia shivered at the chiming of the bell above the door. It still welcomed her, but Clyde did not. She struggled to take in everything that had transpired over the past two days. Ruby's comment when they'd spied the racing ambulance during their luncheon had been closer to home than any of them could have known. That siren blared all the way to Clyde's butcher shop.

But help was too late.

He was already gone.

Clyde went in early that morning, as he always did, to slice up the luncheon meats for the day's customers. He'd finally taken on some part-time help, but he didn't trust them around his slicer. When his employee came in around noon to relieve him so the old butcher could go ice fishing, he'd found Clyde unresponsive.

Celia hated the idea of him on the floor like that, all alone.

After she'd dropped her friends at home following their lunch, Celia had swung by the large grocery store closer to her house to pick up a few things. When she finally got home, the light on her answering machine was blinking red, hard to miss in the afternoon dusk.

Clyde had listed her as his emergency contact. Perhaps that was the saddest note of all. They'd known each other for years, and while she'd helped him with some tasks his brother used to take care of when Clyde struggled to keep up with it all, Celia had never felt particularly close to the man. They were friends, yes, but people deserve to have at least one close confidant in their life. Clyde apparently didn't have that anymore, with his only brother dead.

She should have tried harder. He was a private man, and she'd respected that. But in the end, he'd died alone.

She might have failed Clyde in life, but she wouldn't fail him in death. He had no remaining family. Just a few years ago, at her insistence, he had agreed to have simple estate plans drawn up through Jack, Celia's lawyer. When she got the news of Clyde's death, Jack was the first person she called to find out what she could and couldn't do as far as his store and any personal property went. It wasn't as if she could put it off. There was a cooler full of perishable meat to contend with.

Per Clyde's wishes, she'd called the local shelters. Representatives of all three were meeting her here at the butcher shop this morning.

As she pushed the door open, the familiar jingle of the bell above the door greeted them. Ruby was close on her heels, rubbing her hands together in the frigid morning air.

"Can we turn some lights on?"

"Ruby, it's not that cold in here. Why are you shaking?"

"I think the cold has permanently soaked into my bones. Eleanor might be on to something."

With a sigh, Celia checked the time as she set her handbag on the heavy old counter—the same counter where Clyde had transacted business with shoppers in this neighborhood for fifty years. It was the end of an era.

Ruby dropped her coat on top of Celia's. "Where did they find him?"

"Right there, according to the police officer I spoke with." Celia pointed to the roomy area behind the counter. "I hope it was immediate. I hate the idea of him lying there all alone."

Ruby shivered. "I hope his ghost isn't still around. It smells funny in here."

Celia lifted the end of the counter to gain access to the back portion of Clyde's shop. "It's bound to smell off. They've been selling raw meat out of here for decades. But Clyde and his brother worked hard to keep it spotless. And don't joke about ghosts hanging around."

Ruby crossed her arms, rubbing herself as if to warm up. "I'm sorry. I shouldn't have said that. I know you've always had an inkling that Beverly's spirit somehow stayed in your house after she died there."

"What can I say? I live alone. I need someone to talk to. But don't let my family hear you say that. They'll stick me away in a home somewhere."

"Your secret is safe with me," Ruby said. "All right, I suppose we should get to work. What do we need to do?"

Celia nodded and stepped through a swinging door into the very back of the store. Ruby followed.

"We'll need to use these boxes on the floor here to gather up any of his paperwork. Karen is going to help me get the final financial statements pulled together and tax returns filed. Thank God I have her to help with that."

"Karen? As in, *Helen's* Karen?"

Celia nodded. "I helped Clyde with his basic bookkeeping, but I don't know tax laws, so I referred him to Karen."

"She must keep busy," Ruby said. "Okay. I can take the boxes to her. Is there any cash or checks here that we have to worry about?"

Celia walked over to the north wall and removed a decade-old paper calendar from the wall. Behind it was a small safe, embedded in the wall. "There might be a little cash in the register out front. I'll check. But he kept most of it in here. I wanted him to go to the bank every day, but he didn't want to be bothered. We'll gather it all up now and you and I can take it down and have it deposited into his business account when we're done today."

Ruby opened a drawer in Clyde's old metal desk. "What will happen to all of it? Did he leave everything to you?"

"No, thank heavens. I would have felt awkward about that. When I talked to Jack yesterday, he said Clyde wanted a small sum to go to me when they settle the estate, but I already told Jack I want that donated, too. They'll sell this building and his home down on Fourth. Jack is supposed to split the net proceeds between a few charities Clyde specified. He had a soft spot in his heart for the animal shelter, too."

Ruby stopped cleaning out the drawer and faced Celia. "Tell me that poor man didn't have a dog or other pet we need to find a home for."

"Oh, God, no. To keep it simple, Jack agreed we should donate all the food right away. People from a couple different shelters will be here shortly."

Ruby wandered over to a rickety bookshelf in the corner, piled with miscellaneous papers and odd junk. A framed picture of two men sat on the top shelf. She picked it up. "He used to run this place with this guy, didn't he? He looks familiar."

"He did," Celia said. "That was his older brother. After he died, Clyde had trouble keeping up with things here. That's how I got involved, actually."

Ruby set the picture back down, shaking her head. "You are kind of like an animal shelter yourself, you know that? Picking up strays along the way. But instead of puppies or kittens, you pick up businesses."

Celia smiled. "I'd hate to be bored."

The bell above the door jangled. Celia excused herself to get started with dispensing the food. The two women and three men who came were all thankful for the donations. It pained Celia to hear that they were all facing shortages of various staples, now that the holidays were over.

"People are always more generous around the holidays," one of the men shared, "but come New Year's, many forget there are people in need all year long. This will help." They all nodded emphatically.

When there was only one small section of dry goods left to be boxed up and sent off to the shelters, one of the women approached Celia. "Say, do you know if you'll be selling that old chalkboard out there? We could use something like that at the entry of our building."

Celia almost told her to take it, but paused. She remembered how meticulously Clyde would update that board, neatly printing out the list of fresh meats he was offering. Something about the memory made her say, "I'm sorry. That actually isn't available."

The woman shrugged. "No problem. I just thought I'd ask."

Within the hour, the volunteers were all gone, along with the food. Celia tucked the cash in her purse, ready to head to the bank—and it was only three thirty in the afternoon. They'd accomplished more than she could have hoped. Two of the shelter people were even kind enough to transfer the boxes of paperwork to Celia's car before they left.

"Are you ready to go, then?" Ruby asked, pulling on her coat.

She'd been a trooper, helping Celia all day without complaint. Celia decided she'd treat her to an early dinner when they finished at the bank.

"Not quite," she said.

She ducked into the back of the store again, quickly returning with Clyde's tall step stool.

Ruby frowned. "I don't think you should get up on that thing."

"You're probably right, but there's something I need to do. Jack is meeting two people here tomorrow, a realtor and a man who buys and sells used equipment like the coolers and meat slicers. I'm not sure if I'll be back. I want to take two things. Clyde wouldn't mind."

She opened the ladder below the old chalkboard, much as she'd watched Clyde do many times. Ruby grunted her disapproval.

"All right, miss smarty-pants. If you want to help, get over here and hold the stool."

Reluctantly, Ruby did as Celia asked. Celia prayed the chalkboard wouldn't be too heavy for her to handle.

She should have prayed harder.

The board was hung with a thick wire, which explained why it was often slightly crooked. She could lift it high enough for the wire to slip off its large nail, but the weight of it was too much. The chalkboard slipped from her hands, caught on part of the stool, and thundered to the ground with a crash. Ruby gasped in alarm.

"Son of a bitch," Celia muttered. "I hope I didn't just ruin it."

She climbed down, careful not to suffer the same fate as the chalkboard. She eased off the last step and Ruby pulled the stool out of the way. Celia squatted down to examine the board.

"I suppose the damage could have been worse."

Ruby dragged the stool farther out of the way so she could stand beside Celia. "Is it broken?"

"One corner is dinged, and some of the paint chipped." Celia struggled to stand and accepted Ruby's hand to steady herself.

"What do you plan to do with that old thing? What's"—Ruby peered at the words scrawled across the top—"*The Bird's Nest*?"

"I asked Clyde the same thing once. He told me that's what his mother used to call the treehouse he and his brother played in when they were young. They painted it on here as a tribute to her." As she spoke, Celia ran one finger over the neatly painted letters.

"Ahh," Ruby cooed. "That's sweet. But where will you put it? It's almost as tall as you, and it must be three feet wide. I don't think we can carry this out to your car."

Celia sighed. "Now that it's down, I'm afraid I have to agree with you. But I still want it. Maybe I'll get it out to Whispering Pines someday. There are plenty of bird nests around the resort. I'll phone Jack and ask him to drop it off at my house for now. Maybe put it in the attic. It's special. I can't explain why."

Ruby brushed her hands together. "Fine. Stick it up in *your* attic and let *your* family deal with it when *you're* dead."

"Careful, Ruby, you're starting to sound like Helen."

She shuddered. "Don't joke about that. Did you want anything else?"

"Oh, right. The bell."

Celia could feel Ruby's eyes on her as she retrieved the ladder and set it up inside the main door.

"Careful that someone doesn't come walking in and knock you off that thing."

"Good point," Celia agreed. She flicked the lock.

Taking the bell down from above the door was much easier than the chalkboard. She stuffed it into the pocket of her work jeans and climbed down.

"What in heaven's name are you going to do with that?"

"Ruby, do you have a nostalgic bone in your body?" Celia shot back.

"You know I do, but a bell?"

Celia folded up the ladder and set it against the nearest wall. She was too tired to put it back where she got it. She pulled her mussed sweatshirt back into place and donned her coat. "I loved the way it sounded every time someone came in. Like a musical little 'hello' from above. I thought I'd give it to Frank and Virginia. I think the bell needs a new home above the door in their bookstore."

Ruby shook her head. "You are either daft or brilliant. Who thinks of those kinds of things?"

Celia buttoned her jacket as best she could. It was snug over her layers. She'd have to stop home and change first if they were going somewhere decent for dinner. "There are things in life that are just worth passing on to the next generation, Ruby. I would think you of all people would understand that, what with your mission to save every old building in this town."

She unlocked the door and held it open so Ruby could step outside. A cold wind wound its way through the open door. Celia turned around and faced the empty store that had still served customers only last week.

"Take care, Clyde," she whispered, shutting off the light and closing the door on yet another chapter in her life.

Chapter Twenty-Nine
GIFT OF TAKING THE FALL

SOME CHAPTERS IN LIFE aren't so easy to close, Celia thought.

Staring at the unexpected letter from the IRS, she said aloud, "I don't have time for this right now. I'm leaving in two days."

For the first time in years, she planned to spend a week at Whispering Pines. The Dixons kept suggesting she come out. She supposed she owed them that. They'd been wonderful caretakers for her.

She needed to decide what she wanted to happen with the resort when she passed on. After her birthday, she'd met with Jack. They'd discussed her estate, and he'd given her suggestions. But then the Robinses needed a little extra help with the cleaning company, and then a summer storm caused damage to her house. Life got busy, and she missed her follow-up appointment.

She hated loose ends. She knew better, too. What if she died suddenly, like Clyde Klaus? When arrangements aren't finalized, things can get messy.

This was her legacy. Why was she having so much trouble deciding on things? Her life was full of wonderful people and she wanted to leave them the fruits of all her hard work. The last thing she wanted was for there to be any fighting within her family. She'd never expect that out of them, but she'd learned over the years that money can distort people's morality.

She remembered Will's expression when she'd refused to help him purchase their house. There weren't only blood relatives involved now that her nieces and nephews were adults.

The streetlight in front of her house flipped on. She hadn't realized it was so late. She read the letter again, then folded it up and stuffed it back in the envelope, frustrated that she'd gotten behind with her mail. The postmark on the letter was a week old. If she would have opened it sooner, she might have had this taken care of already. Now she'd be lucky to still leave for the lake on Saturday.

It was too late to call Karen. But since she was the tax preparer, maybe the IRS had copied her on the letter, too. With luck, she would have good news.

An owl hooted outside the window, and the eerie sound made Celia shiver. She switched off the air-conditioner, checked her front door, and headed up to bed. Hopefully she'd still be able to head to Whispering Pines as planned. Whatever the problem was with the final tax returns for the Corner Market, it might have to wait until she got back.

A light drizzle fell on Friday morning. Celia woke to sheets twisted around her legs and a throbbing head after a restless night. She'd have suspected she didn't sleep a wink if it weren't for the nightmares still floating around the edges of her consciousness: a dock, battered by vicious waves, and the exposed underbelly of a capsized fishing boat, visible only when lightning flashed. But then, lightning flashed again, and suddenly there was no boat. Screams echoed behind her, and when she looked back, a young Ruby was running toward her, concern etched into her features. The sun glinted off her friend's blond hair, the storm gone as can only happen in dreams.

Extricating her legs from the damp sheets, Celia eased her feet to the floor and felt around for her slippers. She fumbled for her glasses, wishing again for the perfect vision she'd enjoyed during her first sixty years. Her hand nudged her water glass, and water splashed onto her journal.

She wiped the leather-bound notebook on the bed, thinking she should be sure to take it along to Whispering Pines. Journaling each evening before bed was a habit she'd started on her first trip abroad with Ruby. She enjoyed capturing the wonders they were seeing so she could look back on them when she was home. The habit stuck, even when she wasn't traveling.

She tossed the journal into her open suitcase after finding her eyeglasses. She needed to take something for this blasted headache. Coffee might help.

Heading downstairs, she listened to the *tap-tap-tap* on the roof. Rain was falling harder now. She needed to run to the post office and ask them to hold her mail. She'd do the same with her newspaper—all mundane tasks, easily accomplished when she felt like herself. Today, the errands sounded overwhelming.

She started the coffee, but as the aroma wafted through the kitchen, the smell caused her stomach to churn. She dropped a single slice of bread in the toaster. Food might help. She'd neglected to eat dinner the night before.

Her thick morning newspaper wouldn't easily fit through the mail slot, but her conscientious young paperboy wouldn't have wanted to leave it out in the wet weather. She tugged at the wedged paper, but it barely budged, and she lost her balance.

Stumbling, she grabbed for anything close. Down went the plant stand with the fern she'd been nursing along for the better part of four years. Her fingers grabbed hold of the long drapes. Fabric tore above, but the drapes held enough to slow her momentum.

She leaned against the wall, her free hand over her heart while her other one still clung tightly to her life line. Her beloved fern lay splayed out across the hardwood floor, its earthenware pot split in two.

"I'm lucky I didn't split my *head* in two," she muttered, willing her stiff fingers to let go of the velvet fabric.

The mess on the floor would have to wait. She doubted she'd be able to salvage the fern either way. She hadn't hit her head, but it felt like it.

Easing her way back to the kitchen, she stopped to turn the air-conditioner on. Despite the rain outside, the air felt thick with humidity. She struggled to catch her breath.

Her toast was up, burned but cold, making it even less appetizing. She slathered it with butter and jam to try to make it edible. She set the toast and a small glass of water on the kitchen table, dug a bottle of aspirin out of the cupboard next to the sink.

She must be coming down with something.

Once she got the food and painkiller down, she made her way back out to the couch, careful not to tread through the dirt of the ruined plant.

As she eased herself down, hopeful she'd feel better after a quick nap, something niggled at her. There was something important she needed to take care of, but she couldn't remember what it was.

With a sigh, she adjusted a throw pillow under her head, kicked off the blasted slippers that had done little to keep her on her feet, and closed her eyes. Her plans would have to wait.

Celia woke to the splash of a car driving by on the street. She opened her eyes but didn't move another muscle, waiting to see if her head still throbbed. There was a dull ache, but the shooting pain had subsided. Her mouth felt like it was full of cotton and her stomach rumbled.

A glance at the clock revealed it was almost noon. She'd slept longer than she'd thought. Which was probably good, given how little she'd slept the night before.

She got to her feet, stepping gingerly on shaky knees. She ignored her slippers and her toes felt the grit from her spilled plant. No little fairies had slipped in and cleaned up her mess while she slept.

Her eyes fell on the table where she'd dropped the letter from the IRS the night before. That's what she'd forgotten. She needed to call Karen.

Celia tried to ignore the tiny bits of gravel and dirt as she crossed to the kitchen and her phone. She'd clean up the plant after she sorted out this IRS business.

Karen picked up on the fourth ring.

"Hello, Karen. It's Celia Middleton calling. Did I catch you at a bad time?"

The crinkling sound of paper came over the line. "Hi, Celia. I can only talk for a minute. I'm on my way to a client meeting. But I've been meaning to call you."

"About the letter? The one from the IRS regarding some problem with the final tax filings for the Corner Market?"

"Yes. You obviously received a copy, too?" Karen's voice faded out a bit at the end of her question, as if she was switching ears.

"I did. I just opened it last night. I wanted to stop in and visit with you so we can sort this out right away."

The younger woman cleared her throat. "I really don't want you to worry. I'll handle it. I'm sure it's just a simple misunderstanding."

Celia hoped she was right. There'd been a lengthy IRS audit of the Whitby Company a few years before she retired. It turned out all right, but Tripp's creative accounting practices made for some tense conversations with the auditor in charge. She wouldn't take any chances with this letter.

"That may be, but I want to sit down with you and have a look."

Karen's sigh sounded irritated. "I don't think that's necessary, but if you insist, why don't you stop in tomorrow. Late morning. There's no way I can squeeze you in today."

Celia paused at Karen's tone. Should she back off? Tomorrow was when she'd hoped to leave for Whispering Pines. If she didn't feel better, she might not be up for either the trip or a meeting. But she'd learned that the quicker you address a problem, the better.

"If tomorrow is our only option, I'll be at your office at eleven. Thank you, Karen."

She hung up before she could change her mind.

The aspirin she took held out for another two hours. She cleaned the mess she'd made of her favorite fern, attempted to repot it, and then drove to both the post office and the newspaper.

The sky remained overcast, but the rain stopped. Both the temperature and humidity were in a race to see which could reach the highest peak by midday, and Celia's whole body ached.

By the time she got back home, it was all she could do to climb the stairs to her bedroom. She stared down at her half-filled suitcase, but the idea of traipsing all the way to the basement to retrieve her clean clothes from the laundry held zero appeal. Instead, she lay down on her bed, fully clothed, and sighed in relief when she closed her eyes.

When she woke up, she felt feverish, but the aspirin was down in the kitchen. She got up and headed back downstairs again.

She might need to wait until Sunday to go to Whispering Pines. She could always stay an extra day. She nibbled on saltines and sipped ginger ale. The medicine kicked in again, and she tried to watch two silly sitcoms on television, wondering why she found no humor in the shows. Others certainly enjoyed them. Such silliness.

She listened to the nightly news, then switched everything off and headed back up to her bedroom. The naps throughout the day made it impossible for her to fall back asleep immediately, so she made another entry in her journal. She had little to report after spending much of the day on her back, but she didn't mention how sick she felt. If she ever looked back through her stack of journals, she certainly didn't need to read complaints.

At eleven sharp the next morning, Celia wrapped her knuckles on the locked door of the accounting firm where Karen worked. She felt better, but weak, and she hated it. She might be old, but she didn't like feeling like a little old lady.

She waited, hopeful Karen heard her knock. Since it was Saturday, the nearly empty parking lot behind her wasn't unusual. She recognized Karen's car.

Much to Celia's surprise, Helen appeared at the door to let her in.

"What in heaven's name are you doing here, Helen? Are you taking Karen out for lunch or going shopping with her this afternoon?"

Helen pulled on the door once Celia entered, testing the lock behind them. She offered a quick greeting, but no explanation for her presence. She turned quickly and led the way back to Karen's office. Celia had visited the younger woman before. She wouldn't have needed a guide. Something was off.

The door to Karen's office was closed. Helen reached around Celia and pushed the door open.

Celia took one look at Karen and knew her intuition hadn't failed her. Even when Karen worked on the weekend, she normally dressed like a professional. She'd inherited her fashion sense from her grandmother. Or at least that's how Celia thought of her. This was a whole different Karen, slumped behind a littered desk in her shoebox-size office. Mascara streaked down her face. She looked like she'd slept in her clothes.

Maybe she'd caught the same bug as Celia.

The tight quarters were stuffy, and Celia swore she caught a whiff of stale alcohol.

Helen closed the office door and took hold of Celia's arm, walking her the few steps to one of the two chairs facing Karen. Celia fought the urge to pull away from her friend's grasp. She still felt unsteady on her feet after her mysterious flu bug the prior day, but Helen couldn't have known that. They hadn't visited, and she hadn't mentioned how she felt to Karen on the phone. It was just Helen being Helen, treating her friends like old ladies.

Celia glanced at Karen again, but the woman looked so miserable that she had to look away. She turned to Helen, taking the only other open chair, and noticed a flush on her cheeks.

Helen crossed her legs, folded her hands together, and leveled a look at her granddaughter that could have made a prizefighter cower. "You need to explain yourself, Karen."

Celia knew before Karen even opened her mouth that she wasn't going to like what the woman had to say.

When Karen spoke, Celia couldn't even understand her. The woman tried and failed again, only getting a few disjointed words out before dissolving into tears. Helen didn't let it go on for long. She raised a hand, and Karen clamped her mouth shut, raking a hand under first one eye and then the other.

"I'm afraid we have some troubling news for you, Celia," Helen said. The flush on her cheeks was intensifying, though her voice and tone stayed on an even keel.

"I gathered as much."

Helen frowned at the interruption. "As I was saying, I'm afraid my granddaughter has made a serious error in judgment. She found herself in a financial hole. As I've mentioned to you before, Karen and her husband have been undergoing complicated fertility treatments for a few years now."

Karen sat up straighter. "You *told* her that, Grandmother?"

"Be quiet," Helen hissed. "I gave you a chance to tell your side of the story and you failed. Now *hush*."

Celia recoiled, and she wasn't even on the receiving end of Helen's sharp tongue.

"Yes, I mentioned your struggles to Celia a while back. I told Ruby and Eleanor as well. It's nothing to be ashamed of."

From the look on Karen's face, she didn't agree.

"Can I continue, please?" Helen asked her, her words tight with sarcasm.

Karen only shrugged.

"There's no sense trying to sugarcoat this, Celia. Karen's medical bills got out of hand. Instead of coming to me like she should have, she made a few slightly, shall we say, *inappropriate* entries in the books while assisting you with closing out Mr. Klaus's financials for the Corner Market."

"You barely paid me anything for that work, Celia," Karen interjected, earning herself another piercing look from her grandmother.

Celia could see Helen was struggling to control her temper. She had to feel so ashamed, trying to explain, if not exactly *justify*, what was sounding suspiciously like embezzlement to Celia, even though neither woman had come right out and admitted as much.

Karen stole money from the accounts of the Corner Market.

"Karen, I'm not here to help you make Celia feel one ounce of responsibility for your error," Helen said. "I suggest you don't either. This is on you. Not her."

Karen burst into fresh tears, at which point Helen let out a huff and angled her body to face Celia, effectively removing the blubbering woman from their exchange. "I'll do everything in my power to help sort out this issue with the IRS in a way we can avoid bringing in the authorities. I'll take care of any financial implications. For example, any fines the IRS levies for underpayment of taxes."

It was Celia's turn to cut Helen off. "Excuse me, Helen. I need to understand something. Karen, did you steal from Clyde's accounts when you were helping me close everything out?"

Karen gave a slow nod, her breaths ragged as she fought more tears. "But, Celia, please understand! It was a perfect storm. All Clyde's money was heading for either charities or taxes. We'd just found out another round of *in vitro* failed—my body was out of whack with all the hormones they keep pumping into it—and collectors wouldn't stop calling. We were six months behind on my medical bills by then, and my husband was ashamed we'd fallen behind on our mortgage. His father owns the bank that holds our mortgage!"

A fresh wave of tears hit, rendering Karen speechless again. This was probably good, because Celia was having trouble summoning much sympathy for a woman who, at least from appearances, should have plenty of resources to support her lifestyle.

Finally, Karen garbled out one last attempt. "I'm so very sorry, Celia. I know it was wrong. I gave in at a moment of weakness."

Celia's head was pounding again. "Karen. I need you to be one hundred percent honest with me right now. Have you stolen from any other businesses in town? I've referred you to many of my friends and business acquaintances. I had the utmost faith in you. Both your mother and your grandmother are dear, dear friends of mine. How could you put me in this position?"

Helen reached over and touched her hand, but Celia snatched it away.

"Celia," Helen said, "my granddaughter's husband will run the largest bank in town within a few years. That bank is an integral part of this community. You must understand, it's imperative that Karen and her husband maintain a stellar reputation."

Celia would have rolled her eyes at the absurdity of the statement if the situation wasn't so dire. "With the IRS involved, Karen could get in a whole heap of trouble over this. You both understand that, don't you?"

"We do. We're not imbeciles, no matter how stupid Karen might have been in her moment of weakness." Helen took another deep breath, then continued. "Celia, you are my oldest friend. We've been through so much together. We've supported each other through thick and thin. We've even had to venture into some gray areas a time or two in the past to help each other out. Is this really so different?"

At these words, Celia felt her disappointment in Helen skyrocket. Was she really going to go there? Hinting at the lengths she and her husband had gone to when helping Celia save Whispering Pines from Tripp? They'd skirted the law, and had certainly abandoned their normally high ethics, to help save the resort. Now Helen clearly thought it was time for Celia to return the favor.

"You helped me *save* the resort. A place we both loved. Tripp still got paid. This isn't the same thing at all. Karen stole money. And now the IRS has flagged it. What a mess."

"I understand that, Celia. And, believe me, I don't take any of this lightly. But I have a plan. I think there's a way we can make this all go away."

Celia couldn't take any more. She stood, looping the strap of her handbag over her shoulder. "I've heard enough. I'm not interested in your plan until I know exactly what Karen did."

Helen snapped her mouth shut, eyes wide.

Celia turned her attention back to Karen. "Pull yourself together. I want you to assemble the documentation that shows me exactly what you did. Deliver it to me by no later than tomorrow morning. I will take tomorrow to go through everything. Then I will decide whether I'm willing to listen to whatever hairbrained idea the two of you have cooked up to make this go away, or if I need to pull in the authorities."

With that, she spun on her heel and took a step toward the door. When Helen got up, Celia dropped a hand on her shoulder and pushed her back into her chair.

"I know my way out. Remember, Karen. I want to see everything at my house tomorrow morning."

As she opened the door and started down the hallway, she overheard Karen's wobbly voice. "I wouldn't have wanted to mess with *her* back in the day."

And Helen's reply: "I assure you, my dear, you still don't want to mess with Celia."

Her brief smile over those last overheard comments had fallen away by the time Celia reached her Cadillac. The door creaked when she pulled it open, and she almost missed the seat when she collapsed into her car. Her eyes felt as if pins were piercing them from the inside. She started the engine, rolled down the windows, and turned the air on full blast. She let her head fall back against the seat as the stream of air turned from heated to icy.

Was she even fit to drive home?

I don't have much choice, she thought.

But she'd give herself a minute before putting the car in drive.

How much had Karen pilfered when Celia was busy taking care of the rest of Clyde's estate? Poor Clyde. He was probably rolling over in his grave about now. Celia had never considered herself to be a gullible person, but now . . .

Karen should pay for what she'd done. No one made a fool of Celia and got away with it.

But then an image of Celia's daughter floated up.

Would Virginia blame herself for this? Karen may have had high medical bills, but she also lived a lavish lifestyle. Helen shouldn't have spoiled Karen with designer clothes and anything else she ever asked for growing up. Celia knew Virginia worried about her mother's influence over her daughter. The shift had been gradual at first. Helen's frustration over Virginia's refusal to go to college resulted in little contact between grandmother and granddaughter until Karen reached school age. But her attitude toward the young girl began to thaw, and when Helen started attending the girl's school programs, a bond formed. By the time Karen reached her tumultuous teenage years, Virginia found it easier to let the girl spend time with Helen, which she begged to do, instead of sulking in her bedroom. She told Celia she worried that her mother was spoiling Karen with too much shopping. Karen was the only granddaughter in the family.

Raising Karen hadn't been easy for Virginia, especially given her continuing rift with Helen while the woman grew ever closer to Karen. Now Celia wanted to protect Virginia from the pain of finding out her only daughter was a thief.

Then another thought wiggled in. Karen was actually Celia's granddaughter. If she turned her in, the woman stood to lose everything. Could Celia live with herself if she allowed that to happen?

"Hey, lady, you okay in there?"

Celia snapped her head up to find two young girls on bicycles, peering through the window at her. They must have been riding by and noticed her in her car. She probably looked dead to them. One girl had long red curls, standing out in all directions despite the ponytails meant to tame them; the other had long blond hair, and it danced on the wind in time with the glittery streamers flowing from her purple handlebars.

The girls reminded her of much younger versions of herself and Helen.

"I'm sorry, girls. I'm fine. I'm fine. I didn't mean to frighten you. I'll be going now." She hoped her voice sounded reassuring.

The redhead gave her an unconvinced look, but they rode away, probably to get far away from the crazy old lady behind the wheel of a big silver Cadillac. As she put the car in gear and turned to look behind her, she noticed her suitcase in the backseat. The latch on her trunk never worked right anymore since she'd gotten rear-ended a year earlier.

"I guess I won't be making that trip to Whispering Pines after all," she said, disappointed.

Maybe she'd had her time at the old resort. Despite how much she'd disliked Tripp, Celia had never gotten comfortable with the extreme measures she went to when she wrestled Whispering Pines away from the man. Was deceit ever justified? While she'd promised Preston she would save Whispering Pines *no matter what*, time had taught her that some things can come at too high a cost.

Perhaps it was time for her to pay the price.

The next three days passed in a blur. Karen delivered the records as promised. Celia's blood pressure ratcheted up as she studied the five checks the woman wrote to herself for consulting fees. Karen included the expense on the Corner Market's tax returns (even *she* had to show balanced books); however, she never claimed the income on her end.

This is what the IRS flagged.

Even more concerning were filings claiming income earned for two employees, both known to Celia, who'd once worked for Clyde but no longer lived in the area. Both were army veterans suffering emotional and physical traumas. The amounts were small enough that, on their own, they wouldn't be enough to require individual tax filings. Karen had banked on not getting caught issuing phony W2s because they were small, and the transient men might fall outside the legal system.

Celia couldn't sleep. Her headaches continued to the point where she finally visited her doctor. After a thorough exam, her physician assured her a stubborn sinus infection, coupled with a urinary tract infection, was behind her ill health and foggy brain.

"No, you didn't have a stroke, and this isn't the beginning of dementia," he'd replied with a chuckle when she'd voiced her darkest concerns to him.

Perhaps if she'd felt more like herself, she may have handled the nasty situation with Karen differently. As it was, she agreed to the plan Helen suggested. The IRS was only questioning the disconnect between the Corner Market and Karen for the consulting fees. Celia would reach out to the agency, apologize profusely for her own oversight of providing Karen with a W9, and explain that because of the complicated financial lives of Karen and her husband, they never noticed her mistake on their end.

The IRS would probably accept Celia's excuse of carelessness and apology at face value, slap them with a fine Helen would take care of, and move on to things of greater significance. In their eyes, Celia was elderly, contrite, and offered a plausible explanation.

The dishonesty of it all appalled her. She worried Karen might have abused her position of trust with other businesses as well, but she had no way to prove it, and Karen insisted this was the only skeleton in her closet.

Celia prayed it was the truth. She'd stand by her decision to take the blame in this case, but she worried it would come back to haunt her someday. Maybe not within her lifetime, but if Karen lied and there were any other transgressions, trouble might follow the younger woman for years to come.

The IRS did accept her apology. Celia hated the sullying of her reputation—even if no one other than Helen and Karen knew the truth. They had even more to lose than Celia if the truth ever came out.

Life had taught her that it was always a good idea to do what you can to protect yourself when dealing with people, such as Karen, with lower personal standards. There wasn't much Celia could do, but she took the time to write a somewhat cryptic letter, assuring whomever might read it in the future that she'd done nothing wrong. It was difficult to articulate a message that might protect her reputation in the eyes of those who mattered most without pointing fingers, but she tried. She took the sealed envelope to her lawyer and made Jack promise to hold on to it. If anything happened after she died that cast a shadow on her reputation, he was to pass her letter on to a family member.

She'd never know if the subject would even come up again. And if it did, the letter may or may not help.

But she had to try.

Chapter Thirty
Gift of New Traditions

"I hate that you won't be with us for Thanksgiving," Lavonne said as she helped Celia retrieve three grocery bags of food out of her backseat. "This will be the first time we won't all celebrate together."

Celia went around to the other side of her car and removed the fern she'd repotted after she knocked it to the floor back in June. She'd nursed it along for months, but half of it still had an unhealthy droop to it. Maybe George or Lavonne would do better with it while she was away.

Lavonne set the paper bags on her kitchen table, then turned to take the leafy plant from Celia. "Is this the same beauty from your foyer? It looks a little worse for wear."

Celia removed a dead frond. "There was a minor incident. I bumped it over a while back."

Narrowing her eyes at her sister-in-law, Lavonne transferred the pot to her kitchen sink. "Don't blame me if I kill it off while you're gone."

"I won't," Celia assured her. "But I thought it stood a better chance of surviving over here than if I had the woman checking my house water it while I'm away. She forgot about my prayer plant last time, and it was dead as a doorknob when I got home. I'd kept that alive since Mother's funeral."

"Ugh. I was glad to see it go. Such a depressing reminder, right there in the corner of your living room."

Celia paused. She'd actually never thought of it that way before. "I guess you have a point."

"Thank you for this," Lavonne said, motioning to the food on the table. "Julie and Robbie have been here all week. I'd forgotten how much food kids eat at their ages."

Celia prided herself on keeping up with the ages of all eight of her brother's grandchildren. Renee's two were eight and five already. Ethan was up to three kids, Jess had Nathan and Lauren, and Val had just had a new baby boy with her husband, Luke. But something about what Lavonne said caught her attention.

"All week? Is Jim not feeling any better, then? Is that why Julie and Robbie are here? Aren't they missing school?"

Lavonne started transferring items from the bags to her fridge. "Yes, to all that," she said as she searched for a spot for a carton of milk. "They're finally getting a second opinion this week. I wish Jim would have gone in when he first started feeling so tired back in June. Did you know he waited until August to see someone?"

Celia glanced at her fern in the sink. When she'd felt so sick in June, she hadn't waited to go in. Men could be so stubborn.

"If he's doctoring now, surely they'll be able to help him feel better?"

Lavonne held up a finger and crossed the room. She listened intently for a second, then turned back to Celia. "The kids are upstairs in our room watching television. You know how George doesn't like to miss his *Jeopardy!* He's not about to give up his remote control, so I sent them upstairs. I'd prefer if they didn't hear us talking about their father, but I don't think they can hear us in here."

"Of course," Celia agreed, lowering her voice. "Are they upset about missing school?"

"No, not really. But their schedules are a mess now. Jim seems to get worse instead of better, and Renee was feeling overwhelmed between her job and going with Jim to his various appointments. It's stressful. She doesn't want to do anything that would put her job at risk, especially since their health insurance is through her. I offered to take the kids for a few days to make things a little easier. They're young. They can miss a little school."

Celia pulled a chair out and sat down. "Heavens. Do you think Jim's illness is serious? Maybe I should cancel my trip."

Lavonne gave a hard shake of her head. "Don't even consider that. Jim would kill me if he found out I made you worried enough to stay home. We all know how excited you've been to go visit Eleanor with Ruby. You'll have a splendid time. You ladies need to travel while you're still able."

"Excuse me? Are you implying I'm getting too old to travel?"

Leaning against the back of a chair, Lavonne smirked. "Celia, I'll turn sixty soon and there are days my knee hurts so bad I can hardly walk. You've got almost twenty-five years on me. I don't know how you do it."

Footsteps thundered down the wooden staircase in the front of the house. The kids' voices reached them before their feet brought them into the room. The racket reminded Celia of how Gerry and George used to pound down the stairs at home when they were young. Their mother hated the noise, but Celia loved the sound of family. It was a welcome sound now.

"Brace yourself," Lavonne warned before turning to catch the tornado of Renee's kids.

Robbie slid into the room first, holding a diary as high as possible. Julie was close on his heels.

"Grandma, make him give it back!"

Lavonne snatched the purple sparkly book out of the boy's hand. "Robbie, you know better than to take things that don't belong to you. Besides, I don't know what you think you're going to do with it. It's locked."

"And you couldn't read what I wrote in there anyhow!" Julie screeched.

"Yes, I could! I can *read*. And I know the key's right there around your neck! Grandma, tell Julie to quit treating me like a baby."

Lavonne handed the diary to Julie and ruffled the top of Robbie's hair. "Maybe if you didn't act like a naughty little brother, she wouldn't treat you like one."

Robbie slapped his grandmother's hand away and stomped out of the room. "I'm gonna go talk to Grandpa."

Julie gasped; Robbie's actions were out of line.

Lavonne only sighed, then finished putting Celia's extra groceries away.

"Grandma, he's not allowed to hit," Julie pointed out, her arms crossed and her toe tapping. At that moment, she reminded Celia of Renee when she was her age. Val used to drive Renee crazy when they came out to Whispering Pines for summer vacations.

"It wasn't exactly a hit," Lavonne countered. "Normally, I'd sit him down and give him a talking to, but I think he's acting out because he's worried about your dad."

"I don't know why. Daddy keeps telling me he'll be fine. You guys all worry too much. At least that's what he says." Julie turned and noticed Celia sitting at the table for the first time. "Oh. Hi, Auntie Cee. I didn't know you were here."

"Hello, Julie. How are you?"

Julie stood a little taller, as if wanting to impress her great-aunt after the scene her little brother made. "I'm fine. Robbie is the problem. You can probably relate. You had little brothers, too, right?"

Celia laughed. "I did. But I was a lot older, so we didn't fight as much as I suspect you and Robbie do."

"How much older?"

"I'm fifteen years older than your Uncle Gerry, and eighteen more than your grandfather."

Julie's eyes widened. She had the good sense not to voice the thoughts going through her mind, but Celia suspected it was somewhere along the lines of Celia being *really old*. Instead, the girl changed the subject. "Did you go to the grocery store, Grandma?"

"No, Celia brought this over."

"Why?"

"Because," Celia answered, "I'm going on a trip. In fact, I hope you won't mind, but I won't be joining you for Thanksgiving this year."

Julie considered this. "Does that mean we'll have to use regular dishes?"

Lavonne burst out laughing. "No, dear. I know we use Celia's china for holidays, but technically she gave me the set when her and your grandfather's mother died."

Celia missed this interaction with children. Julie was a delight.

"But you'll be home for Christmas, right? Because we always go to your house for Christmas. If we changed and came here, Santa wouldn't know where to find us."

Celia was happy to hear she still believed in Santa Claus. She held her arms out and Julie grinned as she walked shyly into the embrace.

"Don't you worry, dear. I'll be back for Christmas. We'll celebrate at my house, just like we always do. Deal?"

"Deal," the little girl agreed, stepping back.

Headlights flashed in the darkness in the back. A car had pulled in.

"I bet that's your mom," Lavonne said to Julie. "Go find your brother and wash up. We'll eat in ten minutes."

Julie started to leave the room, but stopped when she noticed the fern in the sink. "Grandma, you have a half-dead plant in the sink. How are we supposed to wash our hands?"

"Hey, don't make fun of my plant, little missy," Celia jumped in. "I'll have you know I brought that thing back from the brink of death. I brought it over so your grandmother could keep it alive for me while I'm gone."

Julie raised her eyebrows. "Good luck with that!"

She skipped out of the room just as the back door opened and Renee entered, a light dusting of snow on her navy knitted beanie.

"Oh, dear, it's snowing?"

Renee turned to Celia at the sound of her voice. "Hi, there! I didn't expect to see you today. But I'm glad you're here. Mom said you're leaving on another trip?"

"I am," Celia said, watching Renee closely as she pulled off her quilted jacket and hung it on the hook by the door. When her niece turned back to her, Celia searched her face for signs of stress or fatigue. "I had a few things in my fridge and cupboard that won't keep until I get back. And I wanted her to give my plant a little extra TLC after I almost killed it off this summer."

Renee hurried over and gave her a quick kiss on the cheek. Her lips were cold against Celia's skin, and she smelled like fresh air and winter.

"I'm glad to see you looking well, honey," Celia said, squeezing her hand before she walked over to greet her mother in similar fashion.

"It's amazing what a good concealer can do," Renee joked.

"Your mother said Jim still isn't feeling like his old self yet? Renee, if you think it's serious, I should stay home. I can always go to Hilton Head when he's feeling better."

Renee crossed her arms—much as her daughter had done minutes earlier. "I won't hear of it. I want you to promise me you'll go on your trip, as planned, and I don't want to see those pretty blue eyes and red hair of yours until the week before Christmas."

"I'm not sure . . ."

"Celia. Promise me. If all of you act like this is really serious, I might lose it."

Renee had a point. Celia grew up with a sister with a serious heart defect, and their way of coping with the uncertainty was to force normalcy, even when things were at their worst. Hopefully Jim's situation wasn't nearly that serious.

"Did you get him in for that second opinion this week like I told you to?" Lavonne asked, a steaming casserole in her hands.

"Yes, Mother, and we have another appointment with a specialist next week."

Celia had to bite her lip not to smile at the sass in Renee's voice.

"Good. Now set the table, please. Your children are getting hungry."

Standing, Celia crossed over to the back door and retrieved her own coat from another hook. "I'll be going, then. I don't want to hold up your dinner."

"But won't you join us, Celia?" Renee asked, opening a cupboard of plates and glasses. "Mom always makes plenty."

"Thank you, but I have to pick Ruby and Helen up. Even though Eleanor moved away, the three of us are trying to keep up our tradition of going out on Thursday evenings. And since we fly out on Saturday, we need to make some last-minute plans. Helen changed her mind and wants to come on the trip, too."

She pulled her gloves on, then realized she'd left her purse on the floor by the table. Renee followed her eyes, then retrieved the handbag for her. As she handed it to Celia, Renee caught her gaze.

"Remember, Celia. You promised you'd have fun and not worry about us back here. No matter what, I don't want to see you until the twentieth of December. But don't be late either. Christmas wouldn't be the same without you. Promise?"

Celia looped her purse strap over her shoulder. "You are a bossy woman, you know that? Fine. I promise. But please keep me apprised of Jim's situation. Don't keep me in the dark."

Renee opened the door for her. "We're hopeful the specialist will have some answers for us next week and we can get Jim back on the road to recovery. I know he'll be looking forward to your eggnog at Christmas. It's his favorite."

Celia stepped onto the back step and Renee flipped the light on for her. "I'll make a double batch this year. And we'll have a toast to a healthy New Year!"

Renee assured her she'd be looking forward to it.

Her niece closed the door behind her but left the light on. Celia took the stairs carefully, in case the light dusting of snow made the concrete slick. If she fell and broke a hip, she'd never make it to Hilton Head. Ever.

The clouds parted just as she reached her car, revealing a smattering of stars above. A streak of light shot across the black backdrop, so fast she almost missed it. Shooting stars always reminded her of nights spent on the end of her dock at Whispering Pines. She was sorry she'd been too ill, and too busy with Karen's nonsense, to make the trip out there in June. But the problems with Karen seemed to be resolved, Celia's own health issues had cleared with time, and she was going to enjoy this trip to stay in Eleanor's cottage.

No matter what.

Chapter Thirty-One
Gift of Candid Conversations

Summer 2006

"Say, Celia, how is your niece getting along? The poor thing," Ruby said.

They were waiting for their ride inside the library's vestibule. Their monthly historical society meeting had wrapped up fifteen minutes earlier. Ruby's grandson, Seth, was late picking them up and the librarian would have to lock up soon. Summer hours meant they closed at seven, and if they had to wait outside then they'd suffer in the heat.

Celia checked her watch, annoyed. She was tired, and she didn't want to talk about Renee's situation. It broke her heart. "About as well as can be expected, I suppose. It's all such a tragedy."

"It certainly is. Widowed at her age . . . and with two young ones! But I do hope you aren't still beating yourself up for not leaving South Carolina early to come home for the funeral."

"Oh, I would have come back—you can believe that—if not for that blasted ice storm. When I promised Renee that I wouldn't come back early for any reason, neither of us could have guessed Jim was terminally ill."

Ruby, checking the curb in front of the building again, shook her head. "You *are* still beating yourself up. Trust me. Stop. I talked briefly with Jim at your birthday party a few years back, and he seemed like such a kind young man. He wouldn't want you to be so hard on yourself. Is there anything you can do now to make Renee's day-to-day any easier? After my daughter and her husband died,

I had so much support immediately following the accident. But, as time went on, people got busy with their own lives. And I understand that. It's natural. I just think you might feel better if you could do something special for Renee now, when the permanence of the situation has likely taken hold for her by this point."

Ruby, like Celia, had suffered loss. Celia knew her friend meant well. She also made a valid point.

Her niece was trying hard to move on. Not only had Renee lost her husband to a dreadful disease that the doctors were too slow to diagnose, but she'd decided she needed to move her kids into a smaller home now that they had to live off one income instead of two. George and Lavonne were in Minneapolis right now to help Renee search for a new house. Celia worried about Renee living away from family. When she'd broached the subject with her recently, Renee insisted she needed to stay at her job. She made a decent income, and she couldn't take a chance on starting over now.

Ruby was right. Celia had missed the funeral, but maybe she could help Renee out financially. It might at least keep her in her home.

A horn blared outside. Ruby's grandson pulled to the curb and jumped out. His old pickup sported large tires, and he knew his elderly passengers could use a hand climbing in.

"Sorry I'm late, ladies," Seth apologized, his expression sheepish. "Our dishwasher didn't show tonight, so I needed to help get caught up. You can't run a bar without clean glasses!"

Ruby accepted her grandson's arm, but not his excuse. "Seth, you are overqualified to be working as a bartender. Did you call the number I gave you? Their ad in Sunday's paper looked promising."

Seth caught Celia's eye. She could read his silent cry for backup, but all she gave him was a shrug. She agreed with Ruby. He wasn't putting his architectural degree to good use.

He gave Ruby a boost into the front passenger seat. She slid over, and he gave Celia a hand next. "What did I miss in the meeting? Did you talk about the old theater downtown? I hated to miss tonight, but I couldn't help it. Kaylee had another ear infection, and instead of getting her in to see her pediatrician, Dawn took her in to the emergency room, and now I have to help her cover a hefty bill."

He slammed the truck door and jogged around to the driver's side. Once he'd backed up and turned on the street toward Celia's, he turned down the music blaring from his radio and gave another sheepish grin. "Sorry."

"Seth, you know you can come to me anytime you need money for Kaylee," Ruby said. "There's nothing in this world I'd rather spend my money on than my great-granddaughter."

"You've already helped too much," he replied, stopping at a red light.

Celia leaned forward to look over at him. "We're having a special meeting next Tuesday night to talk about the theater. The insurance report on the fire wasn't in yet, but they expect to get it tomorrow. They'll need that before they can decide how to proceed. It should be an interesting discussion. You should come if you can."

The light turned and Seth shifted the truck. The gear stick on the manual transmission forced Ruby to sit sideways, her legs up against Celia's. She grunted when the truck lumbered through a pothole, jarring her against the stick shift.

"Maybe we should discuss getting you a new truck," she muttered, to which Seth laughed.

Celia admired his unwillingness to take handouts from his grandmother. The young man's response was in stark contrast to the way Jess's husband kept coming to Celia with his hand out. She'd told him no when he approached her for help with a down payment on a new house at her birthday party, of course, but then he'd had the nerve to approach her more recently about possibly investing in a business idea he was excited about. He claimed his own funds weren't "liquid" enough, and thought she might want to get in.

His attitude infuriated her. Will was a highly paid surgeon. Ruby's grandson was a bartender, yet he seldom accepted financial help. Celia planned to finally ask George to talk to Will. It was getting ridiculous.

The drive to Celia's wasn't far, which was a good thing, given how uncomfortable Ruby was in the middle.

"Thank you, Seth. I appreciate the ride. Ruby, are we still on for lunch on Friday?" Celia asked once she was safely back on solid ground again thanks to another hand down from Seth.

"Yes. But why don't you come over? I tire of going out all the time."

Seth slammed the door and Ruby rolled down the window.

"What can I bring?"

She waved a hand at Celia through the window. "Just yourself. And maybe a notebook. I have something I want to discuss with you. Now, get inside. It's beastly hot out here!"

Seth's truck pulled away and Celia headed up her front walk. She always enjoyed a little mystery, and Ruby sounded like she had something up her sleeve.

Celia knocked on Ruby's front door two days later, balancing a brand-new notebook in one hand and a delightful angel food cake she'd purchased from the bakery down the street from Virginia's bookshop in the other. When Ruby didn't come to the door, Celia let herself in.

"Hello! Anybody home?"

She heard the faucet turn on in the kitchen off to her right. Sure enough, Ruby was in the kitchen with her back to the doorway. Celia had been telling her to look into hearing aids ever since their time together at Eleanor's the previous winter.

"Knock-knock," she said.

"Holy hell!" Ruby jumped, dropping something into the sink basin with a clang. "Don't scare me like that!"

"I knocked, and I yelled for you. If you won't get your hearing checked, at least lock your doors. Something smells scrumptious. What's for lunch? I brought dessert."

"Perfect, because I burned the cookies yesterday."

Celia snorted. "Let me guess. You didn't hear the timer."

"Ha-ha. Everyone thinks they're a comedian these days."

A fresh loaf of bread sat on the counter, along with a skillet of crisp bacon, two red-ripe tomatoes bigger than Celia's fist, and a dewy head of lettuce. "BLTs—perfect on a hot summer day."

Ruby pointed at the fridge. "Get out the lemonade and mayonnaise, please?"

Together the women finished building their sandwiches.

"Let's go out on the back porch. It's in shade this time of day and the fan I have set up keeps it quite pleasant."

A few minutes later, they settled in comfortable wicker chairs, plates of their light fare in their laps. Celia set her notebook on the floor by her feet.

"I hope Seth can make that special meeting next week," she said.

"You mean the one about the burned-out theater?" Ruby asked. "He'll make it work. He used to go to westerns there with his dad on Saturday afternoons when he was young. I think he'd love to help save the place, or at least salvage some of its contents."

Celia took a bite of a pickle, considering. "He might make use of that architectural degree yet."

Ruby set her plate aside, her sandwich untouched.

"Aren't you hungry?"

"Not especially. I worry about my grandson."

Celia thought Ruby's energy seemed low. She looked like she could use some cheering up. "You should be proud of Seth. Not every young man of twenty-six would be so accommodating of his grandmother and her old friend. When you first told me he was going to be a father, I admit, I worried, too. But he seems to do a good job working through things with the mother. At least that's how it looks from the outside."

"I am proud of him. I just worry about what he'll do when I'm gone."

"Where are you going?" Celia teased.

But Ruby didn't return her smile. "I have cancer, Celia. That's what I wanted to talk to you about today."

Celia's appetite fled. She felt as if she'd taken a punch in her midsection. "Cancer?"

"Now, don't go getting all emotional on me. My doctor feels I still have time. But I need you to promise you'll keep an eye on Seth for me when I'm gone. I know he's not family to you, but other than little Kaylee I'm afraid I'm all he has. Well, and Jack, but you know my son isn't much of a family man. He works more than he should, and he doesn't think about spending time with his nephew."

Celia nodded absently, taking it all in. "What kind of cancer?"

Ruby sighed. "The kind that will kill me. Not today. Not tomorrow. But eventually. I suspect before I'm ready."

Celia suddenly felt off balance, muddled. "Everyone thinks it's so great to live a long life. What they don't realize is sticking around longer than other people comes with a lot of heartache."

"Yeah, it's the shits to get old."

She giggled, despite the topic at hand. Ruby swore so infrequently; when a cuss word slipped out, it packed a special punch. "You can say that again!"

Ruby flipped over the top piece of bread on her sandwich and picked out a piece of bacon. She nibbled on it, lost in thought.

"How long have you known?"

She fished a second piece of bacon out from under a tomato slice. "Celia, do you ever think about the legacy you'll leave behind?"

It was clear that Ruby didn't want to discuss her cancer diagnosis. Maybe it was recent news for her, too. Celia would let her lead the conversation wherever she wished. "I probably don't give it as much thought as I should," she admitted.

"I didn't either, truth be told. Not until this diagnosis. God knows I should have, living through the loss of first my husband, then my daughter and son-in-law. Now it's all I can think about. It's not just about my money or my assets, either. Does that make sense? Maybe it's too late for us now, but I think about what Seth will think of me when I'm gone. Kaylee's only two. She won't even remember me, and she'll never have grandparents of her own. At least on our side of the family—I guess her mother's parents are still living. So there's that, I suppose."

Celia considered Ruby's words. She was no longer hungry, but she forced herself to take a bite of her BLT. She got shaky when she didn't eat, and she didn't need to stumble again like she had the previous summer. That near fall kicked off a chain reaction of nasty occurrences.

She swallowed and said, "You know what I finally understand? The legacy Preston left behind had a dramatic impact on the rest of my life."

"Eleanor's father? You mean when he left you Whispering Pines?"

She shook her head. "No. That's not right. Don't you remember what happened? He felt obligated to leave the resort to his son. But he didn't actually trust Tripp with Whispering Pines. So, he insisted—on his deathbed, no less—that I protect the resort no matter what. I ended up having to get pretty creative—and, dare I say, unethical—to buy it from Tripp."

"Right. *Right.* I'd forgotten you didn't get it directly," Ruby said, dropping the remaining half of the bacon strip on her plate. "But I don't think I knew about the 'unethical' part. Do tell!"

Shrugging, Celia took a sip of her lemonade. "It all happened so long ago, I can't remember all of it. I enlisted Helen's and Warren's help. Together, we caught Tripp in a web of his own making. He had a gambling problem and a roving eye. He was more than willing to sell Whispering Pines to the highest bidder, and the bidder at the top of the list was a developer that would have destroyed the old resort to make room for new. Which was exactly what Preston feared, I think. Anyway, it wasn't that difficult to back Tripp into a corner and force his hand. But it's never really sat well with me."

Ruby's cat wandered onto the porch and jumped up on the back of her owner's chair. Ruby reached back and stroked her. "Celia, you kept your word to Preston. And Preston helped make you the woman you turned out to be. If you had to bend the rules a little, so be it. It's not like Tripp would have thought twice about screwing you over."

"True. He'd have gotten rid of me at the beginning of my career if his father would have let him. Anyhow, my actual point was that Preston's request put me in a tough position. It sucked some of the joy out of how I felt about Whispering Pines after what I did to Tripp. Karma, I suppose. I think that's why I've procrastinated too long to get all my affairs in order. I still don't feel free to sell Whispering Pines all these years later. I feel an obligation to Preston to protect it. But is there anyone in my family who would be up to that task?"

The cat meandered down the arm of the chair and into Ruby's lap. Celia sneezed.

"I'm sorry. I forgot you're allergic," Ruby said, standing and taking the cat out of the room. She shut the French doors. The cat sat on the other side of the glass and shot dirty looks at Celia for getting her evicted. "I suppose Renee might have been a possibility, but with Jim's death and her living in Minneapolis, that couldn't possibly work. I remember you telling me how she used to love Whispering Pines as a child."

Celia nodded. She'd followed the same logic in her own mind. "Maybe Ethan. He's handy. But that wife of his complains a lot. And running a resort almost needs to be a family affair. I don't know what the answer is, but I suppose I better figure it out. As you say, we aren't getting any younger."

"Maybe it's time you consider selling the resort. Preston couldn't have known how long his request would impact your life."

Celia took another bite of her sandwich, giving Ruby's comment serious consideration. But so many of her life milestones had happened at the resort. "I suppose the reality is that I'm not good with change."

Ruby snorted. "I've noticed. Celia, you worked for the same company for your entire career. You've spent almost all your life in the same house. Heck, I'd venture to guess you always loved the same man. It's really no different with Whispering Pines. You can't let anything go."

"It would appear that way on the surface. But don't forget I let go of the most precious thing I ever had," Celia said. She stopped herself from saying more. Oh, she was so tired of the burden of the secret she'd carried ever since her eightieth birthday party. She usually told Ruby everything, but she hadn't yet divulged the bombshell Eleanor had dropped.

It took a moment, but Ruby caught on to her meaning. "True. You gave up your baby. And you spent the last months of your pregnancy at Whispering Pines. Do you think that's why you can't let it go?"

Celia didn't have an answer for that. "I'm not sure. It's part of it. That was a peaceful summer. Do you know, I often sat in an old rocking chair in front of that tiny cabin where you and I stayed one summer, singing softly to my baby as she grew in my womb? I'm sure the other guests thought me a bit mad with grief, seeing as how we lied and they thought I'd lost my husband. But I knew it would be my only chance to connect with my child. It turns out I was wrong about that."

Ruby didn't catch on to the true meaning of her words. "I disagree. Babies can hear your voice when they're growing inside of you. I remember when my daughter would sing to Seth while she was pregnant with him. I would watch her stomach shift when he kicked and rolled to the sound. I'm sure she did the same in my womb, but that was so long ago. We can't underestimate the magic of bringing a new life into this world, and despite the pain it caused you, I'm glad you had the experience, too, Celia."

Celia could no longer hold that secret burden. She felt an overwhelming need to tell Ruby everything. "I'm forever grateful, too. But, Ruby . . . there's more. I had the chance to connect with my daughter later, though I never realized it until my party."

"Party? What party? What in heaven's name are you talking about? Celia. Dear. Don't you remember? You gave your daughter up when she was born!"

She reached over and patted Ruby's knee. The distress in her old friend's voice was real. "Relax. I'm not losing my mind. Or at least not completely, though I seem to misplace my keys daily."

"Stop joking! What are you talking about?"

She took a deep breath as she considered where to start. "Eleanor had news for me at my birthday party."

"Which one?"

"The big one. My eightieth."

Ruby's mouth pinched. "But nothing seemed out of the ordinary that day. You didn't seem upset or anything. Or was I still so self-absorbed with my own problems back then that I didn't even notice? If that's the case, I apologize. I should have been a better friend."

"Ruby, you've always been wonderful to me. I don't know what my life would have been without you," Celia assured her. "No. Eleanor waited until everyone else left that day."

Ruby was clearly trying to recall the events of that day. "I remember now . . . First Helen left, and then I left shortly after. She had me riled up."

Celia could relate. She'd felt more animosity toward Helen than usual ever since the previous summer when she'd practically forced her to take the blame for Karen's misconduct. But that was a discussion for another day.

"Helen has a way of doing that. In fact, what Eleanor shared *relates* to Helen. And to Warren."

"But I don't understand."

"I didn't either. But Eleanor explained everything. Apparently they sold the Whitby Company. No one in the family wanted to run it. When they cleared out the headquarters in Chicago, they shipped a few boxes of miscellaneous records to Eleanor. They appeared to be personal, so someone didn't want to toss them. Eleanor took the time to sit down and sift through it all. And she found something."

Ruby shifted impatiently. "I gathered that. Go on."

Celia knew she was stalling. She wasn't sure she should even tell Ruby this. What purpose would it serve? Was she being disloyal to Helen, even though Helen may not even know Celia was involved in the adoption of their youngest daughter? For all Celia knew, Helen didn't know her adopted daughter and the child Celia gave up were even the same person.

But she'd gone this far with the story. Ruby wouldn't let her put the secret back in its box.

"There was a folder. It contained a legal document pertaining to an adoption Preston arranged. The adoptive parents were Warren and Helen Arbuckle. The dates matched up with the birth of my daughter."

Ruby stared back at her, mouth slack with shock. "What the heck? They *adopted* Virginia? How could Helen never tell us that?"

Celia shrugged. "We'd lost touch with her for a stretch of time. Remember? They lived in Chicago and we didn't see her for a few years. It was right around the time Warren came to work for Preston."

Ruby gasped. "You think Preston gave the job to Warren on the premise that he adopt your baby?"

This conclusion sounded ludicrous to Celia. "Oh hell, I don't think *that*. Neither Preston nor Warren did business that way. Now, I wouldn't have put anything past *Tripp*. But he didn't know about it, or he would have used an unplanned pregnancy against me."

"Well then, why didn't anyone tell you?"

It was a question she'd mulled over time and time again since Eleanor revealed what she'd found. "I think Preston was respecting my wishes. I also think Warren would have looked at it as a win for everyone. Preston might not have revealed who the baby's birth mother was to Warren. And Warren always wanted a big family. Remember how Helen mentioned the difficulties she had with her first two pregnancies? It was when you were arguing with her about the lengths Karen was taking to battle her infertility. For all we know, maybe Helen and Warren adopted *both* of their two youngest children."

"But how could Helen keep a secret like that?"

This question was easier to answer. "Helen has always been good at getting what she wants, no matter the cost. How they built their family really wasn't anyone else's business."

Ruby uncrossed her legs and kicked her orthopedic shoes off. If they'd have been younger, the two women would have grabbed a bottle of wine and gotten comfortable on the floor for a deep conversation like this. Those days were well in their past. "I suppose you have a point. But we've been friends our whole lives. How could she keep this from you?"

"I honestly don't think she knows it was *my* baby they adopted all those years ago. They were in Chicago. I was here. Well, technically I was at Whispering Pines, but you know what I mean. She didn't even know I'd had a child until it came out when you all visited the summer after I retired. She was just as shocked as Eleanor when I told them."

Celia took another drink of her lemonade. The room was getting warm, despite the fans. Or maybe it was her emotions heating her body again. Helen had a way of doing that to her, even when she wasn't present.

"I suppose it's possible she never connected the dots," Ruby conceded.

"Other than Preston's, Warren's signature was the only one on the document Eleanor found."

She nodded. "This actually explains some things for me."

"How so?" Celia asked, surprised. She thought she'd done an admirable job hiding the truth from Ruby and Helen.

"There was a noticeable tension between you and Helen when we were traveling last winter. I thought it was because you were struggling with the situation back home, with Jim and all, and Helen seemed dismissive of it all."

That's because you don't know what Helen forced me to do last summer, she thought. But revealing one secret pertaining to Helen was enough for today. A wave of exhaustion washed over her.

"I suppose finding out that Virginia may be your long-lost daughter is why you've been hesitant to update your will, then?"

She blinked. Was Ruby right? Something had been holding her back, but she'd never considered that factor. At least not consciously.

"Do you think I should leave Virginia any part of my estate? Considering my confidence that she's my biological daughter?"

Ruby pushed out of her wicker chair, moving slowly after sitting for so long. "Oh, Celia, life is so much more complicated than we'd hoped, isn't it? I need a minute. If I don't use the bathroom, I'll be sorry. Hold that thought. I'll be right back."

Ruby shuffled out of the room, closing the door quickly so her cat wouldn't jump in for another visit. Left to her own thoughts, Celia explored the idea of providing for Virginia—and, possibly, Karen.

Should she?

She was already having a difficult time deciding what to do with her various properties, not to mention her small business investments. To add the complexities of a daughter she'd given up decades earlier into the mix would raise so many questions and, potentially, hurt feelings.

It was all more drama than she wanted to stir up, even if it wouldn't be stirred until after her death.

Ruby returned with dessert plates bearing slices of the cake Celia had brought. She was glad to see her old friend eat something. Much of Ruby's sandwich remained on her plate, drying up in the air circulating by the fan.

The earlier announcement—cancer—came rushing back.

"Oh, Ruby, it's scary to think our time here will end, isn't it? You've helped me decide. I'll call your son and finalize everything. What I've done to date isn't enough. You've got me thinking. I've built a pleasant life for myself over the years. What I'll leave behind could make a positive difference in the lives of my family. I think Lavonne could help me figure out how I should handle things. She knows her kids best. I'm going to invite her over tomorrow."

Ruby set the plates down on the table between their wicker chairs, then took her seat again. "And what about Virginia? Will you leave her anything, if she is truly your long-lost daughter?"

Celia paused. "I don't think so. But I'm glad you challenged me to think through that. I've kept my secret, mostly, for all these years. I helped Virginia the most when she truly needed it, and I'd no idea at the time of our true connection. Helen had given up on her, and the girl was a desperate young widow. Even later, I helped her with her business. I did everything I could, and she's happy now. Content with her life and her husband and her bookstore. She knows I think of her like a daughter, and that's what matters most, I believe."

Ruby sliced a forkful of cake, but before taking the bite, she gave Celia a warm smile. "I think that's for the best. Life never turns out exactly how we might have wished. Look at my situation. I won't be here for little Kaylee when she shows up, but I'm hoping you can fill my shoes when I'm gone, at least for as long as you have left."

Celia nodded to the notebook at her feet. "Is that why you had me bring this? To leave me a to-do list?"

Ruby grinned. "You know me well, my friend."

"Indeed I do, Ruby, indeed I do. And now you know all of my deep, dark secrets, too. Well, *most* of them at least."

"You mean there's more?"

Celia laughed at the tinge of excitement in Ruby's voice. No matter their age, sharing secrets amongst best friends was always fun.

"Nothing as exciting as discovering the identity of my long-lost daughter, I can assure you. My frustration with Helen in recent months is more related to a nasty affair that I'd just as soon forget. Hopefully we managed to brush all that unpleasant business under the rug. Let's spend the rest of our visit today focusing on setting your mind at ease, my dear. You deserve that."

Chapter Thirty-Two
GIFT OF A MOTHER'S INSIGHT

CELIA *TRIED* TO INVITE Lavonne over the next day, but of course she'd completely forgotten that her sister-in-law was out of town helping Renee look for a new home in Minneapolis. Lavonne promised she'd come by when she got home. In the meantime, Celia set up another appointment with Jack, promising her lawyer she was serious about getting her estate in order this time.

Her discussion with Ruby cost her sleep. She worried about her friend's health, even though Ruby insisted nothing was imminent. Celia hoped she was right.

A world without Ruby would be bleak indeed.

When she finally found sleep, her dreams took her back to Whispering Pines. She dreamed of the resort's smallest cabin, the one she'd let fall into disrepair. It stood behind her—her safe, happy place. Warm sunlight caressed her upturned face as she rocked, back and forth, below a window box overspilling with bright petunias and creeping ivy. Her baby stirred beneath her palm where it rested on her rounded belly. She drew in a deep, cleansing breath, waiting. Always waiting. Dark clouds scuttled across the sky, blotting out her sun. The air chilled. She stood, shivering, intent on finding her shawl. A figure approached, hazy at first, then the vision cleared. It was a man wearing a brown uniform, a hand raised in greeting. Confused, she glanced behind her, but there was no one there. Where was her rocking chair? The flowers in the window box hung lifeless, dead. The uniformed man walked past her, silent, his eyes trained on her cabin's door. She touched her belly, an instinctive motion to protect, but it was flat, as if there had never been a baby. Where was the baby? The crack of a fist on wood split the air, time and time again. She spun, praying the ruckus wasn't disturbing other guests. The lawns lay silent. No one else was about. When she turned back to face her cabin, the door stood open to a shadowed interior, the man gone. The only sound was her own galloping heartbeat and the sigh of wind in the pines above. It grew darker still, as if night had slithered in when she blinked. A moonbeam broke through, illuminating the doorway just as two figures emerged from the hushed interior. *Iris!* She held something in her arms and her tangle of bleached white hair stuck out in odd directions. Her dress looked oddly familiar: a formal gown of some sort. As she watched, Iris paused at the top of the stairs, her eyes glowing with an unnatural light. Coming up behind her, the uniformed man gave her a slight shove to keep her moving, and as she stumbled down the stairs, she hissed something unintelligible. As Iris came alongside her, the blanket she held fell open to reveal a sleeping baby. Her heart nearly stopped at the sight, and as she reached a shaking hand toward the infant, its eyes popped open and it began to wail. Before she could touch the baby, Iris twisted away, holding the bundle tight to her chest. She spat on the ground, then met her eye. *"How dare you!"* Iris seethed, holding the baby out of reach. She recoiled at the hateful words, her hand again touching her flattened stomach. A sharp pain doubled her over. *"You stole what was ours. Now I'll do the same. No one will ever find peace here again. You ruined it, Celia! You did this!"*

Celia's eyes fluttered open. As she fought to reorientate herself, she felt an echo of discomfort in her midsection, as if her dream—or nightmare—hadn't quite released her. Straightening the blankets, she noted the blush of color in the sky through her bedroom window. She stayed in bed, hoping to drift back to sleep and forget her best friend's cancer announcement, but it was no use.

The dream lingered.

She hated it whenever those disturbing memories resurfaced of the day Iris, Tripp and Eleanor's little sister, was forcefully removed from Celia's favorite cabin. That event forever shadowed happier times: a summer with Ruby, and an even more precious space of time with Beverly. It was the last long stretch she had with her sister. The following year, Beverly lost her battle with heart disease. And after that, of course, there was the summer she'd stayed there awaiting the birth of her baby girl.

She shouldn't have told her current caretakers to ignore the old cabin. A flash of anxiety hit at the notion her cabin might already be too far gone. Was she too late to save it? Why had she allowed the disturbing threat from an unstable woman to diminish the joy she'd held for it. If the cabin became unsalvageable, Iris would win. Which, in a roundabout way, would mean her big brother, Tripp, won, too.

Celia couldn't let that happen.

Later that morning, she called Ed Dixon. Sheepishly, Ed admitted he'd done basic upkeep to the cabin, despite her instructions to leave it alone. Celia assured him she was thrilled he'd gone against her wishes. She ended the call feeling a great sense of relief that the tiny cabin was safe.

For now. But later?

She would need to encourage her family to save that little cabin, no matter what.

The night before Lavonne's scheduled visit, Celia sat down with a pen and paper to craft a letter. Her sister-in-law would probably think she was crazy, but Celia planned to ask her to take her out to Whispering Pines one last time. She'd stash her letter in the back of the closet in the tiny cabin, next to the hidden time capsule her nieces and nephew created during their first visit to the resort.

Celia hadn't thought about that old time capsule in years, but her subconscious mind brought it back to her in her dreams.

Was it still where she and Wayne had stashed it?

Or had someone already discovered their hiding spot?

Celia wandered the empty rooms of her home. Lavonne wouldn't be by until closer to four. She and George stayed in Minneapolis for an extra night to give Renee a chance to look at one more property. Renee's kids were staying at Val's house. Julie loved playing with baby David, her youngest cousin, and Luke promised to teach Robbie how to ride his bike without the training wheels.

Celia admired the closeness Lavonne and George fostered between their kids and grandkids.

Anxious over her upcoming conversation with her sister-in-law, Celia poured herself a glass of wine, forgoing any more coffee. She knew she'd be exhausted by the time Lavonne left, and the wine might help her sleep.

All this focus on Whispering Pines kept bringing old memories to mind. She remembered how her sister would stay up late that summer, long after Celia turned in. She'd sit at the tiny kitchen table, surrounded by journals, paper, and pretty pens, writing until the wee hours. Once Beverly was still at the table, writing, when Celia rose at six to get an early start on her workday.

Later, after Beverly died, Celia moved into her sister's room. The other bedrooms were full. She'd discovered a stack of Beverly's writing in a drawer. Celia couldn't find the fortitude to read Beverly's words until years later, but those pages covered with neatly scrawled cursive comforted her now.

Maybe she'd discover some much needed wisdom in her sister's words as she continued to ponder her best course of action.

The day's weather offered a temporary reprieve from historically high temperatures, and her yellow roses were in full bloom in the backyard. The overcast sky and low humidity felt pleasant. She left a note for Lavonne on the kitchen table and carried her glass of white wine and a shoebox full of Beverly's loose papers to the bistro set out back. The table and chairs—a gift to herself for her eighty-third birthday weeks earlier—were set in the shade of her tallest tree. They'd reminded her of the set she sat at as a young woman, the night she'd enjoyed her first conversation with Danny after sneaking out of the dance at Grand View Lodge with sore feet.

Celia had tied a red silk hair ribbon, one that used to hold Beverly's dark hair back while she wrote, around the box. She pulled it off and wrapped it loosely around her wrist, laid the box's lid to the side, and picked up the top sheet of paper. She'd read her way through the stack many times through the years, reading a page, moving it to the bottom, and going on to the next one. Her eyes had taken all the words in before, but she never failed to discover new nuggets she'd missed. There were short stories, outlines of future potential books Beverly had planned to write but never got the chance, and daily musings.

Beverly had been an old soul trapped in a beautiful body with a warm but weak heart. Celia hadn't fully appreciated the depth of wisdom Bev carried until after her sister died, leaving her with a record of her thoughts scribbled on these pieces of paper.

This box was Beverly's legacy.

What would be *Celia's* legacy?

"There you are!" Lavonne's voice cut through Celia's thoughts.

She placed the romance-heavy poem she'd been reading back in the box. It was the product of an innocent young woman experiencing her first crush. Tripp, Celia's old nemesis, had been the target of that crush. She covered the box and set it safely to the side.

Lavonne came down the back steps, holding her own glass of wine. "I hope you don't mind. I helped myself."

"Of course not. That's why I set a glass out for you. Thanks for coming by. You're probably exhausted after your hunt with Renee. Did she find anything?"

Lavonne accidentally bumped the table as she sat in the second chair. A splash of Celia's wine spilled out onto the white metal swirls of the tabletop.

"Oh, gosh, I'm sorry," she apologized. "I can go grab the bottle if you'd like more."

Celia picked up her wine glass, grinning at it. The glass was still half full. "Depending on how this conversation goes, I may take you up on that."

Lavonne's own grin faltered. "That sounds ominous."

A light, rose-scented breeze skipped through the yard, fluffing strands of Celia's auburn-dyed hair. Patting at the flyaway strands, she laughed, sure the younger woman had gotten a good look at her gray roots. "I didn't mean for it to, but I do have something important to discuss with you. I'm glad you weren't too tired to stop over. But first, tell me how it went with Renee."

Lavonne took a deep breath of the perfumed air, followed by a generous sip of her wine, before responding. "It went fine, I suppose."

"You don't sound like all is fine."

"I'm not convinced moving is the right thing for Renee and the kids right now. I've heard it said that a person shouldn't make any big changes for the first year following a loss like she's suffered. It's too soon to know what's best. Grief still fogs her mind."

Celia unwound Beverly's red ribbon from her wrist, then wrapped it around her finger. "Do you really think her financial situation is the true reason she's considering the move, or is she haunted by memories in that house? Because I can understand that. My sister died in her own room, in this very house." She motioned toward her home. "We were all eating dinner downstairs, but she was too tired to come down. I've always imagined she slipped away in her sleep, gently floating away from the pain and weakness that ruled so much of her life. But it bothered me for a long time afterward. Eventually, I came to look at it all in a different light. Now I imagine her spirit is sometimes still here with me, and instead of bothering me, I find comfort in the notion."

"None of you talk about Beverly very often. Why is that? What was she like?"

"She was special. Gerry and George were young when she died. They probably don't remember much about her. I may not talk about her often, but I talk *to* her—or her spirit, at least—when I'm in the house alone. Sometimes I worry someone will catch me and think I've lost it," she said, her voice light. "This was hers."

"Really?" Lavonne asked, touching the tip of the ribbon that dangled from Celia's finger. "And you've kept it for all these years?"

Celia nodded. "This box is full of Beverly's writings. I pull them out once in a while, read through them. It makes me feel closer to her."

Sliding the box over, she took the lid off again. Lavonne pulled out the poem that Celia had been reading. "What a treasure. I'd love to read through these someday."

Celia motioned for her to put the paper back. She closed the box and set it to the side. "That would be nice. But about Renee. I agree with you. We need to convince her to stay put, at least for a while longer. If you think it might help, I'll call her. I can help her out if she's feeling pinched for money."

"You'd do that for her?"

"In a second. But let's keep it to ourselves. I'd love to help all of them, and I will in time, but I think Renee is the one who might really need it right now."

"I'm sure she'd appreciate it. As long as her pride doesn't get in the way."

Celia hoped Renee would be receptive to the idea. Everyone needs help from time to time. "I'll cross my fingers. But that leads me to the main reason I invited you over today."

Lavonne rocked excitedly in her chair. "I admit, I've been curious ever since you called."

Celia tapped her chest. "I'm hopeful this ticker of mine will carry me through plenty of more years. But I had lunch with Ruby earlier this week, and we had a great conversation about the legacies we leave behind. It made me realize that I've been too passive on the whole topic. As things sit right now, my various properties will be sold off when I pass, and the proceeds of it all will be split between my family."

"That's incredibly generous of you, Celia," Lavonne declared.

"Well, you know what they say. You can't take it with you. But I've changed my mind. I'm not sure receiving a bunch of cash would help anyone much."

She almost laughed out loud at Lavonne's incredulous look. It was obvious her sister-in-law thought a chunk of cash would be very helpful.

But Celia wanted her legacy to feel more personal.

"I need to explain myself better, and make you understand how you can help me. Your four kids have all grown into amazing adults. You and George should be proud."

Lavonne raised her wine glass. "That is probably the nicest compliment you could ever give me."

Celia tapped her glass against Lavonne's. "I mean it. And as their mother, I suspect there is no one in the world who knows them better than you."

"Except maybe their spouses."

"Actually, I'm not so sure about that." She hesitated, unsure she should bring up this subject, troubling though it was. "Can I be frank with you?"

"Of course."

Celia tapped the tabletop, forming her words. Then she dove in.

"I love your kids. You know I think the world of them. But I worry. I admire Jess's head for business, but Will's attitude toward money concerns me. Jim is gone, God rest his soul. I don't feel like I know Val's Luke very well. He seems like a nice man, but I haven't spent much time with him. And then there is Stacey. She and Ethan sure seem to argue."

Lavonne tilted her head. "I can't say you are wrong about any of that, though the warm glow you gave me a few minutes ago is fading quickly."

Celia tugged at the red ribbon, nervous she'd offended Lavonne, and let it pool onto the table. "I'd feel better about leaving all of them—or at least Renee, Ethan, and Jess—something other than just money from my estate."

"But not Val?"

"Val, too, but let's start with the older ones. In fact, let's discuss the biggest decision I have to make that has quite literally been costing me sleep."

"That sounds juicy," Lavonne said, smiling.

"What should I do with Whispering Pines?"

Her smile slipped away. "Whispering Pines?"

Celia nodded. "I can't sell it."

"Can't, or won't?"

"Both, I suppose. Believe me, I've considered it. I never get out there anymore. Any sane woman would have sold it years ago. But, then again, any sane woman might not have worked so hard to buy it in the first place."

Lavonne drained the last of her wine. "I'll admit, I'm surprised you've kept it all this time."

Celia nodded. "I want you to help me decide what to do with it."

"All right . . ." Lavonne dragged the phrase out as she released her pent-up breath, as if unsure how she could help with the decision. "What ideas do you have for it? Have you considered putting it into a trust, having a trustee run it, perhaps?"

Celia had considered it, but the idea held little appeal. "Call me crazy, but I'm seriously considering passing it on to Renee."

Lavonne snorted. Celia wasn't sure if it was in disbelief or humor.

"I'm serious. I know all the kids had fun there when you and George brought them for summer vacations. But Renee fell in love with the place. I could always see it in her eyes."

Lavonne rested her forehead in her left hand, using her thumb to rub a temple. "Celia, those were the eyes of a child. Renee is a grown woman now, recently widowed with two kids, and living at least two hours from Whispering Pines—double that when traffic is heavy. She doesn't know the first thing about running a resort."

Celia nodded. They were valid points. "But she's so *unhappy*."

"Unhappy? Of course she's unhappy. Her husband just died last November."

She tried a different tactic. "Renee's been sick of her job for years. She tolerates it, seldom complains, but there's no excitement. I think taking over the resort would put that light back in her eyes."

"You're serious about this, aren't you? Wouldn't Ethan be a better choice if selling Whispering Pines is off the table?"

"And that is exactly why I'm losing sleep over this. Ethan would be the logical choice. But *logical* doesn't feel right, and I have to make a decision. I can't keep putting it off. My head and my heart are telling me two different things."

Lavonne chewed on her right thumbnail—a nervous tic Celia hadn't seen her do in years. "Celia . . . I know how important Whispering Pines is to you. The logic side of your brain has never figured into those feelings. While I'm still not convinced Renee could handle it, I think you need to listen to your heart on this one. As long as you don't pass it on to her with too much financial baggage, maybe she'd figure out a way to make it work. And we'd all help. But it's a gamble."

"Most important things in life are."

"I think you've made your decision. If you give Renee Whispering Pines, did you have ideas for the rest of them, too? I'm not implying you're obligated to give anyone anything. But you've always been a fair woman. Do you have specific things in mind for Ethan, Jess, and Val, too?"

"I have some ideas. Let me know what you think. I sure as heck won't give *Jess* straight cash."

Lavonne nodded. "You're concerned that's too easy for Will to get his hands on, aren't you?"

"Sadly, yes. Money flows through that man's fingers like water."

Lavonne pushed at the pooled ribbon on the tabletop. "Do you have a better idea?"

"I think I do," Celia admitted. "I have small business interests in Virginia's bookstore and the residential cleaning company. I want to pass those on to Jess, as long as the majority owners approve. I'd also give her most of my stock portfolio."

A car drove through the alley behind the two women, the sound of tires on gravel interrupting the quiet afternoon. When it faded, Celia listened to the hum of a bee while Lavonne considered her idea. Her sister-in-law looked pensive.

"She wouldn't have to spend as much time with Virginia and Frank at the bookstore as I do," Celia jumped back in. "I like to go down there to catch up with Virginia. She's always pressing fabulous new reads into my hands when I leave. Honestly, it is a solution for my boredom once in a while."

"I can't imagine *you* ever get bored. I swear you keep more active than I do."

Celia doubted it, but she also worried that if she sat too long in an empty house, depression would set in. She needed to be around people. "I know how busy Jess is, too. Between their two kids and a job she seems to love, she wouldn't have much extra time. It wouldn't be a problem. Where I worry is in her relationship with Will. While I can't do anything about that, I can try to help give her more financial stability if her marriage falls apart."

Lavonne groaned. "You worry about that, too, huh?"

"I do. Which is why I want to tie up the inheritance I leave to Jess in her name, and it shouldn't be something easily liquidated."

"I'm not sure why you think you need my input on this, Celia. You've put lots of thought into this already. I'd say you're hitting the mark so far. Do you have similar thoughts for Ethan and Val?"

Celia let her eyes travel to the back of the house she'd lived in for most of her life. She tried to view it from an outsider's perspective. The glass in the windows glinted with the summer sun, an almost imperceptible wave to the shimmer, a sure sign of older glass. She hadn't noticed the chipping and peeling white paint in so many places. The siding could use a fresh coat of paint, too. The backside of the house took a beating from the sun, and its pale yellow color was fading to ivory. The windows and siding would have to be replaced someday. But Celia would leave that for the next generation. She'd call Ethan to get the name of a decent painter and make do with that for now.

"I have properties," she said, turning her attention back to Lavonne. "Aside from Whispering Pines. I hate the idea of another family in this house. But look at her. She's seen better days. I suppose the inside is getting dated, too. It serves my needs, but she could use a facelift. I think Ethan would be the only one up for that task, given he has his own construction company and he remodels homes and businesses for a living. He'd be the logical one to take care of my rentals, too. And he's fair. Most of my tenants have lived in my buildings for years. They are elderly, and I don't gouge them. There's some positive cash flow, I've never lost sight of that, but it isn't a lot. Still, it might help Ethan with the expense of college when his kids reach that stage."

Lavonne batted a bee away from her face. "And Stacey is always saying how much she loves your house."

She thinks she'd like living here, Celia thought, *but it's bigger than the house they live in now. Stacey would complain about having to clean it all.*

The only negative in her plans for Ethan was the idea of Stacey living in her house, but Celia kept those thoughts to herself. She'd already said more than she should have about Will. It wouldn't be fair to complain any more about the kids' spouses. Instead, she just smiled, knowing Lavonne was right. Maybe Stacey would be happy here.

"That leaves Val," Lavonne said.

"That leaves Val," Celia repeated. "But first, would you be a doll and run inside and grab my shawl from the front room? Rain must be on the way. There's a chill in the air."

The drop in temperature reminded her of her nightmare.

Lavonne popped up, collecting their empty wine glasses. "Want a refill?"

"Sure. Why not? Between getting these details ironed out, with your help, and a second glass of wine, I know I'll sleep better tonight."

While she waited for Lavonne to return, Celia strummed her fingers on the tabletop, considering again where Val was at in her life. Her niece had elected to stay home after the birth of her first baby. Her husband worked hard doing some type of manual labor. Celia liked Luke. He reminded her a bit of Jim. But she didn't know him as well yet. He was a newer addition to their family.

Celia loved Val. She liked her spunk. The girl was a wizard in the kitchen. She had a knack for it. She could usually be found in the kitchen beside her mom, baking a delicious dessert or pulling something together for potlucks.

Maybe Val could open a catering business.

Or maybe, someday, she'd go back to something else in the hospitality industry. That used to interest her.

"Or maybe she wants to stay home and raise her son," Celia muttered. She needed to be careful not to project her own personality or the things she'd wanted to do at Val's age on to her niece. She should accept they were very different people, shared spunk notwithstanding.

"What was that?" Lavonne asked, setting their wine glasses back on the patio table.

Celia shook her head. "Oh, nothing. I was just talking to myself. Thank you, I enjoy this vintage."

Lavonne took a sip. "It *is* good. I should write the name down. I'm terrible at picking out wine. So. What did you decide about Val?"

Celia ran a finger around the rim of her glass. "In Val's case, I think I need to let her decide."

Lavonne raised her eyebrows. "You want to ask her?"

This made Celia laugh, and she allowed her worry over her indecisiveness to ebb away. "Of course not. Val knows what she wants right now. I'm sure money is tight for them, what with the new baby and one income, but anytime I see her, she has a radiant glow. I think they are learning to live within their means, and that will prove invaluable. I just wonder if there will ever come a day when she wants to do something other than run her household. Maybe that won't even happen until their kids are grown. But I want her to have options."

"And money gives people options."

"That it does. Unlike Will, I trust Luke won't force Val to use any money I might leave to her for his own gains."

Lavonne nodded, seeming to agree.

"I just hope Val doesn't feel slighted at my lack of creativity where she's concerned."

"Celia, you are being very generous with all of them. No one will feel slighted. Trust me. When the day comes—and I hope that is still far off in the future—your thoughtfulness will touch them."

There was a flurry of movement in the tree above them, and a twig tumbled down, landing in Lavonne's wine. Laughing, both women looked up in time to see a squirrel scamper along a high branch and leap gracefully across to a neighboring tree, a second squirrel following playfully behind.

Celia noticed a spot of red above the vibrating branch. Squinting, she saw a cardinal watching her.

She shivered, despite the shawl Lavonne had draped over her shoulders. She believed in the legend behind red cardinals. So many of Celia's loved ones had already made that journey to the other side, she couldn't have guessed which one this might be. She could only hope whichever loved one was looking down on her now approved of the decisions she was making.

Lavonne tipped her glass to inspect her wine, sighed, and dumped the rest onto the grass. "Those little buggers remind me of my grandkids, always getting into something."

"Speaking of—your grandkids, not the squirrels—I'd like to pass something on to each of them as well. I'm not going to put them all through college, but I think I'll try something a little unconventional."

"Celia!" Lavonne coughed, a hand on her throat. "You are doing plenty already!"

Celia waved this away. "Whatever is left, after taking care of all of you, should go to the little ones. I considered stopping at your four kids, and giving any remaining funds to various charities, but I decided I wanted to help get them started on a good foot, too. What if I were to make any gift to your grandchildren contingent on them going on to extra schooling, beyond high school?"

Lavonne nodded. "Sure, I love the idea of encouraging them like that." She looked up. "Do you smell that? The rain is close."

Celia rubbed her arms against the chill, noting the darkening sky. The cardinal was still there, high in the tree above. Sitting patiently.

Lavonne got to her feet, wrapped her fingers of one hand around the stems of both wine glasses, and pointed to Beverly's box. "Why don't you hand me that. I don't want it to get wet. We should go in. As for your idea for the children, I like it. Anything we can do to help give them a good life makes me smile."

Celia stood, shaking out her legs, stiff from sitting so long. She used the red hair ribbon to secure the lid on Beverly's box and tucked it under her own arm. She couldn't trust the precious contents to anyone, not even Lavonne. "I've got it. Hurry! I think I've got every window open in the house, and I don't want to be mopping up water from the wooden floors!"

Chapter Thirty-Three
Gift of Clearing the Air

THE FIRST THING SHE noticed was the scent of pine and fresh-cut grass. Celia inhaled, holding the smell of Whispering Pines deep in her lungs. She waited on the sidewalk in front of the old lodge while Lavonne went back to her car.

"Is the letter in your purse?" Lavonne asked, swinging open the passenger door.

"Yes. It's right there."

Lavonne bent down, disappearing from view.

The letter . . .

Celia was so excited to be back at Whispering Pines she'd practically forgotten why they'd stopped out.

A moment later, Lavonne reappeared, holding an envelope high. "Got it!" She weaved her way through cars and pickups, back to Celia's side. "Boy, it's busy out here. I don't think I've ever seen this many cars in the parking lot!"

Celia hadn't either. The place was running just fine under the Dixons' watchful eyes. She was lucky to have them. "When I called Mary and Ed to let them know we'd be stopping out, Mary warned me it would be busy. There's a huge family reunion out here. It started today and runs for three days."

Lavonne looked around. "They can't all be staying here. There aren't enough cabins."

"They're not, but Mary said the cabins are all full. We couldn't stay the night even if we wanted to. You didn't say anything to George about us coming out here, did you?"

She shook her head, handing Celia the envelope she'd retrieved from the car. "Of course not. You asked me not to. By the time I came downstairs this morning, he'd left. There was a note saying he was going golfing, then he had something to do with Ethan this afternoon. He won't even miss me. I have to be back by six, though. We're going out for dinner with friends."

"I understand," Celia assured her. "This was a spur-of-the-moment visit, and I appreciate you driving me out here. I probably could have driven myself, but I know Gerry and George don't like me going out on the highway anymore. I can live with that, but if either gets the ridiculous idea of taking my keys away, I'll give them a piece of my mind."

Lavonne laughed. "Maybe, if you'd lighten up on the accelerator a little, they wouldn't give you so much grief."

"I haven't gotten a ticket in at least a year," Celia countered before spinning to her left and taking a few steps. Without turning back to Lavonne, she waved the envelope toward the back portion of the resort. "I need to find Ed or Mary. They'll have the key to the cabin."

"Isn't someone staying in it? You said the cabins were all full."

"They are, but we don't use the smallest cabin anymore."

Lavonne caught up to Celia and fell into step beside her. A group of children came running by, shrieking and laughing. The little boy bringing up the rear carried a water balloon in each hand and a smile that said he was looking for trouble. A woman's voice yelled, telling them to be careful.

"I miss those summer vacations when we'd bring the kids out here for a few weeks," Lavonne said, watching the boy chase three girls toward the beach. "Where have all the years gone?"

Celia took another deep breath. This time, the smell of grilling meat made her mouth water. "Coming here feels like we've stepped back in time. There's Ed."

She hurried toward the caretaker. He was stacking firewood next to the bonfire pit. A three-day family reunion would include time around a crackling fire come evening. If she closed her eyes, she could smell the burning oak and taste a charred marshmallow—crispy on the outside and gooey on the inside, just like she liked it.

But she didn't dare close her eyes for fear of falling.

She missed the good old days, too.

"Hello, Ed!"

The man straightened at the sound of her voice. He brushed his hands together and turned toward them. His face lit up with a broad smile. "Would you look at that? Celia Middleton has actually graced us with her presence!"

Celia stopped, hands on her hips, and let him come to her. "I had to come make sure this place hadn't fallen to ruin, but I'm happy to see things look fine—fine, indeed, thanks to your capable hands, Ed."

He nodded a greeting to Lavonne.

"Ed, this is Lavonne, my sister-in-law. Lavonne, Ed and his wife, Mary, run this place. Where is Mary, by the way?"

"Nice to meet you, Lavonne," Ed said, then turned back to Celia. "Mary ran to town. She hoped to be back to say hello before you leave. I'm so sorry we have no room to have you spend the night out here."

Celia glanced around, warmed by the sight of so many guests milling about. It reminded her of her early days at Whispering Pines, before the war changed everything. "Are these people all here for a family reunion? All related?"

Ed shrugged. "Think so. This group booked the whole resort well in advance. The weather should make for a nice three days for them. Say, I bet you need that key to the cabin you mentioned on the phone earlier. I should have put it in my pocket, but it's still in the office. I'll go fetch it for you. I can meet you over there if you like."

Celia crossed the lawn, her eyes drawn to the two oldest cabins. She could picture Leo, Helen's brother, waiting for her on the steps of the larger cabin with fishing poles in hand. She could practically hear the voices of her girlfriends, laughing and gossiping about the fun they'd had at a Saturday evening dance down the road at Grand View Lodge.

She stopped when she reached the base of the smallest cabin's stairs. The screen door at the top burst open in her memories, slamming against the log siding. She imagined the light, wooden door reverberating with the long-ago impact of Beverly's excitement. Her young sister, a newly minted high school graduate, skipped down these very stairs, the pretty yellow skirt of her dress swirling around her knees. A red hair ribbon that matched the tiny roses embroidered around her hem caught up her chocolate-hued waves in a high ponytail.

At a touch on her shoulder the image of her laughing sister dissipated, as transient as a puff of smoke. She glanced back and met Lavonne's concerned gaze.

"Are you all right, Celia? Is the heat too much for you?"

Celia waved away her concern, turning her back to the troublesome cabin and sinking at a measured pace to rest on the lowest step. "The heat doesn't bother me. While I love this resort dearly, the memories are vivid, even painful for me. The older I get, the more difficult it is for me to stay in the present when I visit here. My love for Whispering Pines is rooted in the past. Not in the here and now."

Lavonne took a seat next to her while they waited for Ed to return with the key.

"It's still a lovely place though, isn't it?" Lavonne tilted her head back, watching the way the tallest pines nearly pierced the puffy clouds above, meandering across a crystal-blue sky. "We both have history here. My memories are certainly not as lengthy, or deep, as yours, but they're powerful all the same."

Celia thought back to the summer Lavonne came out to help her recover after her mastectomy. She was still so thankful for the skill of her medical team, and the fact the cancer never returned. With Lavonne's help, she'd healed nicely. Celia tried not to dwell on what could have happened if Karen hadn't kicked her breast while playing on her lap. Her own granddaughter, little baby Karen, helped Celia find the lump early.

It occurred to Celia then, as she sat in a warm pool of sunshine, that one's life is built on seemingly random threads. Friendship brought her to this resort. Her desire to be useful led to her lengthy and rewarding career. Preston Whitby bought this place when his wife left him, and running it gave him a healthy coping mechanism to deal with his loss. He'd hired a married couple to help him with the resort, and Celia was destined to fall in love with their son. Together they made a child, one that circumstances would prevent them from raising, but who would someday have her own child. That very baby would help Celia find the lump in her breast. Lavonne would assist her in her healing process, and, in this very cabin, found herself in a situation which could have blown hers and Celia's brother's world apart.

As if she could read her mind, Lavonne cleared her throat. "Do you remember when we sat right here, on this very set of stairs, that summer I came out here to help you? Jess was still a toddler and we didn't have Val yet."

"I do."

Lavonne nodded, then whispered, "Thank you."

Celia didn't need Lavonne to explain what she was referring to.

"I nearly lost everything that summer. You knew what I'd done, the dreadful mistake I made, but you kept my secret."

But I didn't, Celia thought.

She'd gone to George, discussed her suspicions with her brother.

"George deserves your thanks, Lavonne, not me."

"Believe me, I know how lucky I am that I didn't lose my husband. Possibly my family. And George told me you talked to him about it. I don't blame you. But, to the best of my knowledge, you did as George asked. Not only did you never bring it up again, you never held it against me. You forgave me, and you kept our secret."

Ed came into view, swinging a set of keys.

Lavonne stood, offering Celia a hand. Back on her feet, Celia gave her sister-in-law's hand a quick squeeze before releasing it, whispering back, "That's what family does, Lavonne."

"Got the keys," Ed said as he approached, jingling the large ring of keys. "I'd hoped to get in here and open up the windows, let it air out a bit before you arrived, but couldn't get a chance. I checked it over in early May, both inside and out, and patched a hole in the roof. Darn trees keep rubbing on the shingles on the backside."

Skirting around the two women, Ed climbed the short flight of stairs, pulled the squeaky screen door open, and attempted a key in the lock.

"Dang tags fell off these," he said when the first one didn't work.

The second key did.

"Let's hope everything still looks all right in here."

He pushed the door open and stepped into the shadowed interior.

Celia hung back, waiting. Lavonne lifted her foot to the next step and held out a hand to assist her sister-in-law, but then followed Celia's lead and waited.

The curtain in the front window slid open and Ed jiggled the lower sash. It would only slide up a couple inches. They listened as the man moved around inside.

"Dammit."

"That doesn't sound good," Celia muttered.

If vermin had taken over the cabin or the back wall was caving in, it would be her own fault for letting the little structure fall to disrepair.

"Everything all right in there?" Lavonne asked, louder so Ed could hear.

More shuffling, then Ed reappeared, limping. "Looks like it. I slammed my shin on the coffee table. Power is out. Lights won't turn on, but I've got the curtains on the back window open now to let in some light. I'm gonna have to look at the fuse box."

Relieved, Celia climbed the stairs, moving ahead of Lavonne. Ed stepped out of the way so she could enter.

"Nothing wrong with her legs," she heard Lavonne whisper.

Celia smirked. She loved to prove she wasn't washed up yet, despite her eighty-six years.

As she stood in the cabin's threshold, she paused, allowing her eyes time to adjust.

"It's grimy," Ed said. "Could use some airing out and a thorough cleaning. I wouldn't put guests on the bed back there. It needs to be replaced. But if you want us to get this thing back into useable condition, we could work on it."

Celia stepped inside, feeling torn as her eyes took in the cabin's state. It would take money and time to get it back to a point where she'd be comfortable renting it out again. "Let me think about it, Ed. But thank you for keeping the outside solid enough that the thing is still standing. We'll be fine if you need to go see to things. I just need a few minutes in here, then we'll lock up behind us. We won't leave without saying goodbye."

Ed looked confused at her strange request for time alone in the decrepit old cabin, but he didn't question her. Celia heard him tell Lavonne to be careful and to give him a holler if they needed anything more. As his footsteps faded away, Lavonne stepped inside with a whistle.

"Pretty dark in here, even with the windows open."

Celia nodded. "This place used to be so cute. I shouldn't have let it deteriorate like this."

"The whole resort would probably have fallen into this condition years ago if not for you. In fact, I bet it wouldn't even exist. Don't be too hard on yourself over one cabin."

Lavonne was probably right. Celia took a fortifying breath, then coughed as the dust tickled her lungs. Best not to breathe too deeply until she got back outside again.

"I hope we can see well enough back here."

She entered the only bedroom, shuffling her feet to avoid tripping over anything in the gloom. Instead of going straight to the closet, she headed for the bedside table. She'd gotten in the habit of keeping flashlights in all the cabin bedrooms. Electricity problems were common out here. Even if there was still a flashlight, she wasn't sure the batteries would work.

"Careful," Lavonne said, stopping at the doorway into the bedroom, one hand on the doorframe. "It's pretty dark."

Celia didn't need the warning; she was already taking extra care. She also remembered the layout of the bedroom. She'd been the one to replace the two twin beds that used to fill the room with a more comfortable double mattress. The single drawer in the table stuck, and she had to pull harder. The small table wobbled. Something rattled inside.

"Lavonne, can you give me a hand with this?"

Together, they managed to open it. Celia pulled out the hoped-for flashlight, flipping the switch. Nothing. She slapped it against her palm.

That did it.

"Follow me," she told Lavonne, heading for the closet door, guided by the weak beam from the flashlight. She pulled open the door, surprised to find a jacket hanging inside. "Someone is missing a coat." She pushed the forgotten garment to the end of the closet rod and aimed her flashlight at the lower third of the back wall.

"I don't understand," Lavonne said, peeking around Celia.

"It's in there," Celia said, wiggling the beam of light.

"Really? The kids' time capsule is in *there*? Where, behind that board?"

"Yep." She handed the flashlight to Lavonne, then braced herself with a hand against the closet wall and bent down.

"Wait. If you get down on your knees, will you be able to get back up?"

Celia stopped mid-squat. "I'm not sure."

Lavonne started to giggle. "I should do it. Do you think your envelope will fit through that little gap down there?"

Lavonne's infectious laugh was making Celia chuckle, too. "There's only one way to find out. If we can't push it under there, I'll have to get Ed again. Your knee gives you so much trouble, can you get down there?"

"I can get down there," Lavonne said. "There's just no guarantee I can get up again, either. Give me the envelope."

Celia pulled the letter she'd written out of her pocket, smoothed it, and handed it to Lavonne. She watched as the younger woman eased down to her knees, laid the flashlight on the ground with the light shining toward the gap between the floor and the bottom of the panel, and attempted to slip the envelope through. It didn't go far, crinkling up instead of disappearing. She wiggled the paper a little, then tried again.

"Dammit. It's catching on something," she said, hiccupping over a giggle.

Then she screeched and fell onto her butt. She tried to scoot backward, but she ran into Celia's legs. This just caused them both to laugh harder.

"What did you see?" Celia asked, trying but failing to see anything warranting Lavonne's attempted but failed escape.

"Spider." Shivering, Lavonne reached tentatively for the flashlight. "It was as big as my thumb."

"Oh Lord," Celia said, taking two steps back to give Lavonne more room. "Can't you shove the envelope through that space?"

"No. We need Ed. Or at least a screwdriver to take this panel off. But, to be honest, I'm not crazy about the idea of taking the panel off myself. Who knows where that big-ass spider disappeared to?" Lavonne giggled some more, though this time the sound was tinged with trepidation.

"My guess is you scared it clear down to the lake. Here, get up. We'll go find him. Ed, that is. Not the spider."

She ignored Celia's hand. "Just move out of the way."

With a sigh, chuckles finally subsiding, Celia moved. But when Lavonne scooted out of the closet, still on her bottom, and scuttled across the floor until she could pull herself up using the bed's footboard, Celia dissolved into full-on laughter.

"Everything all right back there, ladies?" Ed's raised voice cut through the ruckus.

She turned toward the voice, wiping at the tears streaming down her face. "Actually, we might need a little help. And bring your toolbox!"

Lavonne backed out of the tight parking spot in front of the lodge, careful not to scrape the white Suburban next to her. "Well, *that* was interesting."

Celia grinned as she tucked her purse down by her feet and snapped her seatbelt in place. "I'm glad Ed could slide the envelope in for us."

"Do you think they'll find it someday?"

She shrugged. "If Renee ever takes over out here, I bet she'll do the work to get that little cabin back in shape. With any luck, they'll find it then. And if they don't, maybe you can jog their memory about the time capsule. They don't know that's where Wayne stashed it, but *you* do now. Maybe make a game out of it. Finding it, I mean. Or have the grandkids search. It might be fun."

Lavonne eased onto the highway at the end of the path leading from Whispering Pines. Celia turned to look back at the sign marking the turn to the resort. Smiling, she hoped the day would come when her family would again make use of this place. She was too old to enjoy it anymore, and there was too much history here for her anyway, but there was a timeless quality about Whispering Pines. It would still be there for them when they were ready.

"I appreciate all of your help over the last couple days, Lavonne. Thank you."

The younger woman nodded, and Celia noticed a ring of smeared mascara under her right eye from the uncontrollable laughter. They'd had fun. Maybe their laughter inside the tiny old cabin had helped to chase some of the negative energy away. Maybe it was even enough to break a curse that may or may not be real.

"I'm honored you took me into your confidence, Celia. It means a lot."

As familiar scenery sped by the windows, she realized how relieved she felt now that she'd made so many important decisions. She'd thrown off the burden of indecision, and now she could get back to enjoying however much time she had left.

With any luck, she still had plenty of years ahead of her.

Chapter Thirty-Four
GIFT OF TRANSITIONS

Late Summer 2015

THE MAN NEXT TO Celia slapped his last playing card down in frustration, and she grinned. "When was the last time we beat these two, Penelope?" he asked, rubbing the bridge of his nose with a gnarled finger. The chair creaked ominously under him as he leaned back.

"Marvin, if you'd paid closer attention to what was led, they wouldn't have taken those last two tricks. And be careful with my chair. Not a one of us could help get you up off my kitchen floor if you break it."

Helen counted the stack of tricks in front of both Celia and Penelope, added the column of figures on the scratch paper next to her elbow, then gathered up the cards. "Good game, you two. Don't be too hard on yourselves. Remember, Celia and I have been playing bridge together for as long as I can remember. We're hard to beat."

Penelope snorted. "And humble, too."

"Few would accuse Helen of being humble," Celia pointed out. She tried to scoot her chair away from the table so she could cross her legs, but it wobbled. Marvin's wasn't the only chair practically falling apart. "You may need to think about investing in a new set of table and chairs, Penelope. I'm not sure how many more bridge games this one can handle. Or you need to accept my invitation to come play at my house."

The blue-haired woman to Celia's right shook her head. "You know I like to host our games. Besides, my Rebecca mentioned she has an extra set I can have. She just needs to find the time to bring it to town."

"Rebecca . . . she's your daughter, right?" Helen asked as she slid the cards into their box.

"My one and only," Penelope confirmed. "She's a busy girl. Haven't seen her in a while. Years ago, she was a friend of Celia's nephew, back when they were in college."

Helen raised her eyebrows. "Really? She knew Ethan? Small world."

Celia nodded. "I remember you telling me that. I keep meaning to mention it to Ethan, but I can't seem to remember anything these days."

Marvin stood and reached for the cookie tray on the counter. "You remembered enough to trounce us in cards today," he pointed out, handing the tray to Helen.

Helen picked out a chocolate chip cookie from the selection and passed it on to Celia. But a pinch deep in her stomach reminded Celia she should pass on the treat. Her stomach hurt most of the time now, and she suspected the source of the pain was something she should see a doctor about, but she'd ignored it as long as possible. At ninety-two, she expected some aches and pains.

All things considered, she thought she was doing relatively well. If a doctor had bad news, she didn't want to hear it. She remembered the news Ruby received years earlier when she went to the doctor for what started out as a backache. Her dearest friend died within a year of that visit. Celia already beat cancer once. Maybe it had finally caught up with her again. Ruby had tried to fight her cancer, and her last six months had been miserable.

She passed the tray of cookies on to Penelope.

"You don't want one?" the woman asked, surprised. "You never pass up my homemade cookies."

"It's getting late, and I have a nice roast in the oven for when I get home. I don't want to ruin my dinner."

Helen's skeptical glance reminded Celia they'd discussed stopping for a quick dinner after bridge, meaning there was no roast in the oven at home, but her friend had the good sense not to point this out in front of their hostess.

"You have more willpower than I do," Penelope said, taking the largest remaining cookie and setting the tray down in the middle of the table. "Are we on for next week, then?"

Celia considered how best to respond. She enjoyed playing cards, but every week was getting to be too much for her.

"I'm afraid I'll be out of town next week," Helen piped in, saving Celia from admitting she didn't want to play again so soon.

"Where are you off to?" Marvin asked. He was never shy about delving into their personal lives.

"I'm accompanying my granddaughter, Karen, to a work conference. I'll be out of town for a week."

Penelope set her cookie down on the tabletop. "Say, Celia . . . I'm sorry to bother you with this, but my toilet has been acting up again. Should I call a plumber, or do you want to get someone over here?"

"I looked at it, but there's corrosion," Marvin said. "I think some of the innards need to be replaced."

Celia grinned at his less-than-professional observation of what might be wrong with his neighbor's toilet. If she remembered correctly, Marvin had worked as an electrician years ago. The retiree's skill set must not extend to plumbing.

"If you know someone, go ahead and call, and send me the bill," she said. "If you have trouble, let me know. I can check with my nephew if you don't find someone. He's a local contractor, so he'd have some names. The guy I used moved away last month."

Penelope nodded. She broke another chunk of her cookie off and took a nibble. "You're so good to us, Celia. I've been meaning to ask you something, and I hope you don't take offense."

Feisty Penelope didn't filter words when she got riled, so Celia braced herself. The woman's grit helped her survive four marriages. Celia suspected Marvin wouldn't mind making it five marriages. He acted as if he might have a crush on his elderly neighbor.

"What's on your mind, Penelope?"

Penelope exchanged a hesitant look with Marvin before replying, as if the two of them had already discussed whatever it was Celia's tenant wanted to talk to her about.

"You've always been more than fair with us here, Celia. But aren't you going to want to sell this place before too long? You shouldn't still be worrying about things like busted toilets and washing machines that won't spin out anymore."

Celia sighed. "Is that darn thing still acting up?"

"I'll mention it to the plumber, too, if you'd like," Penelope offered. "But like I was saying, you probably won't be our landlord forever, and Marvin and me, we're just a little worried about a new owner raising the rent on us. We know you could charge us more."

Celia thought about suggesting the two of them shack up together to save on rent, but then that would leave her with an empty unit she needed to fill, and she hated looking for new renters. Keeping rents low helped minimize vacancies. "I can assure you, I don't have any intention of selling. I enjoy having a little extra pocket money each month from this place."

Helen rolled her eyes. She thought Celia was far too generous with her tenants. But Celia had enough money. She didn't need to make things tight for these fine people renting from her.

"And when I die, this place will pass to my nephew, Ethan. My family is aware of my philosophy behind running my rental properties. I like to keep my rents reasonable, and in return my tenants take care of my properties and seldom leave. Hopefully he'll take a similar approach. Does that help calm your nerves over what will happen when I kick the bucket?"

Penelope grinned and popped the rest of her cookie into her mouth. As soon as she could talk, she shrugged. "You know what I always say, Celia: Ain't a one of us getting out of here alive! And some of us are just closer to the inevitable finish line than others. It'll be the answer to my prayers if they carry me out of here on a stretcher, feet first."

"I wish you wouldn't talk that way, Penelope," Marvin chastised her. "I don't like to think about you getting carried out of here, dead or otherwise."

Penelope winked at the man, causing him to blush. Celia loved Penelope's spirited attitude. And, despite her age, her faded beauty was still apparent. Dear Marvin was clearly under her charms.

"You two are model tenants," Celia said. "Trust me when I say I'll do my best to protect you as long as possible. But there is only so much I'll be able to do from the great beyond."

Helen pulled up in front of Celia's house and parked. "Why did you lie to Penelope about a roast in the oven?"

Celia sighed as she reached for the door handle. "My stomach is giving me a little trouble again."

"Did you try the prune juice like I suggested?"

Dropping her head back against the head rest, she closed her eyes and grinned. "You know we're old when all we seem to talk about are bowel movements and aching joints."

Helen turned off the motor. "Do you remember when we talked about fashion and men?"

Celia lifted her head. "I remember when *you* talked about fashion and men. Vaguely. But that was literally a lifetime ago."

Helen sat with that for a minute, her fingers tapping against the steering wheel. "Are you sure you don't want to grab dinner somewhere?"

Celia glanced at her watch, surprised to see it was only just past four. Why was she so tired? Maybe it was the late summer heat. She could already feel it warming the interior of the car after Helen cut the engine and the air-conditioning.

"I'll pass tonight, Helen. I hope you don't mind. I'm not up for it."

Helen shifted in the driver's seat to face her. "You need to go see your doctor. You aren't acting like yourself. Something isn't right and I'm worried about you."

"I'm sure I'll be fine. Nothing a good night's sleep won't cure. I am enjoying my new bed, by the way. Thank you for the suggestion."

The truth was that the new bed she'd ordered months earlier had done little to help with her sleep, but it allowed her to watch television and read more easily when sleep so often eluded her in the dead of night.

"Just make sure you aren't spending too much time in bed, Celia. You need to stay active. Keep moving."

Helen was right, but Celia still bristled at the condescending tone her oldest friend always used to deliver wise advice. It was time to go in. Socializing wore her out more than it used to. All she wanted to do was get inside and put her feet up—after she took some antacid. She clicked off her seatbelt and opened her door.

Once out on the sidewalk, she poked her head back through the open door. "Thank you for driving, Helen. I'm sorry I'm not up for dinner. I'm sure I'll feel better tomorrow. Why don't you stop back tomorrow afternoon? We'll have tea."

Helen turned her car back on. The late-model Mercedes purred so quietly, Celia couldn't even hear it. "I'll stop by around two. But, Celia, promise me you'll put a call in to your doctor."

Celia stepped back and pushed her door shut, a finger wave her only response to Helen's directive before turning back around to face her house. As her friend pulled away, she straightened her shoulders and headed for her front door, intent on projecting the image of a strong, confident woman in case Helen peeked back at her in her rearview mirror. She needed the woman to stop pestering her.

Her hand clasped the small railing she'd asked Ethan to install at the base of the short flight of stairs that served as a transition between the sidewalk and her elevated front yard. The metal was hot under her fingers. As Helen's Mercedes rounded the corner and disappeared from sight, Celia paused, one foot on the lowest step.

Fall was in the air, despite the day's warmth. She looked forward to the riot of color the trees rimming her home produced every autumn. A few of the leaves on the massive oak on the north side of the house already sported a crimson blush, its crown of lush greenery a glorious sight from her bedroom window. She'd have sworn on a stack of Bibles there'd been no red amongst the green that morning. It wouldn't be long before the transformation from one season to the next was in full swing.

As she rested, her eyes took in the large, cone-shaped blooms of her prized hydrangeas that graced the front of her home. Bronze tips broke up the riot of creamy white. This year she should snip off some of those blooms and hang them in the basement to dry. She could fashion a pretty centerpiece around them later by adding in sprays of evergreen and pinecones.

She'd stopped putting up a real Christmas tree two years earlier. She'd opted instead for a smaller, artificial tree, much to the disappointment of her family when they'd arrived for Christmas Eve. But the tiring process of heading to one of the local tree lots, picking out a tree, having it delivered, watering it every day, and the mess it left once the annual festivities were over and everyone had headed back to their own busy lives, had become too much. She did miss having a fresh tree in her living room. The scent of one always reminded her of Whispering Pines.

A car drove by and the driver tapped their horn, pulling her out of her reverie. It was one of her neighbors across the street, probably arriving back home after her day at the office. She popped out of her minivan, yelled a friendly hello to Celia, and rushed inside.

She has a family to cook for, Celia thought, grasping the handrail tighter to help pull herself up the stairs. An image of two women Celia had worked with years earlier danced through her brain as she proceeded up her walk. Both worked hard at the office, then they'd rush home to get dinner on the table for their families.

While Celia never had a family to rush home to, other than her mother, she liked to think she'd played some small part in paving the way for women to take on more and more responsibility in the workforce. The two women Celia had known did clerical work, but the woman across the street worked in a law firm, not as a secretary, but as a lawyer. When Celia ran into her at their neighboring mailboxes earlier in the summer, the woman had confided that she was on the partner track. Achieving partnership in a law firm wasn't easy for anyone, and that woman still had three children at home. Back in Celia's day, they would never consider a woman for that type of role.

Women were making genuine progress these days.

Celia knew she'd been an anomaly when she was building her career. She'd felt a sense of satisfaction in a job well done, but it was never easy. The fact she was a woman working in a role normally reserved for men prevented her from the level of success she'd craved. It wasn't until years after she'd retired that she allowed herself to acknowledge she gave up too much for work that didn't ultimately leave her as fulfilled as she'd hoped at the beginning of her career.

How different things would be if she was entering the workforce now, as a young woman, instead of back in the late 1940s. She held no doubt she'd have taken over everything for Preston eventually. She grinned, remembering how she'd seldom lacked confidence at work. What she *had* lacked was opportunities, despite Preston's faith in her. Even he, though more accepting than most, had held deep-seated beliefs in the roles of men and women.

At the base of the second set of stairs leading to her front door, she paused again. Another stabbing pain hit her midsection, this one far more intense than the one she'd felt at the bridge table.

"Everything all right, Celia?" the woman across the street yelled from her front yard. She'd come back out, presumably after starting dinner, and now stood watch as their family dog did his business.

Putting on a brave face, Celia turned and waved. "Just admiring my hydrangea!"

Satisfied with this, the woman waved back, then hurried her dog inside.

Alone again, Celia eyed the row of blossoming bushes to her right. Up close, she could better see her spent rose bushes. In early spring and summer, the roses stole the show, but their time this year had come and gone. Beneath them, curling brown petals, with only hints of yellow and pink remaining, littered the ground.

Maybe tomorrow she'd feel up to doing a bit of work out here. She'd prune and sweep up. Fall was glorious in its vibrant colors, but it was also a messy time, and, like all wonderful parties, it required clean-up in its wake.

One last hurrah.

Chapter Thirty-Five

Gift of Honesty

"Did you call the doctor like I told you to?" Helen asked the moment Celia answered her knock on the front door.

"Hello to you, too, Helen. Yes, I agree, we certainly needed this rain," Celia deflected as she let her friend inside and closed the door.

Helen unbuttoned the tan trench coat she'd been wearing on rainy days for at least two decades. "It's too cold for late August, if you ask me. And you didn't answer my question."

Celia took the wrap and hung it next to the door. Despite the garment's age, Celia couldn't see any wear around the wrists or hem. Helen never scrimped on quality. "It's a good thing you're heading to Florida, then. This weather front certainly cooled things down since yesterday."

"Saturday can't come soon enough. This wet weather is terrible for my arthritis," Helen grumbled, heading back to Celia's kitchen. "I'll take that tea you mentioned yesterday."

Celia headed instead for her recliner in the living room, thinking the humidity in Florida wouldn't help Helen's arthritis, either. "I already have the tea set out in here."

Helen stopped at the kitchen entrance. "Why didn't you say so?"

"I just did," Celia shot back. That ache, deep in her stomach, throbbed again. Maybe it was an ulcer, and Helen's insistence that she call the doctor was irritating it.

Helen laughed.

"What's so funny?" Celia asked, dropping into her chair.

"We sound like two crotchety old women," Helen replied, taking a seat on the couch. "When did that happen?"

Celia grinned, despite her irritation with her friend. She should be used to the swings Helen inevitably brought about in her own mood by now. "Let's see. We're ninety-two years old now, so . . . probably thirty years ago."

"That long? No. I'd say it's only been twenty years."

She shrugged.

"I don't know," Helen went on. "Maybe I *shouldn't* join Karen in Florida. The trip might take too much out of me."

Sighing, Celia poured herself a cup of tea. "It's been a few years since I've gone anywhere. Ever since Ruby passed, I haven't had much desire to travel. Hard to believe it's been seven years already. But, I admit, the idea of warm sand on a sunny beach somewhere sounds tempting. If you feel up to it, Helen, go. It's not like it's going to get any easier for us. Besides, you'll be traveling with Karen. She'll see that you get there and back."

"Actually, she's already down there. I'm supposed to meet her at the hotel."

This surprised Celia. She'd assumed grandmother and granddaughter would travel together. "Why didn't she wait for you?"

"She's meeting up with a friend from college. I didn't want to rain on their parade. If I get there Saturday evening, we'll still have a few days to play before her conference starts on Wednesday."

"What will you do while she's in meetings?"

"I'll take a book along. Room service sounds delightful. I'm tired of cooking for myself."

Celia didn't think sitting alone in a hotel room fifteen hundred miles from home sounded like much fun. "Was it your idea for you to fly down there to join her?"

"Oh, it was Karen's idea. She's really excited about it."

"Why isn't her husband going?"

Helen paused. "I suppose he has to work. The man works all the time. Karen said he liked the idea of me going with her so she wouldn't be lonesome."

Celia still found the whole idea odd. It didn't sound like the trip promised much fun for Helen. Flying was tiring, even in first class as Helen always was. What if the trip was too much for the woman?

Selfishly, Celia hated the idea of being the last of their foursome. She and Helen may have their differences, but they'd faced life together since the very beginning. There'd been highs and lows, and gaps through the years when they'd barely spoken, but Helen was always a phone call away. Celia didn't think she could bury another friend.

"Maybe you should stay home," she hedged. "Flying can take a lot out of old gals like us."

"That's probably what I *should* do, but how often does someone get invited on a tropical vacation with their granddaughter?"

How often, indeed.

Celia wondered at this, but she still wasn't sure why the whole idea of the trip felt strange to her. Helen would do whatever she wanted, regardless of Celia's advice, so she let the subject drop. Besides, there was something more pressing Celia was finally ready to discuss with her. The stomach discomfort she was feeling more and more these days filled her with sudden unease. Regardless of which one of them would be the last man—or *woman*—standing, she had to know how much Helen knew about Virginia and her birth parents.

"If you're set on the trip, I wish you safe travels, my friend. But there's something important I've been meaning to discuss with you."

Helen relaxed against the back sofa cushion with a curious smile, arms crossed over her chest. "Sounds like you don't expect me to make it back."

Celia shook her head. "No. That's not it. But this is important to me."

"All right already, spit it out, then."

She took a deep breath and dove in. "Why didn't you ever tell us you and Warren adopted?"

She didn't miss the shock that stole across Helen's face. "What did you say?"

Celia felt a wave of lightheadedness wash over her. Did she really want to have this discussion now, after steering clear of the topic for twelve years? She'd thought about it almost every day since Eleanor told her what she'd found in her father's old things. She reached down and pulled the lever on her recliner, raising the footrest. Elevating her feet might prevent her from passing out over her own audacity to bring this up now.

"Celia, how do you know about that?" Helen asked, still looking dazed over the question.

Celia fought to remain calm. This conversation was long overdue. She needed to understand Helen's silence for all these years. How much did her old friend actually know?

"Eleanor discovered something strange. When she sold Preston's company, someone sent her a box or two of personal correspondence they found when cleaning out the corporate office in Chicago."

Helen nodded. "All right . . . and, based on your question, I assume she stumbled across something unexpected."

"You could say that," Celia agreed. Her fingers gripped the arms of her recliner. *Will I regret bringing this up?*

Almost sixty long years had passed since she'd given up her child. But she couldn't stay silent any longer. She'd lived with the questions for long enough. *Too* long.

"There were adoption papers. Preston's signature was on them . . . and so was Warren's. They signed the papers back in 1956. Wasn't that right around the year Virginia was born?"

The flush of surprise that had washed over Helen's cheeks faded away, leaving an ashen hue. "I swear I didn't know, Celia."

Celia snorted. "Helen, you obviously know you adopted your child. Please don't try to deny it."

Helen sat forward, resting her elbows on her knees and wringing her hands. "Now, hold on a minute. That isn't fair. Obviously I knew we adopted. After having Gloria and Diane, I had difficulties staying pregnant. I had three miscarriages. It was a terrible time. Warren always wanted a large family. We lived in Chicago then, and you and I had lost touch."

She paused for a sip of tea, then went on.

"I did charity work for an organization that helped unwed mothers place babies they couldn't raise. It's where I got the idea. When it became apparent that I wasn't likely to bear any more children, Warren and I talked about adoption. There was so much need. We had a lot to offer."

"You adopted Shirley, too, then?"

She nodded. "But you have to understand. That was our personal business. Warren's and mine. We didn't feel any differently about Shirley and Virginia than we did about Diane and Gloria. They were *our* girls, from the very beginning."

Celia doubted that was entirely true, but who was she to judge her friends' parenting capabilities? "Did you ever tell either of them they were adopted?"

"Of course not," Helen spat out, the color returning to her cheeks. "Why would we do that?"

Celia sat with her friend's response for a moment, mulling it over, while Helen poured more tea from the teapot that originally belonged to Celia's mother. Celia's cup sat untouched on the coffee table between them. She supposed Helen and Warren's reluctance to discuss adoption wasn't uncommon, especially back in the fifties.

Now that Helen had confirmed they'd adopted, Celia had to know the whole truth. "Is Virginia the baby girl I gave up?"

This time, Helen didn't flinch. "I think so. But I swear, Celia, I didn't know. I didn't even *suspect*, not until much later. *You* never told me you had a baby. At least not until decades later, the summer after you retired. But the moment you opened up about it, it was like the pieces of this jumbled puzzle fell into place for me."

Celia relaxed her clenched hands. She'd suspected for some time that Virginia and the baby she gave up so long ago were one and the same—ever since Eleanor stayed after her party—but she hadn't been sure. Helen's response hadn't been completely definitive, but it was enough.

"You weren't involved in the baby's adoption, then?"

Helen shook her head. "Not directly. Not that time. I knew the mother of the first baby we adopted, Shirley's mother, and that proved to be a problem. The poor woman had mental health issues, undiagnosed and unknown to us—at least at first. After we'd had Shirley for almost a year, the birth mother came back with demands. The adoption was legal, and final, but it got ugly. When Warren came to me later with the notion of adopting again, the only way I would agree to it was if everything was confidential and he handled it all. I had my hands full with three little girls, seven and under. I agreed to a fourth child because it was so important to Warren. He was excited, and I knew losing our babies devastated him as much as me."

The knowledge of what actually transpired was giving Celia her energy back. She snapped the footrest of her recliner down and sat forward, fiddling with her tea, giving herself a moment to process everything Helen had shared.

Then, amazingly, she giggled.

Helen's face turned up in a tentative smile. "You aren't mad at me, then? For not telling you what I suspected to be true when you admitted to giving up your own child? I never asked Warren to confirm it one way or the other, so this is all still speculation, of course. But the dates match up, and Warren mentioned once that Preston had somehow helped him. That always seemed a little strange to me."

"Do you think Warren had to agree to take the baby in exchange for his position at Preston's firm?" It was the same question she'd initially scoffed at when Ruby asked it, but now she wasn't so sure.

Helen's hand shook at Celia's words, sloshing tea into the cup's saucer. "Absolutely not. How can you even ask that? Preston and Warren were in discussions about Preston taking over Warren's family business for well over a year before the adoption."

Celia blew out a breath. "That's a relief. I never wanted to believe that might be true, but still . . . I couldn't help but wonder."

Helen pushed her cup and saucer away and eased back on the couch again. "When will we ever learn?"

"What do you mean?"

"Secrets," she said, rubbing the back of her neck. "Secrets are trouble. When we don't know the truth behind something, our minds have a way of filling the void with made-up stories. Warren was so excited when I agreed to take the baby he'd found. To be honest, a tiny part of me worried that maybe, just maybe, the child was the result of an affair he'd had with another woman. I hate to admit it, but that worm of an idea might have made me look at Virginia a little differently through the years. When you admitted you'd given up a child, and the pieces came together in my mind, it was such a relief to realize Warren was probably so happy because he could help an old friend . . . *you* . . . and grow our family. It was a win all around, but I didn't realize it until it was all over."

Helen's initial worry about Virginia's conception rendered Celia speechless for a heartbeat. Warren had worshipped Helen. Celia would bet everything she owned that he would never have cheated on his wife. After the surprise settled, she said as much.

Helen nodded. "I know, but our minds can play nasty tricks on us. False assumptions have torn too many relationships apart."

She made a valid point, Celia thought. Misunderstandings caused way too much heartache in the world. It was time for clarity. "Do you think Virginia suspects I'm her biological mother?"

"I don't think there is any way she would have ever suspected it, and I've never wanted to tell her," Helen admitted. "Now that you know the truth, will you tell her? I hope you don't, but I wouldn't blame you if you did. Believe me, it was always hard for me to accept that she seemed to like you better than me."

The grandfather clock near the front door chimed, pulling Celia's eyes to its familiar face. It had stood as silent witness to much of her life.

She remembered standing in front of it, holding Virginia's baby daughter shortly after inviting Virginia to come stay with her for a time. The slow, melodic chimes of the clock had fascinated the baby. Celia remembered the way the infant's chubby fingers had reached for the clockface, a sense of awe in her shining eyes.

Virginia was so young back then, yet already she was a newly widowed mother of a newborn, and she'd suffered yet another falling out with her parents. Celia knew Warren would have forgiven Virginia for anything, but Helen had a tendency to hold people to unreasonably high standards. It strained Helen's and Virginia's relationship in ways that were never repaired. Celia would have thought her friend would mellow over time in regards to Virginia, but she'd not seen any signs of that yet.

Despite their long friendship, Celia and Helen often butted heads. They were both strong-willed and opinionated, leading to frequent disagreements. Perhaps Helen had always seen the same thing, subconsciously, in Celia's biological daughter.

Karen, on the other hand, loved spending time with Helen growing up. She developed a taste for the finer things in life, things Helen could afford to give her granddaughter, but her mother never could. Helen and Karen were similar, although there was a sharper edge to Karen that even Helen never displayed.

As the reverberations of the old clock's chimes faded away, Celia met Helen's eyes, seeing the apprehension there as her friend awaited her answer.

"I doubt I'll tell her," she finally said. "What purpose would it serve at this point? It would devastate Virginia to learn Warren wasn't her biological father. And, despite your differences, I know she loves you, too, Helen."

Helen's right hand covered her heart. "Thank you, Celia. I'll admit that I've had quite enough drama with Karen, and I suspect learning I'm not actually her grandmother by blood might throw her into a tailspin. Now, it's getting late. I should be going. Tomorrow will be a busy day. I'll need to finish packing, and you know how I hate driving in the dark."

Celia glanced out the window at the deepening shadows. She'd summoned the courage to face a difficult discussion. And now that she had the answer she'd craved for so long, she wasn't sure how she felt about it. Life kept trying to teach her that the answers to life's biggest questions don't always bring peace of mind, but still she kept trying.

Celia tossed and turned most of the night. She should have given up and gone downstairs. Instead, she listened to the ticking of her alarm clock on the bedside table while watching the shadow cast by her curtains dance across the ceiling. Her open window allowed a cool breeze to stir the air. She was sure she caught the hint of smoke in the air. It was late—or early, depending on your perspective—but she'd sat at a bonfire at three in the morning when she was young. She hoped a group of friends was enjoying a similar experience off in the distance somewhere.

She gave up the struggle to rest at half past six. The horizon boasted a soft pink glow through the front picture window as Celia padded toward her kitchen. It was early, but a thought had occurred to her during the dark of night, and she needed to act. After filling her coffeepot with fresh water and grounds, she flipped the unit on and headed back to her office. She hoped the journal would be easy to find.

Her haphazard habit of journaling had ebbed and flowed through the years. Despite the inconsistency, her journals filled an entire row of the bookshelf on the south wall in her office. At least they were in chronological order. She didn't write in a journal anymore; it was too hard on her eyes. The most recent book, the one on the far right, started in 2006 and was only half filled. Precious few words, considering almost ten years had passed since she started that most recent journal.

But she wasn't looking to berate herself; she had something more important to do.

The sun was climbing now, early morning sunshine flooding the room. The journal she needed was the next in line. Her first entry captured the highlights from Christmas 2004. It was fun to read about the childish shenanigans of her nieces' and nephew's kids. She'd forgotten both Ethan's wife and Val were pregnant during that holiday season. Stacey gave birth to Dylan, Ethan's youngest, shortly after New Year's, while Val was still in the cute pregnancy stage with Dave, their first.

Flipping ahead, she found it—her first mention of the letter from the IRS. As she scanned the entries from that awful period in June and July 2005, she felt the anguish over Karen's betrayal all over again. With the benefit of hindsight, Celia felt immense disappointment in herself over the way she'd caved beneath the pressure Helen put her under to make the whole messy affair go away. She'd forgotten how easy it was to convince the IRS she'd been a silly old woman and made a mistake. She may have been eighty-two, but it rankled her now that she'd allowed Helen—and, probably, Karen—to devise a plan that included Celia using her age as an excuse. Pathetic. Helen obviously caught her at a weak moment.

"Why are you even reading this drivel?" Celia muttered.

She pushed up and out of her lumpy old loveseat and headed back to the kitchen with the journal in her hand. Helen's words from the previous day, about secrets and the havoc they can wreak on lives, had cost her sleep the night before. During those hours, as Celia lay there in the dark, she'd decided she needed to toss the journal where she'd written about Karen's embezzlement. The documentation Preston kept about the adoption caused pain and heartbreak years after he died, and Celia didn't want to repeat his mistake by allowing this journal to cause Virginia, her own daughter, heartache in the future. The decision she'd made in regards to Karen's crime still troubled her, but it was done. Jack had a letter she'd written and left for her family on the off chance something would come to light about it in the future. Other than that, Karen's mistake was in the past. Hopefully it was one stupid, isolated incident for Karen, and someone's discovery of it in Celia's journal in the future would serve no purpose.

In a burst of decisiveness the likes of which she hadn't felt in years, Celia dropped the journal holding Karen's secrets in the trash.

Chapter Thirty-Six
GIFT OF CAPTURED MEMORIES

THREE DAYS LATER, CELIA was back in her office. Her fingers ran across the spines of her many photo albums, pulling one off the shelf at random. Today would have been Ruby's ninety-third birthday. She missed her friend and was feeling nostalgic.

She pulled her office chair away from her desk, almost dropping the album when the chair tipped precariously. Celia set the heavy book on the desk and checked the chair. One roller had busted off. Yet another thing in this house, falling apart.

"Most things in here are as old as you," she reminded herself as she straightened. "What did you expect?"

Retrieving the photo album again, she turned for the doorway. It was a good thing Helen would be back in a few days. She was talking to herself too much.

She headed for her recliner, but hesitated when she noted the pillow and blanket draped over it. She was finding it easier to sleep in the chair at night. She'd need to put her bedding away if she didn't want her living room to turn into a quasi-bedroom.

"Later," she said, giving herself a pass. She was in the mood to look at photographs.

Settling instead at her dining room table, Celia flipped to the top page of the album, delighted to see she'd grabbed the one with pictures from her eightieth birthday party. That was the year her family gave her a new camera, so there were lots of pictures. These would be fun.

She smiled at a shot of her dear friends Ruby and Eleanor seated at a table in her backyard. Leaning in closer, she took in their familiar faces. Eleanor died in her sleep a year after they all turned eighty-five. How she missed them both.

"Happy birthday, Ruby," Celia whispered, her finger tapping the priceless photo. "We sure were lucky to celebrate so many together, weren't we? I hope you're having a special, heavenly birthday today."

Her finger moved on to the next two photographs. She remembered snapping these. The first was of a white vase filled with a glorious bunch of yellow roses. When she closed her eyes, she could practically smell them. All these years later, the smell of yellow roses still reminded her of Danny.

When she finished with this album, she should find the one that contained the pictures he'd sent her a lifetime ago, when she was still in college and he'd slipped off to join the war efforts. She'd loved those pictures so much that eventually she'd had duplicates made. She'd nestled one set into frames out at Whispering Pines. They provided a fun roadmap of life at the resort in the 1940s, and she'd felt compelled to leave them out there. But she couldn't bear to give them up, so a second set was the obvious answer.

Danny was gone now, too. In his final years, he became something of a hermit. He told her once that the horrors he witnessed during the wars and bloody skirmishes he covered as a photo journalist forever scarred his soul. When his son contacted Celia with news of his passing, she'd spent two lonely days crying in her own backyard, surrounded by yellow rose bushes. His death came months after Ruby's, and since Helen had never known Danny well, Celia was alone in her grief.

The pain had mellowed since then, and she'd learned to focus on the happy times with Danny. She was finally at a place where reminders of him usually brought smiles instead of tears.

"That's how special people deserve to be remembered," she reminded herself.

The adjacent picture featured the colorful arrangement Ed and Mary Dixon sent for her birthday when they couldn't attend her party. Too busy at Whispering Pines.

What would I have done without the two of them? she wondered, her finger outlining the pretty flowers they'd generously sent on that long-ago day. One thing was for certain: she wouldn't still own Whispering Pines. She'd need to decide what to do about the resort before next spring. Mary was living out east somewhere with her daughter now, after the heart attack that took Ed the previous May, which meant Whispering Pines had sat vacant, boarded up, this past summer. As far as she knew, it was the first time it had closed since it originally opened in the 1930s.

Celia hated the idea of her beautiful resort falling to ruin, but she didn't know if she could summon the strength to hire a new caretaker. With winter fast approaching, she didn't need to decide what to do yet. One year wouldn't mean the end of Whispering Pines. She'd figure out a way to keep it going until Renee was ready to take it over.

The poor girl wasn't ready yet. From what she was hearing, Renee had her hands full in Minneapolis. Her two kids participated in lots of school activities, and she seldom got home to see the rest of her family anymore.

Celia smiled as she turned the album's next page. A young Julie was pulling her father by the hand across Celia's backyard. Jim looked so healthy. She still couldn't believe he'd fallen so deathly ill, not long after her party.

"Knock-knock!"

Celia looked up in surprise at her brother's voice. She'd been so engrossed in her pictures that she hadn't heard anyone at the door. She stood and fought to move the heavy dining room chair out of the way so she could greet George properly.

When he noticed her struggle, he waved at her to stop. "I hope you don't mind that I let myself in."

Resting her hands on her hips, Celia shook her head. "Don't be silly. I don't mind. This is your home, too."

He laughed. "Technically, this place hasn't been home for fifty years, but I appreciate that you still feel that way."

"This is a nice surprise," she said, reaching her hands out to him as he came close and giving them a friendly squeeze. The chair was still in the way and prevented a hug. "What brings you by?"

George released her hands, shrugged off his light jacket, and draped it over the back of a chair. "I thought I'd stop and see what you needed done around the yard. I don't have time to do that actual work today, but I want to see what we need to do so the house is in good shape for winter. The snow will fly again before we know it."

"Bite your tongue, man. It isn't even October yet. Let's get through Halloween before you talk snow."

He clapped his hands together. "That's true! And you know how I love Halloween."

"You've loved it since you were little. I never understood your fascination with dressing up and all the ghost stories and whatnot. Remember when you and Gerry turned the basement into a haunted house? I thought Clarence was going to lose it when your little friends got into his wood shop and messed with his power tools."

Laughing, George shook his head. "I'd forgotten about that. As a grandfather now, I can see why he was so upset. Ten-year-old kids and power tools are a dangerous mix. I'm lucky he didn't tan my hide."

"Sit," she instructed. "Clarence's bark was always worse than his bite."

George pulled up a chair next to her. "He was a good man."

"That he was," she agreed.

"What are you doing?" George asked, sliding the photo album over so he could have a closer look. "Your party! I remember. That was a fun day."

"It was. I like to look at my old albums once in a while."

"Makes sense. Otherwise, why have them? You have quite a collection back there, don't you?"

"I do. Now that you mention it, I have a request."

He pulled the album even closer, studying the photos. "Sure. What do you need?"

"Nothing immediate. But can I have your word you'll take good care of my photo albums? I don't care what you do with all my journals. Burn them, maybe, in case there's anything embarrassing in them. But there's a lot of history in my albums. I'd appreciate it if you took some care with those. I know it's asking a lot. They take up space. But I worry what will happen to them when I'm gone. Maybe it's dumb. I'm not sure why it matters, but it does."

He straightened to meet her eye. "I promise I'll take good care of your albums. I agree with you. There is lots of fun history here. Your family will enjoy having them."

"I like the sound of that. *My* family. I've so often thought of myself as a woman without a family, but I know that isn't true. And you've been very good to me through the years, George. Gerry's been a big help, too."

Tilting his head, George's expression turned skeptical. "This isn't like you, Celia. Should I worry? Is everything all right?"

She adjusted the album so it sat open between them. "George, I'm ninety-two years old. No one lives forever. Looking through these, I'm reminded of that fact. Almost all my friends are gone. I just want to be prepared. When I die—"

"Celia! Do we have to do this now? I just stopped over to check your yard and say hello." Despite this, the grin he gave her told her he understood.

She returned his grin. "Just know that my lawyer, Jack, will help you with my estate."

He nodded. "Yes, dear sister, you've mentioned that to me once or twice. Or ten times. Is there anything new I should know about?"

She shifted in her chair, feeling a pang of unease at his questioning stare. "No, nothing new. I am going to make an appointment to see my doctor one of these days. Just routine. But I wouldn't mind some company. Would you come with me?"

"Just let me know when, and I'll take you."

"Thank you. Would you look at this picture? Can you believe Julie was ever that young? What is she now? Sixteen?"

"Seventeen," George corrected her. "And Jim looked so healthy then."

"I was just thinking that when you poked your head in. Lauren is even younger here. I bet it's been a long time since she smiled at her dad like that." Celia pointed to a picture of a miniature Lauren sitting in Will's lap. "I got the impression when we were at Lizzy's high school graduation party last spring that Lauren is fed up with her father."

"Lauren and pretty much everyone else. I feel bad for Jess. I feel like her marriage is headed in the same direction as Ethan's. Sometimes I wish she would just throw in the towel, but she puts on a brave face."

"Are Ethan and Stacey divorced, then?" Celia asked. "I hate to say it, but I never figured those two would make it."

"You didn't? I admit, I didn't see the breakup coming. When Ethan called to say she'd left, I was as shocked as he was."

She couldn't see how Ethan and George could have been surprised. The woman had seemed unhappy for years. She couldn't have been easy to live with, and Celia hoped Ethan would take this chance to rebuild a different life. But co-parenting with her wouldn't be easy either.

"Who is that?"

Celia squinted at the person George pointed to in the photograph, a dark-haired woman sitting next to Will and Lauren. "Oh. That's Karen."

"Hmm . . ." He leaned closer to the album page for a better look. "Karen Lark, right? The banker's wife?"

"Yes. She's my friend's granddaughter. Helen's. In fact, Helen is in Florida with her this weekend. Why Helen agreed to *that* trip is a mystery to me. I bet Florida is unbearably humid and buggy right now. Karen's mother is Virginia. You remember Virginia and Frank, don't you? They own the bookstore I help with once in a while."

George nodded, but Celia could see his mind was elsewhere. She reached to turn the page, but he put his palm out to stop her.

"Do they know each other?" He pointed between Karen and Will.

Celia looked from her brother's face to the smiling image of Virginia's daughter and Jess's husband. "I guess I don't know. They were sitting together in this picture, but I don't know if that was just by chance, or what the deal was. Why do you ask?"

George sat back in his chair, crossing his arms and rubbing his chin with his right hand. The gesture was one he did often, similar to the stance Clarence used when he was deep in thought. "Oh, I'm sure it's nothing."

"No, you don't. Don't shut down on me, George. I know you. Something's bugging you."

"It's just strange," he said, uncrossing his arms and motioning to the picture.

"What's strange?"

"Jess and the kids are coming over for dinner tonight. Will is out of town. Again. I could have sworn Jess said he was in Florida at some medical convention."

She laughed. "Maybe he'll run into Helen and Karen. Wouldn't that be a coincidence?"

"That would be a hell of a coincidence, all right," he agreed, but his expression didn't hold an ounce of humor.

"George, I can practically see the wheels turning in that brain of yours."

He shook his head and turned the album to the next page. "It's just strange," he said again. "Remember when you asked me to talk to Will a couple years ago? When he kept coming to you for financial help?"

"I do. And he's never asked again, so thank you for that."

George flipped the album page back to the one Celia was looking at when he first came in, tapping his index finger on Karen's face. "I met Will down at the Coach House for a drink. I swear I bumped into her coming out as I was going in. We greeted each other, and she kind of acted like she recognized me, but I couldn't place her. Huh. I'm sure it's nothing. Life is full of coincidences, isn't it?"

Celia wasn't sure whether George actually believed that, or if he worried he'd just stumbled on something that could cause Jess even more pain. She wasn't sure either. It would be a leap to assume anything, but maybe there was more to the story.

Before she could reply, George stood.

"Let me know when that doctor's appointment is, will you? I'm going to check around outside quick. I need to be home in an hour and traffic will be heavy. Lavonne will strangle me if I'm late, what with Jess and the kids coming over. I'll come by sometime this week and get started on the actual yardwork. If you think of anything else you need done, just make me a list."

She closed the album and stood, allowing her brother to move her chair out of the way.

"George, you're busy. I can hire someone to do the yard. Maybe I'll call Seth. Remember him? Ruby's grandson. He's always offering to help me out, and I promised Ruby I'd keep an eye on him."

George turned back to her as he reached the front door. "Isn't that the kid you lined up to help with the stained-glass windows at church?"

"That's him. Although he's not a kid anymore, I suppose. He must be in his mid-thirties by now. Today would have been Ruby's birthday, you know. Gone seven years already. He's probably missing her, too."

George clasped his hands and gave her a sorrowful look. "I'm sorry, Celia. I know you must miss her. Give this Seth kid a call, say hello, but don't ask him to come over. I want to help you. Let me do that, okay?"

Grinning, she agreed. It felt good to have someone fuss over her. "If you insist."

When he turned again to leave, he noticed the pillow and blanket on her recliner in front of the picture window. "Celia, are you sleeping in that chair?"

"Not right now."

"Don't be smart with me," he shot back. "First you mention a doctor's appointment, and then this. Now I am worried. If these stairs are giving you too much trouble, I can get some help over here and we can move that new bed of yours down to the main floor. Remember when we turned that room back there into a bedroom for Mom after the accident?"

Celia was sure her face turned white at his suggestion. She stood straighter, ignoring the pain in her stomach. She hadn't felt it all day until this stupid suggestion. "George, I may be old, but I can go up and down those stairs as many times a day as I choose. I'm not ready to be turned out to pasture yet, and don't you forget it."

His eyes grew round at the harsh rebuke. "Forget I mentioned it. Boy, sis, I forget what a tough old broad you are."

She softened at his teasing tone. She'd overreacted, but the notion that she might not be able to manage in her own home sent a chill down her spine. "Don't let it happen again."

With a salute and a smile, George left the house, closing the door behind him. "Lock this door!" she heard him yell from the other side.

She did as he asked.

As she passed the grandfather clock, she noticed it was nearly four. She'd meant to get that appointment made, and she hoped to catch Virginia at the bookstore. After her discussion with Helen the previous week, she wanted to spend time with her daughter.

The phone numbers were in her address book next to the fridge. She walked into the kitchen, pulling up short at the sight of the garbage bag near the back door. She should have asked George to take it to the alley for her. After calling to arrange to see her doctor in two weeks, and inviting Virginia to stop by the following afternoon, she decided to take the garbage out herself before it started to stink.

At the bottom of her back stairs, she stopped, remembering what was in the garbage bag. Her journal. The one that documented Karen's embezzlement from the Corner Market.

George's words floated back to her. She wasn't a big believer in coincidences. Karen may be with her grandmother now, but Helen had said she'd gone to Florida early to spend time with an "old friend" for a few days before her grandmother's arrival.

It was probably nothing, but Celia felt a sense of unease over throwing the journal away. Her fingers struggled to untie the plastic bag, but she persisted until she finally pried it open and fished out her journal. Old coffee grounds clung to the cover and Celia gave it a little shake. Some journal entries might prove to be too important to throw away.

Chapter Thirty-Seven
GIFT OF A DAUGHTER

CELIA REACHED FOR THE light switch in the darkness, her other hand keeping a tight grip on the handrail. She had no desire to tumble down the attic stairs. She'd tucked her old journal she'd retrieved from the garbage under her armpit. It still smelled faintly of coffee. She brought the photo album from her eightieth birthday party, too. It waited at her feet until the stairs were safely lit.

When she reached the top of the attic stairs, she looked around. All kinds of junk had found its way up here. There was no longer a clear pathway where George's kids—or grandkids now—could ride their bikes like they used to.

A long life, lived in the same house, made for lots of junk.

Ethan could deal with it all later. Maybe they'd have fun rifling through her things after she was dead. She certainly didn't have the energy to deal with it.

"It'll be a small price to pay for a free house," she reasoned out loud.

The sigh of the wind, whistling through the pipes in that way that used to scare the kids when they played up here, was the only reply.

She'd come up to find her blue trunk. After looking through the album with her brother, and saving the old, incriminating journal from the landfill, she felt compelled to put both items somewhere other than on the shelves in her office with all the others. Maybe she was being silly. Karen had probably just spent a few innocent days with an old college roommate or some such acquaintance, and was now tiring from more time with her ornery grandmother. Will was probably back at the hospital, working, despite a draining few days away at a medical conference filled with boring lectures. This trip up to the attic was probably, *hopefully*, completely unnecessary.

But if Karen hadn't reformed, Celia felt compelled to leave behind what evidence she could regarding previous misdeeds.

The large, enclosed clothing stand off to her left caught her eye. Pulled by what she knew to be inside, she set the album and journal down on a discarded bedside table and made her way over to the portable closet. The zipper was tricky, but Celia took her time opening it. Inside, Beverly's dresses seemed to shiver with delight as Celia ran her hand over their fabric. Or maybe it was *Celia* shivering in remembrance.

How she missed her sister.

It occurred to her then, as she toyed with a red flower along the hem of one dress, that she'd stopped talking to Beverly's spirit. Why was that?

"I'm sorry, Bev," Celia whispered, but only the wind sighed in reply.

She should have Ethan look at those pipes. They scared him as a child, but maybe he could fix them now.

"They aren't hurting anything," Celia heard. She turned around, unsure. Had she said that?

Shaking her head, she realized she needed to stay on task. Memories could overwhelm her. She zipped the cover on the rack and retrieved the two items she'd brought upstairs.

"Where is that trunk?" she asked, but of course there was no one to answer her.

She spied the chalkboard she'd salvaged from Clyde's store after he died. She remembered seeing her trunk over in that part of the attic when young Nathan carried the heavy board upstairs. She headed toward it. At first, all she could see were boxes containing her old Christmas decorations. She'd ask George to bring those down for her when he came back to work in the yard. If he put the boxes in a spare bedroom, she could get at them when it was time to decorate for the holidays again. On the floor next to the boxes was Clarence's old toolbox. She wondered if Ethan ever used the tools she'd given him out of that box so many years earlier.

Where is that trunk?

Then she glimpsed the unmistakable blue color dear Clarence had painted her trunk. The boxes of decorations had hidden it from view. She moved them out of the way, then fished the keys out of her pocket.

Why did the trunk have to sit so low to the ground?

"Get down there, Celia, and quit acting like a feeble old woman. Don't worry, Beverly. I'm back to talking to myself again. I'll be talking to you again, too."

A car door slammed outside, and she checked her watch. It was too early for Virginia to be here yet, but she needed to get this done so she'd be back downstairs in time to greet her. The sound of a car driving away meant it was probably her neighbors, coming or going.

Celia unzipped her sweatshirt and got down on her knees, pain shooting up both legs. She tried the lock, and on her second attempt it snapped open. Pushing back to her feet, she pulled the lid open. It felt heavier than she remembered. Or maybe she was weaker.

The scent of cedar wafted out to meet her. This part of the attic was dark when there was no natural light, but now the sunlight from the nearby window illuminated the contents of the open chest.

Her much younger face smiled up at her from a yellowed newspaper. Celia picked up the paper, squinting so she could read the date in the corner: *November 21, 1955.* She did the math.

"I was only thirty-two years old," Celia whispered, gazing in amazement at her youthful face.

This article was Danny's excuse to come back and see her that Thanksgiving. They'd conceived Virginia that very night.

Celia shuddered. So many memories.

She pulled back the white tissue paper and let her fingers roam across the fragile white linen of the christening gown. Would anyone else in her family, any of George's descendants, ever wear it as she and Beverly had when they were newborns? It bothered her a little to remember Karen also wore it as an infant.

Under the miniature gown was the wedding gown her grandmother had gifted to her.

"Such a shame . . ."

Her fingers danced over the pearl button at the back of the neckline. The exquisite dress deserved to clothe a beautiful bride someday. Celia didn't have the strength to pull it out to look at it, but she could remember the intricate lace that lined the arms and bodice, and the heavy silk that formed the skirt.

With a sigh, she dug a little deeper, careful not to damage either dress. A shade of blue was there on the bottom, lighter in color than the trunk but recognizable all the same. She reached for the booties, the soft yarn caressing her fingers. Beneath the booties that Beverly had so lovingly crocheted for her during her last days was a slip of paper. Celia pulled that out, too. She held the booties in one hand and angled the paper to catch the light, not remembering what it was. The writing was hard to distinguish, faded with time, but it was a sales receipt. She remembered then. Clarence gave Celia this trunk just after Beverly died. Celia let the paper slip from her fingers with an anguished sigh. Poor, beautiful young Beverly, gone much too soon. Celia buried her nose in the handmade booties to get her mind on something other than the receipt for her sister's cemetery plot.

"I wish I'd have remembered these were in here," she whispered, admiring her sister's handiwork. She would have passed them on to George when Ethan was born.

And that was it. There was nothing else.

These treasured items represented some of the most critical choices Celia had made in her life. She could have gotten married, but she'd picked her career instead. She could have kept her child, but she gave her up. It was what society demanded of her back then. During the middle of the last century, single working women didn't have—or, at least, didn't *raise*—babies out of wedlock.

Another car door slammed outside. This time, it sounded closer. It might be Virginia.

Part of her longed to show Virginia her nearly forgotten treasures in the old trunk. After all, they were technically part of *her* heritage, too. But Celia had decided she wouldn't divulge this final secret to her daughter. There was too much at stake for people that meant a lot to her.

She'd have to hurry. She set the booties back inside, rearranged the wedding dress, and laid the christening gown back inside, too, covering them all with the tissue paper. Then she added the photo album and journal on top, careful to keep the tissue between the books and the fabric. She closed the cover with a grunt, careful not to let it slam or catch her fingers. She slid the padlock back in place, dropped the keys in her pocket, and glanced at the boxes of decorations.

The doorbell rang below, and so she left them on the floor. George should still be able to find them. Celia hurried over to the stairs, careful not to trip, and headed down, a tight grip on the handrail again. She was halfway down when she realized she hadn't put the newspaper back in the trunk.

"Probably for the best," she muttered. The acid in the newsprint wasn't good for the fabric inside the trunk. No one would care about a silly old article anyhow.

She snapped off the light and stepped back into the upstairs hallway, shutting the door behind her. Hopefully Virginia would be patient, she thought, as the doorbell rang a second time.

"If you want to meet my daughter, Beverly, follow me," Celia whispered, grinning at the notion of her long-dead sister's spirit silently observing their tea from the stairwell.

As their laughter died away, Virginia reached for Celia's hand.

"I hope you know how much I appreciate all you've done for me through the years. You are like a second mom to me, only better. You know: fun, supportive, giving. All the things my real mother never was to me."

Celia patted the back of Virginia's hand. "And you were like a daughter to me, Virginia," she said, squeezing the younger woman's fingers before sitting back in the recliner. "I'm so glad we've stayed in touch for all these years."

Stifling a yawn, Celia stared at the woman sitting on her couch, in the same spot Helen had sat while sharing tea with her the week before. Today, she and Virginia spent the better part of an hour laughing and reminiscing about the early days, when Virginia had brought her baby to live with Celia following the death of her estranged husband.

"You saved us back then."

"Please don't make me out to be the hero here. I had room. You needed a place to stay while you rebuilt your life. You are the hero in this story, my dear."

Virginia grinned at Celia's words. "I did raise a daughter all by myself, didn't I? At least until Frank came along. And it wasn't easy. I suppose I could give myself a pat on the back, too—if I could reach it. But I'm not quite that limber anymore."

Celia laughed, flexing both her own knees, trying not to grimace. "Don't complain to *me* about your body, Virginia Fisk. I've got thirty-two years on you. You aren't even sixty yet!"

Virginia reached back with her right hand and tapped her left shoulder. "Close enough."

"I refuse to discuss aging bodies with you. That's all I seem to talk about with your mother these days."

At the mention of Helen, Virginia's hand fell and her smile slipped.

Celia hated the animosity between the two. "Ginny, dear, will you do me a favor?"

"I'd like to say I'd do anything you asked of me, but I'm afraid what you're about to say has something to do with my mother. Must we ruin a perfectly good gab session by bringing her into this?"

"She really isn't that bad, you know. The two of you just rub each other the wrong way."

Virginia shrugged. "It wasn't always like that. She used to treat me like a princess. Both her and Daddy. But that all changed at some point. I think I was in junior high. I'm not sure what happened, but Mother suddenly objected to everything I did or said, and nothing ever changed her mind. Daddy was much kinder."

Celia nodded. "I remember those dynamics. I suspect your mother struggled with how best to handle you when you started developing interests in areas she knew little about."

Virginia's cynical snort spoke volumes.

"What? It's true. You love poetry and romance. Your mother, on the hand, has always been a very practical woman."

"*Snobby* woman, you mean."

"Maybe a bit," Celia conceded. "But she was raised that way. A silver spoon and a tongue sharper than most."

Virginia crossed her legs and tugged at the rose-colored skirt riding up over her knee. "If that's what you think of her, why have you been friends your whole life?"

"That's simple. Beneath your mother's prickly exterior is a person loyal to those she loves to her very core."

Still picking at the hem of her skirt, Virginia said, "Too bad she never loved me, then."

Celia sighed. "You don't believe that. Your mother loves you. She just didn't know how to *like* you very much when you were younger. And believe me, she's not proud of that. I think she's worked so hard to forge a strong relationship with your Karen to atone for the countless ways she's afraid she failed you."

Virginia sat with that for a moment, a single tear creeping down her cheek. "I'm not sure I believe you."

Celia thought she understood. Helen's harsh treatment of Virginia through the years would leave anyone doubting her love. But Celia did believe Helen loved

Virginia. "I don't think there is another relationship on earth more complicated than the one between a mother and her daughter."

Virginia flicked away another tear and sat up straight, a tentative smile replacing the frown. "True. It's not as if my relationship with Karen is all flowers and sunshine. Sometimes I just don't understand that woman."

Laughing, Celia tapped on her own chest. "I was plenty headstrong, back in the day, and I'm sure some of my decisions left my mother shaking her head and losing sleep at night, too. I think we put too much pressure on ourselves with this most important of relationships. Aren't we all just trying to do our best, clashing personalities and all?"

Virginia picked up her tea cup and drained what was left in the bottom. Celia noticed she held the cup exactly as Helen did. The women weren't as different as they both thought; they were simply too close to see it.

"Thank you for inviting me over today, Celia. As always, it's been a pleasure. But I should be going. That's the third time you've yawned in as many minutes, and I don't want to wear you out."

Celia clasped a hand over her mouth, embarrassed that she hadn't even noticed yawning so many times. "But I don't want you to go. This is so much fun."

Virginia stood and gathered their cups and saucers, as well as Celia's prized teapot, onto the silver tray. "Don't get up. I'll set this in the kitchen quick."

Celia watched Virginia disappear into her kitchen. She didn't know if she'd made any progress in convincing the woman to give Helen another chance, but she'd tried. If the wounds Helen imposed on Virginia ran too deeply, there was nothing more Celia could do. She'd helped Virginia through the years, when she needed it the most, before she had any inkling at all that she was her biological mother. The maternal instinct was strong, no matter what the thinking mind thought. Celia had spent too many years mourning the loss of her child, when she was actually here all along.

The best blessings can't be explained.

Chapter Thirty-Eight
Gift of Wisdom

Celia eyed her bed with apprehension. Sleeping in her recliner downstairs was more comfortable, but after George's comments, her stubborn streak demanded she keep using her upstairs bedroom. Her brother was trying to be helpful, but the notion she was losing her ability to manage the stairs held an ominous ring. She didn't want to be one step closer to either the Grim Reaper or the ground.

Besides, a ground-level bedroom meant she'd have to give up her office; a preposterous idea given all she still had to do. Her office was where she conducted all her business.

Seth would be by in a few days so they could update his business plan—an annual task she enjoyed immensely. Time with Seth was the next best thing to time with Ruby.

Virginia dropped off the most recent bank statement for the bookstore, too, when she'd stopped over for tea. Celia liked to help Frank keep things up to date.

She was less involved with Homes Sparkle these days, given Joyce and John's daughters were taking over, but they might still need her expertise, too.

Celia wouldn't allow herself to slow down. Things in motion stayed in motion. *She*, therefore, had to stay in motion.

She left her bedroom to retrieve Beverly's box of writings from their old bedroom. Reading one of Bev's stories before bed might help her relax enough to enjoy a decent night's sleep.

At least, that tactic *used* to help.

Her tenacity kept her upstairs in bed all night, but her sleep was fitful. Will appeared again, his hand extended. After that, poor Helen floated into her dreams, dazed and confused in a busy airport somewhere, unable to find her way back home. Celia stood beside Preston's bedside, promising to protect Whispering Pines, no matter what.

When the singsong of birds woke her in the morning, the sheets were tangled around her legs and her flannel nightgown was damp with sweat. Despite the state of her bedding and pajamas, the surrounding air was chilly. She'd have to forgo the pleasure of sleeping with an open window until springtime. Summer had tiptoed into autumn.

Celia fumbled for her glasses and did her best to straighten the sheets and blanket around her. She fought the urge to jump out of bed and get started on her day. It wouldn't hurt to stay where she was for another ten minutes. Her fingers caressed the silk binding along the top edge of the blanket one of her nieces had gifted her the previous Christmas. She'd thought it superfluous when she first saw it; the blankets she'd used for years were fine. She did have the good sense not to admit as much during gift opening, and later, when her old blanket was in the laundry, she'd tried it. The soft, luxurious feel of the new blanket reminded Celia of the beauty in life's simple pleasures.

She tossed her old blankets that same day.

Shivering in the chill air, she pulled her new blanket up to her chin, watching the leaves waltz on their branches outside of her window. The inevitable kaleidoscope of greens, soft yellows, deep goldenrod, and magical glimpses of red, had begun. Nature's riot of color would be short lived, replaced in short order with a bleached blanket of white. The only breaks in the snowy view would be the black skeletons of naked trees and the deep green of pines.

Even in the dead of winter, her Whispering Pines would boast more color than the view out her bedroom window. The pine trees would stand sentinel around the resort, protecting it until it could spring to life once again. The dark smudges of vacant cabins nestled in the snow, their doors and windows popping with red-painted trim, would wait patiently for another season of campers to descend. They'd leave their troubles at home and remember how to laugh again.

Celia jolted awake. The *beep-beep-beep* of a garbage truck in the alley pulled her out of her dream. She must have dozed off.

It was a treat to travel back to Whispering Pines, even if it was only in her mind.

Would Renee appreciate the gift of Whispering Pines she'd receive at Celia's passing? Or would her niece curse her for it? Taking on the resort would be an enormous task—a fact Celia knew all too well.

Should I call Renee to come over today? I could sit her down and talk to her about it, explain my notion that the resort could ultimately be a lifesaver of sorts for her.

Celia's stomach rumbled with hunger. When was the last time she'd eaten anything? With a sigh, she folded her blanket and sheets out of the way and rose from her bed, careful to confirm her legs would support her. She donned her robe, found her slippers, and made the slow journey downstairs to the kitchen.

No, she wouldn't invite Renee over. Her bequeath to her niece wasn't up for discussion or debate, which was what could happen if they discussed it face to face.

A letter would be better. That way Renee wouldn't be able to convince her to change her mind. Celia still felt her niece might need Whispering Pines more than the resort would need her niece.

Preston's request, made to her mere moments before he drew his final breath, had proved to be a decades-long dilemma for Celia. She wanted to avoid that for Renee. For all of her family, really, when it came down to how they would use the legacy she'd leave for each of them. She'd write each of them a letter, explaining her logic behind the decisions, and provide them with an escape clause of sorts. She didn't want to make anyone suffer under the weight of obligations.

She'd love to leave them with all of her hard-earned wisdom, but that was never possible.

We learn about life by living it.

But perhaps she could give them a few guideposts that might help along the way.

Her hunger forgotten, she padded back to her office and rummaged through a desk drawer. An unopened box of monogrammed stationery was in there somewhere. She might as well use it up. Only her own father had shared her initials, and he'd died when she was five.

She found the stationery and used her letter opener to break the seal on the box. She'd tucked the opener into her purse the day she retired—a souvenir after forty years on the job. Inside the box her fingers felt the silky texture of the quality paper. The stationery would serve her purpose nicely.

She set the first sheet at a comfortable angle on her desktop, the fancy scroll of her initials at the top, and smiled at the ostentatiousness of it all. Helen probably used pricey paper like this all the time.

She found her favorite pen in the pencil cup. Her eyes caught the dusty wine bottle behind the cup; the few remaining stems of once vibrant flowers she'd plucked from her eightieth birthday bouquets still protruded out the top of its neck, brittle after twelve years. But both the bottle and the dried blooms were precious to her. They represented lifelong friendships.

Those were the types of things she wanted to impress upon her nieces and nephews.

She let her eyes drift shut, recognizing the size of the task she was undertaking. Crafting poignant letters for each of her beloved family members might be her last chance to help them on their own life journeys. Her upcoming doctor's appointment would be a turning point. She could feel it, deep in her bones. That gave her two weeks. Writing more than a dozen letters would take her days. Her eyes would suffer. But she was up for the task. Few things had defeated her in the past. She'd complete this, too.

With a deep breath and one last glance at her vintage wine bottle, Celia set pen to paper.

September 1, 2015

My dearest Renee,

I feel the time is near to say my goodbyes to you. I do not know exactly when the Good Lord will call me home, but I suspect it won't be long now. My body weakens and my vision fades. Leaves will soon turn golden outside my window. It may be their last glorious show I will see, these trees which have sheltered my home most of my life. The wind will again turn sharp and cold, whisking the leaves away for another winter from which I may be absent.

I believe the time has also come for me to do something special with my resources, before I no longer have a say in matters.

Celia sat back. She needed to get to the point.

What wisdom—assuming I've gained any in my ninety years—do I want to leave Renee with when I'm dead?

Flowery prose wouldn't help the dear girl.

Not that Renee was a girl anymore. She was a grown woman, doing her best to survive in a challenging work environment while raising two kids alone. Renee's family structure had suffered a tragic blow when Jim died.

She tried again, adding two paragraphs she hoped would let Renee know how proud she was of the way she was moving on with her life. Celia attempted to draw parallels to her own life, and the way the death of her father impacted her when she was so young. Losing a father was different from losing a husband and partner, but still devastating to their family structure. Renee was still learning to navigate her loss.

Maybe it'll help if I can let her know how my relentless focus on work impacted my life.

Ignoring the growling of her stomach, Celia dove back in.

The time also came in my life when I could have stepped back from some of my hard work. My brothers were grown. My savings would have kept my mother comfortable for the remainder of her days. I could have made the effort to share my own life with someone. Instead, it was easy to stay with the routine I knew best. People at work respected me and felt like family. It was easier to stay there. But each evening, my coworkers would go home to a spouse and children of their own. I often worked late because no one was waiting at home for me. Never being a mother to a child of my own is one of my few regrets. Another is not having a husband at home to greet me at the end of a long day.

Celia squirmed in her recently repaired desk chair, the old wood creaking. She reread her words. Was she getting too preachy? Were her words too vague to be relatable?

She had given birth to a child of her own—but Renee could never know that—and then given her baby up because that was what society expected back then. Celia could see now, in hindsight, that the cost of compliance was too high. But she'd committed to taking the truth of Virginia's parentage to the grave.

She was also tempted to articulate her nontraditional love affair with Danny to Renee, but what would be the point? Her history with Danny was too complicated to capture in a few paragraphs, and bringing him into the picture at this late date would confuse everyone. Celia would die an old spinster. At least that's what she'd allowed most everyone, other than her closest girlfriends, to believe. It was too late to change the narrative now.

So, rather than shock Renee with the full story, she stayed true to the storyline her niece was already familiar with.

Leaving Renee Whispering Pines would come as enough of a shock.

You will never have the regret of missing out on raising your own children. You were blessed with a husband you loved, but you lost him too soon. Don't give all of your time and energy to your work and your children. Save enough of yourself so you have the strength and desire to forge strong relationships with people who will light your days and carry you through to your own sunset. Don't depend on your children to do that for you. They need to build lives of their own.

Celia reread the last paragraph and shook her head. Why did she keep arching back to relationship advice? In reality, that was her own greatest weakness.

Her next paragraph spoke to the career she'd built. Celia might have enjoyed her work more if she would have changed companies once Tripp began making life so difficult for her, but she'd never found the courage.

Courage is what she wished for Renee.

She hated to admit her career wasn't as fulfilling as it might have been, since she'd dedicated her whole life to it, but it was the only way she could make Renee understand.

My only other significant regret is something I never shared with anyone. Most people think because of my success that I must have loved my work. I enjoyed the work and the people; however, it always felt like something was missing. I longed for a deeper connection or sense of peace and fulfillment from my work. I never found it. Some lucky people do. I suspect you have not yet found this type of connection either, my dear Renee, but my hope is that you will.

Please do not misunderstand me. I know I have lived a blessed life. I have always felt the strong bonds of family with all of you. I loved being a part of all the important and mundane moments of your lives. My work provided me with the means to help many people throughout my life as well. Material possessions are meaningless if they cannot be used to lighten the burdens other people carry and to make the world a brighter place.

Celia set her pen down, flipped over the filled page, and pulled out a fresh sheet of paper. She had to shake out her cramped hand. If she didn't switch to her decision to leave Renee Whispering Pines soon, she'd have a short novel written before she'd even reached the main purpose of the letter.

Maybe food would help.

Relieved to find a carton of yogurt in the fridge that wasn't expired and an unopened sleeve of saltines in the cupboard, Celia ate enough of both to quell the rumbling of her stomach. As her strength returned, she peeked in the freezer. A lonely miniature pot roast sat in a back corner. It would be better than nothing.

She ran the crystalized packaging under a stream of warm water, then wrestled it out of the pliable plastic wrap. More water helped her break the frozen Styrofoam off the bottom. She dropped the still-frozen hunk of beef into her trusty roasting pan, noting how pitiful it looked in a pan meant to cook a family-size meal. She scoured two potatoes and added them.

It would have to do.

She shoved the pan into the oven and headed back for her office, this time with a cup of peppermint tea. If the food bothered her stomach, the tea should help. She'd need to head to the grocery store when she finished Renee's letter. If she didn't get a proper supply of food in the house, George and Gerry might press for her to make some changes. But she'd made it this long in her own home, and she wasn't moving in with one of them or to a nursing home now. But, as her old tenant Penelope said during their recent bridge game, her goal was to leave this place feet first. As morbid as it sounded, Celia shared the same sentiment.

She got comfortable again and picked up her pen.

Do you remember traveling to the lake and vacationing at Whispering Pines? You used to stay in the cabins for two weeks each summer, before all of you kids got too busy as teenagers.

Years ago, when I was in my forties, a business acquaintance was unable to pay a debt he owed me. Eventually, he signed over the deed for Whispering Pines to me to settle his debt. It wasn't worth much back then. There were a handful of cabins and one home, but our family spent many glorious vacations there.

Hopefully, the transition to talk of the old resort wouldn't be too sudden. Renee probably seldom thought about it anymore. But Celia's eyes were tiring, and she needed to finish this first letter. If she didn't pick up the pace, she'd never get through them all.

She considered sharing more details around how she obtained Whispering Pines in the first place, given the situation was so unusual, but she wasn't particularly proud of the lengths she'd gone to. Instead, she gave Renee an abbreviated update on the current state of the resort, ending with the most crucial part: that it was now vacant after the death of her old caretaker.

Then she realized she hadn't actually told Renee why she was talking about Whispering Pines in the first place.

She intended to ask Jack to have her family read these letters before there was any formal reading of her will or other estate documents. It might be unconventional, but it was how Celia decided she wanted things to play out. It would be her last chance to dictate anything, so she'd play it up.

Grinning, she attempted to explain her thought process behind bequeathing the resort to her widowed niece.

I have put much thought into whether or not I should keep Whispering Pines in the family or sell it. The property has always held a special place in my heart, even though I have spent little time there during the last few decades. I always hoped to do something more with it. My days spent there were some of my most peaceful.

After much deliberation, I have decided to pass the deed for Whispering Pines to you.

Celia stopped writing, much as she imagined Renee would quit reading after that last sentence. She tried to imagine what her niece would be thinking. Probably either that she'd misread it . . . or that her dear departed Aunt Celia had lost her marbles near the end of her days.

Since her goal wasn't to cause Renee undo stress—or leave her with the impression that Celia was crazy—she added a paragraph about the financial buffers she'd put in place. Running a resort was expensive, and Renee would be starting from ground zero. If, that was, she even agreed to Celia's terms.

Celia prayed she would.

As she neared the bottom of the third page, Celia took a deep breath and added what she felt was the most important point of all: the escape hatch. She didn't want Renee to think she had to keep Whispering Pines forever.

If you choose to accept my gift to you—or even if you choose not to—I have but one request. Please do not sell the property for at least five years. Give yourself time to come to love it as I did and find a way to make it work for you. I have left further instructions with my lawyer; he will work with you on the transition.

Always remember to work hardest not on someone else's dreams, but on your own.

If this single statement doesn't yet resonate in your heart when you read it, you aren't yet ready to appreciate the meaning behind the words. I pray in time you will come to understand their wisdom.

Stay strong, my dearest Renee. Use your God-given talents to make this world a brighter place and enjoy each and every day.

All my love,
Celia

After signing her name with a flourish, Celia dropped her pen in the cup and pulled off her glasses. Her eyes ached, as did her right hand.

Would the words be enough for Renee? Would they help her understand one of the biggest complications in Celia's life?

No. That was too much to expect out of a simple letter. But it was the best she could do. Life is messy, and death leaves holes. There was no way Celia could avoid it.

She could only hope Renee's memories of the limited time she'd spent at Whispering Pines as a child would be enough to pique her interest. Young Renee had loved the resort. Later, as an adult, she'd often stood in front of the Christmas tree and inhaled the pine scent, telling Celia how it reminded her of those early vacations.

Celia lifted the three-page handwritten letter to her nose. Nothing. How fun would it be if she had a pine scent she could spritz on the odorless paper? She laughed out loud when she thought of the evergreen-scented deodorizer in her bathroom.

"That wouldn't work," she said, her tired eyes watering with humor.

Then she remembered. Renee's daughter, Julie, always used to say Celia's house smelled like roses in the summer, inside and out. But in the winter, the smell disappeared. One Christmas a few years ago, young Julie was proud as punch to give her a pretty glass perfume bottle filled with rose water. Celia loved the scent of it, but she developed a slight rash when she spritzed it on her skin. She hadn't had the heart to toss it, so it remained atop her dresser, on the glass tray holding various scents. She didn't use any of them anymore . . . but what if she could use Julie's thoughtful gift to make her last letters more memorable?

Revived, Celia headed upstairs, the climb less tiring than usual. She found the pretty pink bottle immediately. Back in her office, she tested it on a crumpled piece of paper she pulled from the garbage can next to her desk.

The light mist had no impact on the ink from her favorite pen that she'd also used to write the discarded to-do list, thankfully; and, even better, it left a light scent behind. It was possible that by the time her family actually opened their letters the scent would have faded away, but she'd try. Ever since her first summer at Whispering Pines, the scent of roses would bring memories of Danny to Celia's mind, and the special love they'd shared. Maybe a whiff of the flowery scent would do the same for her family when they opened her letters, only they'd be remembering her. She spritzed the first completed letter.

Content she'd given the task her best, Celia folded Renee's letter once the mist dried, eased it into a matching envelope, and addressed it to her niece. She licked the envelope, pressed the seal shut, and took a sip of her peppermint tea to chase away the bitter taste of glue.

"One down, many more to go. But I still have time," Celia whispered as she placed her niece's envelope between her pen cup and the wine bottle.

No one was there to witness her progress, but she wondered if Beverly's spirit was silently cheering her on from nearby.

Celia settled into a routine over the next two weeks. Drafting a letter or two each day was emotionally draining. She needed to make each one as special as possible. Her nights were restful. Maybe she was finally used to the new bed Helen had encouraged her to buy, but a part of her knew that it had more to do with the letters. Sitting down to write those letters to her family members had served as a wonderful chance for Celia to reflect on many parts of her life. She'd concluded hers was a life well lived.

With one day to spare before her doctor's appointment, Celia sealed the final envelope. It was to her brother George (she'd finished Gerry's letter the day before), and she hoped she'd done an adequate job of expressing her appreciation to him for allowing her to be part of his wonderful family of children and grandchildren.

When her mother married Clarence so long ago, and later gave birth to Gerry and George, Celia had felt more like their mother than their big sister, given the age gap. But as time went on, age became less of an issue in their relationship. And as the inevitable struggles of aging impacted her everyday life, her brothers were always willing to help.

She'd prided herself on being fiercely independent, and it vexed her to accept their help, but George reminded her once that he was simply returning the favor.

Even though he'd been young when Clarence died in that terrible car crash, George remembered how much Celia gave up to move home and help their mother raise him and his brother.

She supposed he had a point. It made it easier to accept his help.

She considered asking him if they could swing by her lawyer's office after her appointment the following day, but she decided she'd prefer he not know about the letters yet. Instead, she called Jack and asked him to stop by. She didn't feel like driving to his law office.

Besides, she had something else she wanted to give Jack, too.

Now, as she stood on her front step and waved goodbye to her trusted lawyer, she sent up a prayer of thanks for all Jack helped her accomplish through the years. He'd been young when they started working together, inexperienced, but Celia gave him a chance, and he had never failed her.

She hoped he'd enjoyed their working relationship, too.

His joy when Celia handed him her favorite framed photo of her and her best friend warmed her heart. Jack promised the picture of her and his mother would take prime real estate on his desk at the office. He joked that if anyone asked who the women were, he'd tell them of the many ways he'd helped Celia amass a small yet impressive fortune through the years. She'd be good press for him, he'd teased.

She hoped Jack would retire soon, make some kind of life for himself outside of his career. They had plenty in common. Jack should make the most of his later years, just like Celia had tried to do.

Alone again on her front step, Celia looked down on her prized hydrangea. Her letter writing had kept her too busy to cut any of them for drying. Tomorrow she'd ask George to do it for her. If she remembered.

Chapter Thirty-Nine
GIFT OF FREEDOM

WHAT A DAY, CELIA thought. It was such a relief to have her letters written and turned over to Jack. They'd be safe in his capable hands.

She picked at her small plate of roast and potatoes. Her stomach ached, and her appetite had deserted her again. But her doctor would insist on bloodwork in the morning, and she'd be miserable if she was weak from not eating.

The clock chimed seven—later than Celia realized. The angle of the sun was lower outside, a sure sign summer was over. Leaves littered her front yard.

After eating as much as she could, she headed for her recliner. She spied the new novel Virginia had brought when she'd come for tea. Summer was over in Minnesota, but the book's cover hinted at a lighthearted story set on a sunny beach somewhere. She eased her tired bones into her trusty recliner and picked up the book, flipping it over to read the description on the back. The large print was a pleasant surprise. Virginia was always so thoughtful.

The book's synopsis spoke of a long-overdue reunion of old friends. Celia was missing her friends, so the storyline appealed. Helen caught a cold on her Florida trip, so they hadn't gotten together since her return.

Celia cracked open the book, hoping to escape the loneliness that was now a constant in her life. The font size on the page made the reading easier, but the fading light did not. A lamp stood on the end table, but when she turned the switch, there was only a *click*. No light.

She kept forgetting to change the bulb.

The first few pages were good, but it was getting too dark. Unable to read more without straining, she set the book aside. She'd try again tomorrow.

The stairs creaked, but as her gaze traveled up their length, she knew they'd be empty. It was the old house, creaking around her, just as it had for as long as she could remember.

A shimmer of red caught her eye. The last of the sun's rays streamed through the stained-glass transom above the front window. The square of unexpected color on her lap reminded her of the church windows she'd worked with Seth to refurbish. Saving them was the highlight of her work with the historical society.

The wind sighed through the trees outside, causing the stream of light to flicker. The red square danced on the dark wool of the blanket she'd pulled over her lap, almost like it was flying. It reminded her of Danny's story of the red cardinal, a notion she'd passed on to her family over the years. Celia grinned and tried to run her finger around the outline of the red square, but it kept moving.

She really should get up and turn on a light. The house would be dark soon, and moving around would be a tripping hazard. But she was so relaxed, all she wanted to do was rest. Her stomach didn't hurt at the moment. Maybe the little bit of food she'd managed to eat was helping. Or maybe the pain stemmed from an ulcer, and without Helen around to irritate her it was improving on its own.

She chuckled at the idea. Helen may be as irritating as a pebble in her shoe, but she was a loyal friend. They'd *all* been loyal: Helen, Ruby, and Eleanor, much like the old friends in the book she'd just started.

She let her eyes drift shut, promising herself she wouldn't sleep in the chair for the entire night. A flush of red danced in front of her closed eyelids, and she forced them open again. She couldn't remember ever feeling this tired.

Standing in front of her, wearing the pretty red dress Celia would always remember her in during that stolen summer at Whispering Pines, was Beverly.

Celia snapped her eyes shut. Her mind was playing tricks on her. She might enjoy talking to Beverly's spirit once in a while, but her sister never appeared to her like this. Or she was dreaming. Beverly would by gone again by the time she opened her eyes.

But it felt good to rest. She'd pushed too hard, writing all those letters. Her doctor's appointment was just a silly, arbitrary deadline. She should have given herself more time.

Celia took a deep breath, eyes still closed, willing the tension to ebb away that had flooded her body with Beverly's unusual appearance. She imagined herself sitting at the end of her dock at Whispering Pines, alone in the sunshine, contemplating life.

The hot sun bathed her shoulders, and she knew she was dreaming. She didn't want to go upstairs to bed. The warmth felt too delicious.

Glancing down, Celia recognized the chair she was lounging on, and the dark sand of the beach. Ruby and Eleanor were locked in a heated debate next to her. Their brothers, Tripp and Leo, tossed a frisbee around. Tripp caught the disk with his left hand—the hand he'd been missing ever since the war.

I wonder where Helen is?

Celia looked toward the lodge, spotting Preston and Mrs. Bell out front, probably discussing the menu for the week.

Everyone had someone to talk to except for Celia.

Then she spotted him.

Danny, walking toward her, his ever-present camera hanging from the beat-up leather strap around his neck. He tossed his head and pushed the heavy fall of hair out of his eyes with one hand. The jagged scar along his hairline, earned while covering a war assignment, no longer marred his smooth forehead. She hoped the small bunch of white daisies and yellow roses in his other hand were for her. His smile was brighter than the sun overhead, and it filled her with more warmth.

It felt so good to be back at Whispering Pines; she didn't care if she ever woke up.

EPILOGUE
SEPTEMBER 2019

Sparks burst like fireworks against the darkened October sky, competing with the bright smattering of stars above. Renee sat back in her lawn chair and watched them float higher and higher.

"Watch those sparks, Nathan," Jess warned, angling the newspaper she was trying to read so the light from the bonfire would illuminate the print. "I'm so glad you pulled this out of the burn pile."

Nathan spared his mother a glance from the other side of the flames, adding more to the firepit as the rubbish from Ethan's cleaned-out attic burned down. "I hope we're not burning any other important papers," he said, checking the folder he held in his hand before tossing it in. "What's that article say about Aunt Celia?"

"This?" Jess asked, rattling the newspaper. "She really was incredible. Sometimes I forget how different the world looked, back when she was building her career. She was a woman before her time."

"That's what Grandpa always says," Robbie chimed in. He set the wheelbarrow he'd used to transport another load of junk from his uncle's truck over to the bonfire. "But in what way? What was so different about her?"

Renee sipped from her water bottle, listening to her son and her sister discuss the woman whose generosity had provided her with the opportunity to build a whole new life. Her eyes scanned long, narrow shadows cast by the bright moon above. There was mystery and magic in the dark; ghosts of the past and hints of new beginnings.

The fact they were all back at Whispering Pines, relaxing after a hectic day, spoke to Celia's unique life and accomplishments. As a child, Renee had absolutely idolized her aunt. As a grown woman, Renee still aspired to *be* Celia, at least in some respects. But she also understood there were things her aunt would have done differently if she had her life to live over again.

No one escapes life without a few regrets.

Jess shrugged at Robbie's question. "Celia was different in lots of ways. Back then, most women worked in the home. If they worked in an office, it was usually in a secretarial role. But not Celia. She helped manage projects and sold big deals to clients. That was almost unheard of back then. She did tell me once that one of her bosses was a real jerk, though. He started to make life miserable at the office. I think she was happy when she could finally retire."

"Bosses can still be jerks," Robbie muttered.

Renee grinned. Her son was right.

She pointed to the newspaper in Jess's hands. "She got her start when the man that owned her company took her under his wing, right? He owned this resort, too. He was a real mentor to her."

"Right," Jess said. "That's Preston Whitby that you're remembering. He *did* sound like a good man. I think it was his son that gave Celia trouble. Maybe Preston was retired by then. His son took over."

Val, relaxing in the lawn chair nearby, looked between her sisters as she cracked sunflower seeds and tossed the spent shells into the fire. "I guess I should have paid more attention to Celia's stories. I have no idea what you two are talking about." The sweep of headlights pulling into the resort's parking lot caught her attention. "There's Julie and Lizzy. I hope they remembered the wine."

Renee shook her head. "And based on *that* comment, I'd say you still don't care too much about Celia's story."

Val poured more seeds into her hand. "That's not true. I care, but my body hurts *everywhere*. Cleaning out Celia's old attic was a lot of work. Plus, since Luke and the boys are all at the Twins game, I only have a small window for myself here. I need to make the most of it."

Renee watched Jess give up on reading Celia's newspaper article by firelight. She folded it up and tucked it under her chair, but Renee held out a hand. "Give it here. I'll put it in the picnic basket for safekeeping."

Jess handed the paper over, and another burst of sparks lit up the sky. Nathan was making progress on the pile.

"Nathan, you stored that white shoebox full of stories and poems someplace safe, right?" Renee asked.

"You know it," he confirmed, bending down for another armful of papers. "It's in the trunk of my car, tied tight with that red ribbon. I thumbed through a little of it. There's some good stuff in there. Tell me again who Beverly was . . . ?"

Ethan, ignoring the conversation until that point, looked up from his phone and sat up straighter. "She was a sister to Celia, Dad, and Gerry. She was just a couple years younger than Celia."

Nathan nodded. "Got it. She's the one who died young, right? Polio or something?"

"Close. Heart problems. Dad said she was only eighteen, if I remember right."

Renee had forgotten how young Beverly was when she died. *The same age as Robbie is now,* she thought with a shudder. *I barely survived my husband's death . . . I think losing a child would kill me.*

Maybe the idea of someone dying at eighteen bothered Robbie, too, because he turned to Ethan, changing the subject. "Any news on the game?"

Ethan wagged his phone in the air. "Yeah. Drew and Dylan are texting me. Twins are down."

"Great!" Val cried. "I'll have five depressed males descend on my kitchen tomorrow afternoon if this continues. *Lizzy! Julie! Did you remember the wine?*"

"*Yes, Aunt Val!*" one of her nieces hollered back from the parking lot.

"They'll have fun no matter how the game turns out," Jess countered. "I'm glad Dad went along. I'm sure Luke and Seth could have handled the boys just fine, but Dad will enjoy it. And thank God Mom watched Harper for me today. Having a two-year-old underfoot in that attic would have been too chaotic."

Renee turned at the sound of someone approaching from the direction of the duplex. "Oh, hi, Lauren. What were you doing?"

Jess's daughter grinned as she entered the circle of light from the fire. "I was hanging up those amazing vintage dresses we found in the attic today. Thanks again for letting me take those, Ethan. I brought more chairs, too."

Ethan groaned. "Would you guys stop thanking me for stuff? It was all Celia's. Just because she left me the house doesn't mean she left me everything in it, too."

"True," Renee said, grinning at her big brother. "But thanks for letting us be part of cleaning it out. It was so fun to be up there again. I'm glad we waited for a while before we did it. Can you believe it's already been four years since she died?"

"No, I can't. I still catch myself calling it *Celia's house*," Ethan said.

Lauren set up three more chairs and plopped into the one closest to her mom. "I'm just glad Grandpa wasn't there to claim those dresses. I bet he'd have wanted to add them to his costume room in his basement."

Jess deposited a bottle of water into the drink holder on her daughter's chair, ignoring the eye roll Lauren gave her. "He loves all things Halloween. And don't give me that look. You aren't twenty-one yet. You aren't drinking any of the wine."

"Mom, I'm twenty. And in college. Close enough."

Renee might have agreed with Lauren, but Jess shook her head. "Rules are rules."

Robbie snagged one of the chairs Lauren brought.

"That's going to tick Lizzy or Julie off," Lauren warned.

"You snooze, you lose," Robbie said, grabbing Lauren's water bottle and chugging it.

Lauren made a disgusted face, but then grinned. "Now I'm going to *have* to have wine, Mom. There's nothing else to drink."

Renee laughed. Lauren, one point; Jess, zero. Why was it so fun to watch her siblings battle with their near-grown kids, but it still drove her nuts when she was doing the same with her own?

Robbie didn't look fazed. "I hear you about thank-yous and all, Ethan, but that was cool of you to let us take the stuff nobody wanted but was too good to burn. I'll sell it and use the cash toward replacing that boat motor Nathan blew up this summer."

"You are such a shit, Robbie."

Robbie replied by flipping Nathan off. He must have learned that from his sister, Renee thought with a sigh. "Boys. Language."

Robbie ignored her. "Got any beer for me, sis?"

Julie smacked his baseball cap as she reached his side and then yanked him out of the chair—an impressive feat given Robbie had a good six inches and thirty pounds on his big sister. Nathan whooped in delight.

"Mom!" Robbie whined.

"Seriously?" Renee shot back. "You're going to pull that card?"

Julie sat before Robbie could beat her back into the chair and Lizzy did the same, a bottle of wine in each hand.

"Thank God," Val said, pointing at Renee's picnic basket. "Tell me you have cups in there."

Renee tossed the cover of the basket back. "What kind of resort owner would I be without supplies? I have cups. Plastic flutes, even. And a corkscrew, just in case the girls picked out a bottle that didn't have a screw-off lid."

Julie set the twelve-pack of beer on the grass and tore it open, tossing the first one to Ethan. "Is that the right brand?"

"Perfect, thanks," her uncle said, popping the top and knocking back the can. He burped. "Man, I'm pooped."

Jess wiggled her fingers at Julie for a can, then smiled at her brother. "Turning fifty will do that to a guy."

Ethan settled deeper into his chair. "Shut up, Jess. You aren't that far behind."

Renee saw the gold chain on Julie's wrist sparkle in the firelight. She stood, wanting to inspect the piece her daughter found in an old jewelry box in Celia's attic. "Robbie, if you take my chair, you're grounded for life."

Robbie crushed his empty water bottle. "I'm too old to ground, Mom."

"Don't test me. Let me see your wrist, Julie," she instructed, reaching for her daughter's arm. "I'm so glad you found this." Julie was trying to dig out another beer at the same time and Renee was having a hard time seeing what the charms were in the dim light. "Take it off, will you? I want to look at it."

Pulling her arm out of Renee's grasp, Julie tucked her wrist under her bottom. "You can't have it. Ethan said *I* could have it."

Ethan groaned again. "For the millionth time, it wasn't mine to give!"

Both women ignored him. Renee said, "Don't worry, honey. I want you to have it. I just want to see what the charms are again."

"Fine," Julie conceded, giving her mother access to her wrist. "But don't lose it in the grass."

"I won't lose it, promise."

Renee had to stick her face close to her daughter's hand in order to remove the bracelet. The clasp was tiny, and she'd broken a nail during the day's work. Once she held the bracelet, she pulled her chair closer to the firelight to see.

"I think this is real gold. I wonder where Celia got it? These charms are delicate, well made. Look, here's the Golden Gate Bridge! And the Eiffel Tower."

"Let me see it when you're done," Jess said, taking a sip of her beer.

Julie shook her head. "You guys are going to lose it in the grass."

"Oh, stop it, Julie. We won't lose it," Jess scolded her niece. "Hey, Renee, maybe *Danny* gave it to Celia."

Renee grinned. "Maybe!"

Val grunted as she pulled the cork out of one of the wine bottles. "Who's Danny?"

"No idea," Jess shrugged, leaving lots of bewildered faces around the fire.

Giggling, Renee fingered a tiny golden pine tree on Julie's bracelet. Or was it a Christmas tree? "Remember when Jess helped me change out the pictures by the front door in the lodge this past summer?"

"You mean those frames that were hanging there before you had me install that window?"

"Exactly," Renee said to Ethan. She held the bracelet up for everyone to see. "We found a picture of Celia with a cute guy that none of us recognized. The shot was fuzzy, but even Dad didn't recognize him. The names on the back said *Celia* and *Danny*."

"And don't forget, there are those initials on the steps at the duplex that say *CM* and *DB*. We're guessing Danny was Celia's 'one that got away.' "

Julie grinned. "I love that. Aunt Celia had a mystery man. Do you think maybe he was a pilot and traveled the world? If he collected those charms for her, maybe it was during his travels."

"Nathan, you should do some research on this Danny guy," Lizzy joined in. "It shouldn't be that hard to figure out who he was. Maybe he was somebody famous."

Nathan abandoned his fire-feeding job to help himself to a beer. "Might be kind of fun."

"Jess, catch!"

Renee tossed Julie's bracelet in her sister's direction. Julie screeched, but Jess snagged it out of the air like a pro.

"I think the Twins could use you on their team," Val said, relaxing in her chair with a very full cup of wine.

Julie dropped her head between her knees. "You guys are going to give me a heart attack."

Lizzy poured herself a glass of wine, then set the bottle in the grass. "I'm glad Dad gave me the old tool chest we found up in the attic. I'm going to display all the old chisels and stuff in my office at the construction company. I doubt Renee and

Jess will want to play catch with those rusty old things around the fire. Thanks again, Dad."

Ethan's three sisters all raised their drinks in a simultaneous toast and shouted to the stars, *"They weren't his to give!"* before falling into fits of laughter.

Ethan stood, dropped his empty beer can in the grass at Julie's feet, and waved a disgusted hand at his sisters. "You three are too much. There's a perfectly good dock out there, just waiting for me in the moonlight, and I think I'll go out there and ponder the meaning of life. It's too noisy up here."

Renee wiped at her tears of laughter and watched her big brother make his way toward the water, a slight hitch in his step. Celia always used to tell her that dock was her favorite place on earth, and she was sure she'd have loved to know Ethan was heading out there to enjoy the peace and solitude of Whispering Pines.

Thank you for reading **Celia's Legacy**. I hope you enjoyed the rest of Celia's story.

I loved bringing these stories together in a complete circle. The series wouldn't have felt complete without going back to explore Celia's life story, too.

The Gift of Whispering Pines series focused on a special family. Celia lived an extraordinary life and taught those around her the value of both family and lifelong friendships. Growing up, Renee was also fortunate to be part of an extraordinary group of friends. They met at summer camp when they were only twelve. As so often happens, they would drift apart for a while, but they're back together now and I invite you along for the fun in The Kaleidoscope Girls series. It all kicks off with Jackie, Renee, and three other special women in **Better with Friends**, Book 1. Come experience the magic of female friendships!

Be sure to visit www.kimberlydiedeauthor.com to sign up for my newsletter to get the latest on new releases and more.

ACKNOWLEDGEMENTS

The legacy of my great aunt, Mary K. Nierling, served as the inspiration behind my Gift of Whispering Pines series. Mary was my grandmother's oldest sister, and our real life "Celia." She was the matriarch of our family on my mother's side.

We lived down the street from Aunt Mary during my high school and college years. In hindsight, I wish I'd taken the time to get to know her better, but I was young and intimidated by her forceful presence. She died the year I graduated from college. I have snippets of memories, along with countless questions I'll never have the chance to ask her. I wish I could sit down with her now to hear a firsthand account of the full life she lived. Or at least however much of it she'd be willing to share!

These books have allowed me to connect with distant relatives. I owe a big thank you to Sylvia Nierling for sharing some unique memorabilia she found while sifting through trunks filled with old family photos. These items confirmed some stories I'd heard about Aunt Mary through the years.

I doubt many 34-year-old women could claim to be the State President of a highway contractors association the way Aunt Mary was for North Dakota back in 1937!

Among the items Sylvia shared was the eulogy Monica Nierling gave at Aunt Mary's funeral. Thank you for permission to share some of your heartfelt words here, Monica. It was great catching up!

Excerpt from Mary K. Nierling eulogy:

You were, indeed, a woman before your time. Your hard work, brilliance, and perseverance in your professional life earned you the respect of your business associates and stature in your community.

You always willingly and generously shared the fruits of your labor with us. More importantly, you gave yourself to us, your family. Oh, you were domineering and, when you spoke, we listened. As we grew in maturity, we began to appreciate your total commitment to your family. You opened your home and your heart to us in numerous loving, caring ways. When your nieces and nephews were young, you would listen intently as they related their news or crisis of the day and then you would exclaim in your quiet voice, "Well, for pity sake." You cared–and we knew it. As the family circle grew, you graciously accepted spouses and offspring into your network of love, concern, and care. In turn, they, too, have been blessed and enriched by your wisdom and zest for life.

Your presence was always cherished at special family occasions and milestones. We were so proud to have you with us. You shared our joy. You shared our accomplishments. You shared our pain. You shared our sorrow. You were our matriarch, the hub of the family wheel.

Now, dear Mary, you have been released and set free from the bondage of your earthly body and you can soar like the eagle. We shall always treasure you as a golden thread in the tapestry of life. You mark the end of an era. You were so special, so unique. You have left us a legacy. We hope and pray that we can follow in your footsteps and know, love and serve our God, our family, and our community as you did. You fought the good fight. You finished the race. You kept the faith. (March 26, 1992)

I'm not sure I realized how much of Aunt Mary found its way into Celia's story until I read this again.

As I've noted in the back of other books in this series, I wouldn't be able to pursue my dream of writing without the unwavering support of so many. My husband and kids have been amazing. Friends continue to encourage me as I transition to dedicating even more of my time to pursuing a new career in writing.

In a crazy world of upheaval, I'm so thankful to my editor and to my cover designer. Thank you!

Most of all, a huge thank you to my dedicated readers. You fuel me when life happens and I'm not always able to publish as quickly as I'd like. You took a chance on a brand-new author, and I'll be forever grateful.

Labeling every chapter in this series as a *Gift* continues to remind me that life is a gift. Every day is a blessing, even the hard ones, and each of us is building our own legacies with how we spend those days. I love that these books, inspired by Aunt Mary, a woman before her time, can be part of my legacy.

About the Author

Kimberly Diede writes contemporary novels that weave together family, friends, hope, and romance. She writes family sagas, suspense, and women's fiction that you'll find hard to put down. She truly believes we are never too old for second chances in life.

Kimberly enjoys spending the short months of her Midwest summers on the lakeshores of Minnesota and North Dakota. Nothing beats writing and hanging out with family and friends at their cabin. Her love of tradition and all things vintage comes through in her decorating and her stories.

Be sure to follow Kimberly on social media to catch glimpses of the junk she drags home to repurpose and to get updates on her latest books.

Website: https://www.kimberlydiedeauthor.com/
Facebook: https://www.facebook.com/KimberlyDiedeAuthor/
Instagram: https://www.instagram.com/kimberlydiedeauthor/
BookBub: https://www.bookbub.com/authors/kimberly-diede